I0673287

Dedication

To Becca, many grateful thanks for all your hard work!

Acknowledgements

As always, my very grateful thanks to everyone who has helped me with, or who has read (and especially left a nice review of) my Artesans of Albia series. I could not have done it without you.

To Dave; to my parents, Barbara and Dennis; to my brother Dave: I love you all!

To Milly and Milo: thanks for all the cuddles and walks.

To my editor Diane Dalton: special thanks for your expertise and for saving me from potential embarrassment.

To Mikey Brooks: I do believe that this is your best cover yet! I adore it.

To NTN (David Snell, David Shepherd) and to Susan Mallett: many grateful thanks for the music and the fun.

To Bob Watson: for website advice and maintenance.

To Janet Morris: special thanks for that wonderful endorsement.

To anyone who has reTweeted, posted to Facebook, or otherwise helped spread the word through social media, and to anyone who has taken the trouble to write and post a review.

I hope you enjoy this book!

Praise for the Artesans of Albia series:

"Cas Peace's *Artesans of Albia* trilogy immediately sweeps you away. The series propels you into a world so deftly written that you see, feel, touch, and even smell each twist and turn. These nesting novels are evocative, hauntingly real. Smart. Powerful. Compelling. The trilogy teems with finely drawn characters, heroes and villains and societies worth knowing; with stories so organic and yet iconic you know you've found another home—in Albia. So start reading now. I, for one, can't wait to find out what will happen next.

~Janet E. Morris, author of *The Sacred Band of Stepsons* series; the *Dream Dancer* series; *I, the Sun.*

✣ ✣ ✣ ✣ ✣

"I have just loved this entire series. Cas Peace is a master storyteller, providing a depth and breadth of information about her worlds and their people that is just staggering. Her characters are complex and multi-dimensional, and I have very much enjoyed reading this series. I am also looking forward with great anticipation to her next novel in this series. I heartily recommend this series to anyone who enjoys epic fantasy, strong world-building, and beautiful storytelling. Highly recommended!"

~K Sozaeva, *Amazon Vine Voice and Top 1000 Reviewer.*

✣ ✣ ✣ ✣ ✣

"As a fan of the late great David Gemmel I think I have finally found an author who is similarly inspiring. It's how fantasy should be written. Less about the world building and more about the characters. I didn't want to stop reading."

~ML. H, *Amazon reviewer.*

✣ ✣ ✣ ✣ ✣

"A superb read. Non-stop intrigue and action. I literally could not put it down. Anyone needing a good series to read should take up Book 1 and get started. Cas Peace has created an unforgettable hero(ine) in Sullyan, and a world that ranks alongside Middle Earth and Westeros."

~David C Snell, *Amazon reviewer.*

Published by Albia Publishing 2015

First American Paperback Edition

This is a work of fiction. Names, characters, places, and incidents either are the product of the author's imagination or are used fictitiously. Any resemblance to actual events, locales, or persons, living or dead, is entirely coincidental. The publisher does not have any control and does not assume responsibility for author or third party websites or their content.

Copyright ©2015 by Caroline Peace
Editing by Diane Dalton
Cover art by Mikey Brooks, www.insidemikeysworld.com
Author photo by Dave Peace

All rights reserved.
No part of this book may be reproduced, scanned, or distributed in any printed or electronic form without permission. Please do not participate in or encourage piracy of copyrighted materials in violation of the author's rights. Purchase only authorized editions.

Visit Cas Peace at her author website: www.caspeace.com

ISBN-10: 1-939993-68-7
ISBN-13: 978-1-939993-68-7

Other titles in the Artesans of Albia series:

Trilogy One: Artesans of Albia

Book One: King's Envoy

Book Two: King's Champion

Book Three: King's Artesan

Trilogy Two: Circle of Conspiracy

Book One: The Challenge

Book Two: The Circle

Book Three: Full Circle

Trilogy Three: Master of Malice

Book One: The Scarecrow

The Scarecrow

MASTER OF MALICE
BOOK ONE

Cas Peace

Albia Publishing

The Kingdom of Albia in the Realm of Albia. (not to scale)

Realm of Andaryon. (not to scale.)

Chapter One

Lerric, aging client-king of Bordenn, stood in the dark doorway. A damp, noisome smell assailed his nose, the drip of water reached his ears. Lerric shivered, his reaction not wholly due to the chill in the air.

Deep within the lightless room he detected a hint of movement. Creaking leather, a hiss of pain. Lerric stepped one pace farther from the door's protection and raised his lamp. As soon as the faint yellow light touched—and flinched from—the dark form huddled on the truckle bed along the far wall, a vicious curse sounded. A crooked hand flew up to shield eyes that could no longer bear good, honest light.

"Put that out, you bloody fool! Would you blind me entirely?"

"Ah … your pardon."

Lerric shuttered the lamp and gloom reclaimed the cell. When his eyes grew accustomed to the darkness, the king assessed the cell's lone occupant.

Habitually dapper and well-fed, his body had assumed scarecrow proportions. A parody of his former self. The fastidiously clean and expensive raiment was replaced by a thin, shabby robe of dusty black. A darker blot amid the shadows, it barely disguised the gaunt frame it covered.

Gone were the arrogant swagger and confident poise, replaced by a savage desire for revenge, a thirst for retribution. Three years of incarceration and hopelessness, of nursing raging grievances, hadn't lessened the pious fervor and deeply-held beliefs. Thirty-six interminable months of imprisonment and deprivation had served only to deepen his determination to rid the land of those to whom he owed his life. Those without whose mercy he would have suffered a horrific and agonizing death.

His eyes, damaged and unable to focus, peered peevishly at his visitor as he levered his skeletal frame upright. The tortured creature that had once been Baron Hezra Reen stood, leaning on a wooden cane as gnarled and lined as the liverish skin of his face, and bared his yellow, decaying teeth at the well-dressed man by the door. His host.

"Well? Are you going to stand there all day gawping, Lerric?"

His harsh tones lashed the older man. Lerric winced and pried his eyes from the cane clasped so tightly in the other's hand, thinking—hoping—it must be a trick of the gloom that made it glow a gory red.

His daughter had convinced him that this withered being held the key to avenging her disgrace, yet Reen's shocking physical aspect and aura of menace eroded Lerric's confidence in the wisdom of allowing Sofira her way. How could she still profess to love this ill-tempered, wrinkled shell of a man, this ranting, obsessive bigot? He only had her word that the scarecrow's mind was still sharp, undamaged by years of incarceration. After all, Sofira only had his letters on which to base her assertion.

It suddenly crossed Lerric's mind that those letters could have been written by someone else purely to convince Sofira of the Baron's sanity. Although who on that gods-forsaken island—or was that a contradiction in terms?—Reen could have found to write them for him, the aging king could not imagine. It was nothing less than a miracle he had even found a carrier for his messages, given his status as prisoner and traitor. But gold was gold, and there was always someone willing to risk the High

King's wrath for a price.

And even though he had played his part, Lerric had yet to learn the full story behind his unwelcome guest's liberation.

Despite his curiosity, Lerric had been reluctant to make this visit. His own men had retrieved Reen from captivity, brought him south laboriously by boat and by land after plucking him, half-dead and raving, from the sucking arms of the sea. The operation had gone off without a hitch, yet something about their eyes and manner had alerted Lerric to the possibility not all was as it should be. His men had been unwilling—or unable—to speak of what disturbed them, and it had not escaped the king's notice that none of them had come near him since. Two of them seemed to prefer the uncomfortable duties of the watchtower, while the third had not been seen at all. Remembering their furtive looks and uneasy shifting as they reported Reen's arrival, Lerric experienced a shudder of unexplained fear.

Placing the shuttered lamp on the floor, he advanced into the cell. The scarecrow watched him approach, peering myopically, beckoning Lerric closer within range of his failing eyesight. Almost mesmerized, Lerric obeyed.

The unimaginable tortures Reen had suffered during his exile, agonies which had warped and twisted his body and rendered his skin painfully sensitive to daylight, had turned the once-arrogant little man into a human mole. Reclusive, given to fits of ranting interspersed with hours of religious chanting, he was a figure of nightmare. Lerric wondered what his daughter's reaction would be when she finally saw the man she professed to still love. The man for whom Lerric had agreed to pawn his kingdom—and maybe, he thought with an icy shiver, his very life.

Sofira had assured her father she and Reen had long since forgiven each other their mutual betrayal at Reen's sham of a trial. Reen understood she had only been trying to protect her position and her children. He knew she was only posturing when she had insisted upon his execution; she would never have let it be carried out. She would have rescinded the order had she retained her crown. And *she* knew, she avowed—although her father heard the hidden note of outrage quivering just below the surface—that Reen's impeachment of her that was the cause of her losing her husband, her children, and the crown that was rightfully hers, had been forced from him under severe duress by their powerful and scheming archenemy. The enemy who was still riding high on the triumph of that success, and who still held the High King in the palm of her hand.

"Sit, sit," grumbled the scarecrow, waving a bony claw toward the only chair in the room. Lerric sat, his aging bones aching in the moldy damp, feeling far less a king and more the supplicant under the fervid light in the other's dark-gray eyes. Casting a look at the leather-sprung truckle bed as the wasted man sat once more, Lerric summoned the courage to speak.

"Are you sure this is what you want? Wouldn't you be more comfortable in the palace, or even a private house? I have plenty. I could vacate one for you. No one need know you were there—"

"*Fool!*"

The cane's heel struck the stone floor with such a violent crack it made Lerric jump. The word was spat with force and Lerric fell silent. The wizened claws gripping the cane turned white with the preternatural strength of their grip, and the lined, hawk-like face thrust close. The all but useless eyes, their whites now yellow and veined, snapped with anger and a thin line of spittle hung from the cracked lips.

"Have I not told you I must hide?" the dreadful voice wheezed. "Have I not told you the reason why I may never walk in daylight? Did I not tell you why I must languish like this, hidden deep in the rock of the earth? If I do not they will find me, Lerric;

they will root me out like hounds on a scent and tear me to pieces. They are merciless. They are godless. They are vengeful heretics. I have told you all this, and yet you offer me your comforts? Pah!"

Lerric leaned away from the spray of spittle that accompanied this rant. There was an unholy light in the feral eyes, a sly twist to the mouth. He was surely unhinged. What had he done, thought Lerric, what had he unleashed by giving way to his daughter's tearful pleading? Oh, but it was too late now—far too late.

"No," the wheezing scarecrow went on, leaning back, the demonic glint fading, "I must stay well hidden. And I no longer need what you would call 'comforts,' not after three years of incarceration in a living hell. *She* saw to that. But the tables are turning. I have learned why I was seemingly abandoned by my God and left to rot. I am the stronger for it, believe me. I have learned secrets they've never even dreamed of. Secrets they wouldn't want me to learn. Oh, yes."

The emaciated form leant forward, crooking one long-nailed finger under Lerric's nose. "I am the stronger now. Do you hear me? I have unlocked the powers granted me by God; granted me through suffering in order to do his will. I have the power to defeat them—to defeat *her*—and no one can stop me. With your support we can finally drive them out, rid our lands of their blasphemous ways, their unnatural powers, and restore your daughter—my Queen—to her rightful place. With me to guard and guide her, we will be invincible. No one will touch us, no one will harm us. You will see your daughter reign supreme and all Albia will revere her!

"Once she and I are wed—ah! Then, Lerric, then you will see!"

Lerric hid his face in his hands to blot out the terrible sight of this gaunt figure, scrawny arms raised high, the thin and threadbare robe falling back from limbs devoid of muscle, skin devoid of life, bone devoid of blood. Horror stole over Lerric as he listened to the creature he had agreed to champion, and to whom his beloved daughter had pledged her body. For surely it was no longer human, this skeletal, ranting fanatic; and for one redeeming moment Lerric was sorely tempted to slide his dagger from its sheath and plunge it into the breast of the treacherous creature that had once called itself Baron Hezra Reen.

And maybe it would have saved Albia, Lerric, and many, many others much misery, anguish, and horror.

✤ ✤ ✤ ✤

"Daughter, forgive me, but I must ask you again; are you sure, are you *completely* sure this is what you want? You haven't seen him yet, you haven't spoken with him. I have to tell you, he is not the man you remember, no matter what his letters suggested."

Lerric was sitting with Sofira on the bed in her luxuriously appointed chamber, autumn sunlight streaming through the window. Its warmth helped alleviate the horror he still felt after his earlier meeting with the creature Sofira had begged him to save. The king held fast to his daughter's hands, mainly to disguise the tremble of his own, but also to convey his intense unease. He looked earnestly into her hard gray eyes and willed her to hear his concern. Despite his fear, he was loath to reveal precisely what had taken roost in that fetid cell far beneath the palace floors.

Sofira stared back at him, hearing his care for her, seeing his distress. But it seemed she could not understand his concern, for her brittle eyes glazed with tears. "Don't you want me to have back what was taken from me, Father?" Her colorless face was animated with hurt. "You know how unhappy I've been since I was forced to return here. You know how I ache for my children."

Lerric nodded. "I know it's been hard for you. At least at the castle Elias allowed you access to them—"

"Access?" Sofira snarled. "What use is *access* to me? Never allowed to be alone with them, never to take them out of my prison, never to walk in the park with them? He doled out time with them as if giving tidbits to a dog, and kept me kenneled like one, too. And I a Queen! How could you condone that?"

Lerric thought better of reminding his daughter she had ceased to be a queen when Elias dissolved their marriage. And in light of what she had done—misled by Reen or not, she couldn't pretend ignorance of the risks she had run—Lerric considered her fortunate not to have suffered the death penalty. Not that he could tell her that, either.

He spoke soothingly. "I didn't say I condoned it, daughter, and you know I never wanted to see you separated from Eadan and Seline. It's just that … Sofira, are you absolutely convinced Hezra is sane?"

Sofira froze. She stared at her father, a biting retort on her lips. But then she realized he was only trying to protect her, clumsy though he was. She relaxed her spine and smiled.

"Oh, Father, of course I'm sure. Do you think I wouldn't know if something had affected his mind? It's a clever ruse, a ploy he's devised to make them relax their vigilance. Didn't you read his letters? Didn't you feel the sincerity in his words, his deep desire to restore all I've lost? And don't forget, my restoration will also benefit you. You'll be more than recompensed for your trouble and the support you continue to give us. We'll not forget you or Bordenn when I am once again Albia's High Queen."

Lerric doubted that. He had seen the light of fanaticism in the scarecrow's eyes, the driving desire to control, the fervid lust for revenge at any cost. Reen might be willing to accept the title of consort for now, but Lerric would not bet much on him being happy with a supporting role for long, not once the reins of power were in his hands. Sofira was clearly already under his spell. He had cunningly charmed her from within his prison, writing her words of contrition, loyalty, and love. In her beleaguered state of angry, lonely sorrow, brought on by the conditions Elias had imposed on her, she had been easy prey.

Lerric shivered. Why should that word—*prey*—cause his heart to constrict? Why did it conjure images of ragged carrion birds feasting on a corpse?

Sofira's hands tightened on his. "Father, are you unwell?"

He gave himself a mental shake and the specter of doom withdrew. He half-smiled for his daughter and shook his head. If his words of caution could not sway her, he would have to hope the sight of the man himself would give her pause. She expected Reen to appear unchanged. He was still relatively young, after all—not yet forty years of age—although his current shriveled appearance suggested a man in his eighties. Sofira was bound to be horrified by what she saw.

Reen had thus far refused her earnest pleas to be admitted to his convalescent cell. He was not yet ready, but when he was, when he finally emerged, Lerric would be there to support her once she realized the awful truth.

✤ ✤ ✤ ✤ ✤

Midnight came and went. The palace lay wrapped in silence. Sofira stood shivering in the dark hallway. She told herself it was just the anticipation of this long-awaited reunion causing these strange sensations within her. Why he had made her wait so long, she had no idea. The questions she had begged her father to convey elicited no response. He would come when he was ready, that was all she was told.

She felt guilty for her impatience and had to remind herself of the dreadful ordeal he had suffered; the long and lonely months surrounded by disapproving clerics, forced to listen to their monotonous chanting and endure their pious rituals. Small wonder he needed space and time to recover. The world must seem a strange and changed place to him now.

But she would compensate him for what he had borne in her name. Although she had paid the dearer price by her reckoning, she had never faced the death penalty. She had never been confronted with her own terror of death in agony; had never suffered the humiliation of having to grovel for mercy at the feet of her direst enemy. And it had been she who had brought him to that pass, she who had inflicted that deepest shame upon him. It was up to her to show him how grateful she was that he had found it in his heart to forgive her and was willing to use his knowledge and cunning to win back all that been so unfairly ripped from her.

She scrutinized the darkened hallway, assuring herself all was as he had specified. It was the dark of the moon; no stray ray of silver would touch his form. The windows were all covered with heavy black drapes so not even a twinkle of starlight could find its way through. The one small lamp her father had brought rested on the floor, its feeble glow the only relief in the intense, velvety dark. And at the first indication of his presence, even that light must be smothered.

Her heart lurched in sympathy for the torments he must have borne. How could they have been so cruel? Her father had told her something of Reen's words when first he was rescued from his long incarceration. Lerric's voice had trembled as he described that first meeting, and his daughter had seen how Reen's piteous condition had affected him. How Sofira had begged and pleaded to be allowed to tend him, but Reen remained adamant. She must curb her impatience until he was recovered enough to meet with her. It had been hard and, in the end, she had to wait a full month. Now, the waiting was over.

She started. She could hear his footfalls on the stair. He was coming to her! She turned triumphant eyes to her father, who stood in silence beside her. Lerric too had heard the sounds and bent to the feeble lamp, turning down the wick. His hand shook and he glanced nervously up at his daughter. But Sofira had turned back to the yawning maw of the stairwell, quivering with anticipation.

The footfalls drew nearer and Sofira held her breath. She had imagined this moment so many times, had tried out the words she would speak to him, felt and lived the emotions they would both experience. But now the moment was here, she felt empty. What could she say to him, this much-wronged man, this betrayed but loyal confidante? How could he trust her after what she had done?

Shivers wracked her, raising gooseflesh on her arms, making her acutely aware of the soft robe she wore and the way it clung to her body. Her senses seemed heightened; her hearing was sharpened and her eyes cut the gloom like a creature of the night. She almost felt him pushing the darkness aside like a curtain as he slowly ascended the stair. Finally, he emerged from the portal before her.

Sofira gave a great gasp and felt the start her father made. She was dimly aware of the waves of fear radiating from Lerric, but she had scant interest in his strange behavior. The focus of her attention was riveted by the shadowy figure in the portal and the brief, impossible impression of two ruby glints in the darkness, as if demonic eyes were staring.

As if propelled by some outside force, Sofira moved slowly forward. He watched her come, his dark gray eyes fixed on her face. One hand gripped the cane by his side, the other was held out toward her, as if in supplication.

Sofira halted before the scarecrow, one slim hand to her mouth. She stretched forth her other hand and heard Lerric stir behind her.

She brushed Reen's outstretched fingers and felt an electric thrill run across her skin. Soft, dark eyes smiled gently at her and she gazed trustingly back. She stepped closer and took his hand in both of hers, clasping it to her breast. She could find no words to offer him, had no idea how to express the regret she felt for the torment he had undergone. She could see the effect of it upon him and knew him changed, yet it hardly registered. She watched for some sign of his mood, some indication of his feelings, and was suddenly afraid. What if he railed at her? What if he refused to aid her now he was freed from duress?

Reen stepped closer. His smile widened, and she felt her heartbeat slow. A connection seemed to form between them and her trepidation fell away.

"My gracious Lady," Reen whispered in the darkness, "the sight of you gladdens my wounded eyes. Sore they have been for lack of beauty to comfort them."

His gentle words lightened Sofira's habitually stern expression. Her heart swelled with joy and places within her soul, barren for so long, seemed to fill with forgotten sensations. She could hardly control her breathing and felt lightheaded and giddy. Words she scarcely knew she had formed came from her lips.

"Oh, my lord, I hardly know what to say to you. That you have survived such dreadful torment is no surprise to me; you have inner strength such as I have never known. But to think you can bear to look upon me when I caused you such wrong ... that you can forgive me and offer me your aid and support ... that I had not looked for. But you are very welcome here. My father and I will do all we can to ease your soul, and I will pledge myself to you as I promised.

"Now that we are reunited, we will put right what is wrong in this realm. We will restore our Matria Church to her glory. Together, we will repay Elias and his minions for their cruelty and overturn their ill-considered policies, and Albia will be better for it. This I vow with all my heart."

11

Behind her, she vaguely heard Lerric make an odd noise, as if words were strangling in his throat. But Reen was smiling at her, and she forgot her father. Reen stepped closer, pressed his body to hers and slipped his arm around her back. As he increased the pressure she melted against him, and offered him her lips.

Reen took them hungrily and as his mouth fastened on hers she saw, for the fleetest of moments, a sullen ruby glow in his eyes. Something within her struggled to scream, but then joy washed over her and all was forgotten.

Her champion had returned and the world would be hers.

Chapter Two

High King Elias Rovannon of Albia stood behind his four-year-old son, well out of reach of the little wooden sword the boy was brandishing. Eadan was as likely to connect with his father as he was with his opponent's weapon, and Elias already had bruises to show for it.

A sharp crack of wood echoed as Eadan's sword was knocked away. "Foul!" roared the King, pointing an accusing finger at Eadan's young opponent. "That was a foul stroke, and you know it."

"Was not!" cried Morgan, turning indignant blue eyes on the aging swordmaster who was scoring the bout. "Was it, Master Ardoch?"

Ghyllan Ardoch chuckled and cast a sly eye at Morgan's parents. "It was a winning stroke, Morgan laddie, and that's what counts."

Morgan's mother, Brynne Sullyan, sat at ease upon the ground, her slender back against a tree, her golden eyes half-closed. Her left hand stroked the dark, curling hair of the young man whose head lay in her lap, an indulgent smile upon his handsome face. Robin Tamsen raised himself on one elbow, the better to watch his young son.

Morgan Sullyan was only three and a half, but already showed signs of the talents he had inherited from his parents. He had

Sullyan's delicate build and amber skin, still bronzed from days under the warm summer sun, and his father's dark hair and blue eyes. A quiet boy until something caught his attention, his curiosity had led him into trouble ever since he could walk. It was fortunate his innate Artesan talents had manifested early, for his ability to call out to either of his parents from the moment of his birth had already saved him from injury more than once.

Robin was about to reply to the swordmaster's sly look when a delighted cry rent the air.

"Tad's coming, Tad's coming!"

They all looked up at Eadan's high-pitched shout, and his sister, the Princess Seline, let out an excited squeal at the sight of the two men who approached from the direction of the garrison. Seline hurriedly composed herself, a look of self-disgust on her face. She was seven years old and every inch the haughty royal Princess, especially in the absence of her mother. She considered herself far above the demeaning antics of the younger children and had agreed to join the picnic in the castle park for one reason only.

Seline had fallen hopelessly in love with the dashing seventeen-year-old swordsman, Tad, and took every opportunity to be in his presence. But screaming childishly was not the way a well-bred young girl should behave and she hastily smoothed the rumpled velvet of her warm winter gown to regain her composure. She tried a coy smile as the two men came closer, but the younger of them had no time to notice her, for he was suddenly set upon by three screeching devil children hell-bent on bringing him down.

"Help!" cried Tad from beneath the wriggling bodies, casting an appealing glance at the man who had accompanied him across the park.

"Unhand him, you brigands!" yelled Cal, the dark-skinned captain diving for Eadan's discarded sword before rushing into the fray. "Come help us, Taran, we are outnumbered and sore beset!"

Almost helpless with laughter, Taran Elijah, Adept-elite and Court Artesan to King Elias, rose from his comfortable place at the side of his partner, Jinny, and dashed to the aid of his friends. More of the little wooden swords were snatched up from where they lay, and Robin turned to grin at Sullyan as their son and Cal's daughter, Elisse, moved to stand shoulder to shoulder. They fended off Taran's mock attack with creditable coordination.

"She learns fast," commented Sullyan, glancing at Elisse's mother.

Rienne Arlen tore her attention away from the fussing toddler in her lap to watch the antics of the fighters. Her son, Taric, only a year and a half old, was teething and inclined to be fretful. She smiled to see the collaboration between her daughter and Sullyan's son.

"I wonder if they'll always be so close," Rienne said, and then snorted with laughter as the High King of Albia let out a yell, having received yet another bruise from the hand of his son as he got too close in his efforts to advise the boy. Ardoch was urging Morgan on to wilder and wilder swings with his wooden sword, Elisse following his every move.

"Aeyron! Robin! Come on, we need your help if these dastardly invaders are to be repulsed."

Robin exchanged glances with Elias's royal guest, Prince Aeyron, co-ruler of Andaryon, and the two surged to their feet, unable to ignore their comrades' distress. To whoops of joy from the young terrorists, they too caught up weapons and joined in the mêlée.

"C'mon, Sellie, come help us!" Prince Eadan called to his sister, but the young Princess turned a scandalized expression upon him, resolutely staying where she was.

Sullyan could see Seline would dearly love to join in but was reluctant to drop her poise in case Tad should see her make a fool of herself. Seline was at that delicate age when she was still enough of a child to sometimes be tempted by rough games, but was also beginning to realize she would soon become a young woman. The appearance of the dashing, gallant Tad among the King's Guard had hastened that realization.

Since Elias's ill-advised invasion into the realm of Andaryon three years ago, major changes had been made to the garrison at Port Loxton. This had imposed similar changes on the routine at the Manor. Mathias Blaine, General-in-Command of the King's fighting forces, had been deeply disturbed by the ease with which the Baron and Queen Sofira had been able to work their treachery, and although the Baron had been exiled and the Queen divorced and stripped of her power, some unease had remained in his heart. He had grimly vowed that such things would never happen again. Once the traitors had been dealt with and the personal lives of two of his most trusted and powerful officers returned to something approaching normality, the general began his reforms.

The most obvious change he made was to ensure the presence of a senior military officer at the castle garrison at all times. This meant either the general himself or one of his two colonels. Since none of them wished to move to the capital on a permanent basis, he devised a rota system which saw the Manor forces divided up between himself, Colonel Jerrim Vassa, and Brynne Sullyan. At the head of their respective companies, each high-ranking officer spent four months at the capital, thus ensuring a fresh set of eyes, and an exchange of new ideas.

The past year had seen another major change to life at the Manor. Taran Elijah, Adept-elite, had finally accepted the position of Court Artesan. Taran's decision was partly influenced by the young blonde woman sitting by Sullyan's side, whose eyes were currently filled with tears.

The Baroness Jinella, niece of the traitor Hezra Reen, had

fallen deeply in love with the tall and handsome Adept. Their relationship hadn't had the best of starts due to Taran's futile commitment to Sullyan, but as time went by and they saw more of each other, they had grown easier together. Taran also stood as mentor to little Morgan, and now that the boy's embryo Artesan talents were beginning to bud, he would be more involved with his training than ever. But Sullyan's regular tour of duty at the castle meant Taran could fulfill both roles at the same time, and so he had allowed Jinny to persuade him to accept Elias's handsome offer.

Taran was independently wealthy, thanks to Elias's generosity after the Adept helped rescue his son from the Baron's clutches, and so he felt no obligation to Jinny whenever he stayed at her mansion. He was there because he wished to be, and he was surprised to discover that he wished to be in her company more often than not. He was genuinely fond of the woman and enjoyed spending time with her. He found release for his passions in her bed and she shared his delight and enthusiasm.

Sullyan was relieved Taran seemed to be settling down to life with Jinella. Brynne Sullyan loved Taran almost as deeply as he loved her, but the trust and loyalty of her heart was given without reservation to Robin, her true life mate, and she had despaired of Taran ever committing to another woman. Knowing the depth of his emotions and the wealth of love he had to offer, she had grieved over the waste. But his developing relationship with Jinny seemed to enrich and satisfy him, which was why the Baroness's tears were so puzzling to Sullyan now. She shared a brief glance with Rienne before she spoke, not looking at the sorrowful heiress beside her.

"Why the tears, Jinny?"

Jinella startled, swallowed, and used a delicate lace-edged cloth to dry her eyes. Beside her, Rienne snorted with laughter again as Morgan finally inveigled the old swordmaster into joining the fight on the children's side, which was the cue for the adults to discard their toy swords, snatch up practice foils, and fence in earnest.

This was a favorite game and the three women knew what would happen next. The children would choose their champions. Morgan always chose Robin and Taran, Elisse picked Cal and Aeyron, and Eadan wisely went for his father and Tad, which was the only way he could guarantee Seline would join the game. Ardoch was pressed into awarding points as they fenced against each other. The old Torlander was in on the game and always made sure Elias and Tad won by one point. Seline never knew how much her brother enjoyed seeing her blush as Tad gallantly bestowed the champion's kiss on his lady's hand.

Jinella twisted her fingers in her lap as she watched the skillful swordplay. Sullyan knew that she admired the grace of the fighting men and these shows of steel and strength usually thrilled her to the core. But today she seemed troubled, and the sight of her man pitting his blade against his friends failed to lighten her mood.

Sullyan did not press her. She could see Jinny needed to order her thoughts before speaking. Rienne, tactful as ever, stood and carried little Taric to where he could watch his father more clearly. Jinny watched her go.

"Brynne …."

Jinny faltered. Sullyan turned to face her, sending silent encouragement. Jinny had no innate Artesan talent, though she had sometimes shown intuition above normal levels. Sullyan was sure there were times when Jinny felt the power of the Artesan.

The Baroness took a breath and rushed into speech. "Brynne, how intimately do you know Taran?"

Sullyan raised her brows. The tack of the question had taken her by surprise. She took care over her answer. She and Jinny had not always shared an easy relationship, as Jinny had seen her as a rival for Taran's affections.

"I am not sure exactly what you mean. I know Taran Elijah very well. You know that we, as Artesans, can hold no secrets from each other. I know the wishes of his heart and I know the depth of his love and commitment. But there are aspects of his life that are closed to me. We do not seek to invade each other's privacy."

Jinny closed her eyes. "I'm being clumsy. I'm not really sure how to ask what I want to know."

Sullyan regarded her. "I can see you are troubled. Does it concern your relationship with Taran?"

Jinny nodded. "Oh, this is so difficult! I've wanted to ask you … ask someone … but I wasn't going to do it right now. I've been unhappy for a while, but this lovely picnic isn't the right time. But I was watching the children, and I was thinking about something Taran said to me earlier."

Sullyan's enquiring expression encouraged Jinny to continue.

"Taran told me he was sad your tour of duty was over and that you and Morgan would be leaving tomorrow. He's so enjoyed his mentoring duties, and he's so good with Morgan, and it made me realize what a good … what a …" Jinny gulped down a sob.

Sullyan's voice was soothing. "Just say it, Jinny."

The younger woman took hold of her courage and blurted, "Do you happen to know if Taran has ever fathered a child?"

Sullyan's eyes widened in surprise. "What a strange question." She hesitated before replying, "Not to my knowledge, although I doubt it very much. Rienne could answer you better than I. She has known Taran much longer. But Taran is too honorable to risk an unwanted pregnancy, and if he had fathered a child he would have taken responsibility for it."

Jinny hung her head, her face pale. "Yes, I thought you'd say that," she whispered. "It must be me."

"What must be you?" Sullyan asked the question although she

already knew the answer.

"I think I must be barren," Jinny murmured, "or else I would have conceived by now. We've not exactly been restrained in our relationship. We've had ample chances to make a child over the past three years, but nothing's happened. And I'm so afraid he won't want me if I can't give him children. Do you think that's why he's never asked me to marry him?"

Sullyan caught Jinny's tearful gaze. "Has he ever said so? Has he ever discussed having a family with you?"

Jinny shook her head sadly, causing Sullyan to purse her lips in annoyance. Damn Taran and his honor!

She became aware of Jinny's hopeful look and her heart turned cold. She was afraid she knew what the girl was going to ask her now, and her guess proved correct.

"Brynne, could you use your powers to tell me whether I could ever bear a child? I know I have no gift myself, but Taran says you can ... touch ... someone ungifted provided they're willing. And I really do want to know."

Sullyan cursed Taran for the second time that day, and wondered how she could let Jinny down gently without hurting her feelings or telling her an outright lie. Sullyan knew very well why Jinny had not conceived, and her opinion of Taran was undergoing a swift revision. How could he let her believe this? How could he not have told her?

She was spared the necessity of answering Jinny by a sudden rush as noisy children converged on them, throwing themselves down on the blanket, their pleading cries loud in the winter air. The fencing bout had ended in the usual way, with the contrived win of Elias and Tad, and now Prince Eadan and Princess Seline demanded their prize: the thrill of watching Sullyan fence with—and defeat—both King Elias and Tad at the same time.

Sullyan was tugged to her feet by her overexcited son. She

extended her hand for the practice foil held out by Eadan. She saw Jinny's hopeful look turn mournful and gave the girl what truth and cheer she could.

"I could not promise that using my powers in the way you have asked would tell you what you want to know, Jinny, but one thing I will promise you. I will speak with Taran Elijah about what you have said. Try not to concern yourself. This matter will be resolved."

She was dragged away by the yelling children, and the air was once more filled with raucous cheers and screams of encouragement as she proved herself yet again one of the most skilled swordmasters Albia had ever seen.

Chapter Three

The cold dark of evening had descended once more, but it was warm and pleasant in Elias's private dining hall. Twin fires crackled merrily in their hearths at opposite ends of the large room. Candles and lamps mellowed the air while decorative tapestries and heavy drapes kept out the winter chill. The cloudless day had given way to rapidly falling temperatures and it was a widely held opinion more snow was on the way.

The room buzzed with conversation above the soft playing of the minstrels, although there was an undercurrent of sadness beneath the jokes and stories. Sullyan was aware of the King casting her wistful looks across the table and resolutely refrained from catching his eye. She would speak with him later when, no doubt, she would be forced to refuse yet again his heartfelt plea to remain in the castle.

There was a good crowd in the King's private rooms, as it pleased him to entertain those who were leaving his immediate service to return to the Manor. By surrounding himself with as many friends as possible, Elias strove to hold off the depressed loneliness that had haunted him since his wife's betrayal. They might not have shared an intimate marriage, but Elias had always trusted her loyalty. Discovering how deeply she despised him, and how thoroughly he had been deceived, had badly shaken his confidence.

At his table this evening were all the adult attendees of the picnic, as well as Elias's First Minister, Lord Levant, and his

chamberlain and secretary, Lord Kinsey. The other members of
Sullyan's company, including young Tad, were being entertained
over in the barracks by Major Denny, who had been promoted to
Commander-in-Residence of the King's Guard the previous year.

Under normal circumstances, Cal, who was a captain by rank,
would not have been included among the King's guests, but his
marriage to Rienne and her inclusion among the King's circle of
close friends guaranteed him a place in this gathering. Rienne, as
an empath, was highly valued by Sullyan's team of Artesans due to
her greater insight into what they might be suffering. She was also
Sullyan's dearest friend. So when General Blaine devised his rota
for the guarding of the King, Rienne was included as part of
Sullyan's command.

In this, the General had shown his cunning as well as his
willingness to accommodate his most powerful officer's familial
limitations. Sullyan was Robin's commanding officer and was
understandably reluctant to take the field at the same time as her
life mate due to the huge risk this would pose to their son. She had
no intention of leaving Morgan an orphan, as she herself had been,
but also would not shirk her duty to her King. With the inclusion of
Rienne in the party, not only could the healer provide for Morgan
should the unthinkable happen, but she would also be on hand to
treat any injuries as soon as they might occur. Sullyan felt
immeasurably safer with Rienne along.

The dark-haired healer was content with the arrangement as it
also meant she need not be parted from her own life mate for four
months at a time. And Cal need not be parted from Rienne and his
two children. The system worked well for all concerned, and
Rienne spent her four-month tour of duty working in the castle's
infirmary.

The main topic of conversation this evening revolved around
the only non-human in the group. Prince Aeyron was good-

naturedly fending off the barrage of questions and advice being flung his way. After some long years—and constant nagging by his father, the Hierarch—the thirty-five-year-old Prince had finally announced he was courting and hoped soon to be betrothed. This visit to Elias had been arranged partially in order for him to make this welcome announcement to his human friends and allies.

Brynne Sullyan, his adopted sister and Princess of Andaryon, had been informed some weeks previously, but had been constrained to secrecy until her royal brother had the opportunity to make this courtesy trip to inform Elias himself. Now she smiled in deepest pleasure to see the flush brought to Aeyron's handsome face by the congratulatory and often downright derogatory remarks cast his way by his friends.

Aeyron had taken many months to recover from the effects of his torture at the hands of the Baron. His right hand had been maimed in order to send a gruesome message to his father, and it had taken much careful nursing to mend not only the physical hurts, but also the mental trauma. Andaryan nobility set much store by physical perfection and strength of arms, and these ideals were especially important in the person of their ruler. Aeyron's confidence had suffered deeply with his loss, and Sullyan had played a vital part in the total recovery he eventually made. His gratitude and love for her had never waned.

Unfortunately, as with Taran, Aeyron's understandable but misplaced emotion had hindered his search for a mate. Knowing full well he could never wed Sullyan even had she been free—her blood was hybrid, a unique mixture of human and demon—his deep attachment to her left scant room in his heart for another. He had also become disaffected with the traditional and prejudicial social mores of his realm, which dictated that women were good for bed and breeding only. Having seen Sullyan in action, both in a military and a diplomatic capacity, Aeyron desired a life mate who would be capable of ruling by his side. Such a woman was hard to find in Andaryon.

During Sullyan's pregnancy, while she was resident at the Hierarch's Citadel, she and Aeyron began the reforms which Aeyron hoped to continue once he found a suitable Princess. Although there had been some outspoken dissention, none of the Andaryan nobles dared rebel openly.

Since Morgan's birth and Sullyan's return to the Manor, Aeyron had been bereft of her advice and company. Yet he found an unexpected ally in the form of his birth sister, Idrimar, whose husband, Ty Marik, was an old friend of Sullyan's and a staunch supporter of her far-reaching ideas. Marik encouraged his wife to take an active part in the running of her father's realm, and since Marik and Aeyron often relieved Pharikian of his many duties, Princess Idrimar was now a familiar and accepted presence at the council table.

So it was to Sullyan's relief and great pleasure when Aeyron announced he had found the soul mate he desired; a woman of noble birth who had a brain and could be encouraged to use it. Now, his friends wanted details and would give him no rest until they had them.

"Come on, then, Aeyron, what does this paragon with a brain look like?" teased Cal. "How long are her teeth? How many men has her father tried to foist her off onto? Have you seen her mother yet? Have you checked her confirmation or bloodline?"

Rienne gasped in outrage at her husband's inference that not only was the Princess ugly, but that her mother must be a horse. Her soft gray eyes widened in indignation and she turned to the tall Andaryan at her side, laying a hand upon his forearm. "Ignore these jealous, petty men, Aeyron. Tell *me* what she's like. I'm genuinely interested. What's her name? I suppose Brynne's met her already?"

Sullyan shook her head as the men bridled at Rienne's casual dismissal of them. Aeyron grinned broadly. He had anticipated this barrage of insulting banter and had already fended off similar reactions from his fellow countrymen at home.

"Her name is Lirina," he told Rienne, "and her father rules a small, sea-bordered province many miles to the south of our realm. We've not had much to do with the Dalkians in the past. They're so far away they never attend any of the gatherings at the Citadel, and as they've never caused my father any trouble, we rarely have contact with them. Lirina's father, Lord Seyakin, came to the Citadel forty years ago in order to declare his fealty to the Hierarchy when he acceded to the rule of his province, but since then we've heard hardly anything from them."

Rienne noted the flush in Aeyron's cheeks and the diffident way he spoke the Princess's name. "So how did you come to meet Lirina?"

The tall Andaryan smiled, taking an appreciative sip of the ruby vintage in his goblet. "Word got out I was looking for a wife. Emissaries came from far and wide, offering me gifts and bribes and all manner of other, ah, inducements to encourage me to consider this or that heiress or Princess. Among them, at the end of last summer, was an ambassador from Dalkia, and he carried with him a portrait of Lirina. Once I'd seen it and heard the man's opinion of her character, I decided to pay her father a visit."

"Risky," came the gruff voice of the Torlander across the table. "How did you know yer man was telling the truth? Anyone can paint a flattering portrait. Anyone can tell a good story."

Aeyron replied equably. "Agreed, Ghyllan, and I would have made no promises nor accepted any gifts until I had seen and spoken to the lady in question. But I was persuaded to the journey by the letter which arrived along with the ambassador and his portrait; a letter from an eminently trustworthy source."

Aeyron glanced slyly at Sullyan and she sharpened her gaze as she realized there was more to this tale than she had yet heard.

She laughed. "Go on, then, my brother, seeing as you have now so cleverly piqued my curiosity."

Aeyron grinned. "The letter was written by an old friend of yours. Someone you haven't seen for a few years now."

Sullyan's brow creased, but then her expression cleared. As she sorted through what she knew of Lirina and her home province, the answer became clear. After all, there were not so many candidates to choose from.

"Ky-shan!" she exclaimed. "How is he, Aeyron?"

The Prince inclined his head. "He is well, Brynne, as is his son, Jay'el. My father is very pleased with their services to our shipping concerns, and not least for the profit they make us."

"So how does Ky-shan know Lirina?" Rienne asked.

Aeyron glanced at her. "Ky-shan had been plying the seas about Dalkia's coastline, scouting possible new trade routes for the fleet. A large and unexpected late summer tempest blew up, forcing him to run into Dalkia's main harbor for shelter."

"That must have been some storm," said Sullyan, knowing Ky-shan's reputation for seamanship.

Aeyron nodded. "It was a freak, and it caused some damage to Ky-shan's vessel. He put in for repairs and while he was there, he investigated the capital's trade potential. Using my father's seal, he gained an audience with Lord Seyakin and they discussed mutually beneficial trade possibilities.

"During his visits to Seyakin's palace, he met Lirina and her younger sister, Kyrie. Lirina handles most of her father's business interests. Knowing how rare that is and how it would intrigue me, Ky-shan gave his letter to the ambassador when he heard he was leaving for the Caer. He didn't tell Seyakin what was in the letter; he didn't want to raise the man's hopes should his daughter not catch my eye."

"But she obviously did catch your eye, and also your heart," smiled Rienne. "And now you are to be betrothed! Well, I'm very happy to hear it. May you find the fulfillment you desire. Might I ask the age of your intended bride?"

"Lirina is twenty-eight," the smiling Prince replied. Deliberately, he added, "Her sister is twenty-three."

"Jay'el is twenty-three." Sullyan spoke casually, not looking at Aeyron.

He narrowed his eyes and breathed an exasperated sigh. "How do you *do* that? I was saving that revelation to startle you with."

Sullyan allowed herself a small grin. "Forgive me, my brother."

Aeyron frowned in a pretense of irritation. "Well, since you are so clever, perhaps you can tell me the import of the request I have been asked to convey to you?"

Sullyan already had a good idea of what Aeyron was hiding, but she enjoyed stretching out the suspense to amuse her friends.

"Let me see," she mused. "Let us suppose Jay'el has fallen for the charms of the young Kyrie and is desperate to impress Lord Seyakin as a valid suitor. Ky-shan is understandably keen for him to do so. After all, a link by marriage to the Hierarchy of Andaryon is not something to let slip away. But Jay'el, of course, does not have the status of a Prince of the Realm, and so must look to what talents he does possess in order to convince Seyakin of his suitability. As the winter season in Andaryon often keeps the fleet in port, Ky-shan feels he can manage without his son for a while, and this would leave Jay'el free to learn new skills with which to court the young Kyrie." Sullyan glanced at her brother. "Am I nearing the mark?"

"You know full well you are, you witch!" Aeyron's growl brought general laughter.

Sullyan turned to Elias, who watched this intimate byplay with envy and some puzzlement. "Elias, it seems your College will have its first non-human student."

In the three and a half years since its inauguration, the College had grown slowly but steadily. With the much-publicized exile of the Baron—the Artesan craft's most outspoken opponent—the populace was being led carefully toward a greater acceptance of those born with the gift. King Elias had undertaken a series of progressions through the main parts of his province, spreading the word of his approval of Artesans and the existence of the College, even going so far as to offer recompense to families who would lose the skills of those keen—or at least willing—to learn how to use their talents. After some time, during which the King despaired of influencing the long-held beliefs of his people, a trickle of candidates began at last to appear at the Manor gates.

Now, while still not at anything approaching full capacity, the College at least had a fair number of trainees. Elias was beginning to feel proud of his innovation and foresight. He grinned at Sullyan.

"I trust you will make him welcome, Brynne. Perhaps it will even be a good excuse for a royal visit."

Sullyan was aware there were two very compelling reasons why Elias should wish to visit the Manor while she was there. His loneliness and deep-seated need for her was only one of them. The other was currently fast asleep in the nursery, worn out by the excitement and exertions of the day. She gave her sovereign a look full of sympathy, which brought a flush to Elias's complexion.

"He will be completely safe with us," she murmured. "You have my sworn word on that. You know I will guard him with my life."

Elias did know this. She had already laid her own life on the line in his service more than once. He had no doubt she would do so again, despite all she now had to lose. As always, he was humbled by the depths of her love and commitment.

Their eyes met as if there was no one else in the room. "I do know that, Brynne." Well used to their sovereign's behavior around Sullyan, the others tactfully looked away or spoke of other things.

It had taken Sullyan some time to convince her monarch Eadan was ready to begin training in the handling of his emerging Artesan talents. Elias had no traces of the gift and neither, as far as either of them knew, did his mother. General Blaine, who had known Elias's father, thought the talent probably came from his side, but as none of them knew much about Sofira's family history, this was pure speculation.

Elias had always been a supporter of Artesans. Growing up in his father's court and listening to the intrigue that went on as a matter of course, Elias, who had a lively mind and never suffered from prejudicial thinking, was quick to see the advantages of surrounding himself with loyal servants who possessed valuable talents. The fact they were reviled and mistrusted by most of the populace and, more seriously, a large portion of the ministers at his father's court did nothing to dissuade the young Elias. The civil war that resulted in the death of King Kandaran left the new High King with a clearer field in which to practice his beliefs. The fact there were still those who plainly disapproved moved Elias not one whit, nor dampened his fascination with Artesans. It came as a complete shock to him when Sullyan blithely announced his baby son would one day exhibit the gifts that so impressed him.

That was three years ago. Since then she had kept a close eye on the little boy and his embryo talent, and Taran's move to the capital a year ago meant the Adept-elite could also report to her on Eadan's progress. It had become clear over her recent tour of duty that Eadan would now benefit from a good grounding in the basics of the Artesan craft.

She had felt guilty about mentioning it to the King. She was well aware how close Elias and Eadan were. Since the boy's abduction at the hands of Reen, Elias had become understandably more protective of his son and Heir. Sullyan knew how desolate Elias would be to lose his son's company, even though he knew he would be as safe—if not safer—at the Manor.

And then there was Eadan himself. The boy was full of life, full of fun, and very fond of his father. Although she was not to blame for Sofira's actions, Sullyan felt responsible for Eadan losing his mother. She was an orphan herself and understood only too well how the loss of parents could affect a child. Yet it was Sullyan's actions that saw Sofira impeached for her treacherous activities, and her subsequent exile from Port Loxton.

Once their marriage was dissolved, Elias imprisoned Sofira within the castle, placing strict limits and conditions on her access to her children. It was never his wish to deprive his children of their mother, but Sofira, always vocal in her opinions, railed constantly against the strictures placed upon her, making a misery of her children's visits.

It was Seline who felt it most. The young Princess had been close to her mother and was very like her in temperament. She was spoiled and haughty and guarded her privileges and status fiercely, permitting no liberties. She had been brought up with certain expectations and was wholly convinced of her mother's innocence. Despite the guards and carefully selected ladies who accompanied the children every time they visited their mother, Sofira managed to instill in Seline the conviction that the King had treated her harshly, and that she was the victim of a sly and invidious plot. Seline had been heard on numerous occasions berating her father bitterly for her mother's plight.

Seline's character and demeanor worsened, and soon Elias

could ignore it no longer. He put a stop to the children's visits, and when this only deepened Seline's resentment and anger, he banished Sofira from court. Having obtained her signed affidavit that she would never again rebel against him on pain of death for both her and her father, Elias had Sofira transported back to Bordenn, there to live her life in obscurity.

Seline reacted very badly to her mother's absence.

Although Elias had never felt the depth of affection for Seline that he did for Eadan, he nevertheless recognized the girl's pain, realizing she was too young to understand all that had happened. In an effort to placate the girl and show her he wasn't completely heartless, Elias permitted the letters Sofira sent her daughter to reach their intended recipient. He did, of course, read them first.

Eadan had been too young for Sofira to influence as she had Seline. She had attempted to bond the little boy ever more firmly to her by giving him treats and permitting him whatever he wanted while trying to poison his mind. It hadn't worked, for Eadan seemed to intuit what she was doing and gave no credence to her malicious lies. Sullyan privately believed that Eadan, even then, was able to sense both his father's integrity and his mother's duplicity, and was only confused and upset by Sofira's spite. But the fact remained Eadan had lost his mother's love, and now Sullyan proposed he be removed from his father also.

So she smiled her understanding at Elias, and the High King ducked his head and flushed again at the depth of commitment in her eyes.

The party broke up shortly after. There was much to organize for the morning and Sullyan wanted to inspect the barracks and check on the men before going to her rest. Colonel Vassa would arrive sometime in the morning, granted access through the substrate by Lord-General Anjer in Andaryon, and she needed to ensure all was in readiness. She left the King and his other guests to their after-dinner liquor and moved through the castle toward the outer doors.

Loxton Castle had undergone some structural changes since those dreadful events three years ago. The Queen's apartments were in the east wing, and Elias had caused these to be walled off from the main castle after her impeachment. Her private rooms had remained untouched, but there was now only one access door to the entire wing.

Since Sofira's departure a year ago, the east wing remained deserted. The children's nursery had been moved into the main castle, nearer Elias's apartments, and the door to the Queen's wing remained securely locked. Sullyan would pass this door as she made her way outside.

As she came abreast of the stout iron-bound door, she halted mid-stride, arrested by the strangest feeling of foreboding. Prescience was not considered an Artesan talent, nor was it even widely accepted as existing, and Sullyan herself, for all her mighty powers, was skeptical. Yet she couldn't deny there had been times in her life when momentous events seemed to affect her psyche, and she had even acted upon such feelings. They had rarely let her down.

She searched her mind for what had caught at her senses, trying to pin down this vague sensation of wrong. As so often happened, the more she chased it, the more elusive it became. She had no patience with this. Her other talents were there for the asking. Her training, her knowledge, and her power allowed her access to her metaforce and psyche at will. Her gifts were as readily accessible as the senses of sight, touch, or smell. So she wasted no time in fruitless wonder, merely tucked the feeling away within her mind, to bring out and examine at a later date should she feel the need. She walked on, ignoring the faint, natural sound of wood as it settled.

Chapter Four

Within the cheerless cell deep beneath the palace, the scarecrow grew weaker. He lay helpless on the uncomfortable bed, staring angrily at the leprous growths covering the slimy rock walls. He viciously cursed the ache gnawing at his body, the lassitude dragging at his limbs.

Damn the boy! Surely he had possessed more strength than this? Surely Reen hadn't used it all in the desperate escape from his island prison? But there was no denying the facts. His physical strength was waning fast and he would be forced to do something about it. He might as well do it now, and he blessed the foresight that had prompted him to take the action that would ensure he could renew his fading strength without revealing his true nature too soon.

Reen was well aware that his host was suspicious. He clearly felt the waves of fear and revulsion given off by the older man and wondered briefly whether he ought to have expended more of his unsuspected powers to bind Lerric to him as he had Sofira. But his resources were finite, and he must spend them wisely.

Soon, this would change. Once he had Sofira completely under his control he could act as he wished, and he would have both her backing and her authority to bolster him. Already she had unwittingly provided him with the means to implement a very important aspect of his plans. He could afford to relax once the next phase had borne its intended fruit, but for the moment he needed Lerric, and it would cost him more than he was prepared to pay to control the client-king's will.

Physical strength, though, was a priority. Angrily, gripping the livid wood of his cane, Reen exerted his will.

Within minutes two of the men Lerric had sent to accomplish Reen's rescue descended the winding stair to the cell of their new master. Reen's hollow, hawk-like face broke into a sneer as he heard their reluctant progress. The door to the cell opened slowly with no courtesy, but the scarecrow expected none. He stared into the terrified eyes of the two men before him, an evil leer on his face. The tremble of their limbs was plain to see, and the abject fear they exuded fed him like an elixir. He breathed the scent of their horror deeply.

"Come here."

The man he had addressed, the younger of the two, hesitated fractionally. Reen, mightily displeased by this unexpected display of resistance, lashed the man with his hatred; though he could ill afford the effort it cost him. The youthful face contorted with pain and tendons stood out in the strong neck as the man strove to scream. Sweat broke out over his body and his companion moaned in terror.

"I said, come *here!*"

The man obeyed, all sense of self smothered by the Baron's controlling will.

"Help me up."

Reen gleefully absorbed the rank miasma of the man's terror, even this slight power lending him strength as the muscled arm reached out, pulling the feeble wastrel to his feet. The dreadful, wheezing voice came again.

"Remove your shirt."

Hands fumbled with the fastenings of the sweat-dampened cloth, the man's eyes bulging with fear. As the fabric came away and fell to the filthy floor, an angry circle of skin in the center of the man's chest was revealed. Swollen and crusted with old blood and unwashed dirt, the affected area glowed with a sullen ruby light.

Reen cast a swift glance over his shoulder to check the second man. He could not afford to be disturbed or have the man cry out. He needn't have worried. Eyes screwed shut, sweat pouring down his face, teeth chattering in terror, the other servant was past all conscious thought or action.

Well and good! Reen turned back, staring into the eyes of the man before him. He bared his teeth in a decaying smile. He slowly raised the tip of his cane and heard the faint, pleading whimper that escaped the captive's throat. Drinking in the man's essence, Reen placed the tip of the gnarled cane against the raw patch on the muscular chest. He leaned on it, hard.

Immediately, he was falling, surrounded by terror, blasted by screams. The scarecrow's arms cartwheeled as he flailed for balance, but the sensation lasted only a second. This was the moment of vulnerability; the one moment when he could be thwarted, cast out, denied. But he already knew the fellow no longer had the ability to resist him. This cataclysmic wailing and shrieking was the only release permitted the tortured man, and even this fed the scarecrow's black soul.

As he fed, Reen felt himself swelling. Twisted bones straightened, feeble muscles grew strong, and his skin regained a semblance of youth and vitality. Briefly, Reen regretted the weakness that prevented him from absorbing what he needed the other way, the more pleasurable way. Then he reminded himself sternly that such activities would have to wait. Much as he craved them, his need for physical strength was such that he must take it the simplest way possible, with the least cost to himself. Those other pleasures, the darker pleasures, would come later.

Before he damaged the man too severely, Reen withdrew from

his essence. He removed the tip of the cane from the man's bubbling flesh and watched dispassionately as the drained body crumpled to the floor. Let it lie! It would recover soon enough. He couldn't afford, just yet, to reduce it too much. Soon—ah, soon, he promised himself—he would do as he willed and not have to concern himself with the well-being of his creatures. For now, much as it galled him, he needed them alive.

He turned toward the other man, his body now firmly fleshed, his movements sure. His lips once more broke into a sinister smile as he registered the blind panic on the older man's face. He approached the gibbering servant, savoring the moment, drinking the terror, laughing at the tears that flowed as the captive's gaze swung from the glowing tip of the cane to the ruby red points deep within the terrible gray eyes.

Once again, silent screams rang in Reen's mind.

⁜ ⁜ ⁜ ⁜ ⁜

"I'm not sure I can do it, Brynne. How can I bear to let him go? Are you sure you can't stay and begin his training here at the castle? I could have rooms made available to you—a whole suite if you like! You'd have free rein; you wouldn't be distracted by the duties of the garrison, you could devote all your time to my son …"

And to you.

Brynne Sullyan faced the distraught King of Albia. They stood in the quiet of the sunlit nursery. Seline was nowhere to be seen and Eadan had just gone scampering off in a state of high excitement to fetch his favorite wooden sword, without which he'd go nowhere. Sullyan sighed as she faced up to the inevitable battle of wills she had been both expecting and dreading this morning.

"Elias, my friend, you already know my reasons for insisting Eadan come to the Manor. I am not free. I have a duty to the

General and my company, as well as to you. The facilities of the College are what Eadan needs. The support and experience of his peers will go far toward encouraging his emerging talents. And besides, you saw how keen he is. Have you not promised him this from the moment he could understand your offer? How could you disappoint him now?"

Elias's blue eyes misted over at her argument and he opened his mouth to reply, but Sullyan was in no mood to endure his stalling tactics. He had made the decision and she would see him abide by it.

"Have no fear, my lord. He will come to no harm with us. We will nurture him and care for him as surely as you would. He is one of us, and precious, doubly so as he will grow to be the first Artesan King of Albia. Do you think any of us would see that jeopardized?"

"Of course not, Brynne, I understand that. It's only that I will miss him so much, and you know how I'll also—"

"I know you will miss him, my friend." Sullyan didn't want to hear the rest of Elias's sentiments. "And I am sure he will also miss you. I will be in regular contact with Taran as usual, and you will get a daily report on his progress and well-being. You are always welcome at the Manor, you know that, and Eadan will want regular visits from you so he can show off what he has learned. Let him go, Elias. You know you must."

The sandy-haired King gazed into Sullyan's warm eyes, hearing her unspoken plea. He knew she referred not only to his protests over Eadan, but also his desire to keep her near him. He sighed, a sentiment she silently echoed. She knew he couldn't help his feelings, and feared he would not be able to dispel the specter of loneliness that would descend once she was gone.

He dropped his gaze and Sullyan saw capitulation in the weary slump of his shoulders. His defeated aspect pained her; it was what made her dread the end of each tour of duty at the castle. She longed to reach out to him, take him in her arms for comfort, but she didn't dare. She had to keep her distance, for both their sakes. If she did not, if she once let slip her guard, they might well step beyond safe boundaries which could never be re-erected.

Fortunately, Eadan reappeared at that uncomfortable moment, clutching his toy sword. He was followed by his nursemaid, Bessie. The little boy was in a state of rare excitement at the thought of his coming adventure, and he capered around his father, waving his sword, crowing his delight and dispelling Elias's somber mood. It was hard to feel despondent when Eadan's joy was so infectious.

Despite his closeness to his father, Eadan obviously felt no fear of leaving him and traveling with Sullyan to the Manor, two days' fast ride away from his home. During his adventures following his rescue from the Baron's clutches at only one year of age, he had shown no anxiety at the many strange sights and sensations he experienced. Indeed, he seemed to form an attachment to Sullyan even then, due in part to her ability to perceive and understand his emerging psyche.

He was also close to her son, and to Rienne's daughter. They were always at the castle when Sullyan was there, and to Eadan, they were part of his family. So although he was leaving his father behind, he was going with people he knew and trusted. Morgan's colorful and exciting descriptions of life at the Manor whetted the little Prince's appetite all the more. That and the promise of training both in metaphysics and in sword play—Eadan's chief joys—would have persuaded him even had he been reluctant.

Elias could not hide a smile as he watched his son's antics.

"Oh, very well. I won't be difficult. But I shall expect daily reports, as you've promised, and I'll be over to see him very soon.

"Eadan," continued Elias, having to repeat the boy's name

39

firmly to get his attention. "Eadan! Come here, I want to speak with you."

The little boy stopped brandishing the toy sword and stuck it through his small belt. Sullyan noticed with a smile that someone had made for Eadan a replica of her own leather weapons harness, which could be worn either around the hips or crosswise over the chest. Years ago, when she first began her own training, Ardoch had suggested this arrangement as it enabled her to draw her sword from across her back with either hand when she fought on horseback, a valuable talent which she had unwittingly developed before the more conventional teachings of the King's swordmaster could train it out of her. She wondered whether the Torlander had been encouraging Eadan to do the same thing.

Elias knelt down in front of his son and regarded him seriously. Eadan's eyes were a blue-gray, softer than his father's.

"Eadan, I want you to behave yourself while you're at the Manor." Elias held up a hand to forestall his son's protestations. "I'm not speaking as your father now, but as your King."

This statement had an immediate effect on Eadan. He straightened his back and lifted his chin, well aware of his status as a Prince.

"I want you to remember, while you're learning, that you are the Heir to the throne," Elias continued. "You must work hard and obey your teachers, and you must not let me down by behaving badly. I want to be proud of you, Eadan, do you hear me?"

"Yes, Papa." Eadan gazed up at his father trustingly.

"And there's something else." Elias glanced slyly up at Sullyan where she stood smiling down at them, Bessie beside her. "I want you to look after Brynne for me. Can you do that? Because I love her very much, you know, and I think you do too, don't you?"

"Yes, Papa." Eadan approached Sullyan and took her hand, his young voice firm and serious. "I'll look after her, don't worry."

His tone and the look in Elias's eyes caused Sullyan's heart to lurch. She stared at Elias in defiance, knowing he was paying her back for her resistance to his wishes. He knew she had scant defenses against either his or Eadan's love.

She tore her gaze away from Elias and turned to the little boy. "Do you have everything you need, Eadan? We had better go. Major Tamsen will have gathered the men by now and we must not keep them waiting."

Bessie smiled at Eadan and ruffled his blond hair. "I've sent his things down already, Lady."

The boy released Sullyan's hand and scampered out of the room, heading toward the stairs. Elias and Sullyan followed at a slower pace. They emerged into the chilly morning sunshine, the hard frost of the night before glittering on the cobbles. Sullyan was stirred as always by the sight of the ordered ranks of men waiting obediently behind their captains; her life mate and lover at their head. She pulled her sheepskin-lined leather jacket tighter against the cold and nodded to Robin as she walked by Elias's side toward the smaller group awaiting them.

Elias went to speak to Prince Aeyron, as the tall Andaryan was returning to his own realm this morning, and the two of them moved apart from the others to exchange farewells. Sullyan smiled up at Rienne where she sat atop her gentle spotted mare, a well-wrapped Taric cradled sleepily in her arms. Elisse was sitting on the saddlebow of her father's iron-gray, and Morgan was on Robin's horse, twisting around to watch Eadan as he ran over to Sullyan's huge warhorse, Drum, and began petting the great black's nose.

Sullyan gazed at him before turning to the last member of the party, the one who wouldn't be returning with them. At the end of Sullyan's sojourn at the castle, Taran's fulltime duties as Court

Artesan would recommence. She usually had a word with the Adept before leaving, but today she had more than King's business on her mind.

"Taran, will you walk with me, please?"

He raised his brows. This wasn't her normal leave-taking.

She moved some way apart from the others, aware of Robin's eyes upon her. Taran regarded her curiously as she turned to him. He had no idea what was on her mind. Jinella wasn't in attendance that frosty morning; she had already returned to her mansion.

Sullyan gazed up at the tall Adept. "Taran, are you happy here?"

The question took him by surprise and he frowned.

"Yes, Brynne, you know I am. I'm sorry to see you all go, of course. I can't help missing your companionship when you're not here. And I've enjoyed teaching that young scamp you call a son. He's been keeping me on my toes, I can tell you."

"You have made a good start with Morgan, my friend. Robin and I want you to know how much we appreciate what you can offer him. He already knows not to take his talents for granted. That is a very valuable lesson and confirms we were right in asking you to help him learn."

Taran ducked his head, uneasy at her praise, a legacy from his father he still found hard to shake.

"There's no need to thank me. I'll do whatever I can to help him. And he's not a difficult lad to like."

This gave Sullyan her opening. "You are very natural with him. So natural, in fact, that I confess I am a little surprised you and Jinny have not yet started a family."

Now Taran did blush and Sullyan plainly saw his discomfort. "We're not wed," he said shortly.

"And why is that?"

Her question made him glance at her sharply. "Has Jinny said something?"

"Can you blame her?" Sullyan allowed some of her irritation to show. "I, of all people, know what it is like to believe yourself barren, and to fear the person you love will not want you because you cannot bear children. Is it a wonder she is unhappy?"

"Barren?" Taran frowned in puzzlement. "I didn't know she thought she was barren."

Battling Elias's inappropriate emotions and wheedling had thinned Sullyan's patience. Her voice was sharper than usual. "Oh, Taran, for goodness sake! What did you expect Jinny to think? How long have you been together? Three years? And you have not exactly been celibate all this time, have you?"

Taran flushed crimson. He never could get used to her complete disregard for modesty or the sensibilities of others.

She stared at him, exasperated. "Why did you not tell her you were preventing her conceiving? And more to the point, why are you? Do you not want children?"

The tears that came into his eyes melted some of her frustration. He was an honorable man, a gallant one, but his sentiments sometimes made him go further than necessary. She sighed deeply and touched him on the arm.

"Jinny is unhappy. She thinks you have not asked her to marry you because she has not conceived. You need to talk to her. You must tell her what you feel and you must make up your mind about what you want."

Taran hung his head and Sullyan softened.

"She is good for you, my friend. She makes you happy and she shares your passion. That is what you need. Do not deny yourself the chance of happiness just because it is not quite the happiness you truly desire."

Taran turned away. That was the crux of the problem and they both knew it. Taran could enjoy Jinny's company, he could make love with her and find release for the intensity of his emotions, but, in his deepest heart, he felt it was second best. And that was unfair to Jinny, who gave herself freely and honestly, loving him while still being aware of a special part of his soul that she could never touch. And that, Sullyan knew, was why Taran held back, why he used his powers as an Artesan to prevent the conception of a child. For a child would cement their relationship and bind them together forever. Taran wasn't sure either of them was ready for that.

"I'll talk to her," he said shortly, unhappiness evident in his voice.

Sullyan had to be content with that, despite the unease she felt. "Be sure you do. But be gentle, Taran."

She turned away as he glanced at her in sharp surprise.

Feeling somehow disquieted, Sullyan returned to the men. Elias and Aeyron had finished their leave-taking and Aeyron had mounted his stallion. Sullyan saluted her monarch before clasping Prince Eadan around the waist and boosting him, giggling, onto Drum's back. She swung up behind him.

"Settle down, my Prince," she advised when the boy kept wriggling around, trying to see everything at once. "We will soon be crossing the Veils."

As she spoke, Aeyron turned to Elias once more. "Lord-General Anjer sends his greetings, my lord, and bids me inform you that Colonel Vassa and his command are ready to make the crossing."

Since Elias's hugely embarrassing and unnecessary invasion of Andaryon, the changes to his security arrangements were not the only new innovations. Concerned lest her King throw obstacles in her path regarding her return to normal duties now she had a young child to care for, Sullyan had entered into diplomatic discussions with the Hierarch of Andaryon and brokered an agreement between the two sovereigns that permitted the movement of troops between each realm. This remarkable concession was granted to each monarch's immediate forces only, and permission had to be sought before such advantage was taken.

Due to the skill and strength required to open a specific trans-Veil access, as opposed to one that opened at random, only those of Master rank or above could perform the feat. But the convenience of being able to move a body of men about the country at a moment's notice was so valuable that the slight restrictions didn't matter. And so, a journey that would have taken Vassa's company of foot soldiers three days to complete could now be accomplished in a matter of minutes.

Earlier that morning, General Blaine at the Manor had bespoken his counterpart in Andaryon, Lord-General Anjer, and had transferred Vassa and his men to the Plain surrounding the Hierarch's Citadel. Now, Anjer had bespoken Aeyron to complete the maneuver. Elias gave the tall Prince a wave of his hand, and the Artesans present could feel the Master-ranked Aeyron parting the substrate to allow Vassa access to the castle.

Opening a trans-Veil tunnel anywhere near human habitation was normally considered a risky undertaking and was only attempted under duress, especially by those of lesser rank. But Robin had already supervised the clearing of the spacious parklands surrounding the castle, and Major Denny was even now out in the grounds ensuring they stayed that way. The concentration required to place the opening of the tunnel so precisely, however, was good exercise in control, and as Aeyron was working toward Master-elite, he needed all the practice he could get.

Through the courtyard gates, Sullyan watched as Aeyron's Earth-based structure blossomed in the grounds. She had a vague glimpse of the snowy Plains around the Citadel before Vassa's company came marching through and obscured her view. She made Elias one last obeisance, and then gave Robin the order to move out.

As she came abreast of Colonel Vassa at the head of his men, she stopped to exchange a few words. She was in daily touch with General Blaine, but it was courtesy to allow Vassa to pass on any last minute instructions. She also formally handed over responsibility of the King's security and watched Vassa lead his men up into the courtyard. He dismounted to greet Elias.

"Carry on, gentlemen," she called to her company, and rode beside Aeyron as they entered the tunnel.

Aeyron collapsed the structure as the dry cold of the Andaryan winter surrounded them. Anjer's men, drawn up in battle formation on the Plain as a courtesy to Vassa's troops and an honor guard for Aeyron, cheered and saluted their Prince and Princess. Anjer grinned and greeted them warmly.

"We are pleased to see you safely returned, my Prince," he boomed, bowing to Aeyron. He turned to Sullyan and made a deeper, more lavish bow. "Highness, you are most welcome."

She heard the men's good-natured laughter, both demon and human, and glowered at the enormous man. "Anjer!"

His unrepentant grin didn't fade, and the fact he'd used her title so pointedly gave her pause.

The large man shifted, and she saw that two other men had been concealed behind his bulk. Smiling broadly, their bronzed, weather-beaten faces alight with pleasure, the two men bowed before her as she slid down Drum's ebony shoulder.

"Ky-shan, Jay! I did not expect to see you here. Are you well?"

She held out her hands to them and looked them over. She hadn't seen them in years, but had received regular reports from either Pharikian or his son. She could see they had hardly changed.

Ky-shan was now in his middle fifties and was as stocky and powerful as ever. His blue eyes twinkled merrily in the dark skin of his face and he held out a meaty hand toward her. She took it, and her small hand was nearly crushed by the strength of the ex-pirate's pleasure. His son, Jay'el, was a slimmer version of his father. He had grown a narrow mustache like Ky-shan's, which added maturity to his youthful face. She gazed into his eyes and read deference there. Her smile widened.

"I have been hearing news of your conquest, Jay, and of your desire to learn new skills with which to impress your chosen lady."

Jay'el smiled. "You did say I could come and learn if ever I wished."

"I did indeed, and you will be very welcome. Is it your intention to come with us now?"

Jay'el turned to his father. "If you're sure you don't need me with the fleet?"

Ky-shan shook his shaggy head. "I've already told you you're free for the winter season. Just be sure you're back for the spring sailing. And make sure you work hard at your lessons. I don't want Seyakin complaining his new son-by-marriage is useless."

Sullyan raised her brows. "Have you made the betrothal already, then?"

The older seaman struck his son a playful blow on the shoulder. "She couldn't take her eyes off the young blade!" he guffawed, causing Jay'el to redden. "But her father seemed to think a courtship of two months too short a time to acknowledge a formal betrothal. And he wanted some sign of this pup's commitment to his daughter, so I suggested he might be willing to spend the winter in the study of his talents, seeing as he's never troubled to do so before."

"I take it Seyakin has no gift himself?" Sullyan guessed, and Ky-shan nodded. This made Seyakin's willingness to accept the untitled Jay'el as a suitor for Princess Kyrie easier to understand. The lord of a far-off province whose eldest daughter was likely to be taken from him when she wed Prince Aeyron would value an

Artesan in the family to receive and convey messages from her, and from Pharikian at the Citadel. The more useful Jay'el could make himself, the more chance he had of convincing Seyakin he was suitable.

"We will be pleased to have you, Jay," she said, "although you will have to be prepared to work alongside others much younger than yourself."

The young seaman announced himself willing to do whatever was asked of him. He took leave of his father and went to renew his acquaintance with Robin.

Sullyan turned to her brother and took an emotional leave of him. "Convey my love to our father, and to Ty, Idri, and the twins. Tell Timar I will try to visit him soon. But for now, my brother, I must go. I wish you good fortune in your new-found love, and I look forward to meeting the woman who has captured your heart. My soul will be easier knowing you have found someone able to share your duties as well as your bed. Take care of yourself, and call me if you need access through the Veils in order to visit her again."

They clasped each other tightly and parted. Aeyron still experienced pangs of uncertainty whenever she left him, and she feared he would never fully lose the dependence he felt. Hopefully, Princess Lirina would fill the empty portions of Aeyron's soul and he would then, once more, be complete.

She returned to Drum and seated herself behind Eadan, who had waited alone on the great black stallion with no sign of fear or apprehension. Sullyan reached through her psyche and took hold of the substrate. Her touch was sure as she caused it to part, and she led the men, their number increased by one, back to the Manor.

Chapter Five

In the darkened room, the scarecrow leaned back upon the bed pillows and gave himself up to the ministrations of the woman beside him. He felt the cool touch of her hand upon his brow and permitted himself an unseen smile.

He had finally "allowed" Sofira to persuade him into a more comfortable room than the dank, unwholesome cell beneath the palace. It suited him to accede to her request, not because he craved the comforts she offered, but because in bowing to her desires he encouraged her to believe he was responding to her care. And that bound her ever tighter.

Two months had now passed since his escape from exile, and he was beginning to understand the parameters of his new condition. Under the guise of recovery from torment—not an entirely false pretext—he was able to explore the capabilities he now enjoyed without exerting himself unduly. It quickly became clear his needs were changing. He had to improve the arrangements for the renewing of his physical strength, and easier access to the main parts of Lerric's palace would facilitate this.

It was also more fitting to his status as Sofira's betrothed.

Before agreeing to her pleas to nurse him, he insisted on certain strictures. He convinced her that the complete absence of daylight was vital to his recovery. She accepted this readily. Whatever he needed, he must have. Whatever it took to restore him to her, she would do. It was, she told him, her way of showing her deep contrition for the anguish she had inflicted upon him at his sham of a trial, and she would demonstrate her sincerity and commitment to him in whatever way she could.

The very next day, stonemasons and other craftsmen were summoned to the palace. With no thought for the wishes of her father, Sofira ordered all the windows on the ground floor walled up immediately and heavy drapes fitted over all the doors, so not even the glimmer of lamplight should creep beneath them. She had the layout of the rooms altered to allow her beloved the sole use of a full suite, and had a new doorway to the courtyard made so he could walk the moonless nights in private if he so chose. Her father was banished to the upper two floors of his own palace, and Lerric made no complaint.

The palace was largely deserted. Bordenn's harsh winters routinely kept Lerric's nobles away. It might make the process of government trickier, but at least it avoided the problem of awkward questions. The province, which produced mainly foodstuffs such as grain, cereals, vegetables, and meat, needed little in the way of attention through the unproductive winter months. Had it been otherwise, Reen's rescue and concealment would not have been so manageable. As it was, Sofira completed her changes unhindered, and now the palace's ground floor was a dark and gloomy place, inhabited only by Sofira, her scarecrow suitor, and his minions. And these arrangements suited Reen very well.

Lerric showed little interest in his daughter's coming marriage. He had stated that his people, loyal though they were to Sofira and convinced of her innocence, would object to their Princess wedding a convicted traitor. Reen could not care less what the people of Bordenn thought, but Sofira herself came up with a solution to any possible objections.

"I told Father I intend to issue a proclamation, my love," she said, stroking Reen's brow. "I intend to show that Elias was manipulated by false witnesses, and that the conviction for treason should never have been passed. My father will append his seal to the decree, stating that he exonerates you of all taint of treason, and that he supports your inclusion into our family. Enough of our people were angry when Elias cast me off; the decree will come as no surprise."

Maybe not, thought Reen, but his plans for the province might. Bordenn might have been willing to support their king when Lerric joined the rebellion against Elias's father, King Kandaran, but they hadn't been alone then. Three other provinces, all larger with mighty armed forces and strong leaders, acted as buffers between Bordenn and Elias's wrath once Mathias Blaine defeated the rebel forces. It was only Lerric's abjectly sworn statement pleading coercion by the other rebel leaders that saved his neck once the war was over. And now Lerric was under pain of death should he rebel again. Appending his name to a declaration such as Sofira planned was tantamount to signing his own death warrant. Yet Sofira was adamant Lerric would accede to her wishes, and Reen believed her. Her relationship with her father was one of the reasons Reen was here.

Tiring of her ministrations, Reen feigned weariness and bade her leave him to sleep. It was coming on to midnight and the men he had summoned earlier ought to return soon.

A shiver of evil pleasure shuddered through Reen's flesh. He had been able to refresh himself from the same source once more without arousing suspicion, but he could not keep on that way. He needed servants who were whole, not half-devoured, and it was unsatisfying to restrain himself before he was fully sated.

He had sent his minions out with very specific instructions and told them not to return until they succeeded. He knew it would take them some while, but he also knew they would do as he bid them.

They were aware of the consequences of failure, and they had no independent will of their own. And tonight he intended to feed to his heart's content.

He watched Sofira depart with a stir of anticipation. The pleasurable fulfillment he would savor tonight was only one aspect of his new life. Soon, once he had full control and could relax his guard a little, he would sample once more the other pleasure, the darker pleasure, and he would have his fill.

He was fairly quivering with anticipation when the call finally came. He moved to the heavily secured door that led to the outer courtyard and slowly drew the iron bolts. Without opening the door, he stepped back. The night was clear; there would be starlight. It was not as hurtful as the glow of the moon, but he preferred to avoid it if he could.

In a voice saturated with displeasure at the long wait, he growled, "Come."

The iron ring that worked the latch turned and the door swung slowly open. As he had instructed, they had two captives. Both were tightly bound, their mouths stopped with cloth and rope. They were fully conscious. Reen could tell this without the benefit of functioning eyes. He could taste the fear, smell the terror. Then his heart swelled. They had done it! They had fulfilled his request to the letter. Fighting down the urge to crow with unholy glee, Reen rasped, "Bring them in."

The two men dragged their struggling captives into the abyssal gloom. Reen closed the door swiftly, the knowledge of what was to come enabling him to bear the feeble spark of starlight that prickled his withered skin. His servants jumped as the door closed; they hadn't seen him move.

The younger of the two spoke in a dull, lifeless voice. "We have done as we were bid, master."

"Yes," rasped Reen, mounting excitement flooding his voice,

"you have done well. Bring them through here."

The scarecrow moved across the room and opened another door leading into a short corridor. At the end of this, in another small room, a muted flicker of firelight showed. Despite his unnatural condition, Reen still felt the cold, especially when he was weakened by hunger. Firelight was less painful than the light of sun or moon and he could endure its low glow with no great effort. After all, it had been Fire of a sort which was mainly responsible for his present condition.

His two servants, faces blank, said nothing, manhandling their captives down the corridor and into the small room.

"Secure them," grated Reen, feeling sullen ruby points of light glow deep within his eyes.

Avoiding his demonic gaze, the two men deftly secured their whimpering prisoners to the iron rings set into the walls, retying the bonds so that each captive was fastened hand and foot to the rings and unable to move their limbs. The cloths in their mouths remained.

"Now get out."

Without a backward glance, the men fled the dreadful room, closing the door soundlessly behind them. Reen dismissed them from his mind. He could easily recall them when the time came to clear way the debris of his feast. He moved slowly to stand before his two captives.

They were both male, as he had specified, and both were relatively young. They appeared strong and healthy, and he recognized the fire of resistance in their eyes as well as the fear of the unknown. They weren't tall—Roamerlings never were—and they had the tanned, swarthy skin of their race, their dark eyes made darker still by the absence of whites. Reen amused himself for a moment trying to guess which one of them was gifted, which of these unnatural creatures from beyond the Veils held the knowledge he intended to absorb.

He stepped closer to the one on his left and extended a hand. The dark, terrified eyes watched him. He was not hiding his true aspect as he did with Sofira, and the trembling Roamerling flinched in horror as the withered, claw-like hand grasped his shirt and violently ripped the fabric away, baring the dark skin of his chest. Reen heard the growl of anger and fear which was the only sound the man could make.

Almost gently, he laid his hand on the man's skin, over his laboring heart. Yes, his guess was correct. It was the other, slightly older man who possessed the power Reen so desired. But it didn't matter which was the vessel. Both would provide him with strength, and the fact the gifted one was older only meant he should have more experience, more control, which suited Reen's needs very well. His servants had exceeded his expectations with this first haul. It was almost a pity, for they were unlikely to do as well next time.

He spared a glance for the second captive and was pleased to see he couldn't take his terror-widened eyes from the scene beside him. Reen grinned. He would give the creature something to watch. Something to soften him up, weaken his resistance.

Closing his eyes, he grasped the gnarled cane. The desiccated flesh of his hand seemed to fuse with the strange gray wood. He raised the cane and brought the dimly-glowing tip toward his victim's bared chest. The Roamerling watched it come, terror and confusion bulging his eyes. The cane's glow brightened as it sensed the warmth of the man's sweat, and Reen pressed it to the flesh, centering it over the frantically beating heart.

Terror and pain swamped Reen, and he flailed within the Roamerling's horror. But these extreme emotions were what the scarecrow craved, and he drank avidly of the man's panic. The sensations faded as he drained the outlander of strength, and Reen once again felt himself swell with youth, potent with energy, and reveled in the triumph of his renewal.

The captive's throat strained to scream; tendons stood out starkly and blood flecked his face where small veins had burst with the force of his agony. But he was denied release, and a strangled whimper was all his comrade heard. The older captive watched in horror as his friend's contorted body subsided and hung limp, all resistance gone. But the eyes held intelligence still. Reen was not yet ready to take the final step, to absorb the final gift.

He emerged from his feeding frenzy and stared into the face of the second man. His lips stretched into a horrible smile. Never taking his eyes from the second man's face, Reen leaned harder on the livid wood of his cane.

The flesh beneath its tip was ripped and ruined. It had erupted the moment the cane's heel touched, but now it boiled. A charnel reek filled the air as flesh crisped and spat. Reen once more plunged his senses into the helpless captive and saw his route was open. Hungrily, he surrounded the Roamerling's life force and dragged it out, absorbing, devouring. The body gave one final heave at this most fundamental of violations, and was still. The life light went out of the dark eyes, snuffed and absorbed, secreted within the swelling husk that stood before it.

Reen flung his head back and laughed. The strength he felt was incredible! His body seemed young, his muscles supple, his flesh strong and firm. It felt so good after days of weakness, and he knew now that he would never have to suffer that again. This had been an experiment, a double experiment that was only partially concluded. But now he was sure. If this Roamerling's physical strength was compatible with Reen's ruined body, then he had no doubt the gifts of the other would be too. He would take the strength of this second man, but it was not his physical power Reen craved now. Oh, he would show them—he would show *her*! He would grow more powerful than she could ever imagine and she would be helpless against him. And once he had that final power, the control he craved the most, then he would take his revenge and she would be unable to counter him. She would be destroyed, rendered weak and useless, and he would win.

His face stretched into a grimace of evil triumph as he ripped the shirt from his second captive. Reveling in the man's terror, he gleefully absorbed the powers of the Roamerling Artesan.

Chapter Six

The atmosphere within the main room of the healer suite was tense with strain and effort. There was no sound but the labored breathing of the two occupants, although they sat as still as stone. The air was charged with grim determination and it was building toward an overload. Suddenly, inevitably, it snapped.

"Oh, I can't do this, love. I'm nowhere near breaking through. It's too hard."

Robin's handsome face was white from his efforts and sweat ran freely over his body. His every muscle trembled and he could hardly keep his hands still. His breathing was ragged and harsh and his heart pounded fit to burst.

"Try again, Robin, do not give up yet."

The voice of his life mate was, if anything, even more strained than his own. Her golden eyes were closed, her face pasty, and her brow furrowed. She too was covered in sweat, although the air in the healer suite was chill. There were currently no patients within its quiet confines and the two Artesans had no need of braziers or the warm air of the under floor furnace to regulate their temperatures.

Brynne Sullyan was at the pinnacle of her powers, a Senior Master in rank and the highest ranking Artesan in Albia. Indeed, she was one of the highest in all the five realms. She was certainly the most powerful Artesan Albia had ever known.

Yet she was not one to be content with her own achievements. She was well aware that her vast powers needed exercise if they were to stay honed and sharp. Even as with her weapons skills, she trained regularly in order to stay in control.

Robin and Mathias Blaine, with whom she trained most often, were both of Master rank, although Robin was nearing the level of skill and strength necessary to support being raised to Master-elite. He was working on the element of Air, the most capricious of all the elements and the most awkward to control. To be raised to Master-elite, he only had to influence Air, not master it, but he was finding the task extremely difficult. This was not, however, what he was currently engaged in.

Sullyan, knowing there were Artesans in the distant past who had reached the rank of Supreme Master, was not quite ready to explore what she was convinced would be necessary to attain that final achievement. There were those who believed Spirit, the so-called "fifth element," was purely mythical, but Sullyan's experiences during her twenty-seven years of life had convinced her it was real. The question of whether it could be influenced, however, was another matter entirely and one she would explore only when she felt the time was right.

Instead, she had decided to tackle a problem which had exercised her mind for the past few years. There existed a substance, a naturally occurring metallic ore, which could affect an Artesan's metaforce and psyche. Commonly called spellsilver, the activated metal ore could, when it came into contact with the skin, either block or enhance the flow of power through the psyche, depending on the silver's polarity. Having experienced its dreadful numbing effects more than once in her life, Sullyan was determined to see whether the phenomenon could be circumvented.

She had already succeeded in breaching the debilitating void around her powers while wearing spellsilver, and had called out to those who had the power to hear her. She had also accessed the psyche of her unborn son whilst surrounded by spellsilver, and had used his embryo pattern to save herself and Prince Aeyron from death. But the circumstances under which she had done these things were extreme. In both cases she had labored under severe duress, and she was convinced the peril of her situation had contributed to her astonishing achievement. Yet the fact remained she had done it, and so a pathway must exist, a method of negating the ore's effects.

This was what she and Robin were currently trying to find.

Her life mate, encouraged to one final effort by her words, gasped in pain. "It's no use. I just don't have the strength."

Robin could no longer even keep hold of the tiny fragment of dull gray metal in his palm. His hands trembled violently and his face was tinged with green. He dropped the ore as if it burned him and bowed his head over his arms as he wrapped them around his chest. He took a long, shuddering breath.

"Ah, Robin, do not be so hard on yourself. Remember, I was Master-elite when I breached the spellsilver, and I was also desperate beyond measure."

Robin glanced at his love where she sat cross-legged on the floor beside him. She laid aside her own sliver of ore. Her tone was distant, her eyes clouded, looking back into the past at that fearful memory. She knew her words triggered a recollection in Robin's mind also. He, too, had experienced the kind of desperation that had caused his beloved life mate to so seriously consider taking her own life, and this was what had lent her the strength to breach the silver. He had also attempted the ending of his existence, but, unlike Sullyan, it was lack of courage that prevented him rather than the love of his friends.

She sensed his guilt and saw his face flush at this false

thought. It was actually his foreknowledge of Tad's inevitable grief that had stayed Robin's knife—the thought of what his suicide would do to the boy who worshipped him as his hero.

But there was no opportunity for Sullyan to reassure Robin. She knew well the scars that terrible time had left, and by mutual agreement they never referred to them. She and Robin were closer now than ever, and that was all that mattered.

There came a light tap on the door and Sullyan glanced up as Tad entered the room. Relief showed on his face to find them unoccupied, although worry shadowed his eyes at their disheveled state.

"Are you all right?"

Sullyan smiled, brushing stray tawny hairs from her damp face. "We are well, Tad, just exhausted. What can we do for you?"

"General Blaine's asked for your attendance, Colonel. He's had a message from the King."

Sullyan rose at once. "Is it urgent, or do I have time to wash?"

"I think he'd like you to come straight away," Tad said.

Sullyan smiled at him. He was so very young—only seventeen—and yet he was already a valued member of her company. He was a skilled swordsman and a gifted horseman; he could fight as well from the back of a warhorse as any of them. He was an Artesan-Journeyman and it was Sullyan's opinion that the rank of Adept would be within his grasp in no more than a year. He was as diligent in his metaphysical training as his military. She and Robin were trying hard to include him in their circle of close friends—Taran, Cal, Rienne, Bull, and Dexter—but Tad still felt awkward and deferential, too young and too aware of the high status of his two heroes. Tad could never forget it.

"Very well, Tad, Mathias will have to forgive my state. Did he give you any indication as to the message's import?"

Tad replied in the negative and they left together, leaving

Robin to pick up the fragments of spellsilver and return them to their polished granite box.

When she reached his office, General Blaine answered her knock and waved her to a chair. She took in his preoccupied air, a shiver of premonition running down her spine.

"What has happened, Mathias? Is the King well?"

Blaine shook his head. "There's nothing wrong with Elias, not in the way you mean. But he's had an unsettling message and he wants you to hear it. Taran's standing by with the details."

Sullyan raised her brows but wasted no more time on questions. She reached within for the complexities of her powerful psyche and held the pattern belonging to Taran before her mind's eye. She had hardly quested for contact before she felt him respond.

Brynne. Elias is in a bit of a state and he wants me to ask you how he should respond to a message he's just received.

She was surprised. *He wants to ask* me *how he should respond?* Elias was a capable monarch; he had never yet asked her advice on matters of state.

You'll understand when you hear it, Taran said darkly. *I'll skip over the formalities and give you the gist. It's written by the Cleric Patrio of the Serna Bay order and dated almost three months ago: 'I write to inform you of the death of the prisoner Baron Hezra Reen, whom you sent into our keeping three years ago. We believe it to be a case of suicide, as it appears the Baron slit his wrists before casting himself into the sea from the island's highest point. Despite a search by the fishermen who supply us, I regret his body could not be found.'*

Sullyan was silent when the Adept finished reading, absorbing what she had heard and sorting through her feelings. It had taken some time for the letter to reach Port Loxton; the island off Serna Bay was both distant and inaccessible, which is why it had been considered ideal. She heard Taran's voice again.

Brynne? Elias is waiting for your reply.

Is the messenger still there? she asked.

There was a brief pause while Taran relayed her question to the King. *No, Elias let him go. It's not as if an answer was expected.*

I thought he wanted to know how to respond? Was it brought by a member of the order?

Again there was a pause. *No, it was a runner from the nearest garrison. One of the fishermen who supply the island took the Cleric Patrio's report to the garrison commander, and a runner brought it from there.*

She gave a mental shrug. *So what exactly does Elias wish me to advise him on?*

This time the pause was longer. Sullyan sat trading looks with Blaine while she waited for Taran to reply. The General, of course, already knew the contents of the message.

Taran's voice came through once more. *He's confused and unhappy, Brynne. I don't think he knows what he feels about the Baron's death, and he's looking for some kind of reassurance from you. He hasn't actually asked me to convey this, but I think he'd like you to come and discuss the message with him.*

What is there to discuss? No, Taran, do not pass that comment on to Elias!

Sullyan broke the link to speak with her general. "You know he wants me to go to the capital?"

Blaine sighed. "I expected as much. You'd better go, Brynne. If he's getting himself worked up over this he'll not settle until he's talked it out."

"Talking will not alter what has happened. I should have thought he would be relieved by it, not worried."

The General stared at her. "He's never got over what they did to him. He'll never forget what they made him do to you. You'll just have to accept that he's dependent on you now and hope that, in time, his shame will recede and he'll be able to move on. Until then, we have to do all we can to help him. It won't take up much of your time, after all."

She stood, accepting his words. "Sometimes, Mathias, I regret my own cleverness in forging the agreement with Timar. Crossing the Veils like this may be just too convenient now."

Blaine smiled. "You don't mean that."

Sullyan shook her head and relayed her agreement to Taran. The relief she felt from him was palpable.

Within the hour she had washed and changed and was sitting in the King's private audience chamber, drinking fellan and reading for herself the parchment the King had received.

The message had brought all the bad emotions flooding back for Elias. She wouldn't have thought this news could upset him so. He should have been dancing for joy that the traitor was dead, not feeling the empty dread and nagging sense of foreboding that exuded from him. He was annoyed with himself now she was here, she could tell, and ashamed of his weakness. Diplomatically ignoring his turmoil, she laid the parchment aside.

"Suicide," she murmured, her eyes unfocused. Elias leaned forward expectantly. She gazed at him, her expression reassuring. "I can see why you were so … concerned. The Cleric Patrio says the body was not recovered."

Elias gripped the stem of his goblet to steady his hand and took a healthy swallow of brandy. "The runner who delivered the message told me the fisherman searched the seas for hours once Reen's disappearance was discovered. But because of the blood they found—"

"I would give much to have seen that blood," Sullyan said. "I cannot understand why the Baron should throw himself into the sea if he had already slit his wrists. And how would he have the strength to climb the crags to where he is supposed to have jumped?"

"Yes, exactly. You don't think I'm foolish to have these feelings of ... unease?"

Sullyan gazed at her worried sovereign, her own expression serious. "No, Elias, I cannot think you are foolish. I confess I feel much the same way. If there was a body ...."

"What do you think I should do?"

"There is only one thing you can do. Send me to the island to speak with Patrio Ruvar and do what I can to satisfy you of the circumstances."

Elias's eyes widened. "You'd do that?"

She smiled. "I am in your service. I will do whatever you bid me."

The King ducked his head and she frowned. He still couldn't get over her willingness to forgive and forget the shameful way he had behaved after his son had been abducted. In his eyes, he had forfeited all rights to her loyalty, thrown away any claim on her respect. She was a Princess in her own right, and a powerful Artesan. What right did he have to command her? Yet she had told him her Oath of Allegiance still bound her; she had never rescinded it and had no wish to. Her only desire was to serve her sovereign lord and he had no choice but to grant that wish. He would just have to bear the shame.

"When will you go?" he asked.

She didn't miss the fact he had not given her an order. "I will return to the Manor tonight and discuss the matter with Mathias. I would not go alone, and Robin has duties at present. I need to arrange for Morgan's care while I am away, but I will leave as soon as I may. I will inform Taran when I am ready."

She left him, knowing he would go to his rest feeling easier. If anyone could discover the truth, it was Sullyan.

✣ ✣ ✣ ✣ ✣

Taran had been released from his duties for the day as soon as Sullyan had arrived. He was rarely needed in the evenings and spent most of his free time in the garrison with either Major Denny or Swordmaster Ardoch. Sometimes both. Tonight, however, he had another duty to perform, and it would likely prove both uncomfortable and painful.

Yet Taran could not shirk this unpleasant duty, couldn't wait for Jinella's next visit to the castle; that would be cowardly in the extreme. And no matter how deeply he wished he didn't have to be the bearer of these tidings, Taran Elijah was no coward.

Or was he? He considered this as he mounted the beautiful blood-bay stallion that had been a gift from Elias and rode out of the torch-lit castle courtyard. His face burned as he realized how much time had passed since Sullyan had commanded him to talk with Jinny and tell her why he was preventing her from conceiving. He shouldn't have put it off; he should have gone to her immediately and got it over with. Instead he had used the resumption of his Artesan duties as an excuse, and the fact he and Jinny saw significantly less of each other when he was actively engaged in Elias's service only made the evasion easier.

Yes, he berated himself as he passed the night guard at the gates and returned the man's greeting, *you have been cowardly*. Well, now he had an unpleasant duty he *couldn't* avoid. If he must do this—and he must—he would do the other at the same time. If Jinny was to be upset, he might as well upset her all at once. At least then he could be on hand to comfort her. If she still wanted his comfort after what he had to tell her.

Bucyrus was fresh and fast; it didn't take Taran long to reach Jinny's home. His arrangement with Jinny was such that he treated her home as his own whenever he desired to be there. He was well known by her servants and never needed to announce himself. He rode round the side of the solid square building and dismounted in the gravel-laid yard. A groom emerged from the lamp-lit stables to take Bucyrus from him.

"I won't need him again tonight, Matty, but I'll probably have to return to the castle early in the morning."

"Right y'are, sir," the young lad said cheerfully, touching his cap as he led the stallion to the stables.

Taran had status in Port Loxton now, not only because of his position in the King's service, but also because of the part he had played in the rescue of Prince Eadan from this very mansion. He still wasn't comfortable with the deference of Jinny's servants.

He strode into the mellow warmth of the mansion, stamping his feet to remove the light dusting of snow that had fallen during the day. *It's definitely getting colder. There'll be some serious snowfalls soon.* He pulled off his boots and stepped into the soft house slippers Jinny insisted he wear. He left his boots where they were; it always scandalized Jinny if he cleaned them or put them away himself. She often asked him scathingly what he thought servants were for. "I don't pay them good wages to watch you work, Taran!" she would say.

He moved through the huge house, looking into various rooms, and finally tracked her down in the kitchens going through the herb store with Alice.

Alice had joined Jinny's household after the Baron's trial. She had once been nursemaid to Seline and Eadan, but had been cast out by the Queen—or, more accurately, by the Baron—on the pretext of being unreliable. In reality, it was because she had seen too much. Whatever the reason, she'd been forced to leave with no character reference and had fallen into the trap most unsponsored young girls did: prostitution.

Rescued by the intervention of Sullyan and the contrition of the King, Alice had been offered her old position at the castle. Though overcome with gratitude, she was uncomfortable at the thought of returning there, especially as the Queen was still in residence at the time. When Jinny heard of her distress she offered Alice the position of housekeeper at the mansion. Alice had served Jinny faithfully ever since.

Both girls looked up in surprise as Taran appeared in the herb store doorway. The Adept noted Jinny's welcoming smile with less than his usual pleasure. She wouldn't remain glad to see him for long.

"Taran!" The Baroness came over and kissed him. "I hadn't expected to see you tonight. Why didn't you send me a message? I could have arranged a special supper."

Taran spared a warm smile and a quick greeting for Alice as he took Jinny by the arm and led her from the room. "I hadn't expected to be here myself, Jinny. The King received a message and I need to tell you about it. And there's something else I need to talk to you about."

Taran's serious tone and averted eyes transmitted his mood to his partner. Jinny was used to Taran's character by now; she could tell when he was happy or sad, or when he had something difficult to say.

"What is it, love? What's happened?" She clasped his hand in an effort to halt him.

"Let's go into the drawing room. This is private business and I don't want to be overheard."

Puzzled and alarmed, Jinny allowed him to steer her into the lavishly decorated drawing room. As it was only used when Jinny entertained, he knew it would be deserted and none of the servants would blunder in while they were talking. He closed the door behind them and crossed the carpet, bidding Jinny sit on the settle. He seated himself beside her and took up her hands, feeling her tremble as she always did when anticipating bad news.

"Oh, Taran, tell me what it is! You look so serious; it must be something dreadful."

The Adept took a deep breath. "Forgive me, Jinny, I don't mean to upset you. The truth is, I don't really know whether you'll consider this bad news or not."

"Is it my mother? Has something happened to her?"

Taran shook his head. Jinny had fallen out with her mother after Jinny's elevation to Baroness. Her mother's opinion was that Jinny ought to remember her roots and return to her mother's modest estate and use her new wealth to benefit her immediate family. But Jinny had no intention of leaving court—of leaving Taran—and merely sent her mother some gold in recompense. It obviously wasn't enough. Now the two women corresponded rarely, apart from her mother's frequent letters demanding more gold, and Jinny had never even invited her mother to see her new lands.

The hard glint in Jinny's green eyes told Taran she wouldn't have been too upset if her mother had fallen on hard times.

"No, it's not your mother. It's your uncle."

"My uncle?" Jinny frowned, but then her expression changed to one of fear. "You mean my Uncle Hezra?"

"Yes." Taran clasped her hands tighter. "The King has received a message from Cleric Patrio Ruvar, the head of the holy order on the island where your uncle was exiled. It seems the Baron couldn't stand the loneliness or disgrace of his banishment any longer." Watching her, Taran saw Jinny's eyes mist over as she guessed what he was about to say. "I'm so sorry, love, but it looks like your uncle took his own life."

Jinny remained silent while Taran spoke. The moisture in her eyes did not spill over and she didn't crumple as he had feared she would. Reen had treated her very harshly before his conviction, and it was Jinny herself who had provided much of the evidence that helped expose him. He had reviled her publicly and thoroughly for her lack of familial loyalty once she turned against him. The gnawing guilt Jinny felt over her actions hadn't entirely been erased by the exposure of his treachery.

She took a steadying breath. "How ... how did it happen?"

Taran was proud of her. In moments such as this, she could be much like Sullyan.

"He slit his wrists one night and then cast himself into the sea. He was seen at the last moment by one of the clerics, and a beacon was lit to attract a fishing boat from the coast. They searched for him as best they could at first light, but it was no good. He couldn't have survived anyway, not with the cold of the sea and his wounds."

"When was this?"

"Nearly three months ago. The clerics of the order did a search of the island and asked the fishermen to scour the coast for any signs of the Baron's body. Once they were sure they weren't going to find him, the Cleric Patrio wrote a report of his findings and sent it to the nearest garrison. There are no Artesans at that garrison, and so the report was sent by runner. That's why it took so long. Patrio Ruvar thinks the body must have been swept farther out to sea—apparently the tides around there are very strong—and so they never stood a chance of recovering the Baron. He told Elias they conducted a Service of Passing for your uncle and that his possessions have been packaged in case you'd like to have them."

Taran made no mention of the King's disquiet over the Patrio's message, or that he had summoned Sullyan to the capital to read the note for herself. The Adept had been strictly forbidden to voice any of their concerns in Jinny's hearing. Elias knew how troubled she had been over Reen's perfidy and he wouldn't add to it.

The Baroness sighed. "So that's that. I don't know whether to be relieved or sorry. If he was so distressed by his imprisonment, then I suppose I'm glad he's out of it. I know the King would never have pardoned him; he would have remained exiled until he died, however it happened. But I think a very small part of me was hoping he'd repent, offer to atone in some way. Then perhaps he could have been released to some easier place where he could have done some good with the rest of his life. Ah, well, it wasn't to be. I hope he's at rest now.

"So, what was the other thing you wanted to tell me?"

Taran's heart sank. *I really must be the world's worst coward.* He didn't like to admit how much he had been hoping Jinny would be so upset over her uncle's suicide she would forget what he'd said. Her distraction would have given him the perfect excuse not to mention the other matter. Now he had no choice.

He couldn't sit still. He dropped her hands and stood, feeling her green eyes upon him. A frown creased her brows. "This is going to be difficult for me, Jinny, and you're not going to like what you hear. I only hope you can forgive me and that you'll try to understand why I did it."

"What have you done, Taran? Tell me. I won't be angry, I promise."

Jinny made it sound as though she thought he was confessing to cleaning his own boots again. Her attempt to reassure him only made matters worse. He faced her as best he could.

"When we had our picnic at the castle a few weeks ago, you spoke to Sullyan. You told her you feared you were barren, and thought that was the reason I'd never asked you to marry me."

Jinny's face paled and then colored. "Yes, yes, I did."

Taran sensed her guilt and despair, as if she thought she had done wrong by confiding in Sullyan and Taran might break off their relationship as a consequence.

"I've been so unfair to you," he blurted, turning crimson himself. "I should have spoken to you long before this, but we sort of drifted into our present arrangement and we never formally made an agreement between us. At first I was waiting to see how it went and whether we were suited, and I suppose I was content to let things carry on as they were. But that's no excuse.

"Jinny, there is no reason to think you might be barren."

She opened her mouth to speak, but he held up his hand. "Hear me out, please. You can yell at me later if you want; I probably deserve it. The reason I've never mentioned marriage is because of the difference in our status. You are a Baroness and a very wealthy young woman. Regardless of my recent good fortune, I am no more than a peasant from an obscure little hamlet in the south of the province. No matter what you might feel for me, you can't deny I'm no match for you. Because I was half-expecting you to realize this, I … took steps to prevent us from making a child. I didn't want you to feel pressured into marrying me."

Taran fell silent, watching Jinny's face. A closed, hard expression settled over her features. "What do you mean, 'took steps'?"

Taran ducked his head. Discussing such things always embarrassed him. "As an Artesan, I have control over my own … fertility."

He heard her sharp intake of breath. When she finally spoke, her voice was brittle, with an edge of real distress.

"Are you telling me that since we've been together … every time we've made love—*all* those times—you were holding back? Deceiving me? But how could you *do* that, Taran? How could you feign all that passion? How could you lie to me? I thought you *loved* me!" Her voice spiraled higher as she spoke, her last words delivered on a note of angry hysteria.

Tears came into Taran's eyes. He couldn't bear to see her so distraught, especially as she had misconstrued his meaning.

"I *do* love you, Jinny," he said, starting toward her. "I didn't mean I'd … I give you my word, I never feigned anything. My feelings are real, the passion is real. It was only that I was so sure … I mean, I never let myself believe you would want to actually *marry* me. I thought we were just enjoying ourselves; that you were only waiting until someone more suitable came along. I never lied to you, I swear. My only deception was that I never told you there was no possibility of a child. That was my fault, I'll admit. That you might think you were barren never entered my head."

"It never entered your head." Jinny's tone was devoid of emotion.

She sat straight-backed, regarding him coldly. Her hard expression was a mask. He could sense her inner feelings were in turmoil. She seemed to be caught between two warring emotions: bitter anger and reluctant understanding. In trepidation, he watched the conflict. What could he do to put things right?

He spoke softly into her silent fury. "I was only trying to protect you, love. Please forgive me. My honor would let me do no less."

She slowly raised her face, her countenance white. Two spots of color flamed high on her cheekbones, a febrile glitter in her emerald-green eyes. Taran went cold.

"Well, damn you, Taran Elijah," she hissed. "And damn your bloody honor."

Shocked, he spread his hands. "Jinny—"

"Shall I tell you something, my honorable lover?" she continued as if she hadn't heard him. "I was only waiting for one thing before I broached the subject of marriage between us. I knew you'd never do it and I understood why, even though I've told you I don't care about your background. I've been convinced for months now that even if the most handsome Duke or Prince in the entire realm should come seeking my hand, he could never touch my heart as you have. I knew I would never feel as deeply for anyone else as I do for you, and that if you refused me, I would never wed another. All I was waiting for was that magical moment when I could tell you I was carrying your child. The thought of the look in your eyes when you heard you were going to be a father: *that's* what I was waiting for. I've seen how you love little Morgan, and how good you are with Eadan. I knew a child would make you complete."

She inhaled deeply, shakily.

"But all this time you've been ... when I think of what I went through ... blaming myself, worrying myself sick, desperate not to lose you ... and all this time all you've been worrying about is your *damned honor!*"

Jinella surged to her feet. Fearful, Taran backed away from her fury. He had expected her to be upset, but this? "Jinny, I'm—"

"Don't you dare!" she yelled, her temper alight. "Don't you *dare* say you're sorry! It's too late for sorry, Taran. What am I going to do now? How can I ever trust you again after this? Do I even want to?"

He stared unhappily, only now realizing what a terrible and fundamental mistake he'd made. What had seemed to him like protection, consideration, had seemed to her a betrayal. He had misjudged her feelings and the depths of her commitment and had, albeit unwittingly, belittled what she had offered him in their relationship. He wouldn't blame her if she could never recover from this, could never rekindle the closeness they'd shared. And that made him very sad. For he did indeed love her. He had known it for months, but he just hadn't allowed himself to believe she could feel the same way about him.

Well, he knew now. Probably too late.

"I *am* sorry, love," he said, his eyes misting as she turned abruptly from him, her hand cutting the air in disgust. "None of this is your fault. I've been stupid, I've been blind. I should have confided in you, shared my concerns, and I should never—ever— have deceived you. I can only tell you that I do love you, and that I want to share the rest of my life with you. You can pour scorn on my honor if you wish"—her snort was loud and emphatic—"but I couldn't tell you how honored I'd be if you could find it in your heart to forgive me. All I can say is that I deeply regret the hurt I've caused you, and if I've done irreparable damage to the love and trust we shared, then I will spend the rest of my life trying to atone for it. I don't suppose you want me to stay around tonight, not after what I've done, so I'll go back to the castle and leave you in peace. But I'll wait to hear from you. If you need me, you only have to send for me.

"I really am terribly sorry."

He turned and walked to the door, hoping she would call him back and hold out her arms to him. But there was no sound from her and he left the room despondently. He made his way back to the stables, apologizing to young Matty for undoing all his hard work on Bucyrus's harness as the lad readied his mount.

He glanced up to the windows as he mounted and rode away. Was that her outline, watching him behind closed drapes? Or was it just his desperate heart, hoping against hope she'd forgive him?

Chapter Seven

"**W**ho will you take to the island?"

Brynne Sullyan considered her general's query. It couldn't be Robin; he had duties of his own at the Manor, and there was also Morgan to think of. One of them was always at the Manor to care for their son. She would, however, need another Artesan to stand for her. This was a given rule as well as a sensible precaution to take. Now that there were more Artesans at the Manor, it was easier to do. Yet of the four she could choose from, only two fitted her requirements. Bull, who would once have been her natural choice, was currently engaged in training the new College students. Besides, his weakened heart meant he rarely participated in strenuous duties these days. Jay'el was still very new to his powers and was there purely to learn, not to accompany Sullyan on missions for the King.

"I shall take Cal and Tad," she said finally, and the general nodded. "I have informed Taran of my intention to leave this morning, and he has passed this on to the King. All I need now is the location of the nearest garrison, if you would be so good?"

Though the agreement between Pharikian and Elias concerning travel through the Veils made reaching far-flung portions of the realm a much simpler matter for those on their monarch's business, it was still necessary for the Artesan concerned to know where they were going. It was not enough to know a place was in the north or south of the land. There had to be physical knowledge of the terrain and intended destination or the transfer couldn't work.

Sullyan had never visited this particular garrison, but Mathias Blaine had, albeit many years ago. He could pass her an image of where she must go, and so he accepted her tacit request to mesh psyches and held the location of the remote outpost in his mind. Neither of them had ever been to the island where the Baron had spent his exile, so this garrison was the nearest point to which she could transfer. The soldiers stationed there would give her directions to the fishing village which served the clerics on the island. Once there, she could request the use of a boat to reach the island itself.

Fixing the image of the garrison firmly in her mind, she thanked the general and assured him of her swift return once she had satisfied herself as to the truth of the Baron's demise. Blaine shared her opinion that the circumstances should be examined very carefully indeed. He was under no illusions as to the Baron's feelings where Elias and Sullyan were concerned, let alone Artesans in general. If he yet lived and was free to work his schemes, the consequences could be catastrophic.

"Be careful," he admonished.

Once all was in readiness, she made her way to the horse lines. Tad was waiting alongside three harnessed stallions, three packs at his feet. Cal was also there, giving Elisse one last hug, and Sullyan suddenly found herself enveloped by the arms of a small boy. She smiled down at her much-loved son and swung him up into her arms.

"Take care of Papa while I am away, and see that he gets some rest," she told the giggling boy. "When I return, I want to hear how well you have behaved. Now, run along and find Uncle Bull. I believe it is time for your lessons."

Elisse grabbed Morgan's hand as Sullyan set him down and

they raced off in the direction of the College, laughing and dodging the stallions' legs. The horses turned their heads in mild curiosity as the shrieking children passed.

Cal fixed his pack to his saddle. "Poor Bull. I sometimes wonder whether he regrets volunteering to train those two hellions."

Tad snorted. "Bull's more than a match for either of them. You want to sneak up on them one day and watch him. He knows how to impress them into submission. If he can cope with a barracks full of cocky cadets, he can cope with two three-year-olds."

The young man leaped into the saddle of his liver chestnut. Tad was the proud owner of one of Drum's first colts, but the dark bay was too young yet to ride on a mission such as this. He was still being trained under the watchful eyes of both Sullyan and Stablemaster Solet.

He glanced at his colt's sire as Sullyan vaulted lightly into the saddle. At twelve years old, Drum was in his prime and a magnificent specimen of male horseflesh. He was huge, strongly-muscled, sleek and fit; his coal-black coat sparkled in the frosty daylight and his silken mane flowed over his arched and graceful neck. Sullyan saw Tad's admiring look and grinned as she gave the order to move out.

They rode down the track leading toward the ridge, their mounts' hooves crunching through a crust of snow. It was bitterly cold and they had all brought their thick sheepskin-lined combat jackets as well as their heavy oiled leather riding cloaks. The journey to the garrison wouldn't take them long, but they still had the ride to the fishing village and then a sea voyage to endure.

Neither Tad nor Cal had ever been in a boat and Sullyan wasn't sure they were looking forward to the experience. They had asked Jay'el what to expect and the young seaman had regaled them with horror stories about winter voyages on freezing, stormy seas. Fortunately, they eventually recognized the gleam of mischief in Jay'el's eyes and an impromptu wrestling bout ensued. Tad had redeemed his honor by winning.

They reached the ridgeline, their favored place for making the crossing into Andaryon, and Sullyan quested for contact with Lord-General Anjer. His permission for her short appearance on Andaryan soil was a formality, but she had too much respect for her adopted father to flaunt rules she herself had recommended. As she broke the contact she turned to the younger of her two companions.

"Journeyman, will you construct the tunnel for us?"

Tad was daydreaming and took a moment to collect his wits. "What? Oh ... yes, of course, Colonel."

Sullyan smiled as she watched Tad center his concentration and attune himself to his psyche. He should have been prepared; she had already warned both men she would not be doing all the metaphysical work on this trip. Tad hadn't been on so many missions like this that he was inured to the novelty. He would do well enough. Once she had sprung a few surprises on him, he would learn to stay alert.

She watched critically as he formed the trans-Veil construct. As a Journeyman, Tad possessed insufficient strength and skill to determine the opening of the Andaryan end of the tunnel, but for this crossing it didn't matter. It was the second crossing that counted, and she would add her own strength to Tad's for that one. She examined the structure once Tad anchored it.

"What do you think, Captain?"

She saw Tad's satisfaction when Cal was just as startled to be asked his opinion. Cal covered his surprise better than the younger man and studied the tunnel with a practiced eye.

"Looks strong enough to me, Colonel."

She smiled and bade him prove his confidence by riding through first. He nudged his stallion and passed along the shimmering structure, knowing Tad was proficient in this now and there was no danger of the tunnel collapsing. Sullyan's question was intended to sharpen them up, not imply any lack of faith.

She followed him through and Tad brought up the rear, collapsing the structure behind him. He received her approving nod and turned to repeat the process. This time, Sullyan overlaid her psyche with his and he had to contain himself firmly as he experienced the momentary disorientation such profound depths of power always caused in those of lesser rank. His developing psyche had a long way to go before it matched the complexities of a Senior Master's.

Through the blossoming structure they saw the snow-covered hillside that was their destination. Sullyan knew the garrison nestled at the foot of those hills, sheltered by them from the worst of the weather. The three companions rode swiftly through the tunnel, emerging once more onto Albian soil.

They were now hundreds of miles north of the capital and the weather was harsher than in Albia's more temperate regions. The snow was deeper and it was frozen solid. The horses' weight broke the surface, but it had been frozen for so long they only sank up to their fetlocks. The three riders pulled their cloaks even tighter and expended a little power to keep warm. Sullyan nudged Drum into the lead and led them in the direction of the garrison. They came within sight of the small outpost an hour before midday.

Sullyan was gratified to see the sentries were alert even in this poor weather. She heard the horn call that attended their sighting, and a guard awaited them as they rode up to the gates.

The little garrison consisted of a few stone buildings huddled against the hillside, with stabling and storage barns carved into the face of the hill itself. The whole enclave was surrounded by a stout wooden palisade wall, breached by a single gate. The outpost was manned by only twenty men, relieved every four weeks by their fellows, all of whom were drawn from local villages. The duty captain came forward to give his name and greet his unexpected visitors.

Sullyan swung down from Drum and threw back her heavy cloak to reveal her rank insignia. She introduced herself and her companions. The captain was a rough-looking fellow in his late forties, with silvering brown hair and shrewd green eyes. Those eyes stretched wide when she spoke her name and he accorded her a very respectful salute, although his expression betrayed anxiety over the reasons for her coming.

"Colonel Sullyan, you are very welcome here, but I confess I'm surprised to see you. We had no foreknowledge of your visit. Is there some problem in the area? I've had no word of any unrest ..."

"Be easy, Captain Giel. It is not trouble that brings us here and we will not trespass upon your hospitality. We are bound for the island housing the Order of the Wheel and will trouble you only for directions to the fishing village that services the needs of the clerics."

Giel's expression intensified, but then cleared. "Ah, would this be in response to the message sent by Patrio Ruvar to the King?"

"That is correct. The King wishes me to speak to the Patrio concerning the circumstances surrounding the traitor's death. I take it there have been no sightings of his body along the coast?"

"None, Colonel, and I've had my lads scouring the shores daily ever since we heard of the Baron's suicide. We'll not find him now, though. The tides will have swept him right out to sea. They're fearsome fast round here in winter."

Sullyan nodded. "All we need then are directions to the fishing village, if you would be so good."

"I'll send one of the lads to show you the way," offered Giel, but Sullyan shook her head.

"Thank you, but we cannot wait for you to detail one of your men. We need to reach the village quickly. I wish to be on the island by nightfall."

Giel's eyes widened. "Tonight? I'm afraid that's not possible, Colonel. There won't be any craft left in the village. They'll have gone out at dawn to make the most of the light and the tide. And besides, there's no wind. It's a good two-hour sail even with the tide and a breeze in your favor. You'll have to spend the night in the village and catch the early tide with one of the fishermen. You'll have ample time to take one of my lads as guide."

"The arrangements for our crossing are my concern, Captain," she said. "Just tell us the way, if you please."

Giel capitulated, although it was clear he expected her to find things as he'd said. He pointed out the road to the village, which was simple enough, and they rode away from the garrison, Giel watching from the palisade wall.

Tad and Cal hadn't ventured an opinion while she was speaking with Giel, but she had seen their puzzled glances. Now Cal nudged his horse closer to Drum and caught her eye.

"Colonel, how are we going to reach the island if there're no boats and no wind?"

She smiled. "We are going to a fishing village. There will always be boats, no matter how many are out at sea. As for the wind, I am sure there will be a suitable sea breeze when we want one."

She left them pondering her intentions as she led them on toward the coast.

They came out of the hills and onto the coast road within the hour. Sullyan led the way up the final rise, and as they topped the slope they saw a good chunk of Albia's northwestern shoreline laid out before them.

To their right, wind-whipped dunes dotted with clumps of sea grass curled and humped their way down to the sea. To their left, their view of Serna Bay was blocked as sand yielded to rock and cliff until a jutting headland could just be made out far in the distance. A narrow track wound its way along the top of the cliffs.

They sat savoring the freezing briny air and listening to the raucous calls of seabirds. Then they turned left and set their mounts' feet to the track along the cliff top. After half a mile or so, they reached a fork. A well-trodden path led a switchback course down through the cliffs, and this they took. It brought them out onto a wide strand of shingle at the foot of the cliffs, and there before them was the village.

It was a picturesque scene. Stone-built cottages and storage sheds nestled into the base of the cliff face. Gray shale slates covered the roofs and fronted some of the houses. The rest were painted white. The village took advantage of a shallow natural bay to the north of the headland, and the villagers had built jetties out into the water, anchoring them to boulders which had fallen from the cliff face over time. Farther out, adding its own protection from the worst of the winter storms, the tips of a reef curled around, leaving a natural passage through to the open sea. A few small craft sat moored to the jetties, but none of them were manned and the entire village seemed deserted.

Sullyan nudged Drum and made for the nearest house, the door of which opened before she reached it. A thick-waisted woman stood in the doorway, a small girl clasping her skirts, peering out from behind at the three cloaked strangers. The woman eyed Sullyan suspiciously.

"What do you want?"

Sullyan ignored her flat tone. "We are here on King's business, Goodwife. We need to reach the cleric's island. Is there anyone here who can help us?"

An expression of scorn entered the woman's eyes. "You'll not get there today. All the men are out."

"*All* of them?" challenged Sullyan, her tone hard.

The woman narrowed her gaze. "Old Jeriko's around somewhere, for all the good he'll do you. You'll probably find him in the net shed." She nodded to the ramshackle cluster of buildings and sheds at the far end of the village.

"We thank you," said Sullyan, turning away as the woman disappeared behind her door. Shaking her head at the manners of fishwives, Sullyan nudged Drum toward the sheds. There was a stout railing nearby and she indicated they should dismount and tie their steeds to the rail. Cal and Tad followed her inside the shed, peering into the interior gloom. They could just make out the bent figure of an elderly man sitting on an upturned lobster pot, sorting through what looked like a hopeless tangle of netting. There were two piles of it at his feet and both piles looked identically useless and ragged.

The man glanced up as they entered the shed. "Who're you?"

"Are you Jeriko?" Sullyan asked.

"Aye. What's it to you?"

"We need a boat. We are here at the King's orders and we need to reach the cleric's island by nightfall."

The seamed face creased as the old man parted his lips in a gap-toothed smile. "Ha! I can tell you know nothin' of the sea, m'lass. Firstly, there's no one here to take you, and second, there's not a breath of wind, nor won't be till tomorrow."

She held his gaze. "We need no one to take us, thank you, and the wind will be sufficient for our needs. Just tell us which boat we can use."

Contempt curled Jeriko's lip. "Didn't you hear what I just said?"

"I heard you, my friend. Did you not hear *me*? There is an

eighteen-foot sloop moored at the end of the jetty which looks suitable for our needs. We will leave this gold to pay for her hire. Will you pass it on to her owner?"

Sullyan held out a small handful of gold bits toward the old man, who transferred his stare to her hand. "That's my boat," he said slowly, "but I don't go as far as the island these days. Besides, King's business or no, there's still no wind!"

Sullyan simply smiled and laid the gold on the table. "You are not required to sail the boat. I can do that for myself. I believe the island is visible from just off the coast. What transit marks do we aim for?"

The old man scooped the gold bits into his weathered palm. They could almost see his thoughts. It was as much as his little craft was worth, and if she was determined to go, what trouble was that to him?

"Very well," he said, "but don't say as I didn't warn you. Someone'll doubtless tow you back in on the evening tide. You sail northwest out past the entrance to the reef, bear away from the headland directly north, and when you come abreast of the red patch on the cliff face and the beacon fire above you, bear due west out to sea. You'll see the tip of the island in the distance. Best of luck, you'll need it."

"Is there a barn where we can leave the horses?" she asked, thankful to have gained his compliance. Receiving his permission to leave the horses in the neighboring shed and his assurances he'd watch over them, she detailed Tad to see to their comfort whilst she and Cal took their packs and walked down the rickety jetty toward their craft.

It was a sturdy clinker-built sloop, with a square-shaped mainsail and a small headsail. With neither Cal nor Tad having any knowledge of sailing, this small craft should be stable yet light enough for them to handle under Sullyan's direction. She tossed their packs into the prow of the small ship and bade Cal embark.

He nearly lost his footing as he gingerly entered the boat. "It's rocking!" he yelped, clutching wildly at the gunwales, which set the craft to yawing even more.

"Stand still, Cal," she laughed. "You are on the water, what did you expect? Move slowly and carefully and keep to the center, then you will be more stable. Sit on that bench there, in the stern. You will be our steersman."

Cal groped his cautious way to the bench and sat gratefully, eyeing the length of bouncing craft with a jaundiced eye. Sullyan stepped aboard and loosened the ties holding the mainsail furled along the boom.

"Are you sure you know what you're doing?" Cal asked as seemingly endless folds of ochre canvas flopped around her feet.

"Of course I do. Do you not trust me?"

He couldn't say no, and tried to concentrate as she told him the names of the parts of the boat he would be in charge of. Her familiarity seemed to increase his fear, not relieve it. There were an awful lot of unfamiliar terms.

Once Tad joined them in the boat, the young swordsman learned he was to be in charge of the small headsail and sat toward the front of the boat looking as nervous as Cal.

"Now, Cal," instructed Sullyan, "undo that line from the stern of the boat and push us away from the jetty."

Cal did as he was told, pushing gingerly at the wood of the jetty. The small craft slid forward a few feet to lie still and calm in the center of the bay. They were aware old Jeriko had come out of his shed to watch them, and even the goodwife stared from behind her cottage window, no doubt anticipating a good laugh at their expense.

A preoccupied Cal didn't hear Sullyan's instruction, and had to ask her to repeat it. "What's a halyard?"

"That rope there." She pointed. "Pull on it as Tad pulls on this one; it will raise the mainsail. And watch the boom does not catch you. It will swing about until the wind arrives."

The two men did as they were told and the long wooden beam from which the ochre-colored sail hung rose slowly up the mast. When the sail was taut, Sullyan showed them how to tie the ropes off so the beam was held aloft with no fear of it falling.

Now they had to avoid the swinging boom, the second heavy wooden beam that controlled the sail's base. "Cal, pull the tiller toward you and hold it there," Sullyan said. "The wind will come from over your right shoulder and we want the sail to fill from that side. Tad, when you see the mainsail fill, raise that headsail and tie it off as I showed you. Ready?"

The men nodded wordlessly. They had no real idea of what to expect, so how could they say they were ready? All they could do was trust in Sullyan and do as they were bid.

Sullyan sat in the center of the boat and closed her eyes. It wasn't necessary for her to do this in order to access her psyche, but her companions' anxiety might distract her if she wasn't careful. She had to do this just right. Air was a most capricious element and needed all her attention.

Slipping within her consciousness, she attuned her psyche to the element of Air. The day was cloudy, but the cloud cover was thin. Behind this she could feel the next weather front approaching from the east, and there was wind aplenty here. All she need do was encourage it closer. She centered her will and exerted her power.

The zephyr startled Cal. He hadn't seen it ruffling the water as it came from behind him. The small craft slid gently through the water. "Sullyan!" he called, alarmed by the pressure on the tiller and completely ignorant of what he should do.

Silently, still concentrating on calling Air, Sullyan placed her left hand over Cal's on the tiller, directing his movement. The prow of the little boat came around until it was pointing toward the gap in the reef. She nodded at Tad and he pulled on the rope to raise the small headsail, and the strengthening breeze filled the ochre canvas with a snap. Tad secured the halyard and grasped the other rope to control the fill of the sail.

The breeze grew stronger by the minute and Sullyan could now afford to spare some of her concentration for instructions. She couldn't resist turning to wave casually at an open-mouthed Jeriko, who stood dumbfounded on the strand.

Cal and Tad heard her small, triumphant chuckle. "Oh, I just *love* doing that."

Their eyes stretched wide at this uncharacteristic mischievousness, and she laughed. "Well, gentlemen, what is the point of all this power if you cannot enjoy its effects once in a while?" She sobered. "Although, as you know, I do not condone showing off."

They glanced at each other, clearly unsure how to judge her mood. She grinned again and they relaxed, trying to familiarize themselves with the motion of the boat and the complexities of sailing.

The wind Sullyan had called was cold and smelled of snow. The sea was calm and made little wavelets along the sides of the sloop as it slipped through the icy water. Cal sat in the stern, gradually learning how to make small adjustments to the tiller to keep them on course away from the headland. Tad sat in the prow, watching the fill of the headsail and loosening or tightening the sheet that controlled it, according to Sullyan's instructions.

"Why's it called a sheet?" he grumbled. "What's wrong with rope?"

"How many lengths of rope do you see on this craft, Tad?" Sullyan asked pointedly. "They all do a different job. If I told you to heave on that rope, how would you know which one? And on a larger vessel, with more sails, there is even more rope. Of course they all have different names!"

Tad continued to grumble good-naturedly under his breath and Sullyan let him. She knew he was only covering his nervousness, for they were far off the coast by now and nearing the point when they must turn due west. She could see the red patch of sandstone marring the gray of the cliffs and also the fire beacon mounted on top, as Jeriko had said. She could also just make out the tip of the clerics' island as it rose from the waves.

Attuning herself once more to her psyche, Sullyan checked the state of the wind. They hadn't seen any other craft so far and she supposed the fishing fleet had allowed the morning tide to take them farther out to sea. She hoped her little wind would not cause them any inconvenience; she didn't want to disrupt their trade or prevent them from sailing home when they wished.

Her breeze was behaving as she'd hoped. They turned westward, aiming the prow of their vessel toward their destination. Sullyan herself controlled the mainsail and paid out the sheets, allowing the boom to move out at right angles to catch more of the wind from behind them. She was enjoying herself, pleased to find she had forgotten none of the lessons she had learned whilst sailing with the free-traders of Andaryon.

Chapter Eight

S itting in the stern of the little sloop, Sullyan regarded the island. With the light behind it and fading into the west, the island's rock was black and stark, adding to its forbidding aspect. Frozen snow lodged in the lower crevices of the sharp-edged surface rock, and ice slicked the smoother stone. Not a sign of green could be seen from the water; no trees, no plants, not even any seabirds. Seemingly barren and lifeless, the sharp pinnacle of rock thrust up from the water and loomed above them.

She wondered why there was no snow covering its highest peaks.

"Where on earth are we going to land?" said Cal, leaning over the gunwales to peer beneath the boom. He had surrendered the tiller to Sullyan now they were closer, and she gave him and Tad instructions on how to alter the sails while she guided their craft nearer to landfall.

"There will be a jetty or landing stage somewhere," she said, her eyes on the rocks. She was allowing the breeze to die down, just keeping enough to allow her steerage. "The fishermen must put in somewhere when they deliver their supplies."

"That could be the place," called Tad from the prow. When they looked, they could see a flattened area of stone just behind a low line of rocks, iron rings sunk into its smoothed sides. Sullyan told Tad and Cal to lower the mainsail and they managed to achieve this without covering everyone in wet canvas. Sullyan concentrated on bringing the vessel alongside the slab of stone without crunching the wood. Despite the generous amount of gold she had given Jeriko, he wouldn't appreciate his boat being gouged on the rocks.

Tad, stationed at the headsail sheet, released it at her command, allowing it to flap in the wind as the boat lost speed. Cal was instructed to jump ashore and catch the line thrown to him by Tad, then secure the boat to one of the rings. He landed inelegantly, making Sullyan and Tad laugh as he tottered on the stone as if drunk.

He had his revenge when Tad, in an effort to leap stylishly ashore, found that his legs also betrayed him and he staggered into the sharp rock face. Sullyan eyed them both sympathetically. "Your pardon, gentlemen. Did I forget to mention the effect of a sea voyage on your sense of balance? Fear not, the sensation will fade in time."

Both men directed venomous looks at her as she stepped casually onto land and proceeded to hand out the packs.

Checking the boat was secured against the pull of the tide, Sullyan shouldered her pack. To the left of the landing stage was a rough-hewn set of steps, the only other exit.

The steps were treacherously uneven and slippery with frozen spray. Someone had thoughtfully secured a bight of rope along one side, and they held on to this to steady their ascent. The gradient was steep and unrelenting, but the strenuous exercise helped both Tad and Cal recover their sense of balance.

At the top they were confronted by an iron-barred gate set solidly into the rock. The stair had become increasingly narrow as they ascended, taking on the aspect of an open-roofed tunnel. This gate effectively blocked their onward path and there was no sign of human habitation.

"What now?" panted Cal, leaning against the rock. The ride from the Manor, the stress of the sea voyage, and now this steep climb in the biting cold had sapped their strength. They were ready for a warm fire and some rest. This inhospitable gate did not bode well for their reception.

"We announce our presence." Sullyan indicated the large brass bell hanging to the right of the gate. Its clapper was wrapped in cloth to keep it from sounding when the wind blew strong, and she reached up to unwind the bundled linen. She rang the bell twice.

Silence followed. They could barely hear the susurration of surf on the rocks far below. Tad stirred as if to sound the bell again, but then they heard footfalls approaching. Sullyan threw back the folds of her cloak to display her rank insignia.

"Who comes to disturb our peace at this hour of the day?" came a scratchy voice from beyond the gate. The light was fading fast and it was difficult to make out the hooded figure that appeared from the gloom.

"I am Colonel Sullyan of the High King's forces and I have come at the request of Elias of Albia to speak with Cleric Patrio Ruvar," Sullyan said. "My two companions are Captain Cal Tyler and Swordsman Tad Greylin, also of the King's forces. May we enter? We have had a long journey and we are tired and cold."

The figure moved forward to study Sullyan's array of rank insignia and battle honors. Apparently satisfied, he drew the bolts. "You come on the back of a strange breeze," he commented, holding the gate for them. He relocked it once they were through.

"Yet a convenient one, for all that," she replied. "Frar ...?"

The hooded man inclined his head. "Frar Varian. I am the warder of the gate and I must insist you leave your weapons with me. No one goes armed into the presence of our Patrio."

"Very well, Frar Varian. We mean no offence to your order. We are here purely to ascertain the facts surrounding the death of Baron Reen."

Varian sighed as he beckoned them toward a stone cottage

fifty yards from the gate. Welcoming lamplight glowed in its windows. "Ah yes. That was a sorry business and one we all regret."

Sullyan followed the man into the warmth of the small dwelling. "Why is that, Frar?"

He turned to face her and cast back the cowl of his robe. Frar Varian was an elderly man of maybe seventy-five years, and his thinning hair had been shaved into a complicated spiral design, symbolizing his initiation into this particular Order of the Wheel. He was thin with sunken cheeks, but his brown eyes were shrewd and sharp. He regarded Sullyan frankly as she divested herself of her weapons.

"Baron Reen was a mightily troubled soul," said Varian, accepting Sullyan's sheathed sword and dagger. He laid them respectfully on a wooden rack, showing an unmistakable familiarity with edged steel that narrowed Sullyan's eyes. "He took some months to settle to his life here and to fully accept his fate. In those early days, we despaired of ever giving him ease or succor. He even refused to participate in our services at first, despite his devout piety."

Cal's eyes boggled at this description of the traitorous Reen and he shot Tad a glance. The young swordsman returned the look with raised brows as they too handed their weapons to the elderly Frar. He laid them beside Sullyan's on the rack.

"Eventually," the old man continued, "we began to see improvement. He accepted friendship from one of our number and gradually integrated with us. For some long while he seemed content."

"And then?" Sullyan was acutely interested in what the Frar had to say.

"None of us guessed he would do such a thing." The man's voice, hoarse with disuse, held deep sorrow. "It was pure chance

Frar Durren saw him cast himself into the sea. And then, of course, we discovered the bloodied knife with which he'd slit his wrists. It was only an eating knife and not very sharp. It left quite a mess."

"I can imagine." Sullyan was watching the old man's face. "And you are familiar with the mess a blunted blade can cause, are you not, Frar?"

Varian froze, staring at her in silence. Then his eyes shifted to the rack holding their weapons and she saw understanding dawn. "We were not all born into the order, Colonel Sullyan," he said stiffly. "Some of us had other lives before taking our vows."

She inclined her head respectfully, continuing the conversation. "But you cannot blame yourselves for the Baron's state of mind. He was skilled in cunning and would not have scrupled to hide his true feelings from you. I doubt he would ever have accepted his banishment. The shame and injustice he felt would have eaten through him like canker. I was not surprised to learn the content of the Patrio's letter to King Elias."

Varian frowned. "You speak as if you knew the Baron, Colonel."

She responded softly. "I did, Frar. I knew him intimately."

Her tone made Varian look away, unwilling to pry further. He seemed unsettled and gave himself a shake, as if to dispel some vague disquiet. "I must inform the Patrio of your arrival and your request to speak with him. You will have to be patient. He will be taking the Sundown Service shortly and then he will hear the avowals of the order. Only then will he be free to speak with you. Please make yourselves comfortable here and remain inside. This dwelling place is for the use of the rare guests we receive. You may stay here until your business with the Patrio concludes. There is food in the cold store through that door, and beds through that one. Now you must excuse me or I will be late for Sundown."

Frar Varian gave Sullyan a respectful bow, which she

returned, and then left, pulling his cowl over his head as he stepped out into the darkness. Sullyan regarded the door thoughtfully before removing her cloak and hanging it on the peg provided. The two men did the same and then set about brewing fellan and warming a meal, hoping for a good long rest before the Patrio was ready to receive them.

✤ ✤ ✤ ✤ ✤

"You've done *what*? A proclamation? Are you completely mad, woman?"

Sofira's hand flew to her mouth and her gray eyes widened at the Baron's furious tone. Yet she held her back straight and tried not to show how his flash of temper had unsettled her. He'd taken pains to constantly impress upon her how frail he was, how the slightest upset could rattle him, and always acted contrite when he finally calmed. All of this was carefully calculated to keep her pliable.

Given her eagerness to please him, Reen often had trouble remembering his own decision not to reveal himself to her too soon. Her announcement had shaken him badly and he had to remind himself why he still needed her. His plans concerning Sofira were not yet ripe.

"Madam," he said in a calmer tone, "please forgive me. I am still not recovered, but that is no excuse. I should not speak harshly to you when you have been so kind and so caring toward one who has suffered so much."

Sofira laid her hand on his arm. "Oh, my love, there is nothing to forgive." She didn't seem to notice the quiver of the taut muscles beneath her touch. "I should have told you before, but I wanted it to be a surprise. The goodwill of our people means so much to me, and once this proclamation is issued it will pave the way for their acceptance of our marriage."

Reen went rigid and the tremor of his muscles ceased. "Once it's issued?" he snapped, not troubling to modulate his tone. "Do you mean you haven't issued it yet?"

Misconstruing his displeasure, Sofira hastened to reassure him. "Only to the crier, my love, but don't worry. He has orders to proclaim it at first light tomorrow and throughout the rest of the day."

Reen grabbed her arm in a painful grip. "Madam, you must rescind the order. Rescind it at once!"

She gasped in pain and tried to twist free. "My love, you're hurting me."

"Promise me you'll rescind the order!"

She stared into his eyes and shivered. He realized his guard was slipping and strove for control. He forced himself to release her arm, seeing the bruising on her flesh, and slumped as if exhausted into the chair. She watched him in hurt puzzlement.

"Oh, Sofira, do you see how beset I am?" He passed a hand over his face. The dim glow from the fire, the windowless room's only illumination, hid his true condition from her. "You see what they have done to me, how the merest thought of discovery unmans me? And I am shamed, my love. For more than anything I desire to be a man for you, and yet I fail you at every turn."

As he had intended, his words brought her close to his chair. She cradled his head to her breast and he leaned there, listening to the beat of her heart, feeling her softness surround him. *Soon*, his lusting spirit whispered, *soon you will be strong enough to drop this deception. Soon you will savor your true revenge.*

His body stirred at the thought and he brought himself sternly under control. *Not yet, not yet.* There was still one experiment yet to try, one assurance he needed to obtain before unleashing the full potential of what he was and what he had planned.

Until then, he must play this woman very carefully. For if he was discovered before he was ready—if *she* should discover him—he was dead for sure. He knew, with a certainty beyond any doubt, that if what he feared the most should come about, then even the Execution of the Wheel would be more easily borne than the revenge *she* would wreak upon him.

He shuddered, and Sofira mistook his horror for misery. "Oh, my love, you will always be a man to me," she murmured. "But what can I do to soothe you? How can I help you overcome the terror their cruelty has instilled in you?"

He raised his head and gazed into her face. The fact that he saw only a pale blur signified nothing. He had other senses now with which to confound her.

"You can keep my existence and our intentions secret. Oh, Sofira, I know this is hard for you to understand. You are protected here, safe within the circle of your father's defenses; none would harm you here. But I am a convicted traitor, no matter how falsely accused. Even here, in your father's demesne, I am vulnerable. Do you think Elias would scruple at setting spies within your father's palace? Do you think he does not keep himself informed of your whereabouts or your daily affairs? Do you imagine he is ignorant of your threat to his stability, despite the disgrace he heaped upon you?"

Reen raised himself higher and faced Sofira, warming to his theme. This was always the way to her heart—flattery and guile under a mask of devoted service.

"Elias fears you, my love. You may have been dethroned and cast aside, but you still command power and respect. There are many at Port Loxton who would welcome your return, but there are also those who would crow to see you cast further into disgrace. This, my love, is why we can't afford to give them even the slightest opportunity to guess what we are about. I know you care passionately about the acclaim of your people and you wish them to know how ardently you strive for their well-being and prosperity. You can best serve those ends by giving up all thoughts of a public announcement. Not only is it far too dangerous for either of us—think what Elias's spies would make of it!—but it would also show our enemies our hand far too soon. You do see, don't you? You understand why I ask this of you?"

The passion in his speech brought tears to the Princess's eyes. She was so transparent to him he could almost hear her thoughts. He was so wise, so careful of her, and so fervent for the restoration of what she had lost! How could she have jeopardized what he had suffered for, how could she have risked his intricate plans? She was shamed and her face grew hot at the thought of how careless she'd been. Tears spilled down her cheek and she bowed her head.

"I understand, my love. I hope you can forgive me. I wasn't thinking. It was only my joyful anticipation of our union that made me forget the torments you have suffered. I promise you, it will never happen again."

Mention of their forthcoming marriage set Reen's teeth on edge. He must accomplish his final experiment before that important day. He would have to send out his servants again very soon.

"Madam, it grieves me sorely that our nuptial day must, of necessity, be held in darkness and secrecy. But I will make you this promise. Our wedding night will be an occasion such as you have never experienced. Sensations the likes of which you have only dreamed will be yours for the savoring. And afterward you will have all that you deserve in this world. This is my word and my pledge."

"Oh, Hezra!" murmured the Princess.

Reen dampened his ardor lest the sullen ruby glow of his eyes frighten her. "But for now, my love, although it pains me to say it, I am tired beyond belief. Leave me to rest. I will be stronger on the morrow. And, Sofira," he added sharply as she turned to go, "don't forget to rescind your order to the crier."

"I won't forget, my love. You have my word on that."

He leaned back in the chair with a sigh of exhaustion, muttering furiously at the woman's inconceivable stupidity. He believed she would send word to the crier, but the man could have read the proclamation already, and so he sent out the call that would put his own seal of assurance on the man's silence. The strength he now needed so badly had to come from somewhere, after all.

✤ ✤ ✤ ✤ ✤

⊙he door to the guest cottage opened to admit Frar Varian and a gust of snow-laden air. Varian shook the white dust from his robes as he cast back his cowl and came to stand by the fire. His aging hands sought the warmth of the flames.

"Would you care for some fellan, Frar?" offered Sullyan. "It is freshly made."

"I would, thank you." Varian accepted the steaming mug handed him by Tad. "The winds are freshening and there will be significant snowfall overnight. You should offer up thanks that your voyage was blessed by that vagrant breeze this afternoon. This is not a night for novice sailors to be abroad."

Sullyan smiled gently. "Indeed. It was a truly fortunate breeze."

She noted Tad and Cal watching this byplay, trying to decide whether the Frar knew Sullyan had called the wind for her own convenience. Something in the cleric's eyes indicated he did, but as he made no comment, they couldn't be sure. All they could be clear on was that Sullyan and Varian had put aside the slight tension between them.

Varian looked up from the steaming mug. "Our Patrio bids me

inform you he will be able to speak with you shortly. I am to convey you to his private rooms at the hour of the eighth bell. He thought you would be more comfortable there than in his study, which is not appointed for receiving visitors."

Sullyan inclined her head. "Your Patrio is most kind. We will not trouble him long. I have been asked to clarify the facts contained in his letter to the King, but it is a formality only. The Baron's treachery wrought much damage to King Elias's policies, not to mention the physical threats to himself and his son, and he needs some reassurance as to the final fate of such a dangerous man."

Varian nodded. "I imagine the abduction of his son affected him deeply."

Sullyan caught and held his gaze before replying. "Indeed it did. Elias's Heir is most precious to him. He felt the lad's ordeal like a wound to his heart."

The cleric turned his head at the faint sound of a striking bell. He held out his open hand. "It is the hour of the eighth bell. If you would accompany me?"

They rose and swung their heavy cloaks about their shoulders. Varian led the way into the biting cold, where swirling flakes of snow were already settling on the ground. It was pitch dark; only the soft glow from the guest cottage windows illuminated their way. And soon even that small light was gone. There was no sound except the sough of wind across jagged rocks and the soft footfalls of their guide.

They followed Frar Varian along a pathway worn smooth by countless feet, walls of rock on either side. These provided some shelter from the strength and chill of the wind, but also cut them off from any light there might have been from dwellings up ahead.

They rounded an outcropping and the cleric's quarters came into view. Like the guest cottage, they were all hewn into the rock itself, doors and windows cut into the rock face with wooden shutters to hold out the cold. Only a faint glimmer of lamplight could be seen around the door frames.

Varian halted outside the farthest dwelling and raised his hand to tap at the door. They waited in silence and heard the latch lift, and then the door was pushed open, flooding the night with firelight.

A man stood silhouetted by the leaping light. "Welcome, my guests. Will you step inside? There is warmth and good food awaiting you on this cold and snowy night."

Cleric Patrio Ruvar was a complete surprise and Sullyan understood why Tad stood gawping and Cal failed to suppress a small gasp. Their reactions twisted the Patrio's mouth into a smile.

Dressed casually in a dark linen shirt, overtunic, and breeches, not only was Ruvar as dark-skinned as Cal, but he was also young. Doubtless, Cal and Tad had expected a robed and venerable elder like Varian, who had silently made his departure, not this impishly-grinning young fellow in everyday clothing. They struggled visibly with their misconceptions, and the Patrio's grin widened. It seemed he was no stranger to such reactions.

Sullyan made the introductions and the Patrio shook each hand in turn. He turned laughing eyes on Cal as he took his hand last.

"I take it I am not quite what you expected, Captain Tyler? I'll wager you thought I'd be some wrinkled old grandfather with a long beard and fading eyesight. Am I right?"

"Well ..." managed Cal, looking sheepish.

Ruvar chuckled. "Oh, don't worry. I don't suppose it'll be long before that's exactly how I'll be. That's how the last Patrio ended up, anyway."

He drew them with him along a short passage which emerged into a cheerful and comfortable living space.

Cal looked around with interest. "How long have you held this

… office?" he asked, unsure of the correct term.

Ruvar smiled. "It is now five winters since Cleric Patrio Damas passed along the Wheel." He waved them to seats before the roaring fire. Taking one of the upholstered chairs, he poured fellan from the large jug on the hearth. There was food laid out on a low table between the chairs and he indicated they help themselves.

Sullyan relaxed back into her chair, savoring a mug of hot, bitter fellan. She regarded Ruvar over the rim.

"Frar Varian has already told me something of the Baron's demeanor and behavior prior to his death, but I would hear the tale in its entirety from you, if it is not too much trouble."

Ruvar waved away her concern. "I assure you, it's no trouble. I anticipated a visit from someone at Elias's court when we were unable to find the body to prove the man's death. I must admit, though, I'm surprised the King sent *you*."

She cocked her head. "And why is that?"

Ruvar regarded her steadily. "Did the Baron not cause you much harm, Lady?" His tone had become gentler, more intimate. "I'd have thought the King would have spared you any more involvement with this affair after what you suffered."

Sullyan stared at him for some moments before she answered, and the timbre of the atmosphere between them subtly changed.

"I serve King Elias in whatever capacity he requires. He requires me to satisfy him as to the truth of the Baron's death, and it is my pleasure to fulfill that duty."

Ruvar held her gaze, assessing her. Whatever private thoughts or doubts the Patrio might have harbored, the answer he found in her open gaze seemed to satisfy him. He broke the hiatus with a bow of his head.

"Very well," he said, pouring himself more fellan and giving Sullyan a charming, sideways smile. "I will tell you what I remember of the Baron's time among us, and what I know of the circumstances surrounding his suicide."

Chapter Nine

"Baron Reen arrived here in chains in the first half of summer three years ago," Ruvar said. "He was brought to me by the guards who had accompanied him on the journey from Port Loxton, and he was also attended by Cleric Odren, one of Arch Patrio Neremiah's junior clerics. Odren told me of the circumstances behind the Baron's banishment, and also gave me a parchment containing yet more details of the man's crimes and the reasons why our island was chosen as his prison." Ruvar's tone hinted at disapproval.

"It was not our wish to cause you any inconvenience or force you to become the Baron's jailors," Sullyan murmured. "It was our intention to be merciful. Taking into consideration the impossibility of independent escape from this place and the Baron's deeply-held religious beliefs, we felt he might benefit from the seclusion and silence here, and that this might give him the opportunity to reflect upon his actions and maybe even come to repent of them."

Ruvar regarded her from dark eyes and his mouth was a firm line. "Be that as it may, Colonel, it was necessary for us to deal very strictly with the Baron once his guards struck off the chains and the boat had departed. The man was sorely troubled and not disposed to listen to reason. We had to confine him in one of the penitent's cells for nearly a week until he consented to hear me without the outpouring of venom which had, until then, greeted anyone who tried to speak with him. We learned much during that time of the slights and torments he had endured, and of the base and evil plot he accused you and your kind of perpetrating against him and the King."

"And did you believe his accusations, Patrio?" Sullyan's mild tone was at variance with the hardness in her eyes.

Ruvar waved aside her question along with her challenge. "It matters not what we believed. The man was convinced he was being persecuted and we had to deal with this sense of injustice and betrayal before we could hope to calm his turbulent spirit. Eventually, after some days had passed, I was brought to believe he had come to terms with his situation. I felt the time had come to allow him the freedom of the island. We decided against setting guards on him. It was felt that should he be determined to end his torment and his life, it was not for us to force him to endure. We told him he was welcome to attend our services and that should he wish to join our order, or be given tasks to occupy his time, we would accommodate him. I also made myself available to him should he wish to speak of his spiritual turmoil."

"And did he?"

"Eventually, yes. Although it wasn't my companionship or guidance that encouraged him to integrate into our society."

"Ah, yes," murmured Sullyan, "Frar Varian mentioned the Baron was befriended by one of your order."

Ruvar nodded. "It was Frar Serrin who finally managed to get past the Baron's barriers of hatred. The two of them became fast friends. I believe Reen helped Serrin as much as the lad helped the Baron, for Serrin hadn't found life here as easy or as fulfilling as he'd hoped."

"This Serrin was a young man, then?" Sullyan leaned forward in her chair, watching the Patrio with interest.

"Yes, quite young. When he first came here he was thirteen years of age. When he and the Baron began their friendship, the lad had just turned fifteen. I confess I was surprised by their closeness. Serrin was a reticent boy who consistently spurned all attempts to draw him out of his resentment."

"They sound like kindred spirits." Sullyan's dry comment drew a sharp glance from the dark man opposite. "I should like to speak with this boy, Patrio. Would that be possible?"

Ruvar shook his head. "I regret to say it will not. Not here on the island, anyway."

She frowned. "Oh? Why is that?"

"Serrin left us about a week before the Baron's suicide. I was disappointed in his decision, but not completely surprised. Despite his friendship with Reen, he was never easy with our strict and frugal way of life. He took passage with the supply boat one day and returned to the mainland. I imagine he went back to his family." Ruvar bowed his head and regarded his hands.

Cal stirred in his chair, glancing at Sullyan for permission to speak. She waved him on.

"Patrio, may I ask you something?"

The dark man turned to Cal and smiled.

"You said Serrin was only thirteen when he came here. Is it usual for someone so young to be accepted into your order?"

Ruvar nodded. "There are always misfits in the world, souls who can't find their true path, who feel they don't belong where they were born. For such troubled souls, the paths of faith and discipline can restore their sense of purpose and self-worth. Serrin was sent here by his family to see if our vastly different way of life might be what he was looking for."

Sullyan appreciated the truth of these words. She herself grew up in an environment where she was not wanted, where she didn't fit, and her emerging talents only served to compound her misery. The quirk of fate that led her to her current life was fortuitous in the extreme. Even now she didn't like to think what might have become of her had she not met Mathias Blaine.

"But from what you say, Serrin did not find what he sought in the strictures of your faith," she said. "Did he speak to you about this? Did he tell you of his desire to leave?"

Ruvar's tone was rueful. "Not in person, no. I imagine he was shamed by his failure, and maybe even feared I would try to persuade him to stay, if only for the comfort he brought the Baron. It is to my shame he felt he couldn't approach me. Instead, he left me a letter, which I found only after the supply boat had departed."

She leaned forward again. "Would you have attempted to dissuade him?"

"No, Colonel." Ruvar looked scandalized. "We don't seek to hold those who wish to leave. That's not consistent with our faith."

"Except for the Baron, of course," she murmured.

She saw the look both Cal and Tad shot her. They felt she was baiting Ruvar and could see no reason for it. She ignored them.

The man himself regarded her evenly. "Of course. But those circumstances were very different."

Satisfied by what she had heard so far, Sullyan abandoned her challenge, asking the Patrio to recount the day of the Baron's suicide. Ruvar proffered the fellan jug and she permitted him to refill her cup. He then added more to his own cup and passed the jug to Cal. The small silence that reigned while these domestic tasks were accomplished served to draw a line under what had gone before. When Ruvar took up his tale once more, all was ease between them.

"I fear it may have been Serrin's decision to leave that started the Baron on his final slide into depression. He'd been ill for some while before the boy left. Serrin nursed him devotedly and had himself become exhausted and pale. I imagine he found the Baron a demanding and ungrateful patient, and maybe the strain of it broke their friendship. But from the moment the lad's departure was discovered, the Baron's demeanor changed for the worse. He suffered fits of rage and ranting, and when he was calm, he was silent and withdrawn. Our meager diet had already removed the excess flesh he carried when he arrived, but now he grew gaunt. He adopted a reclusive regime and never went abroad in daylight, or even on moonlit nights. He spoke to no one and grew increasingly frail. He had always used a cane, but now he leaned heavily upon it. We believed he was suffering some deep malady of spirit.

"Then, about two and a half months ago, I was woken in the dead of night by Frar Durren, who told me he'd seen the Baron cast himself into the sea from the island's highest point. I immediately knew that if this was so—and I had no reason to doubt Frar Durren—then the Baron was dead. It is a long drop to the rocks below; no one could survive that fall."

"Would his body have been recoverable from the rocks?" asked Sullyan.

Ruvar shook his head. "There had been a storm the night before. In this region, the waves are often steep and fierce; it takes them several days to calm down after a storm. I knew his body would have been washed off the rocks; nevertheless, I ordered the signal beacon lit. We found nothing.

"The following dawn, one of the fishing vessels from the village put in to the landing stage. I told the fishermen what had happened and asked them to search the area on the off chance of recovering the Baron's body. They told me it would be useless, but they agreed to carry out the search. As you already know, they found no sign of the dead man.

"While we waited for the fishermen to return, I asked Frar Varian to go through the Baron's rooms in case he had left a message of some kind. It was there that the knife was discovered, along with a large pool of blood. I went with Frar Durren to the place where he had seen the Baron jump and we found traces of blood on the path and on the rocks. Frar Durren told me he thought he'd seen blood on the Baron's clothing, particularly about his wrists and hands. We surmised he'd tried to use the knife to slit his wrists but that the blade, being blunt, hadn't done its work properly. The Baron, lacking the courage to cut his wrists deeper, cast himself into the sea."

Ruvar shook his head sadly. "I can only imagine what black despair led him to attempt the opening of his veins. The irony is that the act was totally unnecessary. Even had his fall not dashed the life from his body on the rocks, as it surely did, the sea would have taken him swiftly and with more mercy than he showed to himself."

Sullyan pursed her lips. "So the fishermen returned to tell you they could find no trace of the Baron's body, and then you wrote your message to the King and bid them deliver it to the nearest garrison."

Ruvar nodded. "We found no message in the Baron's quarters, nothing to indicate he intended to harm himself. We gathered his few possessions and I have them here safe. I understand he has a niece. Will you carry them to her?"

"I will, although I doubt she will want them. She, too, suffered at his hands, and most unjustly. Patrio, would it be possible for us to see the Baron's rooms? And would you object if I spoke with Frar Durren about what he saw that night?"

Ruvar shrugged. "You are welcome to move about the island as you wish, and I have no objections to you questioning Frar Durren. Whether he chooses to answer you is his decision. We are a largely silent order and some of us take this vow more literally than others. There are those who will speak only to me. But Frar Durren may well decide to respond to your questions. I only ask that you respect his right to refuse if he so wishes."

Sullyan inclined her head. "Of course. I have already told you, we will cause you no inconvenience if we can avoid it."

She stood, Cal and Tad rising with her. Patrio Ruvar came to his feet and moved toward the passage leading to the door. "Will you need a guide to show you the way back to the guest cottage?" he asked. "We make no more light than is necessary, so there are no lamps to light your way."

"I thank you, Patrio, but we will do well enough. I have already trespassed on your hospitality and goodwill tonight; we will leave you in peace. But one more request I would make before we go."

He cocked his head. "And what is that?"

"Would we be permitted to attend the Sunrise Service tomorrow morning?"

Her question clearly surprised Ruvar. He stretched his eyes wide, but recovered well.

"Of course, Colonel. You and your men will be most welcome. I will send Frar Varian to you at the hour of the sixth bell."

He opened the door for them and they wrapped their cloaks about them as they stepped out into the swirling snow. The glow from the open door didn't fade as they walked back the way they had come, not until they had rounded the first outcropping of rock. It seemed the Patrio's curiosity had been more than piqued by what he had seen and heard that evening.

✣ ✣ ✣ ✣ ✣

"I really think we ought to ask Adept Elijah to contact the General with this news, my Lord. He specifically said he wanted to be kept informed of anything unusual."

King Elias glanced in irritation at the tall man striding at his right shoulder. Colonel Jerrim Vassa was not the King's favorite person at the best of times, capable commander though he was. Elias found him dour and unapproachable, but he was honest enough to admit that the real reason he could never warm to Blaine's second-in-command was simply because his tour of duty followed Sullyan's, and whatever other fine qualities the man possessed, he didn't comfort the King's lonely heart like Sullyan did.

Unaware of his monarch's unflattering thoughts, Vassa carried on. "And you have to admit it's damned peculiar. Roamerlings never leave their dead behind; they always take them back to Endormir to return them to the steppes of their ancestors. Even then, they don't bury the corpses, they burn them. They believe the spirit is trapped forever unless the bodies are burned. Added to the fact that this is the second one found in Lerric's province over the course of the last month and I definitely think we have enough to justify informing the General."

Elias grunted. "Only just within Lerric's borders. You know how the Roamerlings wander. That's how they got their name."

Vassa raised his brows and Elias capitulated. "Oh, all right. If you're so sure my Lord Blaine wants to be bothered over so trivial a matter as two dead outlanders, go right ahead. But don't blame me when it turns out these men killed each other over some family feud and were hastily buried by their shamed relatives or, worse still, slaughtered by some peasant farmer of Lerric's who looted the bodies and was terrified of being found out. You'll find Taran in the garrison. I overheard him saying he'd be playing cards with Denny tonight. Goodnight, Vassa."

Vassa, dismissed, turned on his heel and made his way toward the stairs to the castle's lower floor. Elias strode down the corridor. His second companion, the man who walked at his left and who'd held his peace while his monarch took some of his bad mood out on the colonel, followed.

First Minister Levant sighed deliberately, drawing a fierce look from Elias.

"Go on, then, Rendan," growled the King, "say what you've got to say."

Levant ignored his sovereign's belligerent tone. "Was that really necessary, Elias? Vassa's only doing his job, and you're determined to make it difficult for him. It's hardly his fault he's not Brynne Sullyan."

Elias halted in his tracks, staring at the shrewd and honest face of his most trusted advisor. He had the grace to flush slightly before glancing away. "Am I that obvious?"

Levant smiled. "Only to me. Although I can think of another who'd see through you in an instant."

"Yes, but if she were here I wouldn't be behaving like a small boy deprived of his favorite puppy, would I?"

The King continued down the hall.

Levant raised his brows and his grin widened as he followed. "Now there's a thought. What's it worth not to tell Senior Master King's Envoy Colonel Sullyan that you just described her as your favorite puppy?"

"Go to hell, Rendan! You know what I mean."

Levant caught Elias's arm. The King halted, but would not meet his minister's sympathetic gaze. "You have to stop this, my friend," Levant advised softly. "It's doing you no good. Why can't you settle for her friendship and service? You know it can never be anything else."

The King twisted away from Levant's touch. His minister's use of the phrase "my friend" recalled memories of Sullyan saying it and the emotions it always engendered in his breast. Hearing Levant utter those words was almost too much to bear. He was about to snap some ill-tempered retort when he heard his daughter's voice calling imperiously. Pulling himself up with an effort, he turned around. Levant stepped prudently away.

Princess Seline marched up to her father and stopped in front of him, chin raised defiantly. Elias sighed, recognizing the signs of petulant determination when he saw them. Seline had the trait from both her parents, although Elias believed the haughtiness that went with it was wholly Sofira's. He could hear Seline's nursemaid, Bessie, panting up the stairs behind her charge, and realized they must have had yet another battle of wills. He found himself hoping he could side with Bessie on this one, and then felt guilty for the ungracious thought.

He looked down at the sulky face of his daughter and reflected that, distant as they had become lately, they were both suffering the same malady. He pined for Sullyan's company while Seline pined for the young swordsman, Tad. This was Seline's first infatuation and Elias thought she could have found a worse hero to worship than Tad Greylin. He liked the youth, who was well-trained, polite, and respectful. Tad, realizing he was the focus of Seline's tender young love, went out of his way to be careful of her feelings without encouraging her unduly. Elias had cause to be grateful for the young man's consideration.

"Well, Seline, what is it? The hour is late, I am tired, and you should have been in bed long ago."

"So I keep telling her, your Majesty, but she just won't listen," puffed Bessie, arriving at Seline's side.

"Oh, be quiet, Bessie! I said I would go to bed and I will, but I want to speak to my father first."

Elias raised his brows at his daughter's tone and saw Bessie flush with displeasure. He really ought to have words with Seline. The girl was becoming far too waspish. Far too like her mother ....

Elias strangled that thought. He was depressed enough tonight. Thoughts of Sofira would make him resort to the brandy bottle again and he could do without that.

"Very well, daughter, I am listening. What's so urgent it couldn't wait till morning?"

Seline held her father's gaze defiantly. "There's a fair in the city tomorrow, in the merchants' market. I haven't been out of the castle for days. I want to go."

It wasn't lost on Elias that his daughter wasn't actually asking his permission. He shot a look at Bessie's long-suffering face and decided a day out at the fair would benefit her, too. He knew how difficult she found it looking after his ungrateful and haughty daughter—especially in the absence of the affectionate Prince Eadan—and although Bessie was well paid for her trouble, he wasn't above giving her the odd treat as well. He smiled at the plump nursemaid and nodded to his daughter.

"Very well, Seline. I'll get Denny to detail someone to accompany you."

The Princess's face turned thunderous and she stamped her foot. "*No*, Father! If you do that, you'll spoil the whole thing! I know I can't go alone, but I want to go with just Bessie. How can I enjoy myself with your soldiers trailing around behind me? Can't I go into our own city without some great lumbering bodyguard getting in the way? What do you think is going to happen, anyway? I'm hardly going to get snatched by demons, am I? I'm not going to start another war!"

Elias went white. Seline's spiteful reference to his disastrous invasion of Andaryon shot straight to the hurt in his heart. It was exactly the kind of wounding comment Sofira would have made, and it turned his soul to stone.

"Very well, Seline," he ground out, the words like broken glass on his tongue. "You may go to the fair with only Bessie. But you are to be back within the castle long before dusk, do you hear me? Any later and I will rouse the garrison to fetch you back. Make no mistake that I mean what I say!"

Seline glared at her father. She knew he would carry through with his threat. She didn't make a fuss, however. She had what she wanted. She turned away, a smug little smile on her face. Bessie cast a deeply apologetic look at Elias, but he barely noticed. He had already dismissed his cold, defiant daughter from his mind and turned to resume his interrupted walk toward his chambers. He'd just conceived a pressing urge to spend time with a certain bottle of brandy.

✤ ✤ ✤ ✤ ✤

Seline marched back to the nursery, Bessie trailing behind. It really was high time she had her own suite of rooms, she thought. She was seven years old now, far too grown up to be sleeping in the nursery. Once this little trip into the city was out of the way and her father realized she was capable of getting her own way from now on, she would demand her own rooms. And the services of a *proper* maid. But until that time, she had her secret place.

She ignored Bessie's attempts to see her into bed and firmly dismissed the nursemaid. Seline could manage very well. She could dress and undress herself, brush and arrange her own hair, and she was more than capable of taking a bath on her own. She smiled with satisfaction when she heard the door to Bessie's room close, and she listened carefully to the noises of washing and undressing coming from inside.

When she was sure Bessie had gone to bed, she removed the tiny key from the secret pocket she had sewn inside her gown. It was really only a slit in the fabric, just the right size to hold the little silver key. Then she took out her private box from under her bed and unlocked the lid. She had done this several times in Bessie's presence so the nursemaid could see the box held only a few pieces of gold ribbon from one of her mother's gowns and a bundle of her mother's letters. The Princess removed the latest letter she'd received and unfolded the square of parchment, smoothing it over her knee. As she reread the words from her mother her eyes misted over, and she scrubbed irritably at them.

She was sure she had her mother's meaning right, but even if she had misunderstood, she would enjoy a trip of rare freedom tomorrow. Finding the passage she wanted, she went over the words one more time.

Do you remember, my dearest daughter, going to the merchants' fair last year? How we enjoyed strolling around the booths and watching the peddlers calling their wares? I especially recall how you enjoyed the antics of the man trying to sell those strange curved fruits from Beraxia. Do you remember him? I wonder if he will be there at this year's fair? I feel very sad that I will not be able to go there with you. Perhaps you can persuade Bessie to take you. If you do, be sure to look out for the man selling curved fruits, and if he is there, think of me.

Yes, thought Seline once she had read it through, she was certain her mother was telling her to go to the fair and to visit the stall of the Beraxian fruit seller. Her mother was well aware this man was a regular attendee, so the part about wondering if he would be there this year was completely false.

Seline smiled. Her mother had told her before she'd left that she would try to find a way of communicating with Seline without her father knowing, but this was the first time Seline had discovered a hidden message behind her mother's words.

Sofira knew Elias never attended the merchants' fairs. He was always too busy for such activities and left the provisioning of the castle to Madam Delinna, the chatelaine. He would have no idea what was sold among the stalls. But Sofira had often taken her daughter along, to accustom her to the processes of bargaining and provisioning, and she knew how Seline loved the whole experience. It would be the most natural thing for the Princess to ask to go.

Seline trembled, half with excitement and half with nerves. What would she find at the fruit seller's stall? What would happen there? Despite her earlier scornful reference to demons, the thought had already crossed Seline's mind that perhaps her mother wanted to spirit her away from the castle. That's why she had been so determined to dispense with her bodyguards. Her success in that had surprised her, but it also empowered her. If she could sway her father so easily in that respect, what else could she do? If kidnapping by her mother wasn't the object of tomorrow's jaunt— and Seline was intelligent enough to realize her father would turn out not only the castle garrison but probably the Manor as well if her mother tried anything like it—then she could think of many other demands for freedom she could try her hand at. Any or all of them would make her lonely life at the castle a bit more bearable.

Laying the letter aside, Seline emptied the box and picked at the base with her fingernail. It was a tricky catch, but if you angled it just right … she was rewarded by a click as the bottom of the box came loose. Prizing up the thin wood, she gazed triumphantly at the linen wrapping revealed under the false bottom. She took it out and unwound the scrap of cloth. A larger, heavier key fell into her hand and she clasped it tight.

Bessie would be asleep and snoring by now. Seline took great care to wear Bessie out and keep her up as late as possible when she intended to do this. It would spoil all her careful plans if her nighttime activities were discovered.

Rising from the bed, she took a dark cloak from her wardrobe, wrapped it around her, and opened the door of her room. She could just hear Bessie's gentle snores. Smiling to herself, Seline soundlessly closed her chamber door, crossed the nursery floor, and opened the outer door. She slipped out into the deserted, dimly-lit hallway and ran swiftly on bare feet toward the iron-bound door that was now the only entry to the disused east wing.

Seline inserted the key into the lock and pushed the door open. Unworried by the darkness that faced her, she passed quickly through and turned to lock the door behind her. As she moved down the passageway toward the oil lamp she kept on a shelf nearby, she suddenly froze. Straining her ears, she caught the sound of footsteps.

Heart hammering, Seline stood stock-still, hardly daring to breathe. When she realized the footfalls were coming from the hallway she'd just left she relaxed, letting out a silent sigh. She'd been fortunate. Another minute or so and she would have been seen. She felt herself go cold at the thought of discovery and tiptoed down the hallway toward her lamp.

✣ ✣ ✣ ✣ ✣

Lord Levant was deep in thought as he came abreast of the locked door. He had finally persuaded Elias to go to bed rather than partake of yet another glass of brandy, but he'd seen the loneliness that still lingered behind the King's eyes, unaffected by the amber liquid. He was worried for Elias, not knowing how to bring his monarch out of the depression that reared its head too often these days. He had been turning the problem over in his mind when his thoughts were broken by a faint scraping sound.

Levant stopped by the door, much as Sullyan had done a few weeks ago. Unlike the Artesan, however, Levant had no inner senses to rely on. And he was certain he'd heard something behind that door. He stepped closer and tried the latch, relieved to find the door securely locked. He knew Elias hadn't ventured into the east wing since Sofira's banishment, and there wasn't much chance of him wishing to do so. That door was likely to stay locked forever unless there was a radical change of incumbent at the castle.

Levant stared at the door, wondering whether to mention the possibility of rats to Madam Delinna. If he did, she would have to go to Elias for the key, and that might stir up the King's painful memories. If tonight was anything to go by, that was the last thing Elias needed right now. Levant decided to leave it. If there were rats in the east wing, they were welcome to it. There must be precious little for them to eat in there anyway.

He stepped away from the door and continued on down the hallway, heading for his own rooms and his bed.

Chapter Ten

The sixth bell had only just sounded when Sullyan heard the light tap at the door heralding the arrival of Frar Varian. If the elderly Frar was surprised to see all three of them dressed in their warm cloaks and ready to accompany him, he hid it well.

In truth, Sullyan herself was more than a little surprised. She had asked Ruvar for permission to attend the service mainly to satisfy a growing curiosity and her own theory as to the origins of this rocky bastion of faith, and she'd told Cal and Tad they were not required to accompany her. But as Sullyan woke, well before the sixth bell, and commenced her dressing, she heard the two men doing the same. They met in the living area, still warm from the banked fire, and as Sullyan stirred the embers in order to heat water for fellan, she cast them an enquiring glance.

"I confess I did not expect to see you two so early this morning."

Tad shrugged. "It's not often we get the chance to experience something like this. This place is so strange, I guess we both thought that the more we see of their way of life, the more we might understand what happened here."

Sullyan nodded her approval. "My thoughts exactly. Also, when we arrived here yesterday I was curious as to why there was no snow on the higher peaks, considering how far north we are. I believe I know why that is, and if I am correct, we shall see the reason this morning and the sight will be worth the early rise. But, gentlemen, I caution you to remember we are guests here. When we are conducted to the site of the service, I advise you to keep your eyes open and your mouths closed, unless there are opportunities to join with the service. Remember, this is a silent order and we must respect that."

They'd just finished their fellan when Frar Varian arrived, and they followed him out into the frigid early darkness. There had been a brisk easterly wind and a significant fall of snow during the night, and white flakes lay thick upon the path. As they made their way in silence, the air was still and the white crusting on the ground grew less and less. Sullyan could feel the temperature of the air changing as they passed the lightless windows of the Patrio's private residence and wound their way ever upward, ever more steeply, following the slowly pacing Frar. She felt rather than saw the glance Cal gave her as he, too, registered the slightly warmer air. She was pleased he was keeping his wits about him.

The walls of sharply jutting rock bordering their path loomed toward them as they climbed higher, forcing them to walk in line. Eventually, Sullyan could make out Varian's faint silhouette against the marginally lighter sky and they finally emerged onto a level track.

The constricting rock walls ended abruptly, giving Sullyan the distinct impression of a vast open space before her. As yet, there was insufficient light to see much, but she could tell that the fall of snow hadn't settled here; the ground was only damp. She followed Frar Varian as he turned left and led them farther along the level path, their legs grateful for the respite from the sheer gradient. Soon, he turned to Sullyan and placed a hand on her shoulder, indicating they should wait here. She touched Cal and Tad in turn and they stood facing the vast open space they could all sense as Varian walked away.

Silence settled like a comforting cloak. Sullyan used the time to extend her senses into her surroundings. She now knew what she would see when the light grew strong enough. She could feel the emanations rising from the rock all around her. They suffused her with a sense of antiquated majesty, but they also carried the faint hint of menace such places always exuded. The air was crisp with the clarity that often comes on cloudless winter mornings, and she knew the sunrise would be spectacular. The stars in the west shone brightly, the morning star in the east glittering with silver pulses.

The more she employed her metasenses, the more she could feel people around her. They weren't visible yet, but she knew there were many. They ranged on both sides of her, all standing in silence facing the east, all anticipating the glory to come. She could almost taste the excitement, the tingle of worship, and immersed herself in the sensation.

When the sound began, she almost missed it. It was subliminal, muted, but as natural as breathing. It might almost have been the combined pulse of the island community, each heart joining to beat as one to welcome the coming of the sun. It increased gradually in volume and resolved itself into its separate components, and soon she could hear individual voices chanting softly, each sustaining its own note. There must have been two or three hundred throats giving tongue to that low, humming drone, and it reverberated through the rock at her feet, echoing in the hollows of her soul.

The light grew and the sound grew with it, intensifying and deepening, swelling as the light of the new sun painted the sky with peach. The silhouette of the rocky peaks stood out starkly against the pink-stained east and the voices modulated, rising and falling now in single and multiple tones, building toward a towering crescendo which would erupt into song when the first ray of the new sun glanced over the island's rim.

Sullyan could see them now. Perhaps two hundred and thirty people stood ranged in a huge semicircle to either side of her, robed and cowled, their hoods drawn up, heads bowed before the dawn. As the light increased and the incredible thrum of voices soared toward the heavens, they raised their arms, stretching upward and outward in a gesture of reverence and welcome.

And then the first ray of sunlight burst blindingly over the horizon, cresting the edge of the world and the island as one. Shooting sharply through a narrow slit in the island's eastern peak, its full force struck upon a single man, standing hooded and insignificant until the primal sun limned his figure with gold. Sullyan had already identified Cleric Patrio Ruvar where he stood fifty paces from her, and in that instant of golden glory she saw him throw back his head, his arms upraised, and heard his full-throated Paean to the Sun. The warm, yellow shaft of sunlight flooded down the rock face, spilling like liquid life force into the vast, rocky crater that lay at their feet.

The volcano's bowl echoed and amplified the Patrio's song, and the assembled clerics now abandoned their chant and joined in the psalm, their voices swelling and flowing, melodies twining around a central theme. This triumphant laudation soared toward the heavens, a worshipful greeting and heartfelt thanksgiving for the circle of life and the turning of the Wheel, renewing all creation.

The heady primal power emanating from both newborn sun and the rock beneath her feet flooded Sullyan's being with a force too strong to resist. Caught up in the glory of the moment, she flung back her head, adding her lilting voice to the multitude. She closed her eyes, drinking in the heat of the new sun bathing her with fiery glory, but not before noticing the swift glance of amazement flung her way by Ruvar. She wondered which surprised the man more; her knowledge of the song, or her desire to join the worship.

The song slowly faded, dwindling down as it had spiraled up, and as the burnished disk of the sun rose completely over the horizon, the muted voices stilled. Sullyan opened her eyes and regarded the spectacle before her. It was as if tangible light filled and lapped at the crater of the dormant volcano, bringing vibrant color to the stark, barren rock. Hues of gold and russet, tan and brown, pink and amber were revealed within the bowl, and a faint shimmer of warmth rose from the banked fires deep within the earth's crust.

She stared at this wonder, reflecting that many more people might find their way to faith if they could only witness such rebirth, experience the glory that was in the world and see the mystery of creation revealed with such intense, majestic power. She felt extremely privileged that the talents of her birthright enabled her to sense these ancient and venerable forces so acutely.

She and her two companions stood and listened to the rest of the ritual in silence. It didn't last long. Sunrise was the shortest of the Services of the Wheel. When it was over, the people massed about the crater's rim slowly and silently filed back down the path to whatever tasks awaited them. As they passed the three guests, Tad barely suppressed a gasp of surprise when he saw how many were women. There were even some children among them.

Sullyan turned to leave, but stopped when she saw Patrio Ruvar approaching, a stooped figure by his side. She waited for them, Cal and Tad behind her.

"You have an unusually pure and well-trained voice, Colonel Sullyan," Ruvar remarked as he halted before her, regarding her with curiosity tinged with respect. "I confess that when I granted your request to witness this morning's service, I didn't expect to hear it raised in worship beside us."

She replied levelly. "Did you not, Patrio? Why else did you

think I made that request? Or do you believe as the Baron did, that we Artesans are pagan witches, not fit to follow your faith?"

The intangible sense of challenge was present once again in her tone and she sensed Cal stiffen, wondering how Ruvar would react. But the Patrio had obviously revised whatever opinions he might have held the day before, and he accepted her mild rebuke.

"The Faith of the Wheel is open to all. It's not for me to say who may or may not follow its path. That is for each soul to decide and for God to judge." He inclined his head toward her. "Your joyful contribution to our Paean was most welcome."

"You are kind, Patrio. I hope I did not intrude upon your personal communion."

"Not at all," he assured her. He turned to the man waiting in silence beside him. "Colonel Sullyan, this is Frar Durren, who witnessed the Baron's fall into the sea. He has agreed to speak with you. He will tell you what he saw and then he will take you to the rooms the Baron occupied. Frar Varian will await you there. Once you have concluded your business, it would please me if you and your men would breakfast with me."

Sullyan raised her brows and gave the Patrio a warm smile. "You are most accommodating, Patrio Ruvar. I thank you for your gracious invitation. It would be good to talk over our findings with you before we leave."

The Patrio bowed and withdrew, leaving them with the stooped Frar Durren. He cast back the cowl of his robe, revealing a balding head that at one time had been shaved in the fashion of Frar Varian. Durren was in his sixties and physically frail, but his blue eyes were clear and candid and the smile he turned on them was tentative but genuine.

"I am most grateful for your compliance in this matter, Frar Durren," said Sullyan. "I assure you we will not keep you from your duties longer than is necessary. Might we start by seeing the place from which Baron Reen cast himself into the sea?"

The cleric turned to lead the way. "It is around the other side of the crater. I must warn you, there is a steep climb."

As they walked, Sullyan asked the Frar how he'd come to witness the Baron's demise. In a voice scratchy with misuse, the elderly cleric related what he had seen that night.

"It was an hour past midnight and I was working in the archives. I often lose track of time these days, and when my candle burned low and I rose to fetch another, I realized the lateness of the hour. I left the library and set out for my dwelling. As I came around the edge of the crater, I heard a sound I didn't recognize."

He glanced at Sullyan. "Among a silent order such as ours, sounds take on a special significance. Here on this island, we've become accustomed to the sounds of the sea. Most of us can tell when a storm is brewing, no matter how far offshore, just by the changing patterns of the waves breaking on the rocks.

"It was a cloudless and moonlit night and the sound I'd heard carried clearly. It was a low moaning sound, and as it came again, I realized it was the sound of a body in pain."

Sullyan raised her brows but made no comment. The Frar continued as the path they followed sloped sharply upward once more, his breath laboring with the increased gradient.

"My eyes aren't what they used to be, but even I had no difficulty picking out the shape of a man toiling his way up this track. Concerned, I followed. Being long used to silence, it didn't occur to me to call out. If I'd suspected his destructive intentions, I might have overcome my habitual silence, but I didn't."

There was regret and self-blame in the old Frar's breathy voice, and Sullyan said softly, "How could you suspect, Frar? And I suppose you had no indication at this point as to the man's identity?"

Durren shook his head. "No. The Baron had taken to wearing

the robes of our order and he had become lean and frail, as many of us are. In the darkness, it could have been any of a number of men."

They continued on in silence. The steep track ended abruptly and Frar Durren came to a halt. Sullyan stepped up beside him. He put out a veined hand to catch her arm, a warning in his voice. "Have a care, lady! The ledge is narrow and treacherous. One false step and you would take the same final journey as the Baron."

She looked where he indicated and saw they had climbed one of the island's tall peaks, a remnant of an ancient, earlier crater. The track was well-defined and Sullyan surmised other services of the faith were performed from this spectacular platform.

They now stood upon a narrow, rocky outcrop overhanging the swell of the sea far below. From this point, they had a panoramic view of the entire horizon. The view was quite breathtaking if one ignored the strange sucking sensation that pulled at the senses from the heaving waters hundreds of feet below.

Taking firm control of her muscles, Sullyan leaned out as far as she dared to look at what lay below. When Patrio Ruvar had spoken of the jagged rocks that reefed the island he hadn't exaggerated their threat. If a body were to fall straight down from this point, it couldn't avoid being dashed to pieces on the spikes and ridges of black volcanic rock huddling close to the island's frothy skirts. Even now, without the effects of a blown-out storm, Sullyan could see how the waves sucked and surged among the rocks, and could well believe they would sweep away a human form if one came to rest on such a cruel deathbed.

She stared in fascination at the water far below, thinking the doubts she had harbored about the Baron's death should surely be laid to rest by what she saw. Never mind the lethal rocks: such a dizzying plunge into the sea would certainly dash the life from a fit and healthy body, let alone one as frail as the Baron's. Wouldn't it?

Frowning, she straightened and turned once more to Frar Durren. "What exactly did you see when the Baron reached this point?"

Durren's eyes clouded. "The moaning had increased in intensity, as if the man was in tremendous pain. His hands and the sleeves of his robe looked dark and wet in the moonlight, and later when the light returned we found smears of blood. I saw him clasp his arms about his chest and he shrieked aloud in torment. I tried to call to him, fearing what he might do, but my voice wouldn't obey me. I tried to hurry my steps, but I'm old and the way is steep. There was nothing I could do.

"I saw him move closer to the edge, still clasping his arms tightly about him, still moaning. Then he opened his arms and threw them wide. He screamed most horribly as he cast himself out from the rock with a mighty leap. By the time I reached this point, there was no sign of him."

Sullyan stood in silence, contemplating what the Frar had told her and gazing once again at the scene of the Baron's final act. The three men held their peace and did not disturb her deliberations, all of them thinking their own thoughts.

Finally, she stirred. "I am grateful to you, Frar Durren, for your willingness to relive what must have been a disturbing experience. I now have a much clearer picture of what occurred here." She glanced at the elderly cleric. "Might we now prevail upon you to convey us to the Baron's rooms?"

Durren nodded, cast the cowl of his robe over his bald head, and edged past her in order to retrace his steps. Sullyan followed him and the two swordsmen came behind, neither able to resist a final appalled glance over the sheer precipice to the sea far below.

"Will we find the Baron's rooms unchanged, or have they

been taken by someone else?" queried Sullyan as she walked beside the cleric on the easier descent. When he answered, his voice appeared disembodied coming from the depths of his cowl and it was clear he was tiring and wished to be done with her questioning.

"The room was cleaned of blood, of course, and the Baron's personal effects were collected, but that was all. No one else has taken up residence."

Sensitive to the effort he had made to accommodate them, Sullyan asked him no more. She dwelled on her thoughts as he conveyed them back toward the order's habitations. Just as he reached them, he veered to the right and they entered a narrow and uneven stair winding gently down through the rocks. At the end of this stair was a doorway carved into the rock face, and as Durren opened the wooden door, they found themselves inside the volcano.

Durren left the door open behind them and the daylight allowed them to see where he led. A long, straight corridor through the rock was studded at various intervals by iron-bound doors. Sullyan surmised these led into living quarters and storerooms, and the intrinsic heat of the volcano's magma far, far underground permeated the stone, doubtless rendering the usual necessity of fire within the dwellings superfluous. The air was mild—even warm— and they soon pulled off their cloaks.

Frar Durren stopped outside an open doorway and waved them in. As they stepped past him to enter, he turned and left with no further speech. Sullyan regarded his retreating back speculatively before turning her attention to Frar Varian, who had appeared to greet them.

"I enjoyed your contribution to our service this morning, Colonel," Varian smiled. "I hadn't realized you were familiar with our form of worship."

"The Paean to the Sun is widely used in services throughout Albia, Frar," she returned easily, "although I must admit, I have never experienced it so deeply before. But I have sung the office many times during worship at the Manor."

Varian raised his brows, but made no comment. He waved his hand round the room in which they stood. "These are the quarters of the Baron, where he lived once he was released from the cell we were forced to confine him in when first he came among us. Apart from the obvious, there has been no change since his death. You're welcome to look for yourselves."

With a gesture, Sullyan sent Cal and Tad to look through the suite, investigating the other small areas that led off the central space. One was the sleeping room, the other a small cooking room. The walls were bare rock, although smoothed and rounded. Thin rush matting covered the floor, and the furniture, such as it was, was plain wood and simply made. The facilities were primitive and frugal, in keeping with what they had heard of the order's lifestyle.

Varian watched them move about the room and turned a quizzical smile on Sullyan. "You do not enquire as to the construction of these dwellings, Colonel. Most people's first reaction is to ask how they were formed, how many years of tunneling it took to hew them from the rock."

She gave him a sideways glance. "These are magma chambers off a branch pipe. Even without the heat from below, the smoothness of the walls would have told me that."

He looked surprised. "What do you know of magma chambers?"

She smiled gently. "I am an Artesan, Frar, a Senior Master. My mastery over the element of Earth allows me many insights into the properties of rock and stone. I sense the emanations from the bones of our world very clearly, and this ancient rock speaks most eloquently of its volcanic origins. Either of my men here could have told you how these chambers came to be, as they are also Artesans. Now, if you would be so good, would you please tell me about the pool of blood you found here on the night the Baron disappeared?"

Frar Varian recovered his composure. He moved farther inside the room and indicated a spot on the floor. "This is where we found the blood. It had soaked into the floor and stained the rush matting. The eating knife that caused the wounds lay at the edge of the pool, about here." He pointed to his left foot.

"Can you show me the pool's total extent?" she asked, and he proceeded to indicate a wide area in a roughly circular pattern. When she saw how large the stain had been, she cast a significant look at Cal and Tad. "What became of the knife, Frar?"

The cleric shrugged. "I believe it was disposed of. There are others just like it in the cooking room."

He fetched one at her asking and passed it to her. She took it in a practiced hand, running the ball of her thumb over its edge. The blade barely dented the skin, although the tip was sufficiently sharp to penetrate flesh had she pressed hard enough. She regarded the knife narrowly. Definitely no use for slashing, but effective enough for stabbing. She handed it back to Varian.

Neither Cal nor Tad had seen anything worthy of note within the smaller rooms, and Sullyan thanked Varian for his trouble. She excused him from escorting them back to the Patrio's dwelling. They were familiar enough with the place by now to find their own way. They left the elderly cleric to close up the suite and walked through the corridor toward the light of day. Sullyan had seen more than enough to convince her of the truth behind the Baron's reported suicide. Once their courtesy visit with Ruvar was done, she was eager to return to the mainland. She now had one more task to undertake.

✣ ✣ ✣ ✣ ✣

Seline dressed with care that frosty morning. She was so excited and nervous she even let Bessie help her dress for the first time in weeks. But she did not allow the nursemaid to choose what she would wear. She'd already decided on that.

Despite knowing kidnap by her mother was highly unlikely, Seline wanted to be ready for anything. It was very cold out and if she should find herself bundled into a waiting carriage or whisked away on a fast horse in some loyal swordsman's arms, she would need to be warm. So she chose a green velvet gown which had thick underskirts but wasn't so cumbersome it would hamper her movements. On her feet were fur-lined boots, and over the gown she cast her white silk and velvet mantle, trimmed with white fox fur. The mantle had a matching muff to keep her hands warm.

She was forced to wait while Bessie completed her own dressing and fussed about, checking they had everything they'd need.

"Oh, hurry *up*, Bessie, I'm getting tired of waiting for you! If you don't come this minute I'm going to leave without you."

Bessie came puffing into the nursery where Seline stood impatiently by the door. "All right, Madam, I'm here now. No need to take that tone."

I'll take whatever tone I like! thought Seline, but she refrained from speaking aloud. Another row with Bessie would only delay them further, and she'd burst if she didn't find out soon what her mother had planned. At least she had finally persuaded Bessie to refer to her as "Madam," even if the nursemaid always put that infuriatingly condescending tone on it.

Seline swept out of the nursery, Bessie trailing behind. The Princess fully intended to walk Bessie's plump legs off her today. At least then she would be tired out this evening if Seline needed to visit her mother's rooms again.

The city thronged with people, as it always did on fair or

market days. Seline loved the press of townsfolk, the sellers' cries, the lure of the stalls, and the thrill of making purchases. She ignored the nursemaid, whose breath was already laboring after the long walk down the avenue through the castle parklands and from the effort of pushing through the bustle of crowds. That was another benefit of not having one of Major Denny's hulking swordsmen tagging along, Seline thought in satisfaction. They always cleared the way for her when she walked the streets of the city, and although normally she'd be irritated by the throng, who really ought to know better than to jostle their Princess, today she enjoyed the anonymity the lack of a bodyguard allowed her.

Not that she wasn't easily picked out as high-ranking nobility. Her clothing alone saw to that, coupled with the regal bearing she never permitted herself to drop. Anyone who chanced to turn their head as she approached stepped out of her way, and Bessie was wide enough to forge a way through those who didn't.

She led the puffing nursemaid through the craftsmen's quarter, pausing every now and then to look into shop windows in case there was anything she fancied purchasing on the way back. But she never stopped for long and certainly never long enough for poor Bessie to catch her breath. As soon as the nursemaid caught her up, Seline moved on again. She ignored Bessie's frequent pleas to stop and rest.

They came eventually to the square housing the merchants' market. It was a large and pleasant piazza, full of booths and stalls, bordered by shops and the homes of traders and dotted with trees. Seline stood and looked around the market, trying to spot the fruit seller.

She couldn't see him, and she felt a sinking disappointment. Her face fell into sour, sulky lines. Was she wrong after all? Had her mother's words been just as they seemed, an innocent memory meant to cheer her lonely daughter? Seline trailed disconsolately past the many booths, not taking much notice of what they sold.

Bessie trailed behind, her breath coming easier now Seline had slowed her pace. She was used to the Princess's petulant moods and recognized the beginnings of temper. Seline sighed deeply. This would probably end in another row when Bessie tried to get her charge to return to the castle and rest. Despite her crushing disappointment, Seline wasn't yet ready to end this day of freedom.

The nursemaid came alongside her. *Here it comes*, thought Seline, readying herself for battle. But Bessie was smiling and pointing.

"Look, Madam, there's that dark fellow selling those strange-shaped fruits that come all the way from Beraxia. Do you remember how you loved them last year? You even brought me one to taste when I wouldn't believe the way you described them."

Seline's excitement must have pleased Bessie no end, although she was clearly startled by the whoop of delight. The Princess suppressed it swiftly. She rarely deigned to show her feelings in public and was annoyed by Bessie's private smile. She knew her nursemaid still considered her a little girl. Well, maybe soon she would have cause to revise that opinion.

Bessie bustled in front of her. "Now you wait there, Highness, and I'll go and bargain with that young rogue. I want to buy a good amount of those fruits for his Majesty, and if the trader sees you he'll hike the price way above what it should be. Don't move, I won't be long."

Bessie left her standing there while she went over to the trader's stall. Seline watched her, her heart hammering painfully in her breast. He *was* here! The reason she hadn't seen him was because his stall had been moved and was partially obscured by the draper's much larger booth. She moved a little sideways so she could see the entirety of the fruit seller's stall, but there was nothing remarkable about it. Bessie stepped up to the trader and began selecting some of the odd-shaped fruits, shaking her head firmly at the trader's initial price.

Seline's eyes darted this way and that, ready for … what? She had no idea what she was supposed to be looking for. There were no handsome swordsmen loitering nearby, no obvious strangers that she could see, no one causing a disturbance in order to sweep her away. She turned back to Bessie, who had filled her basket with fruits and was wagging her plump finger at the trader as he grinned mischievously back at her.

Was that it? Disappointment dragged at Seline once again. She must have been wrong. Nothing was going to happen. Tears prickled her eyes and she irritably told herself not to be so childish. Bessie was coming back now; there was no more reason to stay. She turned sharply away, determined to take her bitter mood out on Bessie on the walk home. She nearly fell over the scrawny fellow standing just behind her.

The man put out a hand to keep Seline from falling. "Get out of the way, you stupid idiot!" yelled Bessie. "Don't you touch her!" The nursemaid came up between them and gave the scruffy fellow a shove.

"Your pardon, noble Lady," the rustic mumbled, shuffling awkwardly away from Seline. Bessie glared at him, wrinkling her nose at his disgusting smell. Seline was glad to be steered out of his path. He had a pale and shrunken, almost wasted, appearance.

Bessie gestured Seline ahead of her, grumbling about tinkers and vagabonds and threatening to turn out the garrison to flush all such layabouts out of the city. Seline wasn't listening. She had thrust her cold hands inside her muff, and her fingers encountered something strange.

Exploring it with her fingers as she walked, her excitement mounted. It was a folded parchment. A letter, perhaps? Her breath hitched. Her mother had sent her a secret letter! That dreadfully filthy man must have slipped it inside her muff when she had stumbled against him.

Seline smiled and even allowed Bessie to set the pace on the way back, although her instincts were screaming at her to hurry, to open the letter, to read her mother's words. Yet she schooled herself to patience. She had come this far; she wouldn't jeopardize whatever her mother had planned by making Bessie suspicious. She knew the nursemaid would want a nap when she got back and, for once, Seline wouldn't protest when she was told to lie down for an hour or so. At least, she wouldn't protest *too* hard. It would not do to act differently or it might be remembered.

Hardly able to contain her excitement, Seline even forgot about the purchases she'd intended to make. She had much more important things on her mind.

Chapter Eleven

Sullyan tapped at Patrio Ruvar's door and heard his call of welcome. She entered with Cal and Tad behind her, and they removed their cloaks and hung them on pegs. Ruvar appeared at the far end of the hallway and greeted them warmly. He had changed out of his cleric's robes and once again wore everyday clothing. Sullyan saw Cal shake his head. It seemed he still had trouble equating the revered head of a strict holy order with this very ordinary young man.

Ruvar beckoned them into his living space, where breakfast foods were laid out. The aromas of tea and fellan pervaded the air. The cleric bade them sit and served them himself, holding up a hand at Sullyan's protest.

"There's no formality here, Colonel, except in the execution of our office. We are all equals in our faith; my position as Cleric Patrio is more ceremonial than hierarchical. Any one of us might have been chosen for the role at Damas's passing."

"And why were you chosen, Patrio?" Sullyan asked casually. Cal wasn't the only one to wonder about this cleric's worldly demeanor and casual mode of dress.

Ruvar smiled his charming, sideways smile. "I think we understand each other a little better now, Colonel, don't you? Why don't we dispense with titles and relax our stiff courtesy? You may call me Ruvar. I was selected to become Patrio because I was educated and initiated in Port Loxton, under the guidance of His

Immanence Lord Neremiah."

"Ah!" Pieces of the puzzle fell into place for Sullyan. Ruvar's sideways glances and defensive attitude toward her talents now made sense. He must have feared she would judge him by Neremiah's actions during the Baron's trial. She decided to reassure him.

"I hold nothing against Lord Neremiah, Ruvar. His part in Baron Reen's defense was engineered and directed by Sofira, acting under the influence of Reen himself. I believe he meant no harm toward me and he has made no outcry against Artesans since the Baron's downfall. And my given name is Brynne."

Ruvar inclined his head as he sat opposite her, having served himself with warm bread and soft cheese. "His Immanence and I have corresponded since the trial of the Baron." This drew a narrow look from Sullyan, and his attitude became apologetic. "Neremiah was shocked by the Baron's violent prejudices, and I think he felt guilty for allowing himself to be used by Reen. He was most anxious to know whether the Baron harbored any feelings of resentment toward him."

Sullyan snorted indelicately. "His Immanence has every reason to feel guilty. He could have put a stop to most of the Baron's scheming had he not been so weak. And he need not have asked *you* whether Reen harbored resentment. I could have told him the answer to that."

Ruvar regarded her with sympathy. "Reen hurt you very deeply, didn't he?"

"Hurt me? He damned near destroyed the *world*!"

Sullyan's vehemence shocked them all. Cal and Tad glanced from her to the Patrio in consternation. Ruvar's eyes stretched wide and Sullyan passed a hand across her face. "Forgive me," she murmured, "I ought not to have said that."

"There is nothing to forgive," Ruvar said. "There's clearly far more to the matter than I was told. I was elected Patrio because I was born and raised in the outer world. It was felt my familiarity with such things would relieve others less worldly of the task of dealing with the unknown. Damas never went off the island, and I know he found it hard coping even with speaking to the fishermen who supply us. It is necessary to have someone who knows their ways and can spot the ones who try to cheat us. We are maintained by the Matria Church in Port Loxton and the Arch Patrio would be angry if he found the fishermen squandering the gold he sends them to pay for our supplies. It is one of my tasks to see we are kept adequately provisioned, and that the quality of goods is consistent. So you see, Brynne," he smiled at her, "there's no real mystery behind someone my age holding so august an office."

Sullyan retuned his smile, grateful for his lightening the mood and ignoring her uncharacteristic loss of control. She took another swallow of fellan and he wisely returned to the subject of her visit. "I hope you were able to satisfy yourself as to the facts concerning the Baron's suicide?"

Her voice was soft in the quiet room. "I have gleaned everything I need from the available sources, thank you. I have quite enough information to complete my report to the King. I have only three final questions for you, if I may, and then we must take our leave and begin our voyage home."

"And what are they?"

"The first is this: Both you and Frar Durren mentioned the Baron had taken to leaning heavily upon a cane for support, yet Durren did not see it as he watched Reen's progress up to the peak. Was the cane ever found?"

Ruvar frowned, his dark brows creasing. "Not that I know of. But I can tell you Reen would never have made it up to that peak without his cane. It never left his side and he was unable to walk without it. I suppose it must have fallen into the sea when he jumped. Your second question?"

"Did the Baron enter into correspondence with anyone while he was here? I assume members of your order may send messages to their families via the supply boats?"

Ruvar thought a minute, frowning. "I believe the Baron did send a few letters. But you must understand, I don't pry into my clerics' personal affairs. Letters are placed in a box in my study and are never examined before Varian gives them to the fishermen. Likewise, any messages that return are left in the box for collection by the recipient."

She was disappointed. "So you cannot tell me to whom the Baron's letters were addressed?"

"No." Ruvar's frown deepened, clearly unhappy at her tacit suggestion that he should.

"Do you recall anything about the return letters which might give some clue as to who they were from?" she pressed. "Would Varian?"

He looked scandalized. "Neither of us ever looked at them. Letters are private."

Deciding she would learn no more from him on this matter, she asked her final question. "Can you tell me either the names of the fishermen who ferried Frar Serrin back to the mainland, or the location of the village he came from? I believe it would complete the picture if I could speak with the young man himself. He could probably shed more light on why the Baron chose such a desperate exit from this world when he had seemingly been content for nearly three years."

Ruvar seemed happier with this line of enquiry. "Hmm. I wouldn't like to speculate as to your success with Serrin. He was always a morose and reticent young man and his association with the Baron improved his demeanor not one whit. But you'll discover his character for yourself if you can find him.

Unfortunately, though, I can't help you with that either. We have as little contact with the fishermen as possible; we don't ask their names. It's rarely the same men twice in a row. And the only thing I know about where Serrin came from is that he was unwanted by his parents and sent here as a last resort. He was so resentful and angry over their actions that he never spoke about where he came from. I got the impression his village was farther along the coast to the south. More than that I cannot say."

He spread his hands ruefully. "I am truly sorry not to be of more help to you in these matters. The fishermen should be able to tell you more about who ferried Serrin that day, and maybe they know more than I about where he came from. You will have to stay the night at their village anyway. There's a freshening easterly beginning to blow and you'll have a long and uncomfortable beat back to shore."

An hour later, having taken their farewells and gathered their gear, they made their careful way down the icy steps toward the waiting sloop.

"What did he mean, 'a long and uncomfortable beat'?" asked Cal suspiciously. He had his pack slung over his shoulder, plus the bundle of the Baron's personal possessions. "What is a 'beat,' anyway?"

Sullyan grinned at him. "Beating into the wind, is what you do when you have to sail in the direction from which the wind is blowing. We need to sail east, but the wind is blowing from the east and no boat can sail directly into the wind."

"So how can we get back?"

"We will have to tack."

"What the hell's a 'tack'? First beating, now tacking! I really don't understand all this sailing business."

"Have no fear, Cal. Just do as you are bid and all will become clear. At least I can moderate the strength of the wind, so we will not get too wet. But it would take more power than I care to expend to alter the wind's direction. Tad, step into the boat and take the packs, will you?"

Despite Sullyan's taming of the wind, it was a rough and freezing romp over the waves. The icy spray drenched them from the start as the little craft sliced and drove through the mounting waves. Cal and Tad learned all they cared to know about tacking: turning the prow of the boat through the eye of the wind so they steered a zigzag course closer and closer to their destination. As they finally neared the shore, having taken a good two hours longer over the return journey, the hills and cliffs of the mainland provided some shelter from the full force of the wind and the waves lessened. By the time the entrance to the reef came into sight, they sailed a much calmer sea.

It was coming on for midafternoon and there were other vessels about. Sullyan could see they were generating their fair share of curious stares. The returning fishermen probably recognized the craft as belonging to old Jeriko and couldn't believe their eyes when they saw it was handled by three strangers. Sullyan ignored them, concentrating on navigating the entrance to the bay.

Taking the tiller from Cal, she swung them about one final time and headed for the gap. The wind was on the beam and she told the men to pay out the sheets, allowing the sails to take more wind. The little sloop passed safely through the reef and entered the much calmer waters of the shallow bay.

Instructing Tad to drop the headsail, Sullyan aimed for the jetty. She caught sight of Jeriko standing on the strand and knew the old fisherman had been watching for them. She was determined to bring his craft to rest as easily as she could. Some of the fishermen had already anchored their craft and were unloading the day's catch. A couple of them walked down the jetty to take the sloop's mooring ropes.

Using the last of the vessel's momentum, Sullyan swung the tiller over and brought the boat alongside the jetty. She couldn't avoid the jolt as the craft struck the wooden structure, but all in all she thought they had done a workmanlike job. Tad and Cal threw the lines to the waiting fishermen and Sullyan smiled up at Jeriko as he came hobbling toward them.

He looked his vessel over critically. "Well, I must admit I'm surprised to see you back in one piece. That were quite a blow came up overnight."

One of the fishermen straightened from fastening the sloop's painter. "They was lucky for sure. I ain't rarely seen an easterner drop like that one."

Jeriko held out a hand to Sullyan and she allowed him to help her from the boat. "You see we have brought her safely home, Jeriko. I thank you for her loan."

The old man snorted. "Loan, nothin'! You paid me the worth of my craft and still returned her unharmed. I don't call that loanin'. Here," he said, noticing their wet, bedraggled clothing, "you need to get yourselves dry and warm."

Sullyan agreed. The wind might have dropped, but the sea spray had been icy and they were all beginning to shiver. Jeriko picked up her pack and waved with one hand. "C'mon, lass, you can use my house to dry your things. Don't you worry about your beasts. I looked after 'em well enough. We're havin' a barn feast tonight to celebrate a good catch; you're all invited. I expect you can use a good meal after what them hermits'll have fed you."

They allowed Jeriko to lead them to his small cottage where a welcome fire blazed in the hearth. He showed them where to heat water and then left them. Once he was gone, they stripped off their wet clothing and spread it to dry, using the hot water to warm shivering muscles.

Sullyan waited until they were all dressed again and had

brewed the inevitable fellan. She knew what her own feelings were about what they had learned, but wanted to discover whether the men had come to the same conclusions as she.

She glanced at them over a steaming mug. "Well, gentlemen? Your thoughts, please."

Cal gazed at her as he sipped his scalding brew. "I'm not sure I believe the whole story," he said. She encouraged him and he carried on. "For one thing, I don't like that knife. There's no way he could have slit his wrists if it was as blunt as the one Varian showed us. And for another, there was all that blood."

"Yes," added Tad. "There was far too much blood."

Sullyan agreed. She knew they would pick up that point. They were all well acquainted with how much blood a human body contained and how it bled when injured. "Go on."

"Well," said Cal, "if all that blood did come from the Baron, there's no way he could have climbed that peak. He'd have bled out by the time he reached the passageway. And no one mentioned seeing a trail of blood leading away from his rooms."

That was a good point, she reflected, and one she had not noticed herself. Disregarding the size of the blood pool, if the Baron had somehow managed to slash his wrists with that dull knife, he would have left a trail a blind man could have followed. And Frar Durren said Reen's hands and clothing were still wet with blood when he had seen him toiling up the track. So if it hadn't come from the Baron's wrists ....

"Well done, Cal, I had not thought of that. And Ruvar told us, did he not, that blood was found on the rocks where the Baron cast himself off. So why not on the ground outside his rooms or on the trail? Now, what about Frar Durren's description of the Baron just before he jumped?"

Neither of the two men had picked up the point that most bothered her, and they frowned in concentration.

"I suppose if he had wounded himself badly, he *would* have been moaning in pain," mused Tad, "although I still can't imagine him being able to climb that slope in such a condition."

"Indeed, Tad. And if you remember, both Durren and Ruvar told us the Baron had become very frail. He already leaned heavily upon a cane. Do you not think it strange the cane was never found? Why should he trouble to take it with him when he jumped? Why not simply cast it on the ground? And there is something else troubling me. When I leaned out over that ledge, it was a straight fall down to the rocks below. Anyone who fell from there would be dashed to pieces. And yet the Baron, who was, to use Ruvar's own words, 'in a fragile state,' managed to make a mighty leap out over the water before plummeting. How could someone in his feeble condition, leaning on a cane and with his wrists slashed, be capable of making a 'mighty leap'? And why bother, when a simple fall would do the job?

"The other point that does not quite fit with this picture of a man determined to take his life in despair is the question of the moonlight."

Cal frowned. "The moonlight?"

She nodded. "Do you not remember Ruvar telling us the Baron had become reclusive, never going abroad in the light? He even avoided moonlight. And yet he chose a brightly moonlit night on which to end his life. Why do you suppose that was?"

"Perhaps he'd simply had enough," speculated Tad. "If you were disturbed enough to take your own life, I would think the phase of the moon would be the last thing you'd notice."

She fixed him with a stare. "Even when you had spent the last months of your life fervently avoiding it?" He shrugged. "No, gentlemen," she continued, her expression serious, "I have another theory to fit the known facts. And I do not like the conclusion I am forced to draw from it. I do not like it at all."

After this unsettling discussion, they made their way through the evening gloom toward the bright glow of a huge fire flickering from the interior of one of the barns. They could have found the place without it, for the delicious smell of baking fish wafted out on the cold night air. They were welcomed with food and fellan, and Sullyan found ample opportunity to question the fishermen gathered there.

She discovered that although the village had been supplying the clerics for years, only a handful of fishermen had ever set foot on the jetty, let alone guested there. They seemed to have some strange ideas as to what was done on that secluded, barren island. Sullyan learned, to her consternation, that none of the fishermen recalled ferrying a young lad from the island back to the village.

"What about boats from other villages? Could anyone else have taken him home?"

A seamed and tattooed sailor, brawny hands and arms covered with scars and pits from hauling nets and gutting fish, answered her. "Nay, lass. There's no one else'll go near that place. We wouldn't go, only we gets paid good gold."

She shot Cal and Tad a look, and they shrugged. "Does anyone remember taking the boy out there? It would have been four years ago. He was thirteen at the time."

Another man came closer, removing his pipe from his teeth and trailing a stream of foul-smelling smoke from his lips. "Oh, aye, lass, I remember taking him there. Scrawny little thing, quiet and sulky, and none too pleased to be going, if you ask me. But I was paid good coin to take him and take him I did. I left him on the landing stage and never saw him again."

"Would you remember where he came from?"

He thought for a while and his face brightened. "D'you know, I think I do? His father brought him, and I'm sure I remember him saying he came from Foxdune way."

"And where is that?"

The fisherman told her it was inland, about five miles to the southeast. Cal and Tad gathered they would be making a detour on their way home the next day.

Jeriko offered them a room in his house for the night. While Cal and Tad checked the horses, Sullyan communed with General Blaine.

The bluff man was troubled and said nothing about the conclusions she had drawn, but he approved of the extra journey on the morrow. He decided not to inform the King just yet of her findings, preferring to let Sullyan do that in person. He did, however, tell her about the news he had received from Vassa.

She was surprised. *Two dead Roamerlings? And both on Lerric's lands? Now where does this fit in?*

She felt the general's reluctance. *Maybe nowhere? It could be an isolated incident, nothing to do with this.*

I disagree. If Reen has indeed escaped his prison, who would he most likely turn to? And where was Sofira taken when she was banished from Elias's castle? Who do we know who hates all alien races with a vengeance? Mathias, I hope you will warn Jerrim to be doubly on his guard. I will conclude my journey as swiftly as I may and return to the Manor. I hope I shall find and speak with this young lad, but I very much fear I have discovered the source of the blood found in the Baron's rooms.

But why would he kill the boy, the only one who befriended him? asked Blaine.

Sullyan had no ready answer, but she intended to find out.

Chapter Twelve

It had been the hardest thing Seline had ever done to wait for Bessie to quit fussing over her and retire for her afternoon nap. The young girl spent the time concocting wilder and wilder theories as to what her mother's letter contained. What was she planning? What would she require her daughter to do? How could Seline help her mother regain her crown? Despite her young age, Seline was under no illusions about what her mother really wanted. Sofira was a Princess of royal stock, and no one could take that from her. But to be a Queen—and High Queen of all Albia at that—was the ultimate achievement. Sofira would never accept her mother no longer merited the crown.

Finally, after a lifetime of impatient waiting, Bessie went to bed. Seline waited a little longer before cracking the door open and crossing the nursery. She peered into Bessie's chamber, seeing the plump woman asleep on her bed. Satisfied, Seline returned to her room. Pushing her hand inside her muff, she extracted the folded parchment. Trying to calm her racing heart, Seline curled into her pillows and unfolded the letter.

My dearest daughter, you have been very clever in discovering the hidden message in my last note to you. I knew you would and I am very proud of you. Now I can speak to you without your father knowing, and I can tell you things he mustn't know. But we must still be very careful, my bright and clever angel. You must burn every single letter you receive in this way. Do you understand?

You must never keep even one, no matter how much you might wish to. I shall continue to write to you in the normal way, but it will only be of trivial things, things any mother might say to her daughter. But you are not just any daughter, are you, my love? And I am no ordinary mother.

So, Seline, to the point of all this subterfuge. The man who passed you this letter is a servant of ours. He has come to the capital to carry out our will, and to do this he may need your help. You need not fear him. I know he looks dreadful, but he is a faithful servant and will do you no harm. From time to time, we will pass him instructions and he will carry them out. You may hear of certain things happening that you will not like. I urge you not to think of them and to remember that in order for me to regain my crown, certain obstructions must be removed. I think you know what I mean. But do not fear, my brave Seline, we intend no harm to your father. Once he sees how wrong he has been, he will understand what I have done and we will all be together again, as we were before.

But for now, my dearest child, just be very careful. Look after your brother, but do not tell him of our plans. He is too young to understand. All you need to know is that I will be returning for you both very soon and we will all be happy once more.

Our servant may well contact you again and you may receive other letters or instructions. If you do, try to do as we ask as soon as you can. For now, my dearest daughter, farewell. And remember, burn this letter immediately!

Seline's heart was in her throat. She found herself wondering who the "we" referred to. Clearly her mother had found someone willing to help her, and Seline was bright enough to doubt it was her grandfather, King Lerric.

Despite her mother's urgent order and despite understanding the reason for it, Seline read the letter through twice more, searching for clues as to who the other person was. She knew Sofira wasn't referring to the unwashed servant.

Dismissing the puzzle, Seline read the letter one last time. She worried over her mother's reference to Eadan. She clearly didn't know he had gone to the Manor, which meant her father hadn't told her. Seline frowned, angry. He really should have told her! But that could be remedied. Seline could mention it openly in her next letter. She smiled and continued reading. She wanted to memorize every phrase. Once she was sure she had it right, she took the parchment to the fire and cast it into the flames. She watched it crisp and burn, a triumphant smile on her face.

✤ ✤ ✤ ✤ ✤

The Baron sent the younger of his two servants to find Sofira. He had some good news to tell her which he hoped would improve her mood. The strictures he had placed upon their time together and on the arrangements for their coming marriage were beginning to tell on Lerric's daughter, and although she professed to understand the reasons for them, Reen knew she was far from happy. All this concern over her state of mind and the uncertainty of what she might do without his controlling hand upon her drained his energy.

Reen still suffered tremors of rage whenever he remembered the near disaster concerning her proclamation. On top of that, his servants had to work harder now to find suitable sources for their master's renewal. It seemed the Roamerlings had discovered the loss of two of their race, and the itinerant outlanders had drifted away from Lerric's province. The Baron suspected the disappearance of the Artesan among them must have seriously inconvenienced the troupe the man had led. And although his death had given Reen the knowledge and power to move his servants through the substrate if he chose, he wasn't willing to expend the energy required on a regular basis.

So he had sent them out that evening with orders to find some tramp or beggar—preferably one that was whole and in reasonable condition—and bring him to Reen's chamber. The strength received, although not as sustaining as that from a young, fit body, should nevertheless prove sufficient to enable the Baron to conduct his final experiment. And for that, he needed access to the substrate.

A footfall behind his door brought Reen out of his sadistic and pleasurable reverie. He dampened the fires of his desire and forced himself to relax his hold on the cane he gripped so tightly. It wouldn't do to permit Sofira to see so deeply into him just yet. He would save that revelation for later.

"Come, my love," he called. She had finally learned never to walk in on him, never to disturb him without alerting him to her presence.

The door swung open and she stood in the doorway, trying to see him in the dark. His eyes, so useless in daylight, were able to discern the aura of her presence and he saw her almost as plainly as if they hadn't been damaged beyond repair by the terrible but fortuitous accident that had so transformed his life. He smiled wider to see her so hesitant. Finally, she was learning who was master here.

"Hezra?" She turned her head anxiously.

"I'm here, my love." He moved forward so she could see him. The low glow of the embers warming his room cast deeper shadows into the corners of the chamber, and his black robes absorbed what light there was.

"Oh!" she gasped, half in relief, half in uncertainty. Despite his own decision not to reveal his true nature too soon, Reen was sure enough of his hold over her to let slip his disguise now and then. The glimpses she had caught of the gaunt scarecrow, intangible and dismissed as tricks of the poor light, nevertheless unsettled her. She was no longer so confident in his presence, and he was content she should feel so.

"You called for me?" Her voice was soft and hesitant. He moved closer and took her hand in his. The aspect of the claw was replaced by a younger version and she clasped it warmly. He allowed a smile to permeate his voice.

"I did, my love. Come, sit by the fire. You're cold."

He knew that the gooseflesh prickling her skin, that made her so acutely aware of every touch of fabric upon her body and every movement of his against her, didn't have its origins in the temperature of the air. Reen used his senses to play upon her as if she were some instrument made for his hand alone. Indeed, he reminded himself, he had been molding her long before he'd experienced the heady and dreadful power he now enjoyed.

Back then, when she had first become betrothed to Elias, he had decided he wouldn't be left behind in this small, insignificant southern province. At first he had thought only to be her close and trusted advisor. Then, when Sofira prepared to leave Bordenn to become High Queen, Reen had so successfully persuaded her she couldn't do without him that he thought some lucrative minister's post wasn't out of the question. But once at court, once he realized the possibilities inherent in his unique situation, he saw how low he had aimed. The office of Arch Patrio seemed a worthier and more fitting vehicle for his talents and far-reaching plans.

He had been well on the way to achieving that goal. How far could he have gone had he not been stymied, first by that imbecile outlander Rykan—whose uncontrollable lusts had overcome his better senses—and then by his archenemy? He couldn't even bring himself to form her name within his mind. A hot flare of intense anger flooded him, his entire body flaming with a burning desire to wreak revenge. He trembled in every bone with the depth of his desires and felt his control begin to slip. He forced himself to turn away from Sofira lest she see the ruby glow of hatred deep within his damaged eyes.

"My love?" she faltered, sensing his struggle. "Are you in pain?"

With a huge effort, he controlled himself. He must be patient. He must be strong. Lay the foundations, gather the strength and the power. He wouldn't fail this time. This time he would have his full measure of revenge and *she* would see he was her master. She would taste the bitter despair of his hatred and feel the hopeless yearning, acknowledging in the depths of her pagan soul the futility of struggle as she bowed before the fullness of his power over her.

But all in good time. Damping his rage, he turned to Sofira.

"Sofira, my dear, I have some very good news for you. Your clever daughter has fulfilled your expectations and my servant has made the first contact. We are on our way, my love. We have taken the first steps toward the restoration of your crown and your birthright. Soon you shall return to your place, and we will skulk in the shadows no more. There, my brave Queen. What do you say to that?"

"Oh, Hezra!" Sofira clasped both his hands in hers and brought them to her bosom. He could feel the heave of her breasts and smell the sweetness of her perfume. She gazed adoringly into his eyes. "I knew she wouldn't let us down, she is such a clever girl! Do you have news of her, of Eadan?"

"I have no news, my love, other than what I have told you. My servant was instructed to deliver the letter only. But now that the Princess is alerted to our plans and the presence of my man, we'll be able to communicate with her more readily. And maybe, once we are wed, we'll be able to bring your children here, to be with us. Would you like that, Sofira?"

The Princess frowned. "Well, of course I would. But we'll be going to Port Loxton, surely? I can't be High Queen from here."

Reen took hold of his temper. The sooner he was done with this farce the better. Until then he had to humor this woman, who could be so strong when surrounded by the power of the King, yet so weak and simple in her dependent trust.

"Yes, my love," he said, trying for a patient tone. "Once our plans have come to fruition, of course you will rule from the capital. But we don't know how long that might take, and I thought you might wish to have your children with you before then. I know how much you miss them."

Tears came to Sofira's eyes. "You are so solicitous, my love. Always thinking of my needs. What have I done to deserve such care?"

Nothing except be the vehicle for my *needs!* Reen thought viciously. Aloud he said, "Ah, my Queen, I live only to serve you, as you know. And if you return in some measure the love I feel for you, then I am repaid before ever we succeed."

"You know I do." Sofira moved closer and kissed his lips. The Baron permitted the liberty, although her kiss left him cold. He had never been overly tempted by women, although there had been times when he had taken what pleasure they offered. Later, he thought, once they were wed ... But his tastes ran more to the exotic, and as Reen ran his hands over Sofira's lean body, thoughts of young Serrin came to mind.

He compared the Princess's angular form with Serrin's gentler flesh. The young cleric had been just sixteen when they first began their physical relationship. Before then, the Baron hadn't realized what the boy had been offering him. Reen had been too wrapped up in his own deep despair and vengeful hatred to have any room in his tortured soul for the feelings of others. But Serrin, drawn to this tormented man, had recognized the banked fires within him and gave him companionship without complications. Eventually, seeing the signs in the boy's eyes and his soft, questing touches, Reen began to consider the possibilities inherent in their friendship.

Cautiously at first, and then with increasing confidence, Reen and Serrin explored the ways they could satisfy each other's needs. Giver and taker, master and slave, they had existed together with no friction and each had found release.

The small smile Reen permitted himself in the darkness held something of genuine regret. Poor, simple Serrin. So stunted, so deformed in his soul. He had given his master far more than he'd intended, far more than he had even known he *could* give. Without knowing how, he had kept the Baron alive during the wrenching agonies of his horrific accident, had even helped Reen recover from the dreadful fire and the worst of his disfiguring wounds. And in the end, still without knowing what he did, he made it possible for Reen to achieve what his twisted heart most desired.

Almost—almost—Reen wished it hadn't been necessary … but no. It was folly to feel thus. He now had the means of taking the only thing that could assuage the burning rage consuming his soul; the only thing that could give meaning to those long years of incarceration and humiliation. Serrin had made it all possible. Unwittingly—and unwillingly, at the end—he had surrendered that which his master needed and Reen took it without restraint, without compassion, and without a moment's thought.

Shaking the memory of the agony, the ecstasy, and the blood from his mind, the Baron realized his thoughts had engendered responses in his body that had been noticed by Sofira. Still smiling that cruel smile, he decided not to disabuse her of her misconceptions. Time enough for revelations later. For now, he allowed the memory of the young boy's gentle flesh to override Sofira's clumsy caresses.

✢ ✢ ✢ ✢ ✢

Midnight came and went. Reen sat alone in the darkness of his room, gnawing at the fury in his heart. Why were they taking so long? Surely it was a simple matter to overpower some alley-dweller and bring him back here? There were many such on the streets of Daret, Bordenn's tiny capital, as the Baron knew well. He had been the one to order the last cleansing of the slum districts some years ago, before he'd followed Sofira to Port Loxton. At the rate these half-wits bred, surely there should be more than enough to choose from by now!

Finally, Reen heard his servants returning. The anticipation of renewal, stirring and exciting him as it did, caused him to snap with more than his usual scathing anger when they finally arrived.

"Where the hell have you been? I could have died waiting for you two! And you know what that would mean for you, don't you?"

They did. He had taken great pains to explain it to them after he'd first bound them to him. They were well aware that his goodwill and his unnatural life were the only things standing between them and a horrific death. They glanced fearfully at each other.

"Forgive us, my Lord," the younger one said, trembling. "But since the death of the town crier, the streets are patrolled even more strictly by his Majesty's guards. We had to work hard not to be seen."

"Lerric's guards!" scoffed Reen. "Imbeciles, the lot of them. And they know you, for pity's sake. Why should they suspect or detain you?"

He dismissed their tardiness as his eyes lit upon the captive they held. Gagged and bound securely, he was no more than fifty and he was in one piece. Weakened through lack of good food, maybe, but still serviceable. Reen had feared they would bring him some ancient grandfather with the palsy, or worse still, the wasting sickness. But this individual was still hale, still strong for life, and would fulfill his enforced role adequately.

Reen smiled at his two servants. "It seems you've redeemed yourselves once again. Your continued success ensures your continued life. Now put him against the wall and be off with you. Once I'm replenished, I have another, more difficult task for you. I suggest you get some rest and prepare yourselves. This next task is vital to my plans and I will brook no failure. Do you understand?"

They did, only too well. They bowed their heads and dragged their captive to the rings sunk into the wall. Once he was securely fastened, they scuttled from the room. Reen watched them go in amusement. He could afford the energy to be amused now he had a source of life force before him. Dropping even his scarecrow guise, which he kept up for the benefit of his two minions, who would likely have escaped even his control had they been able to see the reality of his terrible form, he advanced, grinning, on his captive.

The man took one look at the ruined flesh draping the ghastly skull before him and screamed. Even through the gag, the strength of his terror could be heard. Reen halted his advance to listen. He was fairly certain no one would hear the screams, gag or no gag, but he was disposed to be cautious, at least for a while yet. Once his marriage day was over, however ....

Hearing nothing, he moved forward again. His deformed hand reached out to rip away the vagrant's tattered clothing, his fire-damaged flesh stretched impossibly tight over the crippled bones. Had the light been sufficient, the captive would have seen the leprous mottling of what skin was left.

Lifting his other hand, grinning and salivating in anticipation, Reen clasped his dreadful cane in both clawed hands and brought it closer to the man's chest. Fused to his body in the molten pool of fire, it had taken days for Serrin to separate it from the Baron's ruined flesh. Once it had come away, it had retained an essence of him within, burned unnaturally into the transformed wood even as the power had burned into Reen. Now it was a tool, a vehicle for the absorption of the life force that was the only thing keeping Reen's vengeful, fire-ravaged corpse alive.

Savoring the terrible screams of his victim, Reen sucked the life-giving energies into his wasted body, feeling once again the renewal of desiccated flesh, the flow of real blood, the movement of impossibly twisted muscles.

The shattered chest of his captive gaped in a silent howl.

Chapter Thirteen

The inland road southeast of the fishing village was heavy with snow. The icy easterner Sullyan had abated with her powers the day before had returned with a vengeance, and she wasn't inclined to expend any more energy in calming it. So they slogged through the biting blasts with their fur-lined cloaks clasped tightly about them and their hoods drawn up for protection.

Once away from the coast, trees served to shelter the road and cut down the full force of the wind. The snow piled in drifts on one side of the road and the muscular stallions forged a way through the lesser depth on the other side. At least the exercise kept the horses warm.

Their riders, thankful for their Artesan powers, redirected their own body warmth to their extremities, always the first parts to suffer from the cold. Fur-lined leather boots and gloves helped, but the inaction of sitting a horse did nothing for the circulation. They were all relieved to top a rise—exposing them once more to the gale's icy teeth—and see the scattered smoke of a small village.

Sullyan nudged Drum, sending him down the track that led to the village. Icy wind or not, there were still people abroad, and she halted the huge warhorse as they came abreast of a shepherd driving a cart full of fodder to feed his winter-bound beasts.

"Is this the village of Foxdune?" she called through the gale.

The shepherd glanced up at her. His face was partially

obscured by the heavy sheepskin coat he wore, but they could see his eyes, brown and suspicious, taking in their gear, their horses, and their weapons. "Aye. What business is it of yours?"

"King's business," Sullyan said shortly. "Is there an inn?"

The shepherd spat on the ground, causing Cal to draw the first three inches of his sword. Seeing the swift movement—and the disapproving expression on the young captain's face—the shepherd half-raised one arm in defense. His weathered face paled. "Your pardon, I meant no offence. Aye, there's a tavern, if you can call it that. This end of the village, house with a red door. Stabling for beasts round the back."

Cal sheathed his blade with a click, staring hard at the shepherd. Sullyan thanked the man courteously and moved on, leaving him sitting his cart in the middle of the road, watching as they rode away.

"Why are folk always so suspicious?" grumbled Cal, drawing his iron-gray alongside Drum. "You'd think we looked like robbers or cutthroats. They could be polite until given better reason."

Sullyan grinned. "Any stranger abroad in winter, especially in weather such as this, ought to be viewed with suspicion. The common people do not have much. You would be cautious if you were confronted by three well-armed riders. Do not wonder at their mistrust."

Cal subsided, but she could see he wasn't impressed. He knew what it was like to have nothing. He had grown up with a troupe of Roamerlings, and they carried only what they could take upon their wagons. But then, she reflected, Roamerlings were notorious thieves, shunned by so-called honest citizens, so Cal should understand better than most the caution strangers often engendered.

They rode into the village and found the inn. It was the only building with a red door, and copious amounts of wood smoke streamed from its chimney. Riding around the building they found the stables and dismounted. No grooms came forward to take their mounts, so they led them inside and saw to their comforts. At least the place was clean, with plentiful fresh straw, grain, and water.

"Not too much corn," advised Sullyan as they filled the mangers with grain and sweet hay. "We will not stay long. I want to be back at the Manor by nightfall."

Once the horses were settled, they braved the strengthening gale and crossed the yard to the inn. The door opened at Tad's touch and they stepped out of the buffeting wind and into the warm calm of the taproom.

The few patrons inside turned their heads in astonishment at the three armed travelers. The innkeeper, a tall, raw-boned man with a scarred face partially covered by a meager red beard, scowled until Sullyan approached him and removed her snow-covered cloak, revealing her rank insignia. The man's inhospitable expression mellowed.

"Colonel," he said, having examined her gold rank badge. "What can we do for you? We don't often get King's ... er, men in Foxdune."

She grinned at his confusion. She was still the only woman in Elias's fighting forces, although the populace was becoming more used to seeing the many women who served him as runners.

"I am Colonel Sullyan, and we are here on King's business. We would appreciate your help, but for now hot food and drink are our priorities. What can you offer us?"

The inn was famous locally for its mutton stew, and the three of them soon found out how well-deserved that reputation was, although the ale was only passable and the fellan too weak. But the sustenance was very welcome and they thawed their frozen bodies by the roaring log fire before Sullyan beckoned the innkeeper over once more.

He told them his name was Galt, and he had lived in Foxdune all his life. Sullyan accepted the second pot of fellan she'd persuaded Galt to make, this time with extra grounds, and his eyes widened at the gold bits she placed on the table. His demeanor, pleasant enough before, now became positively eager. He ignored his other customers and sat down at their table.

"How may I help you, Colonel?"

"We have come from the fishing village that supplies the holy Order of the Wheel, on the island off Serna Bay," Sullyan said, seeing a wary glimmer of understanding flicker in Galt's brown eyes. "They told me that about four years ago, a young lad from this village was taken to their shores and ferried across to the island, there to become one of the clerics of the order. Would you know of this?"

Galt cast a swift glance over his shoulder to the three other patrons who were sitting at the bar, helping themselves to ale in his absence. None of them appeared to be listening. Sullyan's eyes narrowed at this display of caution.

"That would have been young Serrin," Galt replied, his voice low. "What's he done now? Killed one of the clerics?" Galt's face paled and he stared at Sullyan in horror. "Here, they haven't cast him out, have they? He doesn't want to come back here?"

She exchanged glances with Cal and Tad. Her most pressing question had already been answered. Nevertheless, she determined to wring as much information from Galt as she could. She might learn something of interest.

"I take it the prospect would not please you?" she said.

"Please me?" he barked, only belatedly remembering he was being circumspect. "No one was more pleased than I when they took the young vandal away. There wouldn't be many here who'd be pleased to see him back. Not now his mother's dead, anyway."

"What did he do to turn the village against him?"

Galt scowled. "It wasn't so much what he did, as what he was. He was strange, unnatural. *Things* happened around him, weird things. You know what I mean."

She was only too afraid she knew exactly what he meant, but she wasn't about to let him off that easily. "No, Galt, I do not know. Tell me."

"You know," he repeated, nodding his head at her, "things no one else can do. He bewitched cattle, he made crops fail. It rained just when he said it would and it was sunny when he said so. He was a … you know … a *witch*."

He whispered the last word through clenched teeth and Sullyan lost patience. She had heard it all before. She spoke clearly and with menace as she stared hard at the innkeeper's pale face.

"You mean he was an Artesan, and he was persecuted for it. Well, Artesans are now prized and valued by the King. Have you not heard the proclamations? You should have; they have been cried throughout the land. It is now a capital offence to cry slander on an Artesan, and the penalties for their expulsion or repression are severe. In the King's name, I could impose the direst of reprisals on you and your village for what you did to that poor boy."

Sullyan's anger and the fire behind her eyes cowed the prejudiced innkeeper thoroughly. He drew back before her threats and began, rather desperately, to beg her forgiveness. The customers at the bar slunk swiftly out the door before she could turn on them, too. Sullyan cut off Galt's pathetic apologies with a wave of her hand.

"Enough. You have already told me what I came here to learn. Serrin is not here and has never been back since he was forced to leave. That is well. Were I that poor boy, I would not wish to return here no matter how beggarly I found myself.

"We will leave this miserable place. You have been paid

amply for your hospitality, such as it was. Never let it be said that Artesans of the King's forces do not pay their dues, even to those with such bigoted minds as yours. We bid you good day."

She swept from the inn, leaving the outer door open and swinging in the gale as Cal and Tad hastened to follow her. Neither of them gave the astounded innkeeper another glance.

Tad and Cal caught up with her in the stable, where she was saddling Drum. The low but vicious mutter of invective coming from the black's stall warned them against speaking to her and they readied their own mounts in silence. She led Drum outside and vaulted into the saddle, urging him out of the village at a gallop as if it had the plague. Which in a very real sense, it did.

By the time they rode up to the horse lines at the Manor, she was calm again. Overseeing Tad's substrate construct that facilitated their return journey had dissipated the disgusted fury left by the innkeeper's unthinking prejudice. The King's favor and the King's College might finally be turning the tide of popular opinion, but it would take years, if not generations, to wipe out such pockets of superstition as Foxdune.

She swung down from Drum and gave the huge beast over to the stablemaster. Cal and Tad were dismissed to their own duties and she made a brief and welcome contact with both Robin and Morgan as she made her way to Blaine's office to discuss these latest developments.

Halfway through Sullyan's meeting with Blaine, Robin entered the General's office. Sullyan glanced up at her life mate and he smiled at her as he took the chair next to hers.

"Morgan's with Elisse and Bull," he said, accepting the fellan Blaine held out to him. "Rienne and Cal are, uh, greeting each other. Bull was quite happy to mind the children."

Sullyan smiled at Robin's modest phrasing. Rienne would be pregnant again before she knew it at this rate. But the size of their family was their affair and Sullyan was at peace with her own barren condition. Having Morgan was enough for her. She felt no envy of her friend.

"What did you discover on the island?" Robin asked. Sullyan recounted it once more for his benefit, also relating her experience at Foxdune, which Blaine hadn't yet heard.

The General was silent once she had finished, head bowed, fingers steepled under his chin, eyes unfocused. Robin watched him for a moment and sighed, turning to his life mate.

"Do you really think the Baron could have survived that fall? Even if we discount the slashed wrist theory, if the fall didn't kill him, the cold would have. And he was in no condition to swim for the mainland in any case. It would be too far for the best of swimmers, let alone someone in the Baron's condition. It's surely no great surprise the fishermen found no trace of his body."

Sullyan kept her eyes on the General's face as she replied to Robin. "I believe he could have survived the fall. That 'mighty leap' he was seen to make could conceivably have carried him out far enough to avoid the rocks, and I can see no reason for making such a strenuous effort if he did not expect to survive."

"But why bother, if the sea was too cold? What would be the point?"

She regarded him. "What indeed? Remember, his correspondence was entirely unmonitored."

Mathias Blaine raised his head and caught her gaze. He spoke slowly. "He could have drowned and been swept out to sea. His despair could have driven him to that, without his being so distraught he took no thought for the rocks. Which would you rather as a way out of life: dashing your body against sharp rocks with no guarantee you'd be killed outright, or a swift and numbing passage into oblivion? I know which I'd choose."

Sullyan knew Blaine suspected she was right; he just didn't

want to admit it and she couldn't blame him. She held her peace and returned his gaze.

"So what now?" asked Robin. "Do we assume he's dead, or do we suspect he's still alive? If he is still alive, he can't be in any condition to work more mischief. So what do we tell Elias?"

"And Aeyron."

Sullyan's soft voice filled the room. Her adopted brother had suffered the worst physical torture of any of them at the Baron's hands, and the scars ran deep. Much had been ripped from him with the knife stroke that had hacked away part of his right hand.

General Blaine sighed and looked down, ignoring both questions. "Will you go to Elias, Brynne?"

She nodded wordlessly.

"Just put the facts before him and let him draw his own conclusions. We can't keep any of this from him, but I don't think we should color his judgment with our personal suspicions."

Sullyan agreed, but she knew the first thing Elias would ask once she had given him all the facts would be what she thought about them. She would have to play the interview by ear.

Blaine carried on. "But I really don't think it would be wise to distress Prince Aeyron with any of this unless we have good reason. You might want to talk it over with Timar to see what he thinks. It's not for us to go bandying unfounded suspicions about with no real proof."

Sullyan wasn't happy with this. The almost inevitable but unquantifiable threat the Baron posed to them, if he was alive, was a serious matter. If he was at large and capable of planning any kind of revenge, however small, then she and Aeyron and Elias would be his most obvious and immediate targets. She would speak with Timar, certainly, but she fully expected her adopted father to agree with her. Distressing or not, Aeyron had a right to know.

"I had better leave for the castle, Mathias," she said. "Will you contact Taran? Tell him I am bringing the Baron's possessions to be returned to Jinella."

She left the General's office with Robin beside her. They now occupied one of the grander suites on the top floor of the Manor, due to Sullyan's royal status. She washed and changed in the spacious bathing room, casting wistful glances at the empty bathtub. When she came back into the large living area, Robin eyed her seriously.

"You really believe he survived that fall, don't you? You think he planned the whole thing, faked his suicide to throw us off the scent, and had some rescue set up. But what I don't understand is how he managed it from all those miles out in the middle of the ocean. And why on earth would he murder the one person who'd befriended him? He must have known all that blood would be found. Did he think no one would notice there was too much blood to make slit wrists a credible story? He must have guessed someone from Elias's court would investigate."

Sullyan shook her head. "I do not have all the answers, Robin. What I do know is this: That blood was not the Baron's. There is a missing untrained Artesan boy who was undoubtedly involved with Reen. Important parts of the suicide story do not make sense—although the idea he'd tried and failed to slit his wrists came only from Frar Durren, who saw blood on the Baron's hands. No, there is much more to this affair than we yet know. These Roamerling deaths in Bordenn also bother me, and until we have satisfactory answers to the parts of the puzzle that are missing, or until the Baron's body is washed ashore, I will not rest easy.

"Do not forget what Reen tried to do. Even if the destruction of the Veils is now beyond his capabilities, he could still wreak havoc in Elias's kingdom. Especially if he has somehow persuaded Sofira to shelter him. I would prefer to err on the side of caution and keep us all on full alert for the time being.

"Now, I must go to the capital. Hug Morgan for me. I doubt the King will release me tonight."

Chapter Fourteen

It was warm and comfortable in Elias's private chamber. The lamps gave a mellow glow to the air and the fire leaped and wavered in the grate. A winter wind whined around the castle walls, but it didn't have the bite of the easterner farther north. Sullyan settled into a padded chair at her King's invitation and accepted the mug of steaming fellan he poured for her with his own hand.

She watched him as he sat beside her, noting the worry lines around his eyes, and the slight pallor of his skin. She felt a sudden rush of empathy for him and irritably took hold of her emotions. She must always be on her guard with this powerful and attractive man. She took a steadying sip of scalding fellan.

"Are you well, Elias?"

He raised his head and gazed at her, giving a wry smile. "I must be slipping."

She didn't understand and cocked her head at him. His lips quirked.

"That's the second time in two days I've been too obvious with my thoughts."

She shared his smile. "What was the first?"

He colored faintly. "Ah … perhaps I'll tell you one day. I want to hear what you found on the clerics' island."

She accepted the change of subject and tucked her legs beneath her. Her gaze turned inward, focusing on the conversations she'd had with the clerics and the conclusions she'd drawn. "I will tell you the facts as I heard them."

He nodded, and she began her tale.

"First, I have to say that the clerics I spoke to were not wholly surprised the Baron chose to cast himself into the sea. One of them expressed regret they were unable to prevent the incident, but they all agreed Reen had recently become frail, reclusive, and strangely depressed. Before that, once his initial fury over his humiliation and exile passed, he began joining their services and gradually became easier with the life he was forced to lead. But he was never content, never settled. After some while, he struck up a friendship with a young lad who had been gifted to the clerics by his parents, and who was as disaffected as the Baron himself. It seems they were kindred spirits; both convinced life owed them a debt, both determined to wallow in their misfortune. Although in Serrin's case, his resentment was amply justified."

Elias scowled and leaned forward. "By 'gifted,' do you mean the boy's parents forced him to join the order?"

"That is exactly what they did, and I will tell you why in good time. At any rate, Serrin and the Baron became close. How close I cannot say, but certainly they spent many hours together. For some months, Reen seemed less … unhappy. He spoke with Patrio Ruvar on occasion, but mainly he confided in young Serrin."

Elias's face still bore a scowl. "How old was this boy?"

"Thirteen when he arrived on the island. He would have been seventeen when the Baron left it."

Elias noted her turn of phrase and raised his brows, yet chose not to comment on it. "And do you think they were … do you think their relationship was … improper?" He waved a hand vaguely.

She smiled, amused at his hesitancy. "Are you asking if I think they were lovers?"

The High King was thirty-three years of age and had lived through the assassination of his father and a civil war to regain his crown. She would have thought him worldly enough not to feel so awkward at the mention of such matters. Her brows rose even higher when she saw his face flush again. He nodded and she shook her head.

"I could not say. Patrio Ruvar made no reference to it. But you knew the Baron better than I. Did you ever hear such tales?"

"I can't say I did. I suppose it doesn't really matter. He was friendly with the boy. Let's leave it at that."

She told the King everything she had seen, heard, and learned of the night the Baron disappeared from the island, concentrating only on fact. There was a long pause while he assimilated the information, and he watched her all the while. Then he spoke, slowly.

"You don't believe he's dead."

"Now it is I who am slipping." She gave a small smile and was rewarded by a more natural look from Elias, more like his old self.

"No, you're as open as ever, Brynne. But I can read the clues as well as you. 'A vast pool of blood,' you said. More than enough to be fatal, by the sound of it. And no one who had slit their wrists and left such a quantity of blood behind could've walked up a steep trail and thrown themselves into the sea."

"Indeed."

He regarded her. "I gather there's more? You haven't completed the tale of the boy, Serrin. And whose was the blood, if not the Baron's? I take it this Frar Durren wasn't mistaken; it was actually Reen he saw?"

"Oh yes, there is no doubt the Baron threw himself into the sea. As for the blood and the tale of the boy … I very much fear the two are connected."

"You think it was Serrin's blood? What grounds do you have for that suspicion?"

Sullyan reached for the fellan pot and refreshed her mug, offering it to Elias. She poured for him while she ordered her thoughts.

"No one saw the boy leave the island," she said, leaning back into her chair. "Ruvar told me he would not have tried to dissuade the lad had he been determined to go, so there was no reason for Serrin not to have told Ruvar in person. However, I checked with the fishermen who supply the island—" She stopped and gave Elias a forthright look. "Were you aware the holy order is financed and supported by His Immanence Lord Neremiah and the Matria Church here in Port Loxton?"

Elias nodded, shamefaced. His failure to inform her of this earned him a hard stare before she continued, telling him what she had learned from Galt in Foxdune. When she was done, she captured his gaze.

"Elias, that boy was an untrained Artesan."

"What?" Elias leaned forward. "Did the Baron know this?"

She shrugged. "I have no way of knowing, but I doubt it. At least, not at first. Certainly Ruvar did not know or he would have mentioned it. And I cannot conceive of the Baron conducting a friendship with the boy if he did know. But later on? Perhaps. All I do know is we have a missing boy, a desperate man who reviles all Artesans, and a pool of blood too large to have come from the Baron. And then we have the report of dead Roamerlings in Bordenn."

Elias stared at her in horror. "You're surely not suggesting—? But that would mean he had help, that he planned this fake suicide, that someone is sheltering him, even supporting him! Who in the kingdom would do that, knowing what he did?"

She held her peace, gazing at her sovereign. She understood

how this revelation and dreadful suspicion would affect him. He had never fully recovered from the deep betrayal he'd suffered. But her silence and forthright gaze wouldn't let him go and he had nowhere to hide. He could, however, refuse her.

"No, I don't believe it. I can't believe it."

"Since she left the capital, has the Queen been in contact with Princess Seline?"

Sullyan's question, at such a tangent to their previous conversation, distracted Elias. He frowned in displeasure, as any mention of Sofira made him do.

"Yes, of course, she writes to the girl regularly. But the letters come to me first and I open and read them all. There has never been any hint of subversion or plotting in them."

Sullyan nodded. "As I would expect. Sofira must know you would read her letters. I merely ask whether there has been any change in the frequency of these messages over the past few months."

"No." Elias snapped the word.

Sullyan wasn't intimidated by her monarch's ire and ignored his hot stare. "When the Queen was banished a year ago, what did she say to you concerning her children?"

At first she thought he wouldn't respond. She could see the muscles along his jaw quiver as he fought down the tide of fury her question had stirred. He had to force himself to articulate and Sullyan watched his struggle with sympathy. She wished, not for the first time, she could reach out to him and lend him some strength. But he was no Artesan, and the only other way open to her she couldn't take. The comfort of her arms, which she would have offered to any of her other friends, had to be withheld. It was too perilous.

Elias's voice was harsh when he was finally able to reply. "She said any heartache or misery caused to her children by her banishment was on my head, and the hate they'd feel for me was of my own forging."

She heard the self-blame in his voice and saw the grief in his eyes. She reached out a hand to him. "Oh, Elias."

He shook his head and leaned away from her. "Don't, Brynne. I couldn't stand it."

Helpless, she watched his unhappy struggle. There was no cure for the malady afflicting him. She tried to find another way to help him.

"But your children do not hate you. Eadan worships the ground you walk on. You should see him at the Manor, carrying out your instructions and striving to make you proud. He lives for the day you come to visit so he can show you what he has achieved. He learns and he works only for you."

Elias sighed. "I know Eadan doesn't hate me. You've seen to that very thoroughly. But Seline, I'm afraid, is a different matter. She is very close to her mother and older than Eadan. She's been a very unhappy girl since her mother left."

"I did not have to convince Eadan to love you," said Sullyan. "I merely tried to make up to him some of the care he had lost. And Seline will come to see, as she grows older, that you could not have acted any other way. And if she is never as close to you as to her mother, well, at least she does not hate you. Have you suggested to her that she might visit with her mother—under strict supervision, of course? It might soothe her to think you would permit that."

Elias's face contorted with anger. "I'd sooner die than let my daughter visit Sofira! What the hell are you thinking of? Let her go into the clutches of that scheming harridan? Never!"

Sullyan sat calmly. She understood Elias's reluctance, but she had another reason for making the suggestion. "Very well, you will not let her go. But Sofira does not have to know that."

Her quiet words cut through Elias's fury and he stilled. "What are you saying, Brynne? Speak plainly."

She took a breath. "Let us assume for the moment the Baron is still alive and capable of plotting revenge. Who would he turn to for support? Who of those who might conceivably help him has the power and the means to be of use to him? We know he corresponded with someone during his sojourn on the island, and that he received letters back. To have escaped death by drowning in the icy sea, a boat must have been on hand, and men to sail it. I am convinced the scream he gave was a signal to the sailors. And they did not come from the fishing village, that much we know. But Lerric's lands have a coastline and there must be those among his servants who can handle a boat. He could have arranged transport and lodgings along the way for the laborious overland journey south to Bordenn, if they did not make the entire trip by sea.

"We cannot go to Lerric and force him to answer our suspicions. But if I know the Baron, mere rescue will not satisfy him. He will need Lerric's resources in order to wreak any kind of revenge."

Elias, furious and appalled, turned puce. "Lerric wouldn't dare!"

She shrugged. "He may not have had a choice."

This drew a startled glance from the King. "What are you saying now? That Reen has a hold over Lerric? What could that traitor possibly do to intimidate the king of Bordenn? He'd only have to denounce Reen to the garrison and they'd imprison him immediately."

Sullyan spoke softly, holding Elias's gaze. "He may be controlling something Lerric values. Something the king cannot jeopardize."

Elias opened his mouth to refute her suggestion, but then shut it again with a snap. His face paled and his eyes closed. "Oh, she wouldn't, would she? She can't still harbor feelings for the man after he impeached her? They betrayed each other just as thoroughly as they betrayed me. They'd kill each other on sight … wouldn't they?"

Sullyan remained silent. She had no proof of her suspicions, she just couldn't think of any other possibilities.

Elias shook his head. "No, this is going too far. I can credit Sofira with many stupid things, but I can't believe she'd forgive that treacherous snake, let alone take up with him again."

Sullyan sighed, placing her empty mug on the table. "The alternative is that the Baron discovered his young friend was a fledgling Artesan and killed him in a fit of rage. What he did with the body, I cannot say. He then suffered unbearable pangs of remorse and threw himself off a cliff into the sea, drowning in the icy water which conveniently disposed of his body. We will simply ignore the strange deaths of two Roamerlings within Lerric's borders, dismissing them as unexplained tragedies."

Elias regarded her unhappily. He could hear the wild improbabilities in this theory as well as she.

"I do, however, have a suggestion as to how we might test the idea of Lerric's involvement, or Sofira's."

Wearily, Elias gestured her on.

"You say you do not wish Seline to spend any time with her mother at Lerric's court. But Sofira does not have to know that. A courtesy visit from you to Lerric's palace with the purported intention of discussing Seline's future might just turn up opportunities for investigation. At the very least it should give them pause for thought, if they are indeed plotting against you."

Elias regarded her doubtfully, clearly not liking this proposal. "Do you really think that's necessary? It's hardly practical at this time of year. I can't say I'm filled with joy at the prospect of spending time in Lerric's company, never mind Sofira's. He's always whining about how poor his province is and how unfair my levies are. And how *she* would receive me, I've no idea, but I guarantee it wouldn't be with open arms."

Sullyan shrugged. "The decision is yours, my Lord. It was your disquiet that began this investigation, if you remember—your unease over the absence of a body. I have done as you bid me and given you my opinion based on the facts as we know them. I can think of no other way to test our suspicions, but if you are now happy to let matters rest, then that is what we will do. *Are* you happy to do that?"

Elias glared in frustrated irritation. "Damn you, Brynne Sullyan! You know I'm not."

She held his gaze, waiting him out; knowing his innate caution and distrust would lead him to accept her plan. He knew it too, but held out as long as he could. Dealing with Sofira in Port Loxton was distasteful enough, but walking into her own demesne and spending time under her roof was another thing entirely. Much as he recognized the reasoning behind Sullyan's plan, the execution of it would not be a comfortable undertaking.

She offered no other suggestions, and eventually he sighed.

"Very well. I'll visit Lerric, though if he bores me to death with his protestations of poverty I'll hold you personally responsible. When do you propose we set out?"

"As soon as possible. I will speak with the General first, but my advice would be to set out before you inform Lerric of your intentions. We will make for the nearest garrison to Daret and send a runner from there. We do not want to give them more time than is necessary to cover up what they may not wish us to see. It would be preferable to turn up completely unannounced, but I suppose we cannot do that."

Elias huffed. "Indeed not. I can hardly show up on Lerric's

doorstep, in the middle of winter and with a large retinue, and claim I forgot to tell him I was coming. That would be the grossest insult. I can't take the risk of alienating him, in the event he proves innocent of what you suspect."

She smiled. "A pity. Very well, I will go inform the General and attend you in the morning to finalize the details. Now, if I may be released, I must seek out Taran. I brought the Baron's possessions with me so he can return them to Jinella."

❖ ❖ ❖ ❖ ❖

The Lady Jinella had retired to bed. It was early for her, but there was no reason for her to stay up. She hadn't entertained or seen guests since Taran's cruel revelations three days before. She missed his company, more than she cared to admit, although when he was on duty as Court Artesan she saw far less of him than when Sullyan was on duty there. This struck her as strange when she thought about it.

She lay alone in her great bed, the bed that had seen so many loving nights, so many warm embraces and passionate cries. Remembering them with a pang of sorrow, she suddenly wondered how she could ever have doubted whether what she and Taran shared was real.

He had hurt her deeply with what he had said. Yes, it was utterly like him to want to leave her free to cast him off for someone "more suitable," but the fact he knew her so little as to believe she might actually do such a thing had made her bitterly angry. His assertion that her considering herself barren had never even entered his head was also entirely believable and equally hurtful. Yet she knew his abject contrition had been genuine and heartfelt, and she understood how crushed he was at the pain and suffering he had caused her. He had stayed away as promised, waiting for her to decide on the future of their relationship. That alone had told her how deeply his feelings ran.

She had done nothing but think it over since, worrying at it like an aching tooth. And the undeniable truth of it was, she knew with total certainty Taran couldn't possibly have feigned the love he had shown her.

Tears slid down her cheeks. She'd been foolish in her anger, though he had hurt her with his astonishing admission. If only he had spoken earlier, discussed his reservations, his concerns over his status. She could have reassured him in an instant that his peasant origins meant less than nothing to her. Well, nothing now that she knew him so well. Hadn't she been attracted to him *before* the King bestowed that stipend and the freedom of the city on him? Did he think her so shallow that position and wealth meant more to her than commitment and love?

The realization of the depth of his commitment and love for her hit her like a blow when she recognized that the presence of Sullyan at the castle hadn't drawn Taran from her side. Her face flushed with shame. On the contrary, Sullyan's presence had actually *released* Taran to spend more time with Jinny, and he had taken that opportunity. She could see now that if Taran had been as deeply smitten with the Artesan woman as she'd thought, he would have spent every waking moment with *her*, and not Jinella.

She sniffed sadly then reconsidered. Yes, she had been foolish, but surely it wasn't too late to rectify her mistake? She'd driven Taran from her side, but she could put that right. And if it had to be that the offer of marriage should come from her rather than him, well, so be it. She wasn't so proud she would risk her future happiness on the trappings of protocol.

Smiling, feeling happier than she had in days, she experienced that warm, exciting shiver deep within her that the thought of having him here in her bed once again always brought her. Sighing, Jinny closed her eyes to sleep.

Chapter Fifteen

Not everyone in the Baroness's household had followed their mistress to bed. One servant had been waiting to see the lamp in her room extinguished, and he lingered awhile yet in the hope she would fall quickly asleep. Not that there was much danger of her hearing him.

Seth crept past Jinny's door, treading lightly on the expensive deep pile carpet. He had once questioned the wisdom of parting with so much gold just to carpet the hallways, considering it a vain and wasteful expense. Not that the Baron had taken any notice of his opinions. But now, in the dead of night and wishing to be undetected, the young man blessed the Baron's extravagance and appreciated the irony.

Seth had been the Baron's valet, his personal manservant. He had been part of the household since Reen was granted the estate by Elias at the Queen's request. Seth had been in service since the age of ten, although not initially as a valet. The Baron had elevated him to that particular post, having liked the young man's looks and recognizing his potential in more ways than one. He'd brought Seth into his personal service, replacing the valet who had accompanied him from Bordenn. Seth had fulfilled the Baron's expectations and performed duties for his master far beyond those normally expected of a valet. His silence over those extra duties had earned him certain bonuses and a measure of his master's trust.

After the Baron was exiled, Seth decided he would repay that trust if ever he could. Within the sphere of his own standards, Reen had been good to his servant. As he matured, Seth had become more the reliable retainer and less the passive catamite, although the physical relationship continued. It amused Seth now to think the Baroness knew nothing of his extraneous duties or of his loyalty to his exiled master. If she had, she wouldn't have kept him on. But Jinella had done little to change the mansion's routine and was happy to retain those of the Baron's staff who wanted to stay. Most of them had. Her offer of higher wages for good service did much to overcome any reservations the servants might have entertained. Seth remained with them, although his tasks now concerned organizing Jinella's social diary and planning her dinner parties with the kitchen staff.

This was the one area where Seth found cause for complaint.

He was courteous to Jinella, as his position demanded, although he went cold whenever he thought of the way she had betrayed her uncle. Seth believed the ties of blood-kinship should override all other concerns. He would never forgive Jinny for turning on Reen, who, after all, had been her champion and benefactor at Elias's court. Seth realized he would have to hide his feelings when he decided to stay on, as his main reason for doing so was to be able to take advantage of any opportunity to benefit his true lord.

He did not, however, have to be courteous to any of the Baron's other enemies, one of whom lived under Jinella's roof, having been given a position of trust despite being nothing but a common whore from the city's bordellos. Her inclusion into the household was a deliberate affront as far as Seth could see, and he intended to do whatever he could to change that. However, that was not his mission tonight. Tonight he was keeping an appointment made completely out of the blue, and one which he hoped might provide him with the opportunity he'd been praying for.

Seth crept down the stairs to the ground floor and approached the mansion's rear door. Taking up the lantern he had left in the tiny cupboard on the wall, he lit it from the banked fire in the seldom-used room and left the house.

It was freezing outside and there was sleet on the wind. Seth pulled his thick cloak tighter around his thin frame and cursed the man he was due to meet. Why had he specified nighttime? He had spoken quite openly to Seth in broad daylight in the marketplace. Why all the subterfuge now? Why risk detection and awkward questions when they could have met in one of Loxton's lesser-known taverns and had their conversation in comfort and warmth? Seth didn't know the answers, but intended to find them out.

Raising his lantern against the cold, wet dark, he trudged across the back yard, avoiding the stables where the groom sometimes slept. Usually the lad went home at night, but when he felt like it, or the weather was bad, he made use of the small groom's loft above the stables. Matty hadn't known the Baron like Seth did and the older man was unsure of his loyalties. He was polite to the lad, but otherwise ignored him.

Once he was clear of the mansion's immediate confines, Seth hurried his steps. His destination, the village chapel, was some way off and he didn't want to be out in this sleet any longer than necessary.

✤ ✤ ✤ ✤ ✤

Sullyan found Taran where Elias had told her he would be—playing cards with Denny and Ardoch in the garrison. It was late and she was ready for her bed, but she didn't want to wait until the morning. She strode into the garrison to the salutes and greetings of the men, and found the card school tucked away in a corner of the senior officers' hall.

The eight men around the card table were so involved in the

game that none of them noticed her arrival. She stood in the doorway and watched for her own amusement, taking note of their expressions and eye movements. Denny clearly thought he had a winning hand, as did Ardoch. Taran was unsure of his and would change some or all of his cards. Two of the other men were happy with their hands, and the final three would probably cast theirs.

Taran, who was dealing, gave out the cards and took two for himself. Two men dropped out at that point and Denny upped the stakes. Ardoch matched him, as did Taran. Two of the others then also cast their cards and the third pushed gold across the table. Neither Denny nor Ardoch had changed their hands, and Sullyan could tell Taran was happier with what he now held. There were only four men left in the game.

At the next round, Denny added a heap of gold bits to the pile. Taran stared at him. "Are you sure?"

The old swordmaster waved a hand. "Ach, laddie, let him throw away his pay if he has a mind." Ardoch then matched the gold Denny had staked.

Taran pursed his lips and pushed some of his own coin across. This was too rich for the fourth man, who cast his cards.

Denny had a glint in his eye as he added more to the pot. "Well?" he challenged.

Sullyan observed him keenly, watching the movements of his free hand beneath the table. She also noticed the faint sheen of sweat on the man's brow and smiled. He was bluffing.

"I'll match you," stated the Torlander, pushing more gold across. Taran hesitated, but it was clear to Sullyan he thought he had a winning hand. Slowly, holding Denny's gaze, he matched the other men's stakes.

Denny was perspiring, but managed to disguise it. He kept a smug smile fixed on his face and regarded his dwindling pile of gold. With a deliberate gesture, he swept the entire amount into the pile. The watchers in the room gasped. The pot now contained more than a year's salary for an ordinary swordsman.

Interested to see what Taran would do, and knowing what a good bluffer Denny was, Sullyan moved closer. She glimpsed Taran and Ardoch's cards and knew who of the two would win, but she had no idea what they would do.

Taran was learning fast, but wasn't yet a confident card player, especially not against a chancer like Denny. The likeable young major lived for the bet and had been gambling for as long as he had known his numbers. The amount of gold needed to turn Denny's cards was now too much for Taran. He cast his hand.

Ardoch, on the other hand, was used to Denny's ways and wasn't intimidated. He merely smiled his weathered smile and pushed his gold across the table. "Turn your hand, Denny me lad," he crowed, showing the major his cards.

With a wry smile, Denny did so. There was raucous laughter and some outrage when Denny's cards were seen. His hand wouldn't have won so much as a child's game of "Match the Lady" and there were many ribald comments concerning his eyesight and failing wits.

"Well," he retorted, laughing with them, "but for this old dog's toothless bite, I might have won. Don't you ever give up, you old terrier?"

Ardoch made a pithy remark that set the others off again. Taran gathered his cards and watched the Torlander scoop up his gold, startling when he heard Sullyan's voice behind him.

"Look at Ghyllan's hand, Taran."

He turned to stare at her over his shoulder. She indicated Ardoch's discarded cards with a nod. Turning them face up, Taran hissed. His hand would have beaten the swordmaster's had he summoned the courage to trust it.

"Dammit!" He grinned wryly and shrugged. "Ah well, it's

only gold."

"Indeed," she replied, remembering Taran was now a wealthy man. Not only did he have his stipend from the King, but as Court Artesan he also drew a salary.

The tall Adept rose, laying his cards on the table. "Did you want me?"

Sullyan nodded, and he followed her out of the noisy hall. She turned to face him.

"I have lately returned from the Baron's former prison."

He raised his brows, and she told him the gist of her findings and their suspicions. His pleasant face turned pale and he sucked in a breath. "What on earth do I tell Jinny?"

Sullyan saw his discomfiture and frowned, but she answered his question. "Nothing yet. These are suspicions only, not facts. But I have here the few possessions her uncle left behind. The Patrio thought it best they be returned to her. Can I leave them with you?"

She handed him the small package which he accepted a little hesitantly. Sullyan saw his reluctance. "What is it, Taran? Is something wrong?"

He could never hide his feelings from her, but the reason for them escaped her. He looked at the ground, shamefaced. "Jinny and I haven't seen each other for three days now. Not since I told her why she hasn't conceived."

Sullyan pursed her lips. "Ah. She took it badly, then? Well, what did you expect? She trusted you, and if you have not, in fact, betrayed that trust, you have come perilously close. It will take her some time to come to terms with her feelings. Did you explain why?"

Taran nodded miserably. "That only made it worse. Now she thinks I care more for my honor than for her."

"And do you?"

The brutal question stung him. "Of course not! I love Jinny…" He faltered, frowning when he saw her smile.

She laid a hand on his arm. "But you have never admitted that to yourself before, have you, my friend? You have never really believed it. And if you have no trust or faith in your own feelings, why should Jinella?"

Seeing his misery, she decided to be blunt. "Go to her, Taran. Talk to her. Sort out your feelings, decide what you really want, and then *tell* her. Put your heart into it—that huge and loving heart from which your depth of passion and strength of spirit arise. Let yourself go, allow yourself to love. You will be amazed how easy it is. And that is not advice, my friend, that is an *order*."

"Yes, Colonel." He grinned weakly, and she shook her head.

"What are we to do with you, Taran Elijah? Do not put it off. Do it as soon as you may. The King is going on an official visit and you will have some free time soon. I advise you to make the most of it. Now I am for my bed, once I have spoken to the General. I wish you good night."

The conversation with General Blaine didn't go at all as Sullyan planned. He approved the proposed visit to Lerric, but over one aspect of the journey he adamantly refused to be moved.

"No, Brynne, I will *not* permit you to accompany Elias. You've suffered enough at that traitor's hands. If he is there, I won't give him the opportunity to work more mischief. *I* shall go with the King and we'll take a sizeable guard. You will remain here."

"But, Mathias—"

"No, Colonel. I've made up my mind. Reen hates you with a vengeance and I won't risk you falling into his hands again."

"The Baron hates all Artesans, General, not just me. You'll be in as much danger as I would. If you will not permit me to go, at least take Robin with you. Two Master Artesans ought to be more than a match for anything Reen might have planned. You will need someone to stand for you."

Blaine couldn't refute this argument. Vassa was still on duty at the castle and would remain there in Elias's absence, as there was still Seline's safety to consider. Blaine could choose his company from among those left at the Manor, with Robin to lead them, and Sullyan would command the rest while Blaine was away. He accepted the advisability of taking another strong Artesan with him, and Sullyan was appeased by his accession to her request. If she couldn't go, Robin was her second choice. She retired to bed if not wholly satisfied, then at least easier in her mind.

✤ ✤ ✤ ✤ ✤

The chapel lay wrapped in darkness when Seth pushed open the heavy wooden door. He held his lantern high and peered into the gloomy interior. There came a faint rustle of sound and an inky shadow detached from the freezing blackness. It moved slowly toward him.

He stayed where he was and let the shadow approach. It had an awkward, gawky motion, as if not quite under its own control, and he recalled thinking the same thing when it had accosted him in the marketplace the day before.

The figure shambled to a stop before him and he smelled again the foul miasma rising from the man. It wasn't just the stink of an unwashed body, although that was there in abundance. No, thought Seth with a tiny shiver, it was more like the charnel stink of meat gone bad. He wrinkled his nose.

"You find me repulsive, yet you still came." The man's hissing whisper floated out of the shadows.

Seth shrugged. "You don't have the most savory aroma, but I've smelled worse." He heard the man's gargled laugh. "I only came because you said you had a message from my lord, the

Baron. Can we get on with this? It's bloody freezing. Why you couldn't have chosen a warmer or lighter place, I don't know."

"Afraid of the dark, are you, boy? Well, since you're so curious, I'll show you why this time and place was chosen. Sit down and shutter that lantern."

The scrawny fellow waved at the nearest pew and Seth frowned. This meeting had taken on a surreal and faintly disturbing quality and he was no longer sure he'd done the right thing in coming. But the figure had made no move on him, and Seth knew there was no one else around; he had checked carefully before entering the chapel. He sat.

"Keep silent and attend," the man said, his voice hoarse and unnatural. Seth heard the rustle of cloth as the man opened his cloak. The charnel smell grew suddenly worse. It was gloomy in the chapel with the lantern turned down so low it illuminated nothing but the flagstone on which it sat. There were no other lamps inside, nor outside in the street, so where, thought Seth with sudden alarm, was that sullen, ruby-red glow coming from?

He leapt to his feet in terror when he realized he was looking at the man's eyes. They weren't reflecting any outside light, but glowing with a demonic inner fire. He shuddered violently and tried to turn, intending to run. The hand that clamped his shoulder felt like a claw of iron. It gripped his bones like a vice and he couldn't move. Neither could he cry out. His throat had tightened in horror.

"Seth! Do not fear me. Do you not know your own master?"

Seth froze, his terror abating. "M-my Lord?" he squeaked, looking for the Baron. He had clearly heard Reen's voice.

No one else was there but Seth and the filthy vagrant fellow, who chuckled in the Baron's unmistakable voice. Seth stared in wonder, too amazed to be frightened.

"My Lord Baron! How is this possible?"

"No time for explanations now, Seth. Just accept, and do as I bid you. The man before you is another of my servants and I can speak to you through him. He tells me you are loyal to me and that you're willing to work my will against those who caused my downfall. Is this true?"

The strangely ghostlike voice was undeniably the Baron's, no matter how changed it sounded in the scrawny fellow's mouth. The dreadful smell assailed Seth's nostrils, and the ruby glint of the eyes was disconcerting, but Seth was a practical man not given to flights of fancy. If his lord had found a means of communicating through this fellow, Seth could accept that.

"Command me, my Lord! I will do all I can to aid you."

"Good, very good. First I need some information, and then you will receive your instructions. Tell me, Seth, how is my dear niece, Jinella?"

✤ ✤ ✤ ✤ ✤

Reen broke contact with his servant and slumped to the bed, exhausted. He was pleased. He had been confident Seth would be willing to aid him, but hadn't expected to find his erstwhile manservant still in Jinny's employ. He sneered in the dark. *Stupid, sentimental girl!* Her sense of responsibility to those of lower status would be her undoing—he'd make sure of that.

The start of his scheme should go according to plan with no one the wiser. With any luck, he might even get three at once, although Seth's news about Jinny's problems with Taran had come as a bit of a blow. Still, even if Taran wasn't there, Reen now had two agents in Port Loxton. It was only a matter of time and opportunity.

The other piece of news Seth had passed on was of more serious import. It was a large part of Reen's plan that he should have control over Sofira's children, Eadan in particular. While it was true Seline could inherit the throne if Eadan should die, her rule would last only until she wed a suitable Prince. Having Albia in the hands of a stranger would not suit Reen's scheme at all. If he couldn't get his hands on Eadan, he would have to have the boy killed. Seline could be betrothed to some youngster who could be groomed in Reen's ideals before he grew too independent. This moving of Eadan to the Manor was an inconvenience, but it wasn't insurmountable. He decided against telling Sofira where her son was. Her anger might distract her from the more important issues at hand.

A scratch at the door alerted Reen to the return of his other two minions. He smiled as he rose to admit them, trying to rein in his baser emotions. Now, finally, he could conduct this most essential of experiments, test his control and his strength and his will. He relaxed his hold over his desires, letting the dark anticipation flood through his body. Restraint was no longer needed. Indeed, it was counterproductive. Desire—lust—was necessary if he was to overcome his normal disinterest at the thought of bedding a woman. The success of his wedding night hinged upon the control of his own body's reactions, and the success of all his plans rested on the outcome of his wedding night. Stoking the fires within with thoughts of what was to come, he opened the door.

The two of them stood there, shaking. He could see the ruby light of his eyes reflected in their dilated pupils and their tremble only increased as he smiled cruelly at them. And at what they held.

"Bring her in," he commanded, stepping aside.

They bundled their struggling, whimpering captive into the room, avoiding the Baron's gaze as well as his touch. The young woman they held was dark-skinned, dressed in a bodice and skirts as Roamerling girls usually were, and her long, dark hair fell over her face as she struggled against her captors. They manhandled her over to the bed and secured her hands and feet to the bedposts. Her eyes were black and wide, wild with fear; sweat stood out on her skin. She knew what would happen to her.

Reen regarded her as his servants hastened silently from the room. He was surprised they had managed to find a Roamerling—most of them had left Bordenn by now—and also that she should be so afraid. Roamerling girls prostituted their bodies all the time, which was the main reason he had chosen the race for his experiments. Not only were they an affront to his God by their unnaturalness, but they also profaned the Matria Church's laws on decency and propriety. They deserved punishment and, by God, Reen was going to mete it out.

The pious thoughts running through his mind as he approached the writhing girl inflamed his soul. He was doing his God's will in this, using the holy Fire that had transformed his body and his life, and which burned still within his heart, to snuff out and redeem these pagan outlander souls. He came close to his captive and stared down into her wide, frightened eyes.

The Roamerling girl saw him clearly for the first time and shrieked through the gag. The purple, slumped flesh, the stiffened, clawed hands, the shriveled muscles and wasted sinews, all combined to assault her with nightmares she couldn't bear. And the eyes! They appeared at first as if embers from the fire reflected in them, but the fire was behind Reen now and the sullen, ruby light remained. It glared out at her with the strength of his lust, growing and flaring with unholy desire. He must appear to her as some demon, some monster, and not a natural being at all.

The manner of his being was not important to Reen right now. What he needed was. He reached down and drew the girl's skirts up over her waist. She continued to struggle, futile though it was. The Baron climbed on the bed and knelt between her legs, smiling cruelly all the while. She tried not to look, but was unable to help herself. He knew she could feel the heat of his flesh against her body, and it burned her. It was as if he raged with a fever that should have consumed his flesh, eating it away until only bone was left. But that had already happened. Only his will and the Fire within sustained the outward illusion.

He leaned over her, reaching down to raise his robes. Whimpering in terror, she screwed her eyes shut. The scarecrow shifted his weight, centered his will, and took her.

At his first touch she screamed as if the gag wasn't there. Joined, he felt what she felt. White-hot fire lanced through her belly and her back arched in agony. It flooded every fiber of her being until she was no longer herself. She could feel it eating through her, consuming her from within, pulsing with the rhythm of the scarecrow's thrusting hips, his gasping breath. And with every pulse, she lost more of her self.

Reen was falling, lost in the sensations, totally out of control. This would not do. This was worse than when he used his cane. Surely the lust and the Fire weren't so intense when he had taken Serrin? Surely he'd had more control? If he wasn't careful, he would lose himself too far and the experiment would fail. And that couldn't be allowed to happen. Gasping, desperate, he tried to pull away. But the drive of his Fire was too compelling, the dark sweetness of his pleasure too great. He couldn't let go, couldn't give up such intense ecstasy.

He threw his head back and cried out in rage and fear, forcing himself to slow, forcing his rampant body to obey him. He hadn't bargained on this, hadn't realized how his enforced abstinence would affect him. There had been no one since Serrin, and he now understood how he had hampered his self-control by forbearing. This realization calmed his fervor, soothed the fear. It was easily rectified, this issue of abstinence. It was a remedy he would enjoy.

Calm now and fully in control, he resumed. He could feel the fires raging within him, flowing into his victim, and he could now feel her life force flowing back. This was better. This was what he needed to control. Pure physical desire he could satisfy anytime, and would now that he knew how important it was. But for now, controlling what he received was all that mattered. He exerted his will and altered the flow. It changed, sluggishly, and halted. He smiled a wide grin of triumph and resumed his absorption. The girl's life force flowed to his command and he laughed with the knowledge of his mastery.

He gasped and gave a mighty surge, hearing his victim's shattered scream. He allowed his own cry of release and knew the instant she died. All her young strength, all her vibrant life force, was sucked out, flooding into him, and he was sated. He collapsed onto her lifeless body and lay there panting, his need fulfilled.

After a time, he pushed himself up and stood looking down on her. She lay as if sleeping, although the gray pallor of her skin and the wide, dull stare of her eyes told the true story of her state. He was pleased. Not a mark remained on her body, apart from the obvious, but what among normal men and women was a loving and giving thing had been transformed by the scarecrow's dreadful touch into reaving.

Full of savage joy and feeling strong and fit for the first time since absorbing Serrin's life force, the Baron called once more for his servants.

Chapter Sixteen

Jinella spent the morning in her solar composing a letter to Taran. She took her time, examining every line, every sentiment expressed, until she was certain she had a true account of her feelings. She spared herself no pain and clearly told of her disappointment and anger, but she also told him of her deep love and commitment, her willingness to forgive and forget. She set out her reasons for this change of heart and the brutal honesty of the letter, when she read it back, gave her pause.

She wasn't sure she actually meant to send the letter, or whether writing it was merely an exercise in understanding her own emotions and motivations. Certainly, it helped clarify what she had felt during the night. She was pleased to realize she still believed in the sentiments expressed, painfully honest though they were. Taran should be able to appreciate and comprehend her meaning. She certainly hoped so, for now she had admitted the depth of her commitment, she wouldn't take no for an answer.

Folding the parchment, she slipped it into the little silver box Taran bought her at the last fair they attended. Looking at its delicately chased lid, she smiled at her memories. She had seen the box on the silversmith's stall and tried to wheedle it as a gift from Taran, but he passed it by. He then purchased it without her knowledge and presented it to her later, once she had forgotten the incident. The look of pleasure on his handsome features at her delight still warmed her heart. As did the memory of how she thanked him.

How could she have doubted the strength of his feelings for her? The more she remembered their passionate couplings, even in the cold light of examination, the more she realized how deeply he loved her. It must have been the shock of his revelations and the hurt that he hadn't come to her first with his misgivings that had made her react so badly. It was only his lack of confidence in her long-term plans that had stopped him asking formally for her hand. She knew that now. They were both as bad as each other, and there always had to be one who made the first move. As the one with the most to lose—or share—it was up to her to make that gesture. She was openhearted enough not to resent it.

Feeling a happy anticipation for the reconciliation to come, Jinny trailed her fingers over the silver box as she left her solar to begin the day's business.

✤ ✤ ✤ ✤ ✤

As befitted the Matria Church of Loxton Province, Loxton's Minster was huge. Twin-spired and magnificent, its gilded, carved stonework reared to the heavens in an impressive example of the stonemason's art. Arches, niches, and buttresses all showed signs of the gold spent by previous Arch Patrios to glorify their faith, and the current incumbent, His Immanence the Lord Neremiah, didn't intend to leave his beloved Minster unadorned by his own devotion.

In the early morning chill, Neremiah strolled down the long central nave, admiring the Minster's ornate interior. Intricate marble mosaics were set into the nave floor, the aisles flagged in good local stone. The pillars and arches supporting the vaulted roof were of marble also, decorated with representations of the various aspects of the Wheel. The crossing was plain and unadorned, but the transepts leading to the ancillary altars were paved with more creamy marble. The floor of the chancel could scarcely be seen due to the seating for the choir, and the carved altar beyond took the eye and swept it upward to meet the stained-glass window above, which spiraled the glowing colors of the Wheel down upon the congregation. The gold work of the altar cloth and the delicate crystal of the bowl resting upon it sparkled in the sunlight, lending an illusion of summer to the frigid air of the Minster's interior. Lamps and candles burned in the votive niches, but did nothing to warm the air. On holy days, braziers would flame to take off the chill, but it was the warm breath and bodies of the worshippers that transformed the cold of the vast, majestic building.

Neremiah reached the main altar and turned, gazing back along the nave toward the Minster's huge, wooden double doors. They stood open to the freezing wind and the man beside the Arch Patrio shivered, drawing his rough cloak tighter about his body.

"There, Master Withen—that's where I intend to make my mark." Neremiah flung out one arm, his heavy black robe trimmed with gray silk falling back from his liver-spotted hand.

The stonemason looked in the general direction of the cleric's arm, but was none the wiser. "Your Immanence?"

Neremiah huffed in irritation. "Look, man! In the whole of this highly-decorated edifice to the glory of God, where do you see room for improvement? Where is there a lack, a plainness, which cries out for adornment?"

Now the master stonemason saw what the cleric meant. It was true the crossing had been left plain deliberately, as a definite boundary between the congregation and the choir before the altar. Meant to signify the difference between the secular city and the clerics' holiness, the crossing became a symbol of the altar's purity when one stepped upon it to approach the holy place. Yet Neremiah wasn't content for it to be a symbol. He intended it to be a depiction of what might ensue should one dare to approach the altar—or God—with a less than humble heart. His Immanence intended his addition to the Minster's glories to be the most magnificent yet, the most worthy of note.

He turned to the short, square-jawed man beside him and drew a parchment from his heavy velvet robes. He unrolled it and held it before Withen's eyes. "Here, man. I have laid out a sketch of what I want."

The master mason took the parchment and squinted at it. The Arch Patrio's artistic skills weren't as honed as his oratorical, but Withen valued this contract too highly to say so. Nevertheless, the impression Withen got of what Neremiah intended was as strong as the cleric had hoped judging by the mason's widening eyes.

"But, Your Immanence, this will take months to complete! I'd have to employ others, workers more skilled in the setting of mosaics." He glanced at the Arch Patrio. "It will also be very costly."

"How costly?" The last thing Neremiah wanted was to be told his ideas were beyond his means, but it was essential the work be expensive. No one who came after him should say, in the years to come, he had stinted on his contribution to the glory of the Matria Church.

Withen considered, muttering about materials and the cost of skilled labor. He then named a sum that caused Neremiah to gasp.

"Don't be ridiculous, man. I could rebuild half the Minster for that! This was what I had in mind."

The sum he named was less than a quarter of Withen's, and they fell to bargaining in earnest. Neremiah enjoyed pitting his wits against craftsmen. He always had the last say because they had to give in eventually if they didn't want to endanger their souls. It might have been spiritual blackmail, but Neremiah preferred to see it as obtaining good value for his God.

They finally reached an agreeable sum for the buying of

materials and hiring the necessary workmen. Neremiah then named a further amount for Withen alone, and a bonus amount to be shared among the workers if they finished within a certain time. Withen left feeling more than happy, and Neremiah was finally alone in his beloved Minster, well pleased with what he had achieved.

He walked back to the crossing to stare at where his masterpiece would soon be revealed—a depiction of godless souls being tormented upon the Wheel as they slowly revolved toward the fires of damnation. Above all was the beatific representation of his God, beckoning the worthy and pious to step off the Wheel of Creation and enter his paradise, there to partake of the rewards they had earned before rejoining the Wheel to continue their journey toward spiritual purity. If the figure of God in Neremiah's depiction should bear a striking resemblance to His Immanence, well, that was just a passing fancy. Neremiah wouldn't be the first Arch Patrio to have himself so represented. Whatever awaited him in the darkness beyond life, here, at least, Neremiah would live forever.

Hearing a noise behind him, he turned. The huge doors were still open and a man had entered the Minster, stooped and shuffling. As Neremiah watched, the man stumbled, catching himself on one of the wooden seats. The cleric started toward the peasant, who was obviously unwell. As he neared the man, Neremiah caught the stench of disease and nearly gagged. The fellow needed an infirmary, not his nice, clean Minster.

He reached the man and stretched out his hand in blessing. The man looked up at him from dull eyes and stooped a little more. "Mercy," he mumbled.

Neremiah looked about, but he was quite alone. His fellow clerics were all at their prayers, one of the reasons Neremiah had chosen this hour to meet with the master mason. He didn't want knowledge of his plans getting out until he was ready to make the announcement. He had to have exact figures and times before instructing his congregation in their generosity.

Sighing, he bent to the figure, trying not to inhale the stench. "Here, man, you're not well. Are you fevered? Have you no family to care for you?"

The man shook his head, his breath coarse in his throat. Neremiah could scarce make out the words, but finally caught the whispered plea. "I need to be shriven, Your Immanence."

Neremiah frowned. Such petitions were never refused, but he preferred his junior clerics to deal with them. Yet none of them were about and he couldn't drag one from his devotions without good reason. Besides, this poor soul might not last that long. He sighed in frustration. He had intended to retire to his rooms to begin work on the sermon that would convince the good people of Port Loxton to part with vast amounts of hard-earned gold, but he supposed that could wait. This shouldn't take too long.

"Very well, man, I will hear your avowal. Once you've made it, I suggest you take yourself to the infirmary in the cloister square. You need more than spiritual help today."

The man mumbled his thanks and followed Neremiah to the small set of cells off the western aisle reserved for the hearing of avowals and penitence.

Neremiah entered the nearest cell and lit the branch lamp on the table. The suffering penitent entered behind him and closed the solid door. Neremiah sat behind the table and gestured for the supplicant to do the same. But the man leaned both hands on the table and stared most disconcertingly into Neremiah's eyes.

"Your Immanence, would it trouble you to dispense with the lamp? The brightness hurts my eyes, and besides, I've lost all rights to the comforts of men. I'd feel easier giving my avowal in darkness."

Neremiah pursed his lips. This was one of the more unusual requests, but he had heard many variations on this theme of self-punishment. He saw no real reason to deny the man's wishes, if it made him better able to confess his trouble. He turned down the lamp, intoning piously, "Light was made for all men. It is not for us to judge who has forfeited the right to its benefits."

"Ah, Neremiah! The next few moments may see you change your mind about that. I know others have so judged me."

Neremiah blinked in surprise. Not only was he sure he recognized the voice—impossible!—but he could also see two glowing points of ruby flame. Nothing in the room could have caused such a glow. The cleric felt his blood freeze and his aged hands gripped the wood of his chair. A frown furrowed his brow and he opened his mouth, but the dreadful voice came again, its sound cleaving Neremiah's tongue to the roof of his mouth.

"Yes, Your Immanence, you've recognized me, haven't you? My servant has done well to secure this private audience. I hadn't dared hope to have such leisure to talk with you. Do you fear me, Neremiah?"

The question was rhetorical, for as soon as Neremiah's brain accepted what he was hearing, sweat leaped out all over his body. If not for the foul miasma coming from the figure before him, Neremiah thought the whole of Loxton would smell his fear.

"Hezra Reen? How is this possible?"

A throaty chuckle issued from the vagrant fellow's mouth, prickling Neremiah's skin. Sarcasm dripped heavy in the cold voice. "You of all people should be able to work out how this is possible, my old friend. I will not, however, enlighten you. Not about that, anyway. I haven't come here to explain myself to you. I've come for *revenge*."

The last word was spat with savage vehemence and it caused Neremiah to recoil. The foul aura of rot leaking from his visitor was replaced by the taint of burning, and the ruby glow intensified. Neremiah tried to gasp, but his lungs wouldn't obey him.

"You betrayed me!" the disembodied voice hissed. "You allowed yourself to be swayed by their arguments and you threw me to their retribution. You would have stood by and watched me burn upon the Wheel and done nothing to help me. I trusted you. Neremiah, I *trusted* you!"

The voice sank lower and took on a sinister note of menace. The figure with the burning eyes leaned closer and Neremiah tried to shrink back, move away, defend himself. But he was locked in place, held firmly by the stasis of terror. He could do nothing.

"My vengeance will be sweet." The voice slithered out of some deep pit, echoing with fire. "You are so pious, so devoted, I thought you might like the opportunity to meet your God sooner than you might have expected. What do you think, Neremiah? Will he welcome you? Will he be pleased with what you've done for him over the years? Come now, you must have something to say."

The knife that appeared suddenly at Neremiah's throat and pricked his windpipe prevented the cleric from uttering a single word. The sounds he made were pleading whimpers, and they enraged the Baron further.

"Very well. As you have nothing to say in your defense, we will let God be the judge of your actions. I will tell you this, though. You'll have company where you're going. You are only the first of a select band and you will have much to reflect on once that band is complete. I bid you farewell, *Your Immanence*. We will never meet again."

Neremiah's eyes bulged with terror as the knife moved at his throat. A slice of ice burned through his skin, followed by fiery agony. He saw the fountain of his blood as the knife severed his jugular vein, and gurgled his last onto his expensive velvet robes.

✠ ✠ ✠ ✠ ✠

The scrawny vagrant wiped the knife on Neremiah's vestments and secreted it once more under his cloak. There had been no noise from outside the cell, yet he cracked the door carefully before slipping outside. Closing it behind him, he wrapped his tattered cloak about his bloodstained clothing and made his way out of the Minster. He had already carried out the other task his master had set him and the chaos in the Arch Patrio's rooms would be discovered long before his body. That should give him plenty of time to escape the Minster precincts before the hue and cry arose. He had one more task to perform before he was done.

Swiftly, he melted into the bustle of the city.

✤ ✤ ✤ ✤ ✤

Sullyan sipped her scalding fellan, watching the face of the aged and much-loved man opposite her. The air was pleasantly warm in the Hierarch's rooms, the log fire blazed comfortingly in the stone hearth, and the aroma of bitter fellan pervaded the air.

"Do you think we should tell him, Father?"

Andaryon's seventy-three-year-old supreme ruler stared distractedly into the leaping flames and was silent, his eyes unfocused, his thoughts troubled. He hardly knew what to do for the best. He had told her he appreciated her bringing this problem before him, but she knew he wished she hadn't.

He raised his eyes and smiled weakly. "Brynne, you know my son as well as I do. Perhaps better. I know you shared much while you were held captive by Reen, and the bond you forged will endure for life and beyond. You probably know more of Aeyron's hopes and fears than I do, and I believe you already know the answer to your question."

Sullyan ducked her head, aware as always of her adopted father's perceptiveness. He saw very deeply, this quiet and complex man, and she was moved once again by the closeness he had allowed himself to feel for her, the orphaned daughter of his two best-loved friends. She tightened her fingers around the warmth of her cup and sighed.

"I fear to give him more hurt, Father. Especially now, when he is so happy. I would not see him return to the state of fearful insecurity the Baron instilled within him. It would pain me more than I could bear."

"Brynne, you know I cannot advise you. Only you can decide whether the circumstances warrant a stirring-up of old fears. Perhaps you could wait until Elias has made his visit and see what evidence that turns up. You said yourself your suspicions are just that. It is entirely possible the Baron did indeed perish in the sea, and it would be very like him to leave a trail of false clues. That final twist of malice would appeal to his black heart.

"Yet if you feel that to conceal your suspicions is to deny Aeyron the chance to deal with this in his own way, then I will support your decision. Do not underestimate how the love of his new lady could help him, either. By all accounts, Lirina has won his heart and he is determined to have her. She has transformed his life, and I, for one, am glad."

Sullyan smiled. "As am I, Father. I must meet this lady. Will he bring her to Caer Vellet before they are formally betrothed?"

"I believe that is his plan. He wishes to visit her again to ask her father for her hand, and then, if she is agreeable, he will bring her here to show her what will be expected of her before asking for her decision. He has decided the Trade Fair in late winter would be a good time to introduce her to the Citadel, as it is a time of feasting and renewal. He feels it would also be a suitable time to broach his new regime. Many of our most influential nobles will attend the fair, and much will hinge on our people's reaction to his plans and their acceptance of his bride. Our only disappointment is that neither Idrimar nor Ty will be here to meet her. They are both tied up with their own province and unable to attend the fair. It is a great pity, for their public support would have done much to smooth Lirina's entry into our family, but Aeyron cannot wait any longer. And he wants to be very sure Lirina understands what her new life will entail before she gives him her answer."

"Is that not a radical departure from Andaryan tradition, Father?" asked Sullyan.

Most noblemen of the realm—if not most of the male population of Andaryon—would take whatever woman pleased their eye and only concern themselves with getting an heir. Sullyan had changed Aeyron's opinions as to the value of women, and he was determined to take a wife who wasn't frightened to use her brain. Sullyan's advice to "start a revolution," given lightly and with the intention of distracting the two of them from imminent and cataclysmic demise, had been taken very firmly to heart.

Pharikian returned her look, glad for the lightening of the mood. "Aye, and you know very well how it has come about. Your seditious ideas have taken over my son completely. It will be entirely your fault if my new daughter-in-law turns out to be a tyrant in my own household."

Sullyan laughed. The mere idea of anyone daring to bully Pharikian—or Aeyron, come to that—was unthinkable. But everyone would benefit from a woman who could share Aeyron's ideals. Maybe a new era was dawning for the demon realm of Andaryon.

This pleasant speculation wasn't helping her make up her mind. She must soon return to help the General organize Elias's visit to Lerric, and the weighty reason behind it returned to sit on Sullyan's shoulder like a brooding bird of prey.

"I will not tell Aeyron just yet," she said. "You are right; our fears concerning the Baron are born of no more than unease brought on by the unconfirmed nature of his suicide. I would still be suspicious of him if his lifeless body lay before me. I will wait to see what, if anything, Mathias and Robin find in Bordenn. There is nothing to be gained by dredging up long-buried fears at this stage, and I would not burden Aeyron while he is so content with his life."

She stood and approached her adopted father. Pharikian rose also and took her into his arms. They embraced warmly, each taking comfort from the other's love.

She reluctantly released him. "I must go. I have much to do before Mathias and Robin leave."

"Will you see Aeyron before you go?"

She shook her head. "I think not. Aeyron sees as clearly as you do. I would not be forced into a lie if he notices my uncertainty. But you can give him my love and tell him I am eager to meet his new bride."

She left the Palace, returning through the streets of the lower town to the garrison horse lines. Drum whickered a soft welcome as she vaulted to his back. She saluted the guards and rode out onto the plain.

Chapter Seventeen

A fter the Baron's exile and the changes to the Loxton garrison, brigands in Loxton Forest largely ceased to be a problem. General Blaine spent some time in the city after the trial in order to help Elias come to terms with the betrayal of his wife, and the men he brought with him amused themselves by flushing the criminals from the woods and ensuring they didn't return. Cal in particular had enjoyed that pastime.

Since that initial cleansing, Major Denny had continued to organize regular sweeps of Loxton Forest to discourage fresh footpads and vagrants, but it was so vast and impenetrable it was impossible to be sure they were all gone. While the forest was undeniably a safer place for travelers and reports of ambush were rare, over the past month or so bands of outlaws had resumed prowling the woodlands and waylaying nobles' carriages. Although unwilling to commit a large body of men to deal with the problem, Vassa nevertheless wished to counter their threat.

It was quiet in Colonel Vassa's office where he and Major Denny sat discussing how to respond this latest infestation of brigands. Their discussion was interrupted by the sound of someone yelling Denny's name. Both men looked up as Captain Valustin burst into the office. Denny rose, putting out a hand to steady his subordinate as he skidded to a stop.

"Whoa, man, steady there. No need to burst the door down.

What's got you so rattled?"

Vassa stood also, his stern face draining of color. Denny knew an attack on the King during his tour of duty was Vassa's worst nightmare. "What is it, man?" the Colonel barked.

Valustin swallowed, trying to recover his breath. "Major, Colonel, the Arch Patrio has been found murdered!"

Denny gasped and Vassa's expression turned thunderous. "What? When did this happen? How did you hear of it? Details, man!"

"One of my men sent word to me, Colonel. He was off duty and out in the city. He heard a commotion in the Minster precincts and went to investigate. Some of the clerics were huddled together by the Minster door in obvious distress, and when he asked them what the matter was, they told him the Arch Patrio had been found in one of the supplicants' cells with his throat slit."

Denny loosed a barrack-room oath, but Valustin hadn't finished. "One of the junior clerics went to find him around mid-morning, as no one had seen him since he had gone to the Minster to keep an appointment. The cleric found that His Immanence's rooms had been ransacked and there was no sign of Lord Neremiah. So he raised the alarm and all the clerics turned out to search. They eventually found him in the Minster itself, lying across the table in one of the cells, bled dry from an awful gash in his throat."

"Has anyone moved the body or disturbed his rooms?" Vassa demanded.

"No, sir. My man stayed on to make sure both the cell and His Immanence's rooms were left alone, and then sent one of the clerics to me. I came straight to inform you. The cleric says it's best to hurry, sir. He says as soon as the senior clerics gather their wits, they'll try to get at the body for the Rite of Passing—and likely trample any evidence in the process."

"Well done, Captain. Your man will be in line for a commendation for his quick thinking. Denny, get over there and begin an investigation. I'll go to the King and let him know what's happened." Vassa turned back to Valustin. "Captain, was any more said about the appointment His Immanence had this morning? Do we know who he met?"

"Not yet, sir, but I'm sure we can find out."

Vassa nodded. "Go with the major and do as he bids you. I'll join you later once the King's been informed."

Denny sprinted for the garrison courtyard, yelling for their horses, Valustin on his heels. In short order they were galloping side by side through the city, scattering townsfolk who stared after them in surprise. Word of the murder had yet to get out, though Denny knew it wouldn't take long. Drawing rein outside the Minster precincts, they dismounted and led their beasts toward the hitching post.

Valustin's man was outside the doors to the Minster, keeping at bay a tight knot of clerics, all of whom seemed determined to damn him for his obstructiveness. Denny strode up to them and quietly but firmly requested they move. He was accosted by a small, thin, bearded man who turned sharp blue eyes on him.

"Major, this is sacrilege! Your man here won't allow us access to our own Minster. His Immanence must receive his Rites of Passing. To leave him so unblessed is to profane his memory. I demand you let us pass."

Denny regarded him. "I'm sorry, Patrio ...?"

"*Senior* Patrio Roshan," the man snapped.

"Patrio Roshan, I sincerely regret any inconvenience caused by this, but my man was quite right to deny you access to the Minster—and especially His Immanence's body—at this time. I mean no disrespect, but if we are to stand any chance of apprehending the murderer, it's vital nothing's disturbed until we've conducted an examination. The King will agree with me when he arrives."

"The King?" Roshan looked uncertain, but Denny wasn't listening. Gesturing to Valustin, he sidled past the huddled clerics and entered the chilly Minster.

The awesome building with its air of quiet sanctity always had a profound effect on Owyn Denny. He loved attending services here and watching the clerics as they went about the offices of their faith. He loved the chanting of the choir and the crescendo of the paeans, which often had the building ringing like some celestial bell. The thought that someone had brought murder to this holy place filled him with a righteous rage.

Valustin at his heels, Denny made his way to the supplicants' cells on the western side of the Minster. There were half a dozen, but the one he wanted was obvious. Smears of blood marked the floor and the door was open. He stepped inside and gasped in horror.

Denny had seen corpses many times, some made by his own hand. He was inured to death and gore in battle, but to see the effects of base and vicious murder, and to see it perpetrated upon a man of faith, was somehow disgusting and horrific. He placed a hand over his mouth.

His Immanence the Lord Neremiah had fallen over the table at which he sat. Its wooden surface was flooded and stained with his blood, which had gushed and then seeped from the jagged rip in his throat. The flesh was so ravaged it was as if some animal had gripped the skin and torn it loose. Denny spoke sternly but silently to his stomach and leaned closer. If a knife had caused this, it was a blade both toothed and notched. He wrinkled his nose, straightened, and turned to Valustin.

"What on earth's that smell, Val?"

Valustin, who had also gone pale, shook his head, not trusting his voice. Denny looked around the cell, finding nothing that might have produced that stray whiff of charnel reek. He even sniffed lightly at Neremiah, aware the human body was capable of giving off some very strange odors when suddenly and violently killed. Yet there was no hint of the reek about the Arch Patrio's person, and now it had gone from the air in the room.

Apart from the smears of blood on the floor, there was nothing else to see in the cell. The look of terror on Neremiah's gray face told Denny nothing, nor was there cloth clutched in his fingers, nor any sign of the knife. Denny turned and left the cell, closing the door behind him and Valustin. As they returned down the nave toward the main doors, they heard voices outside. Denny recognized Vassa's gruff tones and then Elias's decisive voice, no doubt dealing with Roshan's ire. Denny smiled. The cleric would get no further with either Vassa or Elias than he had with him.

Elias was indeed dealing with the irate senior cleric when Denny and Valustin emerged from the Minster's doors. He noticed them immediately and raised his brows. Denny could see he was pale and wondered at it. He knew Elias hadn't harbored much respect for the Arch Patrio, and he probably felt as outraged as Denny at the profaning of this holy place, but why he should look quite so troubled the major couldn't guess.

"There are no clues as to the murderer's identity as far as I can see, your Majesty," he reported. "His throat has been savagely cut with a jagged or notched blade; death would have been swift but not painless."

This bald statement, delivered with no finesse or concern for the feelings of the clerics, drew gasps of outrage and horror. Roshan stared at him in dislike, but Denny was in no mood for niceties. A murderer was abroad in his city and that was a personal affront. "Shall we investigate his room next?"

Elias waved a hand. "You go on, Major. Patrio Roshan has

agreed to show you the way. I want to see the body. I'll join you in a few minutes."

Bowing his head, Denny left the Minster in the company of Valustin and Senior Patrio Roshan, who was still glowering as he guided them to Neremiah's private chambers. Vassa went with the King, and the swordsman detailed by Valustin to guard the Minster doors stayed where he was. Until the King gave him leave, no one would enter the building.

"Who discovered the ransacking of His Immanence's rooms, Patrio?" enquired Denny as they walked.

"It was one of the juniors, Cleric Yve," Roshan answered, concern for the fate of his superior plain upon his face. As far as Denny was aware, there had never been a murder committed within the Minster before. He could well understand Roshan's distress. "He's very young and has only been with us a year. He was very agitated when he entered His Immanence's rooms and saw the devastation. I thank all that's holy he wasn't the one to find the body. I believe he might never have recovered from the shock."

"Who did discover the body?"

Roshan grimaced. "I did, Major. Yve ran to me when he couldn't find His Immanence, and once I'd seen the room I called all the clerics and juniors together and we spread out to search the Minster and its precincts. Cleric Lahan and I drew the Minster itself, and he took the east side while I took the west. When I saw … well, you know what I saw … I called to Cleric Lahan and we rushed outside to tell the others, which is when your man came upon us. The rest you know."

Roshan fell silent and Denny let him be. He would see for himself the damage done to Neremiah's rooms; he needn't trouble the man further. Denny and Valustin followed him into the cloistered enclosure where the clerics had their personal quarters.

Simply built and austere, the sandy-colored stone lent an appearance of warmth to the cold functionality of the small, square houses. Roshan led the two men toward the far end of the quadrangle and pushed open a door. He stood back to let them enter and waited outside without being told.

Denny peered into the gloomy house, which was lit only by the open doorway. The room was so plain as to be positively unwelcoming. Simple wooden chairs, a scrubbed table, bare walls and floor. There were candles and lamps set into the walls, but none of these was lit. Neither was there a fire burning in the grate, although it had obviously been lit earlier that day, probably banked overnight. Moving forward into the plain room and ignoring the stairs to his left, Denny saw a second door ahead of him. He pushed it carefully open.

This room was more in keeping with what he knew of the Arch Patrio, he thought, his eye roving over the mess within. The outer reception room must be for show. This inner room, if one ignored the devastation, was much more to Lord Neremiah's taste.

It contained comfortable chairs, now upturned, their rich upholstery ripped. A large fruitwood table, also upended, rested at the far end among scattered papers and texts. Many of these had been slashed and torn, pieces thrown into the still-warm grate, although they hadn't burned. Handsome cabinets lined the walls, all of which had been broken into—some violently—and their contents strewn about the room. The expensive woolen rugs on the floor were scuffed and disarranged. Denny heard Valustin's whistle of amazement as he peered over his superior officer's shoulder.

"They've done a thorough job," he said.

Denny could only agree. "Patrio," he called, "when you followed Yve in here, did you actually enter the room? Did you move anything at all?"

The cleric appeared at the outer door. "Only that big table. And then only to ascertain His Immanence wasn't on the floor behind it. We touched nothing else."

Denny nodded and moved into the room. "Val, look for any clues as to who might have done this. We don't know yet whether this was done after his Grace was killed or before. Did he see the brigand and give chase, or was he murdered and then robbed? Patrio, would you know if anything was missing from these cabinets?"

Roshan moved to the inner door, his face pale. "His Immanence had a locked chest where the offerings of the congregation were kept. It was in that large cabinet under the window."

"*Was*?" Denny investigated. There was no chest. "How large was it? Small enough to carry, even full of coin?"

Roshan nodded unhappily.

The two military men continued their search until they heard the sound of approaching footsteps. Straightening, Denny looked up as a shadow fell across the threshold. Elias stood in the doorway, Vassa behind him.

"Gods, what a mess!" the King exclaimed, belatedly remembering the cleric's presence. "Your pardon, Patrio."

Roshan waved a hand. "Might we have access to His Immanence now, your Majesty? He has been left far too long without the comfort of his due Rites."

Elias flushed at the implied rebuke, but answered levelly. "By all means. I don't think we can learn any more from the body itself. You are free to conduct whatever rites you need and to arrange the funeral. Inform me when it will be and I will announce a day of rest and respect."

"You are most gracious, your Majesty." Roshan bowed, only a trace of sarcasm coloring his tone. He left them and Elias grimaced.

"Why do these clerics always give me the impression they mean the exact opposite of what they say? I'm sure they have no greater hopes of grace than I do, but they always manage to make me feel inferior."

Vassa grunted. "If they didn't you might suspect they weren't needed, and they couldn't have that, could they?"

Elias grinned, but it quickly faded as he turned back to Denny. "Well, Major, have you drawn any conclusions?"

"Not yet, your Majesty. Apart from the offertory chest, nothing seems to be missing from His Immanence's rooms. Neremiah wasn't here when it was taken, by the looks of things, and there's no proof his killer was responsible for this. There's no blood anywhere. So why was His Immanence murdered?"

"What if the thief feared Neremiah might realize who had done this?" Vassa said. "He might simply have killed His Immanence to be sure the theft wouldn't be discovered too soon. Or maybe His Immanence saw the thief leaving and accosted him?"

Denny grunted. Something didn't add up. The murderer wouldn't risk being seen robbing these rooms with bloodstains all over him. And if he *had* risked it, there would be smears of blood in here. Yet if Neremiah had caught the thief in the act and challenged him, the murder wouldn't have been committed in the Minster. The murder itself was too vicious, too savage, to be an opportunist killing.

No. Denny was convinced the theft of the chest was unconnected to the killing. A coincidence. A nasty one, to be sure, but something told him he was nearer the mark with this idea than the other suggestions were.

Valustin straightened, holding a slim sheaf of bound parchment that had escaped the devastation. "Sir, this appears to be His Immanence's appointments diary. Look at this." He thrust the sheaf toward the King and Denny, pointing to a line of script under his finger.

The King read it out. "'Master Withen, eighth hour.'" He glanced up. "Anyone know who Master Withen is?"

Denny nodded. "He's the master mason. Has his workshops over by the wharves."

Elias took the parchment. "We need to see this master mason. We need to know whether he kept his appointment this morning and, if he did, whether he saw anything unusual. He may well be the last person to see His Immanence alive. Denny, we need to search his premises. You and Valustin get over there now and prevent him from touching anything in his workshop. Watch him carefully. Vassa and I will return to the garrison and turn out more men for a thorough search. We might just have found our murderer."

�֎ ✦ ✦ ✦ ✦

Withen could be seen standing at a drawing table in his large, echoing workshop, two craftsmen by his side. Withen had his head bent over a sketch, a charcoal stick in his hand, adding lines here and there. The craftsmen—one young apprentice and one older man—were pointing, making suggestions. All were engrossed in their task and didn't see or hear the two military men until the sounds of their feet scrunching over the stone dust on the floor echoed about the room.

Withen looked up in surprise, puzzled to see soldiers from the garrison. He scanned Denny's rank insignia before speaking.

"Major. We don't often get the military in here. What can I do for you?"

"You are Master Withen?" asked Denny, although he already knew the answer. Withen nodded, the frown remaining on his face. "We wish to speak with you. Is there somewhere private?"

Withen looked irritated. "What's this about, Major? I'm very busy this morning. I've just taken on an important commission and there's much to do."

Denny inclined his head. "Our business may concern that commission, Master, and I assure you it is most pressing. If you have nowhere private we can talk, you might want to accompany us to the garrison."

The two craftsmen widened their eyes, looking from Denny to their master. This sounded serious. Withen stared hard at Denny before sighing. "Oh, very well. We can use my office."

"How many men do you have working here today, Master?" Denny asked.

"Six at the moment." Withen's puzzlement was growing toward apprehension.

"Will you call them all together, please?"

Withen's eyes narrowed suspiciously. "What, now? What *is* this about, Major? My craftsmen and I have better things to do than stand around all day!"

Denny replied smoothly. "I'm sure you have. Nevertheless, you will do as I ask or face the consequences."

Withen stared a moment longer before realizing Denny was serious. Turning abruptly, he gave a yell which was heard throughout the vast workshop.

Three more men appeared from various corners of the building. Two were brawny, muscular fellows hired merely to lift and position the giant lumps of marble and stone Withen ordered from the quarries. The third man was Withen's second-in-command. They came forward to stand with the other three, looks of enquiry on their faces.

Denny held Withen's eye. "Is this all? Has anyone else been here today? Clients, men looking for hire, delivery men?"

Withen shook his head, ignoring the concerned expressions

thrown his way by his workforce.

Denny turned to his subordinate. "Keep them here, Captain, until the extra men arrive. Master Withen, come with me."

He gestured for Withen to lead the way to his office and the man complied, his square jaw set, his eyes showing disquiet. He led Denny to a tiny room partitioned off from the workshop, littered with dust and old papers. He turned to face the major once Denny had shut the ill-fitting door. "I demand to know what this is about, Major. You're treating me like a suspected criminal! What have I done to deserve such disrespect?"

Denny ignored his ire. "Master Withen, can you tell me what you did this morning before coming to your workshop?"

Withen looked surprised. "This morning? Why, that's when I received my commission from the Arch Patrio. Once I'd seen him I sent for the two craftsmen out there, and we came here to begin the initial designs."

"You saw His Immanence? You met with him?"

"Yes, I just told you. I had an appointment with him at the Minster this morning, eighth hour."

"And you left him when?"

"I suppose our meeting took half an hour. I met him outside the Minster doors, we entered the building, he told me what he wanted and showed me where he intended the design to go, gave me a rough sketch, and then we bargained over the cost. I left with the drawing after that." Withen drew himself up, anger mounting. "Will you *please* tell me what this is about? Has His Immanence made a complaint? Has he accused me of trying to rob him? Because if he has, let me tell you, his Grace is a very shrewd bargainer! If anything, he got the best of the deal."

Denny regarded him closely. "It's interesting you should mention theft, Master Withen. But theft is not the main reason I'm here. I have to tell you that Lord Neremiah was found violently murdered this morning, and it must have occurred around the time you say you were with him."

There was a cold, shocked silence.

"M-murdered?" Withen's face drained of color and his hand stretched out to the wall, to support his shaky legs. "But … but I spoke with him only a few hours ago! How is this possible? Who'd wish to murder the Arch Patrio?"

Denny's voice was flat and cold. "That's what we intend to find out, Master. And as the last known person to see him alive, *you* are our primary suspect."

Chapter Eighteen

The King arrived within minutes of Denny's revelation, bringing six swordsmen from the garrison. He ordered them to begin a thorough search of the workshop and its premises while he and Vassa shut themselves away with a shocked and frightened Master Withen in the tiny, dusty office. Denny stationed himself by the door and set Valustin to watching the five men outside. The King had no time to hear the full story before one of the searching swordsmen gave a shout.

Denny hurried over to the workshop's far corner. One of his men was bent over a small heap of marble and stone chippings. He kneeled beside the man. "What have you found, Fergus?"

The swordsman poked at something lying under the spoil heap. "Look at this, Major."

Denny's expression turned grim. What Fergus had uncovered was a thin strip of cloth, and the brown stain on it was immediately familiar to one used to seeing dried blood.

Denny straightened. "Leave it be." He returned to the office and cracked the door. "Your Majesty, you should see this."

Elias stood at once, Withen following suit. "No, Master; you will wait there."

Pale-faced, the short man subsided and the King left with Denny. Vassa stayed to watch the master mason.

Denny showed Elias what Fergus had discovered. "Pull it out, man," said the King.

The swordsman brushed away the dust and chippings, delicately pulling out a long strip of bloodstained cloth wrapped around a slender object. The King's mouth was a stern line as he observed. "Open it."

Fergus complied, and even Denny gasped as the viciously-notched and bloody blade was revealed. Elias tore his gaze from the knife and stared flatly at Denny. "Do you think this is the blade that tore Neremiah's throat?"

Denny glanced back at the awful instrument. "It's the sort of thing I suspected, your Majesty." He felt unwilling to be more definite. Something about Withen's demeanor had struck him as honest. Denny wouldn't have been surprised if they had found no evidence to incriminate the master mason. But even he had to admit this looked pretty damning.

The King grunted. "Keep it safe."

Denny picked up the object and Elias turned toward the office. Then another of the searchers called out, this time from outside the building. Elias stopped in his tracks as Denny sprinted to answer the call. Withen's workforce watched him go, puzzlement and fear on their faces.

Outside the building were storage sheds where large blocks of stone were kept before being moved into the workshop for carving. The door to one of these stood open and the man who had called beckoned Denny inside. It was gloomy within, but when Denny looked where his man indicated, he could just see a gleam of gold coming from behind a large, rectangular block of stone. By turning his body sideways and edging past the block's sharp corners, Denny was just able to enter the space behind.

He crouched down and took up the gold-bound wooden chest he found there. Passing it to his man, he extricated himself and dusted down his leathers. Waving the swordsman before him, they returned to the workshop. Elias was awaiting them and he'd had

Vassa bring the master mason.

Denny approached the group and his man handed the chest to the King. "This was found by Chaz here in one of the storage sheds, your Majesty."

They all recognized the offertory chest, stained with blood though it was, and the pitifully few gold and silver bits left within it gleamed as the King raised the lid. He turned to the bewildered master mason. "Would you care to explain how this came to be in your storage shed, Master?"

Withen opened and closed his mouth like a stranded fish, unable to speak. Elias gestured to Denny. "Show him the other item."

Denny brought out the wrapped bundle and opened it, holding the awful knife before Withen's eyes. The master mason gaped in horror, but Denny couldn't see guilt in his frightened eyes. They flicked to the King's grim face before roving desperately around the other faces surrounding him.

He raised calloused hands in supplication. "I have no knowledge of these things, your Majesty! I didn't bring them here! You can't suspect me of murdering the Arch Patrio? What motive could I possibly have? I've just won a valuable commission from him. Why would I jeopardize that?"

Elias's face was closed and hard. "Yes, but didn't you say His Immanence had the best of the deal? Didn't you just tell me you had to bargain hard to get a fair price? Maybe his intractability angered you. Maybe you decided you could gain more gold by robbing him than you could by completing your commission."

Withen gasped in distress. "I would never do that! I value my business and my reputation. How many clients do you think I'd have if I went around murdering those who struck good bargains? I'd never get away with it, anyway!"

His face, pale and strained, took on a serious look. He gazed at

Elias in frank appeal. "I've always admired and respected Lord Neremiah. You can ask anyone who knows me. I attend Church services regularly, and a goodly amount of the gold that finds its way into that coffer comes from my business. I love our Minster. I've long wished to add my own contribution to the glory of its stone, the magnificence of its aura. I would never jeopardize my chance to do that. I am innocent of this foul murder. I swear it by all that's holy."

Elias considered the mason standing firm before him—still pale, still frightened, but steadfast in his declaration. Denny saw the King glance briefly at Vassa, and caught the Colonel's answering, equally brief, nod.

Elias sighed. "Very well, Master, I will accept your word for now. But the question as to how these items came to be on your premises remains. It's my belief that someone here is involved in this horrific crime. If you aren't the murderer, we must suspect one of your workforce. They would have known of your appointment this morning and could have taken the opportunity to steal from His Immanence's rooms. They will all be taken to the garrison for questioning. Major, if you please."

Denny gave swift orders and soon had Withen's five men secured. Protesting their innocence, through tears in the case of the young apprentice, they were led away to the horses waiting outside.

Withen tried his best for them. "Your Majesty, I will personally vouch for each and every one of my employees. They've all been with me for some years, even young Kerris, and I'll swear for their characters before any court."

The King nodded curtly. "Your words are noted, Master Withen. I hope you don't have cause to regret them."

He strode away, followed by Vassa, leaving an unhappy master mason alone in his empty workshop.

✤ ✤ ✤ ✤ ✤

Sullyan was with General Blaine and Robin when the contact from Taran arrived. Blaine meshed psyches with his two officers and they all heard the Adept's report of the murder and the findings of the initial enquiry. Blaine broke the contact and turned to face his two officers.

He pursed his lips when he saw Sullyan's concerned expression. "This doesn't necessarily have any connection to the Baron's supposed suicide," he said. She just stared at him.

"But if it did," mused Robin, "wouldn't it mean the Baron's back in Port Loxton? Or at least in the immediate area. Do we still want to make the trip to Bordenn?"

Sullyan remained silent and the General stared right back at her. "Well?"

She had the grace to drop her eyes. "You already know what I think, Mathias."

"Dammit," he snapped, "what are we to do, then? Vassa can send out parties to scour the city, but if Reen is behind this he'll be long gone by now. I can't believe he'd risk entering the city, anyway. He's too well known. Who'd risk sheltering him from Elias's retribution? Who did he have in the city with enough power to stand up to the King's will and the might of the King's Guard?"

Sullyan shook her head. "No one. I agree the Baron would not risk himself. If he is behind Neremiah's murder, he is using an agent. Maybe more than one."

"So is it still worth going all the way to Bordenn?" persisted Robin. "What could we find out if Reen isn't actually there?"

Sullyan glanced at her life mate. "I believe it would be worth gauging Lerric's loyalty to Elias. I would be interested to learn of his reactions to the news of Reen's purported death, and also Sofira's to questions on the subject of correspondence with her former confidante. If we accept, for the moment, that Reen is alive, then someone provided the means for him to escape death by drowning, and that will not be coincidence. Someone is aiding him now—someone with wealth and power. Reen would not risk attracting our suspicions and attention if he did not believe himself secure."

Blaine shifted irritably. "Of course, this murder could be the work of some conscienceless thief. Murders do happen, especially in a city like Loxton, and Neremiah wasn't universally popular. He'd spoken out on a number of topics, and never scrupled to berate those he considered less than godly. I think we should be very careful of attributing every strange occurrence to Reen's disappearance."

"Never mind the fact that Reen would hate Neremiah vehemently for failing him at the trial and would be avid for his death." Sullyan's voice was soft in the room.

Blaine glared at her and she shook her head. "Very well, Mathias, I am rebuked. I will keep an open mind on the subject. If you will, once you arrive in Port Loxton, please allow Robin to question the mason's men. He should be able to tell if any of them lie. If he uncovers falsehood, well and good; he will apprehend a murderer and I will bow to your judgment. If not, we will know to look elsewhere and you can instruct Jerrim Vassa accordingly. But I still believe the visit to Lerric is necessary."

Mathias Blaine regarded her with some exasperation before waving a dismissive hand. He knew very well this murder had only increased the strength of her convictions over Reen's supposed suicide. She suspected his own irritation stemmed from the fact that, deep down, he agreed with her.

"We'll depart this afternoon," he said curtly. "Will you be so good as to inform those selected to accompany us? The major and I still have some arrangements to discuss."

Summarily dismissed, Sullyan rose. "Of course, General."

She smiled at her life mate and heard Blaine's heavy sigh as she closed the office door.

Walking slowly down the grand, sweeping staircase to the ground floor, her thoughts were chaotic. She was nowhere near as calm over this trip to Bordenn as her outward demeanor suggested, and Taran's appalling news only increased her disquiet. She was worried Blaine wasn't taking her concerns and convictions as seriously as he ought, and the fact Robin was accompanying him— albeit at her instigation—gave her no ease. Despite the vast levels of power the two men controlled, their safety wasn't guaranteed. How often had she, two full levels above them both, been stripped of her power and rendered helpless? It took only a small amount of spellsilver to incapacitate the strongest Artesan, as the Baron knew well, which was why she had insisted they all experiment with the ore to find a way of overcoming its negating effects. Their lack of success was galling.

She left the Manor building and made her way to the barracks. Voices came from within; Captain Dexter giving his usual last-minute briefing to the swordsmen under his command during the trip. She heard his exhortations to vigilance even as she pushed open the door to the common room.

The barracks common room was similar to the one in the Manor, only slightly larger. The main difference was that the barracks lacked the delicious smells wafting from Goran's kitchen day and night. The barracks commons wasn't used for meals. Fellan and tea were continually available, but the small kitchen was only used for preparing meals in unusual circumstances, such as those surrounding Elias's ill-advised invasion of Andaryon. But the smell of fellan was pleasant and Sullyan moved toward the pot as the assembled men came to attention and saluted her as one.

"Any news from the General?" Dexter asked as he stood the

men down and approached her. They all crowded round, eager for news, for tea, or for fellan, depending on their taste.

"I am to tell you to be ready to move out by midafternoon. There has been a development, gentlemen, and I wish to make you aware of it."

"Listen up, lads," called Dexter, and the men fell silent. Sullyan moved to one of the wooden tables and sat upon the edge, cradling her mug of fellan.

"We have just heard from Adept Elijah at Port Loxton," she said, and told them of the Arch Patrio's death. The more pious among them made the sign of the Wheel. "You all know the reason behind this trip to Lerric's province and that it is not merely a courtesy call on the part of the High King. Lerric was one of those instrumental in the civil war sixteen years ago, and it is just possible that either he or his daughter have been aiding Baron Reen. Now it just might be that the murder of Lord Neremiah is completely unconnected, but I cannot dismiss it until we have firm evidence as to who is responsible. Therefore I ask you to keep your eyes and ears open during this trip, both in Port Loxton and in Daret. The General and the Major will spend the majority of their time with Lerric and his daughter, but you will have just as important a part to play. Mingle with Lerric's men and get them talking. Join any card games, watch them, listen to their gossip. Be alert to any hint of disapproval or fear over what their lords might be doing. Be sympathetic to their grievances. You will hear much that Robin and Mathias will not. Use your position to our advantage. Do not hesitate to bring any suspicious piece of gossip or news to their attention. And, gentlemen, there is one other thing I would ask of you."

"What, Colonel?" asked Dexter.

She heard the concern in his voice and gazed at him. "Look after him, Dex. Look after both of them."

Her heart was in her voice and the men responded. Coming to their feet as one, they saluted her once again.

"With every breath in our bodies and every skill we possess," declared Dexter, the men crying "Aye!" behind him. Their loyalty and love brought tears to her eyes and she smiled in grateful thanks.

"I have every confidence in you. You ease my heart."

By midafternoon, they were ready to leave. Dexter had the men drawn up before the Manor gates, and was himself holding the bridle of Charger, General Blaine's warhorse. Sullyan stood close by, watching Robin attach his pack to the harness rings of Tobias's saddle. She held Morgan in her arms, and he was watching his father intently.

Sullyan tried hard to keep the worry from her thoughts. Her son could pick them up too easily, and the last thing she wanted was to alarm the boy. He was growing in knowledge and control all the time, thanks to a variety of good teachers, but wasn't yet skilled in disguising his emotions. He was too young to understand the need for such deception. So she smiled at him and made comments about what was happening, directing his thoughts to other topics than the imminent departure of his beloved father.

General Blaine strode down the steps from the Manor's grand entrance and took Charger's reins from Dexter. He turned to regard Sullyan before vaulting into his saddle, but uttered not a word. They had already said all that needed saying. She merely acknowledged his tacit acceptance of her concern and afforded him a respectful salute. She turned to Robin as the General gave the order to move the company out.

Sullyan appreciated her superior officer giving them this moment of privacy. Not that she would have cared had the entire world been watching. She gave Morgan over to Robin for a final hug, then fell into his arms herself once he'd set the boy down.

Like the General, Robin said nothing, but his soul merged with hers and shared her feelings. Words were unnecessary between them after all this time together. True life mates, they were joined in spirit as well as body—what one felt, the other did too.

After a short moment, they broke apart. Sullyan felt a hand on her shoulder and turned her head to see Bull behind her. He grinned at Robin. “Don’t be too long, lad, or you may find your place taken when you return.”

“Ha!” Robin leapt lightly onto Tobias’s back. “You wouldn’t dare, you old rogue. Morgan, watch this man while I’m gone. You guard your Mama’s honor for me, do you hear?”

The boy whipped out the toy sword that never left his side. He stood in front of Sullyan and brandished it menacingly. “Yes, Papa!”

Bull laughed and Robin grinned. “You wouldn’t dare touch her now!”

The young Major nudged his mount and waved to his life mate. Then he was gone, leaving only the sound of hoof beats as he raced to catch the others.

Bull threw an arm about Sullyan’s shoulders and turned her back to the Manor. “Come on, Colonel, I need to hear how much extra work you’re going to give this poor old soldier. Morgan, shouldn’t you be with Elisse and Eadan?”

“Yes, Uncle Bull.” The boy skipped off, watched fondly by his mother and the huge man by her side.

✣ ✣ ✣ ✣ ✣

Robin handled the crossing into Andaryon and thence to Port Loxton, exchanging pleasantries with Lord-General Anjer as he did so. He told the Andaryan that Sullyan was in charge at the Manor, and also informed him where the High King would be for the next few days. It was a courtesy agreed between the rulers to inform each other when absent from their capital. It helped cement their relationship and remind their subjects of their close ties.

Before the human forces left the realm of Andaryon, General Blaine sent Dexter's corporal, Wil, ahead of the main party as an emissary to King Lerric to inform him of the High King's intention to visit on the morrow. Blaine had decided Elias would be more comfortable staying at an inn for the night rather than one of Bordenn's garrisons. He told Wil to keep his wits about him while he was in Daret, and to pay good mind to anything he heard or saw. The corporal went off cheerfully, and Blaine saw him emerge from the substrate tunnel into Bordenn's wintry landscape.

Formalities observed, Blaine, Robin, and their company of fifty swordsmen arrived in Loxton Castle's parklands just after noon.

Taran and Denny were there to meet them. Denny greeted them with a formal salute and took Dexter and the swordsmen, along with Blaine's and Robin's mounts, off to the barracks. Taran fell into step beside the General as he and Robin made their way up to the castle.

"Where's Vassa?" asked Blaine.

"Still questioning the men from the mason's workshop," said Taran. "The King's angry and worried, and he's determined to apprehend the culprit as soon as possible."

"Is he convinced one of the masons did it?" asked Robin as they reached the steps to the castle doors.

Taran shrugged. "I think he's *hoping* it was one of them."

Blaine and Robin removed their cloaks, handing them to the servant behind the door. Taran led the way to where the men were held, noting Blaine's piercing look at the way he'd phrased his answer. The General said nothing, following Taran with his expression set. Robin looked thoughtful and exchanged a meaningful glance with Taran.

The Adept led them to the rooms being used to hold and question the mason's men. The interview room was attached to an even smaller anteroom where Elias currently sat, listening through the half-open door to the Colonel's questions and the men's answers. Vassa had shrewdly persuaded Elias to this arrangement, knowing the King's presence would both alarm and fluster the citizens he was interrogating. They were frightened enough without having to contend with the presence of their King.

Taran showed the General and Robin into the anteroom. Elias glanced up as they entered and waved them all to seats.

Vassa was just finishing with the second man he'd interviewed, and the four men in the anteroom heard him release the laborer to the guard. As he was escorted away, Vassa came through to join them, raising his brows at Elias. "What do you think, my Lord? I didn't get the impression he knew anything of significance."

Elias grunted agreement. Blaine turned to him. "I have a suggestion to make. It'll save time if the Major here conducts the rest of the interviews. His Artesan senses should detect any deception or falsehood. You and I need to discuss our visit to Lerric and the arrangements for the security of the castle."

Elias nodded and Blaine glanced at Vassa.

"Jerrim, please show the Major where the men are being held and then join us in the King's audience chamber."

Elias was drawn firmly in the General's wake as Vassa turned to lead Robin to where the mason's men were held. Taran followed. Vassa, relieved to be handing this task to someone else, left them at the door and walked away.

"I take it both you and Brynne suspect the Baron's hand in this?"

Robin looked up at Taran's question, his expression somber.

"She definitely does. I'm trying to keep an open mind, but it's hard in the face of her conviction. I think Blaine's convinced too, although you'll not get him to admit it. He'll instruct Vassa to be doubly vigilant while the King is away, and I'd advise you to do the same. You're not exactly the Baron's favorite person, either. What have you told Jinny, by the way?" Taran turned away, but Robin had seen his discomfiture. "What is it?"

Taran had no choice but to tell him of his troubles, and Robin's expression was serious when he was done.

"So she still believes he's dead?" He shook his head dubiously. "I think you ought to tell her what we suspect, regardless of the state of your relationship. She'll hear the news of Neremiah's murder soon enough, and she's perfectly capable of adding two and two. Do you really want her to sit and stew over the possibilities? Do you want her accusing you of keeping this from her? You ought to alert her to be on her guard, too. I imagine the Baron would just love to get his revenge on her for what she did to betray him. Does she have reliable servants who could double as guards?"

Taran stared in horror. "Do you seriously think he'd try for Jinny? That he's here in Port Loxton? Oh, good gods, what if he's hiding out on the estate? Bloody hell, Robin, I have to warn her—!"

Robin laid a hand on the Adept's arm. "Steady, Taran. You can't go haring off just yet. The King might require your services. And I doubt very much the Baron's here. Sullyan thinks he's working through an agent. So slow down. You can go and speak with Jinny this evening once we've left for Bordenn. I doubt anything more will happen for the time being. Reen must know the city will be swarming with King's Guard for the next few days. He or his agent wouldn't dare try anything else until that's died down."

Taran calmed under Robin's reasoning, knowing the Major was right. Taran wasn't free until the King and his company left the castle. To divert his mind, he accompanied Robin while the Major questioned the mason's five men.

Chapter Nineteen

"As far as I can tell, your Majesty, none of them are guilty of anything more serious than appropriating the odd piece of marble for their own use. Certainly none of them are guilty of Lord Neremiah's murder. And none of them know anything about the knife or the offertory chest."

Elias sighed in frustration and leaned back in his chair, gripping the upholstered leather arms. He stared into the fire in his private audience chamber, General Blaine, Colonel Vassa, and Taran watching to see what his reaction would be. Robin stood before him, at ease after giving his verdict, and Elias regarded him with weary resignation.

"I was afraid you'd say that. Not that I thought Withen or his men were capable of such a horrific act. But this leaves us no closer to an answer and we still have a dangerous killer on the loose—one calculating enough to plant incriminating evidence. So what do we do now?"

The King directed both his gaze and his question to the General. Blaine pursed his lips.

"I know you don't want to leave the city with this unresolved, but we're committed. We have to leave in an hour if we're to arrive at our lodgings in daylight. My messenger will already have alerted Lerric to your visit and we can't back out now. Leave the investigation to Jerrim and Denny. They're quite capable of handling things on their own. And the murderer is probably well away from the city by now, if he's got any sense. He's probably hiding out with those damned brigands in Loxton Forest."

Elias wasn't happy, but he couldn't argue with Blaine's logic. He had no choice, much as he hated the thought of leaving with such a vicious murderer uncaught. He cast his gaze to Vassa. "See if you can't do something about those brigands while we're gone, Colonel. And tighten up the city's security as much as you can. It galls me to think some evil fellow can just walk into Loxton, murder the Arch Patrio, steal all that gold, and then just walk out again. If we have to search everyone entering or leaving in order to stop this kind of thing, we'll do it. Yes, yes, I know the merchants would be up in arms and the nobility would petition for their rights of privacy, but if that's what it takes to keep them safe then I'm sure they can be made to see reason. I *won't* tolerate such brutal assaults and do nothing to ensure they don't happen again. I want to see some progress in this matter when I return. Do you hear me?"

"I hear you, your Majesty," Vassa replied evenly, though Blaine knew he'd be wincing at the thought of all the extra work and the barrage of protests he'd have to field. Denny wouldn't be happy either. Such security measures were unlikely to be effective, not with the amount of trade that passed through Loxton.

Elias had turned to give Taran last-minute instructions as to what he expected to be informed upon while he was away, and Blaine left him to it. With Robin by his side, he made his way to the garrison.

✣ ✣ ✣ ✣ ✣

"What's the meaning of this? A royal visit? Tomorrow? What are you talking about, man? We always get at least a week's notice! Is this some prank? Because if it is, I can assure you—"

Corporal Wil Gerion pulled his orders from his jacket and

handed them to Lerric's Captain of the Guard, the sun-circled crown seal of the House of Rovannon uppermost. He had been greeted with incredulity, unprofessionalism, and contempt by everyone from the gate guards to the stable boy and his patience was at an end.

"No prank, Captain. I believe you'll find these in order. High King Elias will arrive tomorrow morning, escorted by General Blaine and a company of fifty. The General and his Major will expect quarters within the palace. The company and their captain will quarter in the barracks. I strongly suggest you appoint a clean-up detail to work through the night. The High King will not be impressed if he's forced to dismount into ankle-deep muck in the courtyard. Now, if you're satisfied as to the validity of my message, would you be so good as to present me to his Majesty?"

The Captain shut the mouth that had dropped open as he read the parchment. Color rushed to his face as he barked orders at a subordinate, sending the man scuttling off to do his bidding. The Captain's demeanor was improved as he turned again to Wil. "I'm sorry for the manner of your welcome, Corporal …?"

"Gerion."

"Corporal Gerion. It's just that this is such an unexpected development. We've always had plenty of warning before something as momentous as a state visit from the High King. You wouldn't happen to know the reason for it?"

Wil wasn't going to be caught like that. "If you'd just show me through to his Majesty, Captain. I don't think he should be kept waiting any longer, do you? I imagine he'll want all the time he can get to prepare for the King's arrival."

"This way, Corporal." The thin man turned on his heel and led Wil down a corridor; this one brightly lit, warm, and richly adorned with tapestries, a stark contrast to the cold and dreary halls Wil had passed through on his arrival. They met no one on their way and Wil guessed Lerric's palace was largely unused in winter with few nobles in residence, if any, so he chose not to waste gold on heating or torches. This was understandable and was only good housekeeping on the part of the chatelaine, though Wil would have thought a client king of Lerric's standing would have a larger court than this. Why, even the Manor was more comfortably furnished—and vastly more crowded.

They eventually came to a door adorned with Lerric's crest of an athletic hunting dog bringing down some fearsome mythical creature. The emblem was worked in gold on the oak door, and the hinges and latches were all decorated with gold leaf. This was more the style Wil expected to see. He knew from reputation Lerric was a shrewd bargainer and a hoarder of his wealth, but Wil couldn't imagine why anyone as wealthy as Lerric would not display some of that richness for his subjects' benefit.

The Captain rapped sharply on the door, which opened to reveal a glimpse of a sumptuous room, redolent with firelight, warmth, and several appetizing smells that set Wil's empty stomach growling.

The Captain conferred in hushed tones with the servant who had opened the door and then turned to Wil. "I'll leave you to deliver your message, Corporal. Once you're done, come and see me and I'll arrange billeting for you. There's a room you can use within the castle; it'll make up for your lack of proper welcome as befits a messenger from the High King. And the food's better than in the barracks." He grinned at Wil's appreciative expression then turned and left. Wil directed his gaze to the servant who stood just behind the open door.

"Wait here until you are called, please," the servant told him, leaving Wil at the door. Wil could hear his low voice as he informed Lerric of his visitor, and then the sound of his feet as he returned. The servant beckoned Wil forward, announcing his name and purpose. Wil looked around Lerric's private audience chamber with curiosity as he paced toward where Lerric sat in a leather settle in front of a roaring log fire.

The room wasn't large, but it was supremely comfortable. The flagged floor was fully carpeted and many rich tapestries adorned the gray stone walls. Sumptuous red hangings fell in graceful folds at the three huge windows, drawn against the cold. Three intricate chandeliers were suspended from the ceiling and fragrant oil lamps burned in their niches. Wil compared this luxury to the austerity of the rest of the palace and guessed Lerric was more careful of his own comforts than he was of the rest of his court.

As he approached Lerric's chair he turned his scrutiny to the client king. He was around sixty years of age, tall, spare, but still agile. His gray eyes mirrored the sternness of his daughter's, but disillusionment and discontent had not embittered Lerric's gaze as it had Sofira's. His eyes held puzzlement, as Wil expected, but the swordsman could also see a measure of fear, which gave him cause to wonder. The suddenness of Elias's visit was bound to raise wary curiosity, but Wil could think of no reason for fear unless Lerric's affairs weren't as Elias wished them. The Corporal filed away his first impressions to relate to his major later.

He halted a respectful distance from the king of Bordenn, bowed, and went down on one knee. "Your Majesty, I bring you greetings from High King Elias of Albia and present to you this notice of his intention to visit your palace on the morrow. He bids me request suitable lodgings within your palace for himself, his general, and major, and informs you he will bring an honor guard of fifty swordsmen, to be quartered among your own men. I have here his letter. May I pass it to you?"

Lerric nodded, indicating Wil should rise. The king hadn't betrayed one glimmer of his thoughts during Wil's speech, but he had flicked a swift glance at the room's other occupant, sitting straight-backed and proud on a hard chair to his right. As Wil stood and passed the General's parchment into Lerric's hand, he bowed respectfully to Lerric's brittle-faced daughter.

"Your Highness."

Sofira took less notice of him than she would of a scullery maid come to tend the fire. Her stony gray eyes fastened on the parchment in her father's hands, her stern face chalky. Wil would have appreciated time to study her at some length, sensing a strange disquiet within the former queen. He hadn't imagined she would feel pleasure at the thought of her erstwhile husband's visit, but the aura of tense fear she exuded went beyond what Wil had expected. Yet another piece of information to relate to his superiors.

Lerric raised his head from the parchment and regarded Wil. "When will his Majesty arrive?"

Wil noted Lerric's lack of protestations over Elias's timing and hid a smile. "The High King and his escort expect to arrive at your gates an hour before noon on the morrow, your Majesty."

Lerric's face tightened as he turned to his daughter. "Sofira, would you be so good as to inform the chatelaine of the need for extra provisions tomorrow? She will also be required to organize a feast in the High King's honor tomorrow evening. Tell her I authorize the huntsmen to take the hounds out if necessary. This damned weather may well have left the kitchens short of meat."

Sofira nodded stiffly, but made no move or reply. Lerric turned back to Wil, who hadn't missed the inference that Elias's visit would seriously discommode Lerric's household. "You have discharged your duty, Corporal. You are free to find what lodgings you may with the men of my guard. No doubt they can be prevailed upon to feed you, although their rations haven't been plentiful of late. My servant here will show you to the barracks."

Wil bowed himself from Lerric's presence and returned to the hallway. The servant guided him to the Captain's rooms and the swordsman soon had what he most wanted, despite Lerric's gloomy warning: warm lodgings, hot food, and passable ale.

✤ ✤ ✤ ✤ ✤

Lerric stared at his trembling daughter in shock. Her quick, shallow breaths, just audible over the crackle of logs in the hearth, were the only other sounds in the room. Her right hand was pressed to her mouth; apart from that, she hadn't moved.

Lerric's voice was tremulous. "What do you suppose he's up to? Do you think he knows—?"

"Don't be ridiculous, Father! How could he possibly know?"

Lerric stared at his overwrought daughter, seeing her chalky complexion, the fear behind her eyes, and the slight tremor of her fingers. She held out an imperious hand for the parchment.

"What does he say? Let me see that."

Lerric passed her the note and watched while she read it.

She snorted. "Elias didn't write this. That's Blaine's hand."

"His damned general," Lerric muttered, and Sofira nodded curtly. Lerric pursed his lips. "But he's ... you know ... one of those—"

"The term is 'Artesan,' Father," she snapped. "And yes, I know. What of it?"

Agitated, Lerric rose. "But they're who Reen's hiding from! What if they've got a way of finding him? What if they suspect he's here? They must know he's escaped the island by now. What if they don't believe the suicide story?"

His daughter watched him pace before the fire, her expression scornful. "Why should you instantly think Elias's visit has anything to do with Hezra? Why should he think of coming here even if he didn't believe the clerics? Hezra and I didn't exactly part on the best of terms, if you remember, and Elias could hardly suspect *you* of helping the man who impeached your daughter and robbed her of all she had!"

Sofira's spiteful, angry tone caused her father to cease pacing and stare at her. He hadn't heard that aggrieved note since she had recovered from the immediate grief of leaving her children. He had certainly never heard it directed at the man she professed to still love.

Aware of his gaze, Sofira collected herself. She gave a vexed sigh and rose from her chair. "I really don't think you've anything to fear, Father. And you'd better not show this craven nervousness while Elias is here or you'll trigger his suspicions. Now, I must show this parchment to Hezra and tell him of the King's visit. He won't be pleased, I imagine, but at least contingency measures have already been taken to deal with such a situation. We only have to follow his instructions and all will be well."

Sofira swept toward the door, her stiff, unbending back a silent reproof to the doubts and fears of her father—almost, Lerric thought, as though her own fears didn't exist. Yet he knew her too well to miss the telltale signs.

She halted, her hand on the latch, and turned to face him once more. "Has it occurred to you, dear Father, that the reason for this sudden visit may not concern *you* at all? Elias and I were married, you know! We have children, and one of them, at least, misses her mother. Has it not occurred to you that this visit might just be about *me*?"

With that final, spiteful shot, Sofira swept from the room, leaving Lerric worried and doubtful, staring at the space she had occupied.

Chapter Twenty

The vagrant made his way back into the city as the short winter day turned to gloom. There were guards on the Forest Gate, but none looked twice at a stooped and wasted tramp such as he. Beggars often went into the woods to collect what firewood they could to keep their bones from freezing. His mouth twisted in a sneer as he passed right under the noses of the King's Guard and reflected that the Baron's policy of periodically clearing out slum-dwellers had obviously been allowed to slip since his exile.

Well, that suited the vagrant and his master just fine. No one would suspect him of having the strength or the wit to kill the Arch Patrio, and even if he was searched, there was nothing on him to incriminate him. His bloody rags had long since been disposed of. No, he was safe, and now he could turn his attention to the other task set him by his master.

His thoughts revolved around the meeting he'd just had with a certain band of brigands in Loxton Forest. Neremiah's offertory gold had purchased their willing compliance. The gold, and the promise of more once the job was done, went far toward overcoming their reluctance to spend the night in the freezing forest. The wastrel knew there were several caves deep within the woods which could be made tolerably comfortable even in the depths of winter.

He grinned. The promise of additional gold would never be

fulfilled, and there was nothing they could do about it. They would end up doing his bidding for half the agreed sum and never find him afterward.

Satisfied, he made his way toward the city's poorer parts. The streets here were narrow and dirty, full of gritty snow, rubbish, mangy curs, dead rats and live ones. The detritus of Loxton's slums went unnoticed by the vagrant as he limped his way past the ramshackle houses, moldering wooden fences, and mean, tented shelters. He ignored the muttered curses and disgusted looks thrown his way by the slum dwellers; the barging shoulders and obstructing bodies melted away before the foul miasma surrounding him. It was growing worse, but affected him not at all, and he continued his way unmolested, heading for his next appointment.

Now the initial contact had been made it was no longer necessary for the Baron to exert himself and speak to Seth directly. The vagrant could afford to meet him in one of the slum taverns, as the manservant desired—no one would mark their hushed voices or conspiratorial attitudes. They would just be two more peasants among the many such infesting the city's slums. With the King's Guard occupied over the puzzle of Neremiah's murder, attention would be concentrated upon the mason and his men. And before the furor surrounding the churchman's death died down there would be other distractions to occupy their minds.

The vagrant smiled at the thought as he pushed open the rickety door beneath the rotting sign. He was immediately assailed by the smells of stale beer, rancid oil lamps, and too many unwashed bodies. The raucous sounds of the drinkers clamored about his ears, and he shouldered his way through the pack until he could make out the stained and greasy bar through the smoke-filled air. He caught the barkeep's eye and grinned mirthlessly as he registered the paling of the sweaty man's face. The barkeep recognized his unwelcome patron, but had learned better than to protest at his presence. Besides, the vagrant now had more acceptable forms of inducement with which to tempt the barkeep out of his revulsion.

"Ale," he spat, slapping a whole silver bit into a sticky puddle of spilled beer on the bar. The barkeep's bloodshot eyes widened and the silver vanished quickly into his fleshy palm. A full tankard of cloudy ale was pushed across the bar, and the vagrant ignored the greasy marks and the hard deposits on the rim as he took a long pull. Only then did he let his eyes roam over the patrons, searching for his contact.

✣ ✣ ✣ ✣ ✣

Seth had been waiting half an hour and was beginning to feel sick. The dreadful ale curdled his stomach and the foul-smelling air crawled through his lungs like a fungal growth. His head swam from the noise and all he wanted was to be gone. He had almost made up his mind to leave when he saw the wastrel enter the bar. Fighting down nausea and revulsion, he waited.

The vagrant approached slowly, studying Seth. He pushed past two burly ruffians who turned to cuff him for his shoving and then fell back, hands across their mouths. Although how they could distinguish the wastrel's stink from the room's general fug, Seth didn't know.

"I was beginning to think you weren't coming," he snapped as the foul man sat down. Seth's nostrils tried to close of their own accord and his eyes watered.

"I've more important matters to concern me than speaking with you." The man spoke laconically, a thin line of ale running down his chin and soaking into the rough gray cloak he wore. "My master has many plans requiring my attention."

Seth set down his own tankard, the ale within hardly touched.

He had only purchased it for appearances; his stomach could take no more of the acid brew. "So what does my Lord Baron want me to do this time?"

The vagrant turned red-rimmed, cloudy eyes upon him. "You're to be the lynchpin in a plan that'll begin my master's revenge on all those who've betrayed him. By tonight he'll have within his power one or maybe two of his most hated enemies. Did you do as I bid you regarding the servants?"

"Yes." Seth's eyes were alight with the thought of serving his master. "Everything's in place. There'll only be the mistress and the housekeeper inside the mansion; the rest will be in their own quarters."

"And do you have the items I told you to bring?"

Seth reached to the floor and brought up a wrapped bundle. He uncovered a corner and showed the wastrel what it contained. The foul man waved it aside.

"I don't need to see, you fool! So long as they're recognizable and appropriate, that's all that counts."

Seth opened his mouth to protest the fellow's authoritarian manner, but the vagrant turned angrily on him. "Just do as you're told and don't start thinking for yourself! We have our instructions and we must follow them. Don't for one minute think you're important to my master. He'll dispense with your services in an instant if he suspects you might not follow his orders."

The man's face was thrust unpleasantly close and Seth leaned away. He was hurt and angered by the implied criticism and was about to reply in kind, but the vagrant wasn't done. With an evil leer at odds with the very real fear in his shifty eyes, the vagrant put his hands to the folds of cloth over his chest and parted them slightly. Seth gagged, his sense of smell overwhelmed by the charnel reek.

"Never doubt I mean what I say!" the vagrant hissed, his voice strangely altered, his eyes glowing red. "Serve me well and you shall be rewarded, but fail me only once and this shall be your fate."

Seth stared in helpless horror at the ruined, crawling flesh he glimpsed beneath the shabby cloak. His hand flew to his mouth, but he was too late. The rancid ale and the stench of decomposing meat were just too much for his overburdened stomach. He lost its contents over the stained and filthy floor.

The cloak was closed, the vagrant gulping the sour contents of Seth's tankard by the time the manservant recovered enough to sit upright. He wiped his mouth with the back of his hand and found he couldn't meet those red-rimmed eyes in case the sullen ruby glow should still be there. He coughed, trying to force his irritated throat to form words, words which might deflect the anger, appease the suspicion, and reassure Seth's lord of his unswerving obedience. Seth could think of nothing that might induce him to risk the fate this poor wretch had already suffered. He would do anything—even murder—to avoid such a consequence.

"Are you ready to leave?" The wastrel rose to his feet as if the last few minutes hadn't happened. Seth raised his eyes reluctantly, but the manic red glow had faded. There was only the sardonic twist to the wastrel's features that said he knew what Seth was thinking.

The manservant got shakily to his feet and reached for the bundle. The vagabond turned wordlessly and stalked from the tavern, his vile personal shield forging a way through the crowd and persisting long enough to accommodate Seth as he followed. They emerged once more onto the filthy, gloomy street, the younger man breathing thankfully of the outside air, which, under other circumstances, would have smelled rank.

"Where're we going?" he asked when he could catch his breath. The wastrel shot him a glance, but didn't reply. Seth was forced to follow with no idea where he was being led.

✣ ✣ ✣ ✣ ✣

Sir Regus regarded his wife where she sat staring at him from her corner of the swaying carriage. He registered the set of her delicately-painted mouth and the characteristic tilt to her exquisitely-coiffured head. He sighed, heavily but inaudibly. He was going to lose the battle. Years of married life had taught him this, and they had also taught him the futility of what he was about to attempt. Why he bothered, he didn't know. Was it some primeval male urge to dominate? Some deep-seated instinct to master? Was it the pack leader syndrome that took him over and subjected him to this ritual humiliation? He couldn't say. Whatever it was, it was paramount, and Sir Regus obeyed its dictates every time.

His wife, Lady Corina, knew this well. They had been wed for forty-three years and she knew him better than he knew himself. She had discovered very early on exactly how to handle her husband and now the reactions were instinctive. She may even have enjoyed his futile struggles, but she never tried to analyze her actions. Had she done so, she may even have come to suspect he enjoyed their sparring arguments, but the thought never entered her head. She wanted something; he'd try to dissuade her. It was part of who they were together and neither could have altered it to save their lives.

"Didn't I buy you that new gown in Tolk only last week?" Regus protested, staring out the window at the frost-rimed trees as the four-horse team drew the carriage toward the city gates.

Corina's eyes grew round. "That was for Lady Greda's party!"

"What does that have to do with it? It's still a new gown, isn't it?"

Corina sighed loudly and pulled her soft velvet over robe tighter about her plump shoulders. Expensive though the carriage was, its windows were drafty and the winter wind seeped through.

"My dear," she said firmly, "everyone who is anyone was at Lady Greda's party. If I were to attend my next function wearing the same dress, I'd be labeled cheap. I simply couldn't bear that. And I won't hear them casting comments about your generosity or means. Think how degrading that would be. No, my dear, I'm afraid I need a new wardrobe. I'll draw up a list of the most essential items when we get indoors and I'll send a servant for the seamstress tomorrow. That is, if we ever reach the end of this interminable forest."

"Yes, dear," Regus murmured, for once bereft of the energy for his usual heated argument. Indeed, he had hardly been listening to her words, lost as he was in gloomy contemplation of the state of his coffers.

Their three-week stay on her cousin's estate had already cost him dearly. The pouch that held his gold lay depressingly limp against his thigh, and he faced weeks of hard work to replenish his store. Corina's intentions for her wardrobe would only serve to beggar him further even as he strove to earn enough to replace what they had already spent. But such was his lot and he was powerless to change it. If only he could catch the King's eye and convince his monarch to elevate him! But, he reflected morosely, that was hardly likely.

✣ ✣ ✣ ✣ ✣

The men hidden in the trees were unaware of Sir Regus's gloom and wouldn't have cared if they had known. It was pure chance his carriage should be the target. They had not expected a prize such as this so late in the day. Indeed, some in the band had advised waiting until the morrow. It was late, cold, growing dark, and their instructions weren't specific as to time. Yet once the lookout reported the approach of an expensive carriage, the band's leader couldn't resist.

"Why not, lads?" He glanced round at his companions. "Just a half-hour's work and enough gold to feed us for a week. Maybe more. The quicker we do the job, the quicker we get our reward. If we strike now, they'll not rouse the garrison till morning. Ample time for us to choose our ground."

Seeing the eager gleam of their eyes, he turned to the lookout. "Go on, then, get back and tell the boys to run 'em down where we agreed. Once they've taken the coach, we'll come at 'em from behind. Sharp, now!"

The lookout spun his rangy beast and spurred it back the way he'd come. The band's leader, a rough, unshaven fellow with an ugly boil on his neck which he scratched constantly, grinned at his men. "Mount up, lads. There's nobles to rob and profit to be had!"

The ruffians chuckled as they made for their horses and followed their leader into the trees.

✤ ✤ ✤ ✤ ✤

"And don't forget the reception at Lord Pylock's in a week's time; we simply *have* to attend that. I can't wear the red brocade. Lady Sharmel was at Greda's and she saw me. She even remarked upon it, if you remember, my dear ...."

Regus wasn't listening. His wife's voice had long since become a background drone to his melancholy thoughts. He stared out at the deepening gloom, trying to think of a way to boost his income or convince his sovereign he was worth more than his pittance of ten pounds per annum.

He was so deep in his private crisis he didn't see the flitting shadow that crossed the carriage window, nor did he hear the cry of the coachman as the crossbow bolt thudded into his chest, catapulting him out of his seat and leaving the horses driverless. Well trained, they continued on, the wide forest track keeping them on course.

The carriage jolted as it increased speed, jumping over the

uneven ground. Sir Regus, startled out of his funk, bawled a reprimand to the coachman.

"Sorry, me Lord," came a rough voice.

Regus stared at his wife. "That didn't sound like Wrekin."

Corina frowned and opened the window to ask if Wrekin was all right. A rough fellow on a skinny horse appeared at the window and leered at her. She screamed, hands flying to her mouth.

"Regus, *do* something!"

Her husband did the only thing he could think of. He swore.

✤ ✤ ✤ ✤ ✤

The maze of streets and alleys was unfamiliar to Seth. He had ventured to the outskirts of the slums once or twice, but farther than that he had never been. He didn't recognize the dingy gray building where the vagrant finally halted. Judging by the look on the wretch's face, he expected some reaction from Seth, but when he didn't get one he merely grinned and rapped on the door.

"What do we want here?" Seth asked, not really expecting an answer.

"We're about to spend some of the Church's generously donated gold," was the terse reply, leaving Seth none the wiser. The words gave him pause, however, as he realized he was probably looking at the Arch Patrio's murderer.

Seth had no reason to regret Neremiah's death. He had been as furious as the Baron at Neremiah's spineless actions at the trial. That the cleric was only saving his neck and position cut no ice with Seth. Neremiah had betrayed his master as thoroughly as Jinella and death was no less than he deserved. Yet Seth had heard the rumors, already rife around the city, about how Neremiah died, about the horrific wound inflicted on a defenseless man, and looked at his ragged companion fearfully. The afternoon had held enough shocks already; Seth could only wonder what more might befall.

Footsteps sounded behind the door and the bolt was drawn. As the door inched open, Seth caught the gleam of torchlight reflected in a painted blue eye. He heard the soft murmur of voices and a woman's throaty laugh, and knew where they were. His eyes narrowed. Why had the vagrant brought him to a brothel?

The wastrel reached below his cloak and showed his palm. The glint of gold bought him an open door and an invitation to enter. He slid inside, closely followed by Seth. The woman who had admitted them eyed the vagrant with distaste, but reached for his gold nonetheless.

She wasn't young, although her layered makeup disguised the worst of the lines on her face. She wore a simple bodice and skirt, none too clean, the lacings of the bodice awry. They were also loose, hiding nothing of the pendulous flesh beneath.

She grinned as she saw Seth's gaze. He flushed and looked away.

"Yer friend's none too keen," she chuckled as she pocketed the vagrant's gold. The man spared Seth a mocking glance, his lip curling.

"He's not here to sample your charms, Nolah. Have you gathered the girls?"

"Shame. He's young and fresh. Couldn't I—" Nolah saw the vagrant's eyes gleam. "Oh, all right, they're all here."

She turned, leading the way along a shabby corridor. They passed a shadowy stairway and Seth started as a shrill scream sounded somewhere above, followed by the sounds of a scuffle and a man's voice raised in anger. The woman in front of him halted, spat a vicious curse, and ran for the stairs, shouldering past Seth in a flurry of skirts and a waft of cheap perfume. She thumped up the stairs, still yelling curses, and they heard a door slam. Another shrill screech cut the air, and Seth shot the vagrant a look. That scream spoke of real pain. His companion merely shrugged.

A man's raised voice mingled with Nolah's curses, and Seth heard a young girl sobbing. He was beginning to think he ought to investigate when he heard a crack, a heavy thump, and then silence. Alarmed, he moved toward the stairway, but the vagrant hissed for him to be still. Nolah appeared at the top of the stairs, her face red and angry. She massaged her right hand, the thick knuckles grazed and sore.

"Didn't I tell ya what t'do?" she yelled, her voice grating. "Next time remember what yer told and learn t'put up with it. They're not paying good coin t'hear ya screaming. Now get yerself cleaned up, silly wench, and then get Rafe t'chuck 'im out back." She took two steps down the stairs. "And don't forget t'search 'is pockets."

She stumped back down to the ground floor, shaking her head. She stared archly at Seth as if daring him to comment, but he averted his gaze, even though the sobs coming from above were enough to break the heart. Nolah brushed past him and put her hand on the door handle to the room in front of them.

The soft mutter of women's voices within, which hadn't been affected by the commotion above, fell silent. Seth followed as the vagrant entered the room, even more apprehensive now about what the man intended. When he saw the small group of girls gathered there, he thought he finally understood.

Five girls waited in the room, all young and slender, all of medium height, all blondes with shoulder-length hair, although one of them was more strawberry than blonde. This girl was instantly dismissed by the vagrant, and Nolah hustled her from the room, slapping her bottom hard. "Back t'work, me girl."

The vagrant turned to Seth, the nasty smile back on his face. "Well? Worked it out yet? Which shall we choose?"

Seth knew the girls had been selected for their passing resemblance to Jinella, but what the vagrant intended to do was still a mystery. He frowned at his ragged companion.

The vagrant shrugged. "The face doesn't matter. Pick the nearest in height and build. Come on, man, you see her every day."

Seth decided to do as he was bid. No doubt all would become clear in time. He moved toward the girls and looked them over carefully. They all tried to catch his eye, and one of them managed to caress him suggestively. He stepped hurriedly away from her groping fingers. Quite apart from having no interest in women, these jaded and overused trollops would have repulsed him even had he been desperate. He made his choice quickly, as there was really only one girl who fitted all the requirements, even if she was older by a good few years than Jinella. He pointed her out.

"This one's about right."

Nolah chased the three disappointed girls from the room. "Back t'work, the rest of ya." She shut the door and turned purposefully to the vagrant, holding out a meaty palm. "Pay up front, me lad."

The vagrant grinned and pulled more gold from beneath his cloak. The brothel madam stared at the gleaming coins, glancing suspiciously into his face. "What, ya want t'*buy* 'er?"

The vagrant grabbed her wrist and jerked her close against him. Ignoring the way she screwed up her nose against the stench, he gazed deeply into her eyes, raised his hand, and allowed the coins to trickle down the front of her bodice.

"In a manner of speaking. We want the use of a private, ground floor room and as much time as we need. We want no questions asked and no disturbance. We want to enjoy our pleasures in peace and privacy. Understand?"

Nolah nodded, one hand caressing the coins against her breasts. For that amount of gold she was prepared to grant them whatever they wanted.

"Of course, good sirs!" she simpered, affecting a noble accent.

Backing carefully away from the vagrant, she bowed them out of the room, swatting the chosen girl sharply on the arm. "You be sure an' give 'em a good time, honey. If I get any complaints, Rafe'll hear of it."

The girl cringed and hurried to catch up, choosing to hang on Seth's arm rather than braving the vagrant's stench. Nolah brushed past and they followed her as she led them deeper into the brothel, finally stopping outside a door well away from any others. She turned the handle and showed them in.

"This is me best room, gents. I trust it'll suit yer needs?"

The vagrant shoved the girl inside. "Well enough."

Seth followed, bemused, wondering if he would be expected to perform in front of his companion and how it would be received when he revealed his preferences. He heard Nolah close the door with a measure of fear.

Chapter Twenty-One

The vagrant waited until the sound of Nolah's footsteps faded before turning the key in the lock. He regarded the whore who still stood by Seth's side. Mindful of Nolah's warning, she simpered and moved closer.

"Where would you like me, sirs?" Her eyes roved over the room's various possibilities. "On the bed? On the floor? Over the chair? Which of you'll be first? I can show you all manner of delights. I'm one of Nolah's most popular girls. Why, only last week I—"

"Shut up!" The vagrant's command made the girl pout. "What we really want is for you to keep your mouth shut and to do as you're told. Understood?"

She nodded sullenly and the vagrant turned to Seth, indicating the bundle he carried. "Give her that."

Seth handed over the bundle and the girl accepted it resignedly. He imagined it wouldn't be the first time she'd had to wear something strange to satisfy a customer. But when she spilled the silks and satins out of their wrappings, she squealed in delight. Holding the exquisite green silk gown to her chest, she ran to the fly-specked mirror and paraded in front of it.

"Oooh," she cried, twirling to face them, "do I really get to wear this? Can I keep it after? The girls will be so jealous!"

"Just put it on, and be quick about it. If you're good—very good, mind!—we might let you keep it."

She didn't need telling twice and shucked off her shabby skirt and bodice, uncaring of their stares. The vagrant watched her hungrily, but Seth found nothing pleasurable or erotic in her grubby body and prominent ribs. And when she had finally worked out the intricacies of the gown and stood before them, Seth couldn't suppress a sneer of disapproval. He might hate Jinella for what she had done to his master, but seeing this common, dirty trollop dressed in one of Jinny's best gowns made him realize that, whatever he thought of her allegiances and loyalties, Jinella was a true lady.

The vagrant saw his distaste and grinned. "Prefer the real thing, don't you?"

Seth just stared at him, disconcerted by the comment's accuracy, although its meaning differed from his thought. The vagrant grinned wider. "Shoes?"

Seth pointed to the bundle. The girl dived for it, fishing out a pair of green satin court shoes. They were slightly too small, but she didn't care. She tottered gleefully about the room in the high heels in a grotesque parody of a lady's proud walk. It was as much as Seth could do to watch her and he was surprised at himself. He would never have thought he would care so much about the casual profaning of the social world he served.

The vagrant sifted through the material that had wrapped the gown and shoes. "Didn't you bring any jewelry, man?"

The whore paused in her mime, her mouth falling open.

Seth glared at him. "I couldn't get them without her noticing. You said to bring what she'd normally wear, but she always wears the same jewels. Most of them she never takes off, except to sleep."

His companion dismissed Seth's ire. "No matter, we can deal with that later."

The whore flounced away, pouting.

"Stand still, girl," the vagrant snapped, and she left off her posturing. He turned to Seth. "What do you think? Would she pass?"

Seth was still unsure of the charade's ultimate purpose, but answered as best he could. "Her height and build are about right, and her hair's the right color and length. If someone who didn't know Jinella well saw this girl from the back—standing still—they might mistake her for the mistress. But no one who knows her would. It certainly wouldn't fool that lover of hers. Not even from a distance. Her face is nothing like."

The vagrant sneered. "I've already told you the face doesn't matter. A general likeness is what we're after, and it seems we've achieved that. Well then, on to the next stage."

A peculiar expression came over the vagrant's face and Seth's stomach lurched. He felt uncomfortable, unsure what would be expected of him. He backed away a few steps, nearer the door.

The vagrant indicated the bed. The whore turned toward it, flouncing the gown's skirt with her hands. The room was shabbily furnished, the carpeting worn and grimy, the distemper on the walls stained and damp. In contrast, the big bed was amply draped with sheets and blankets and, although faded and thin, they appeared relatively clean. A profusion of limp pillows, their covers marred by faded stains, lay at the head of the bed and the girl leaned back against them, stretching seductively on the creaking mattress. She pushed the gown's wide neck farther down her shoulders to expose the junction of her breasts, and slowly slid the silky skirt higher up her legs, showing what was meant to be tantalizing glimpses of thigh. She smiled invitingly.

Seth's heart beat uncomfortably fast; not with the stirrings of desire, which he definitely didn't feel, but with the wary anticipation of what the vagrant might expect of him. He had no wish to explain himself in front of a whore, not least because it would be all around the brothel after they left. And now the filthy wastrel was turning to him, a nasty little smile quirking his lips.

"Well, my friend? Do you want her first?"

Seth's eyes flicked to the undesirable flesh the girl flaunted. The sight of her grimy thighs and the tangle of hair between them did nothing to decrease Seth's discomfort. He glanced back at his ragged companion, desperate for some excuse to refuse.

The man grinned savagely; his strange eyes alight with a faint ruby glow. Seth recoiled from the malice they contained.

"Oh, don't worry, Seth!" The vagrant's voice crawled sinuously from his mouth, altered, echoing. "I know your desires aren't slaked by the likes of her. I know exactly what pleasures *you* enjoy! So you can relax and leave this to me. I'll need your help again later, but for now your part is done."

The charnel stench flooded the room, causing even the hardened whore to gag. The vagrant turned away from Seth and climbed atop the girl on the bed, his knees pushing between her wide-flung legs. She was still half-propped against the pillows and he leaned over her, a hand to either side of her head. She closed her eyes when he bent down as if to kiss her, but instead he whipped one of the pillows from behind her neck and slammed it hard over her face, holding it firmly.

Seth gasped as the girl struggled, her desperate, muffled cries dimly heard through the pillow. Her arms flailed wildly, tried to prize the pillow from her face, but her tormentor was too strong. Her legs kicked out, but she could do no more than batter his unresponsive flanks with her heels, unable to gain purchase on his body. Grinning all the while, he hung on until her struggles slowed.

Seth watched open-mouthed, appalled and frightened. Whatever he had imagined the vagrant wanted with Jinella's clothing and jewelry, dressing a whore and then murdering her hadn't figured anywhere in his conjecture. He stared dumbly as the man leaned on the pillow, his eyes glinting red and his lips fixed in a mindless grin.

Once all movement ceased he raised the pillow, tossing it carelessly to the floor. He glanced at Seth, a sardonic twist to his mouth, and climbed off the creaking bed, leaving the whore limp and straddle-legged.

"Well, my friend? Now's your chance to see what you've been missing. Want to try her out? You never know, you might like it. Don't worry, I won't say anything to Nolah if you're not quite up to the job. And it's not as if *she'll* tell any tales, is it?" He hooked his thumb at the lifeless whore.

Seth, aghast, stared at the grinning wastrel, disgusted to his very soul. The cold-blooded murder was shocking enough, but the filthy man's suggestion, seriously meant, appalled Seth even more. He wouldn't put it past the fellow to carry out the act himself.

"How could you—" He choked with disgust, unable to express his revulsion. Sickened, he turned away from the vagrant's mocking laughter, wondering what he had let himself in for. He just prayed he would come out of it alive.

✣ ✣ ✣ ✣ ✣

"What do you mean by accosting us like this? Where's my coachman? How dare you waylay us! What the *hell* do you think you're doing?"

Sir Regus tried his best, but it was only bravado. The situation was hopeless and the best he could hope for was a courageous showing in front of his lady. He had to make a gesture in defense of her honor.

The brigands could tell there was no steel behind his bluster. He waved his belt knife, but it was as blunt as a spade and held no edge. Even had it been sharp—even had it been a sword—Sir

Regus knew he wouldn't have impressed these hardened ruffians.

They ignored his posturing and loped around the coach, eyeing its rich fabrics and gold trimmings while their leader stood nonchalantly at the opened door. He pointed the tip of his sword at Sir Regus's ample chest.

"Get down."

Sir Regus couldn't think of a reason to disobey. He had already given up on what gold he had left, as well as his and his wife's jewelry, but he still had hope for their lives. The brigands' faces were hidden beneath cavernous hoods, which implied their victims might be allowed to live if they gave no trouble. As far as Regus was concerned, penury was a better option than death. He got down.

"You too, Madam."

Lady Corina opened her mouth to scream, but caught sight of her husband's warning glance. She was trembling and fearful, but not yet hysterical. She was also intelligent enough to realize what her husband was doing. Furious and terrified though she was, she managed some semblance of dignity as she climbed from the carriage. She spurned the mocking hand extended to help her, looking scornfully from its filthy skin and ragged nails directly into its owner's hooded eyes.

Sir Regus caught his breath. The brigands' leader held Corina's haughty gaze just long enough to see the pride falter, and turned away. Regus nearly fainted with relief.

"Search them."

"You will *not!*"

The ruffian turned back at Corina's shrill protest. "Lady, you will agree to be searched or you will be stripped. The choice is yours."

Her mouth dropped open and Regus feared she would say something stupid. To forestall her, he reached for the limp pouch at his waist and pulled it free. He handed it to the nearest ruffian and then began removing his rings. He stared meaningfully at his wife until the set of her mouth relaxed and he knew the danger was past. She lowered her eyes and raised her hands to the diamond necklace at her throat.

The ruffian leader looked satisfied as he crouched to survey the small pile of gold and jewels. Another pile consisted of clothing, although he hadn't carried out his threat to strip them. It was fearfully cold now and full darkness wasn't far off. It wasn't part of his instructions that they should freeze to death before they reached the city gates, so he had left them the basics. He glanced up as they stood shivering before him.

"It's awful cold. I'd move about a bit if I were you. The walk back'll warm you up. Come on, lads, someone get up on that coach. Those beasts'll fetch a tidy sum and we'll have us a cozy place to sleep tonight."

Sir Regus gaped incredulously as the coach pulled away. The remaining brigands mounted their horses and he ran to their leader angrily. "Here, man, you can't abandon us out here! Surely you don't expect us to make our own way back to the city? My wife can't possibly walk all that way!"

One of the ruffians gave a derisive snort. "Why not? She got two legs, ain't she?"

The leader scratched his neck. "It's not so far, and walkin's good for you. Like I said, it'll warm you up. Better get goin' if you want to get there before nightfall. And just you take care, milord; there's some mighty rough folks about in these woods, don't y'know!"

Sir Regus heard the echoes of their laughter long after they had vanished into the trees.

✣ ✣ ✣ ✣ ✣

By the time Seth recovered from the immediate shock of

witnessing a murder, the vagrant had straightened the dead girl's limbs and clothing. He looked down at her critically, and then nodded. "No marks."

He turned to Seth. Catching the revulsion lingering in his eyes, he grinned. "What's the matter, my servile friend? Too squeamish for the dirty work? Well, that's a pity, for we're not finished yet."

He showed no sign of remorse and Seth was pale with fear and disgust. "You never said we were going to kill her!"

The vagrant sneered nastily. "Oh, and what did you think we were going to do with her once we'd dressed her in your mistress's clothes? Invite her out to dinner? Take her dancing? For the gods' sake, man, use your brains. I know some of the things *you* like doing, my friend, and you're not above a bit of rough stuff yourself. So stop your sanctimonious carping and help me. We're not done yet."

Bending, he picked up the length of material Seth had used to wrap Jinella's gown and shoes and tossed it casually over the dead girl's body. He pushed the limp form roughly onto its stomach and wrapped the folds tightly around it. He shot Seth a look over his shoulder. "Come and carry this."

Seth felt like refusing, but he was committed now, a witness and accessory to murder. And it wasn't over yet. He was afraid he would be deeply involved in at least one more violent act committed this night, if not two. Drawing a deep breath, he moved to the bed and accepted the heavy, limp burden over his shoulder, ignoring the sardonic look in his companion's red-rimmed eyes.

Without thinking, he asked, "How will we get out without being seen?"

"You do like asking stupid questions, don't you?" The wastrel glared at him. "First, I've paid Nolah enough gold to murder and carry off half her girls without her complaining, and second, I chose this particular house of dubious pleasure for one very good reason. There's a tunnel running under the city that leads from the yard of this building right out past the castle and into the edges of Loxton Forest."

Seth gasped. "What? How do you know that?"

"Oh, for pity's sake!" The vagrant was now thoroughly incensed. "I'd have had less trouble from that whore than I'm getting from you! What the master ever saw in you, I can't imagine. How do you *think* I know about it? And if you can't work it out, you can stay ignorant. Now we've still got work to do, so keep your mind on the job, do as you're told, and *shut up!*"

Cowed and humiliated by the vagrant's manner, Seth hitched the whore's body higher on his shoulder and followed his companion, determined not to speak another word. The wastrel went to the door and turned the key, peering out into the deserted corridor before stepping out and beckoning to Seth. The manservant obeyed and his ragged companion closed the door behind them, relocking it and pocketing the key.

He led the way out the back of the brothel, emerging through a rickety stable door into a small yard, dark and dingy. He bent down to a wooden hatch set into the cobbled yard and heaved on a large iron ring bolted through the wood. The hatch came up easily and Seth saw a set of wooden steps leading down into stygian darkness below.

"Set her down and get on that ladder."

Seth did so, treading carefully on the damp, slippery rungs. He soon reached the bottom and found the tunnel was barely high enough for him to stand upright. He stared up at the circle of sky above him and saw it vanish as the girl's body was lowered toward him. He caught her and moved out of the way as his rank companion descended the steps, pulling the hatchway closed after him.

They stood in total darkness, Seth completely at the other's mercy. He felt the wastrel push past him and start off down the tunnel. Not wishing to be left behind in this light-deserted place, he hurried to follow. As he did so his foot caught on something that gave, and he nearly fell. A frightened curse burst unbidden from his mouth, the awful events of the evening and an overactive imagination overcoming any caution he might have felt.

"What the hell is it now?" the wastrel hissed furiously, a disembodied voice in the dark.

"Caught my foot on something," Seth mumbled, hearing the nervous waver in his own voice and hating himself for betraying it.

The wastrel seemed amused and muttered, "Rafe's leavings," under his breath as he set off once more. Seth stumbled as he followed, going cold as he remembered Nolah's instructions to the sobbing girl on the upper floor. Refusing to consider what else might be secreted in the black depths of this cold, clammy tunnel, he hurried on.

The tunnel seemed to go on forever and not a glimmer of light reached their eyes. It was only wide enough for one man—both Seth's elbows touched the dripping walls—but there were no more obstructions underfoot. Fearful of losing his way in the dark, Seth trod so closely behind the wastrel that the charnel reek was constantly in his nostrils. He could even feel the occasional brush of the grubby cloak against his legs.

Despite his burden and the exertion of the walk, Seth was cold. The air was damp and chill with the seeping cold of winter leaking through from somewhere above their heads. Occasionally, Seth could hear the drip of water and feel a movement of fresher air on his cheek. The tunnel must have vents to the outer world, or maybe its structure was unsound. He shied away from that thought. Being buried below ground if the tunnel should give way wasn't a happy thought. He wanted to ask how much farther they had to go, but decided against it. He simply hitched the whore's dead weight higher on his aching shoulder and walked in silence.

The air in the tunnel eventually changed. Seth caught the scent of damp trees and wet earth, and surmised they must be outside the city limits. He allowed himself a sigh of relief. This was expelled as a deep grunt when he cannoned into the back of the vagrant, who had come to a dead halt with no warning.

"Watch it, idiot! Gods, but you're useless."

Seth muttered an apology and backed off, his aching arms pleading to be released of their burden. He heard the wastrel fumbling about in the darkness. It sounded as if he was digging in the ground, or scrabbling at the walls. And then Seth felt a rush of freezing air and could dimly see the night sky before him.

"Come on, man," the vagrant hissed.

Seth hurried out of the tunnel, finding himself in a small cave with bushes at its entrance. He turned around quickly, but the bulk of the whore's body blocked his sight and he didn't see the closure of the tunnel behind him.

"Where are we?" he whispered, uncaring of the vagrant's censure.

"Just on the edge of the master's estate." For once, there was no sneer in the vagrant's voice. "Put her down, man, your arms must be half-dead."

Seth raised his brows at this unexpected show of concern. His arms were painful indeed, as was his back, and he laid the body down, rubbing his aching muscles. "What now?"

"Once you've rested, we carry on to the mansion. I trust you can get us inside the house without being seen?"

"Of course. The mistress will be in her rooms after dinner and the only other servant in the house will be that slut of a housekeeper."

"Ah yes." Amusement colored the wastrel's tone. "The housekeeper. I take it you don't approve of her employment in the master's household?"

Seth didn't even notice his companion's dismissal of Jinny's right to the mansion. His indignation at Alice's appointment came surging to the fore.

"Approve? Of course I don't approve! She's had no training except in how to lie on her back and spread her legs. She's only there because of pity and ignorance. Housekeeper! She couldn't even keep her own maidenhead."

The filthy man smiled. "Calm down, man, I know how you feel. Well, tonight's your opportunity to do something about it. I have specific instructions concerning the master's niece, but none whatsoever about the housekeeper, except to be rid of her. What do you think? Can you take care of it?"

Seth stilled, regarding his companion steadily. "What're you going to do?"

The wastrel shook his head. "Not yet. Come on, enough rest. We must get to the mansion and hide that body till we need it. You think about what I've said and make up your mind. When the time's right, there'll be no more chances. Either you deal with the slut or I will. The choice is yours. Now hurry up."

Seth gathered up the whore's cooling body. It didn't repulse him as much as when it was warm, and he reflected on what the vagrant had said as he once more followed his unsavory companion. He had been correct in his assumption that there would be more violence done this night. He was already a part of it, and neither his wasted friend nor his absent master would betray Seth's involvement. So why not settle a few scores? Why not strike a blow for his master? Why not relieve the burden of injustice the Baron's false indictment had raised in Seth's breast?

How satisfying it would be, he thought, to see the fear in Alice's eyes, to watch her realize she was about to pay for usurping a position under his master's roof.

Yes, he admitted to himself, very satisfying indeed.

Chapter Twenty-Two

Sofira made her way through the dark halls of Lerric's palace until she came to the curtained stairway leading to the lower floor. She knew she would be unobserved. Elias's messenger wouldn't be prowling the palace—not with Captain Bassan keeping an eye on him. Bassan knew better than to let his lord down.

Parting the heavy folds of cloth concealing the door, Sofira pulled it open. She descended the dark stair, lit only by a single torch fluttering in its sconce halfway down. It was barely adequate, but she'd grown used to the dim hallways and stairwells. Besides, it was winter. All large, stone buildings were dark in winter. It was too expensive to heat and light unfrequented areas at this time of year.

Reaching the ground floor, she started toward the doorway to her betrothed's private rooms. She was surprised to see one of his personal servants sitting just outside. They were usually off doing Reen's unfathomable bidding. She wrinkled her nose as she came closer. Why he couldn't get them to wash, she had no idea.

The man looked up as she approached, his expression bordering on insolent. She had learned that such emotions or reactions were beyond these men now; they only portrayed what the Baron felt and possessed no independent thought. The power he held over them was part of what he had become, although she didn't really understand it. It had to do with why he was now ready to take his revenge on those who had wronged him.

Gazing into the servant's blank eyes, Sofira shivered. As much as she shared and supported Reen's thirst for vengeance, this strange power of his left her nervous and cold. She had long ago accepted that Sullyan's shocking revelation during his trial was indeed true. Reen possessed similar, if embryonic, powers to that of the Artesan woman. And although they repulsed Sofira, she acknowledged the aptness of Reen learning to use them against his archenemy. Yet the thought of his body and mind being infused with these arcane and unnatural powers unsettled her. She had to fight to ignore their obvious effects on him whenever she spoke with him.

He had told her it was the unnaturally forced acknowledgment of his birthright that had so warped and changed his body. His suffering and torment were entirely due to the occult energies the vengeful witch had wakened in his soul. Sofira wept when he described his titanic, desperate struggle to retain any of his natural being. He had brought her to her knees with the tale of how he awakened in the night, screaming, terrifying visions of the burning Wheel of Perdition hanging before his ruined eyes. How he pleaded piteously for deliverance from his torment. And how he had been vouchsafed the only route to salvation: the casting down and utter destruction of his archenemy.

Sofira believed and trusted him utterly. Hadn't she heard some of those terrifying screams? And if they hadn't, at first, sounded like the Baron's voice, she only had to think on the dreadful torture he had suffered and the hideous deformation of his body to understand why his voice should be so changed. His moving confession of his darkest fears and terrible weaknesses only served to strengthen her desire to succor him, to aid him, to throw all her weight and support behind him in a fervent effort to restore him to his rightful state.

Now she stood before his door, the parchment from Blaine in her hand, contemplating his reaction to her news. Would he be nervous and afraid, as she was? Would he be furious? Would he rant and rage at her, as he sometimes did when the pressures of his condition were too much for him to bear? Or would he be calculating and calm, as she so loved to see him? There was only one way to find out.

She regarded the seated servant. "I would speak with your master."

He turned blank eyes on her then spoke. "The master bids you enter."

Sofira went cold. This was the first time she had seen firm evidence of the unnatural connection Reen had with his servants. Until now, he had guarded the reality of his abilities, but maybe her sympathetic reaction to his piteous story and her avowal of love and loyalty had eased those restrictions. Much as she needed him to trust her, she could almost wish they hadn't.

Eyes wide, Sofira pushed the door open. A dim glow of firelight met her gaze, but the room was draped in shadow. This was normal. She knew she would never see her beloved in full light. She'd come to think of the shadows as dark friends, wrapping and protecting the man she loved. The amber glow of embers was mysterious and romantic, speaking to the little girl buried far within her bitter soul.

"Come in, my love. I hadn't expected to see you again this day."

The low voice came out of the far corner where a high-backed chair was pulled close to the fire. She moved into his lair, her satin gown whispering across the carpet, and came to stand before his chair.

Reen smiled up at her. The dim firelight softened the planes of his face, almost as if the skin were sloughing off, and it must be an effect of the embers to make it look mottled and ruined. He held out his hand to her and she felt his wasted fingers.

"My love, I had to come. There's been a development."

He frowned. "Oh? And what is that?"

She showed him the parchment. "The messenger arrived but half an hour ago. I came to you as soon as I could. They will arrive before noon tomorrow."

He indicated she should read it out, his ruined eyes no good for such work, and she swiftly told him what the parchment contained. He gasped, his bony fingers gripping the arms of the chair so hard they appeared like fleshless claws. His nails tore the fabric. She could see the tremble of his body and registered the intense fear in his ruined eyes. Her voice faltered to silence, the only sound his hoarse breath.

"My love?" she ventured.

Reen stirred, coughed harshly. He spat a filthy imprecation, causing Sofira to flinch. She'd expected some such reaction, yet the venom in his tone was vicious. He looked utterly, completely, terrified.

He ignored her hovering, muttering furiously under his breath. "I am not ready! It is too soon! They'll sniff out my secrets, question my servants. What of events in Port Loxton, what of my plans there? How will I find the strength—"

Sofira, unnerved by his prattling, laid a tentative hand on his arm. "What can I do to help you, my love? I will do whatever you tell me. I can be clever, you know I can! Just tell me how you wish this handled, and I will do it."

He rounded on her, eyes blazing, spittle flying from his lips. "And Lerric? What of your craven father? Will he do as he's bid? Does he realize his future, as well as yours, lies in obeying my commands? Does he, Sofira?"

She gazed at him earnestly. "He does, my love. But I will

remind him again. He'll not let us down, Hezra, I pledge you that."

"He'd better not! One false move while Elias is here and all of our plans are ruined. Not only that, but both your lives will be forfeit for harboring a convicted traitor. As for me— Well, you know what fate will befall me, do you not? For it was you who begged it for me. Do you remember? Do you recall how you pleaded for my torture, my death, for the dreadful torment of the Wheel? Do you?"

She stared in dismay, his fury and scorn whipping her heart, scoring it with pain. She covered her face, tears leaking between her fingers.

Through her misery she heard his harsh breathing, heard it slow to gasps. Finally, Reen touched her on the arm, his voice calmer.

"Sofira, my only love, please forgive me. I was overwrought. I forgot myself. I don't blame you for your actions that day. I know you acted under duress. You were protecting your children and your position, as a Queen and mother should. It's just that I'm so weak, so vulnerable, and the thought of having to skulk away in hiding while they parade their haughty pride above me fills my soul with fear. Come, my lady. Look at me."

His carefully worded apology worked its usual charm. She couldn't resist his tugging at her conscience and playing on her love. She dropped her hands and gazed on the gentle smile he displayed for her benefit.

"There, my lady! With your help and strength I will endure. Their presence here—and especially that of my archenemy—will pain me beyond measure, but with your help—" She stirred and he frowned. "What is it, Sofira?"

"Oh, my love, I should have told you at once. *She* won't be here. Elias is bringing Blaine with him and his major; you know, the one who killed your spy at the Manor and spoke for the injured cadet at the trial. But your real enemy—the witch—*she* isn't coming."

Reen swooned, and she barely caught his shoulders. It was fleeting and he soon recovered, but in that brief moment Sofira saw something grotesque, something horrific. Instead of the man she loved, she held a monster in her arms, a scabrous, leprous parody of a man with decaying skin and scarecrow limbs. Her hands flew once more to her mouth and she stepped away with a tiny scream.

Reen stood shakily, passing a hand across his brow. He looked frightened and hastened to reassure her.

"I am so sorry, Sofira, my love. I never wanted you to see that. It is *her* influence, her curse upon me. This is what I've had to live with these past years. I've been protecting you, hiding it from you. It is illusion only—yes, she's that powerful—but this is what she would have me become. This is why I need your support and your love. If I thought her malice could destroy your love for me, turn you against me, then I couldn't go on. I'd cease striving against her might and cast myself onto the Wheel of Perdition. It would be preferable to losing your love."

Despite her shock and horror, Sofira was moved. The witch must be vengeful indeed if she could turn a man like the Baron into such a deformed monster.

"Oh, Hezra."

Sofira came close, took him in her arms. She could sense the truth of his words, for the scarecrow semblance was gone, replaced by his normal, if undernourished, body. How could she fail to help him, if this was the future he faced? He needed her strength and commitment as much as she needed his help to regain what she'd lost. They were bound by common goals, common suffering. Her heart had been deformed as surely as his body would be by the machinations of the Artesan witch. They both needed the healing the other could offer.

As she felt Reen's arms around her, his breath upon her cheek, the room seemed to take on a subtle ruby glow, as if the very fire approved their plans.

✣ ✣ ✣ ✣ ✣

Seth was panting hard by the time they reached the mansion. It had taken them a good hour to traverse the estate, but thankfully they didn't have to divert their route to avoid meeting anyone. It was full dark and freezing cold and no one was abroad but them.

Seth's long-suffering gaze was fixed on the uncaring back of his companion. The man hadn't once offered to share Seth's burden and the short respite after they emerged from the tunnel was long since forgotten. His muscles burned with pain and he was sure he now had one shoulder lower than the other.

He stopped as the vagrant held up a hand, realizing that they were in the private grounds of the mansion itself. His grinning companion turned, ignoring the hostility in Seth's eyes.

"Come on, man, this is where your knowledge comes in. Where can we hide that till we need it? It has to be somewhere close to the house."

He jerked his thumb at the dead whore. Seth dumped the body on the snowy ground, ignoring the vagrant's hiss of displeasure. He took his time in stretching the kinks out of his back and shoulders before answering the vagrant's question. He'd had enough of playing the donkey. It was time the wastrel realized Seth had worth and use beyond the obeying of instructions or the carrying of burdens.

"I'm not telling you anything else until you tell me exactly what you've got planned for tonight. You need me. You need me to get you into the house unobserved. You need me to tell you where the mistress is and where the housekeeper will be. You need help with what you have planned and you need to know I won't betray you after. I think that deserves a measure of trust on your part, don't you?"

There was silence in the freezing darkness. The wastrel never took his eyes from Seth's defiant figure, standing as he was with his hands on his hips and a dead whore at his feet. Slowly, very slowly, a ruby-red glow appeared in the vagrant's eyes and a sardonic grin grew about his mouth. The air around him seemed to shimmer and Seth's eyes watered as the charnel reek of maggot-infested flesh entered his nose. An unwelcome memory of the wastrel's ravaged chest rose in his mind and his own flesh crawled. He backed up a pace as the vagrant stepped closer, but an invisible hand closed upon his muscles, holding him firmly in place.

"Let me tell you a few truths, my friend." The vagrant's voice was low and calm, but menace lurked below it. Seth shivered, staring helplessly into the ruby depths of his eyes.

"It may surprise you to know that I don't actually require your help for any of this. I have an intimate knowledge of the mansion, even to the bedchamber of the mistress where she entertains her unnatural lover. I can fulfill my instructions without your help. As to betraying me afterward, well, that would be a foolish move on your part. For the master knows where to find you, never doubt that! And he can work his will upon you even as he has upon me. Perhaps you need a reminder of what your fate would be should you choose to defy him."

The vagrant's hands moved to the cloth over his breast and tore it open. The stench that assailed Seth's nostrils made him retch uncontrollably, and the sight of that crawling, rotting flesh churned his stomach. The strange hold on his muscles disappeared and he fell vomiting to the ground, hands clutching futilely at snow.

There was a low chuckle from the vagrant and the stench faded. Seth raised his sweating face, his mouth damp and vile. He picked up a handful of clean snow and bit into it, rolling it on his tongue until the worst of the bile was gone. He spat it out. A hand clamped on his arm and he allowed the vagrant to heave him to his feet. The man regarded him with what appeared to be sympathy, and Seth thought, just for a fleeting moment, he also caught the echo of a deep and desperate longing. Yet when he looked again the sardonic twist was back on the cracked lips, and he knew he was mistaken.

"Why, then?" he croaked, his throat raw from the bile. "Why bring me at all if you don't need me?"

The vagrant shrugged. "The master thought you'd like a chance at revenge. He needs to know who's loyal to him. When he returns, he'll need trusted retainers to help him hold his power. Why he chose you, I'll never know. But he did, and now it's up to you. You can either make up your mind once and for all to follow my directions, or you can leave. Make your choice, but make it quick. I have other concerns this night."

Seth stared at the vagrant. He knew exactly what he was going to do. He'd just wanted a measure of respect from this wretched creature before they continued. Now Seth realized his mistake. The man wasn't his own master. Far from acting under his own direction, he was a puppet, a tool, no longer a man at all. Seth had no desire to end up the same way. He would treat the wastrel as if he were the Baron himself, and was only glad he had been shown the truth before he'd gone too far.

"I'm with you," he said. "There's a storage barn next to the stables where we can hide the body. The stable boy'll be at his home eating supper and won't return until later to check his charges. And the barn is hidden from the servants' wing. Shall we go?" He heaved the whore's body over his shoulder without being told.

The wastrel grinned and waved him forward to lead the way. Seth trod carefully over the deep-packed snow, making for the back of the mansion. He could see firelight reflected in some of the building's windows, and lamplight glowing in Jinella's bedchamber. There were no fresh hoof-prints in the snow of the yard, so he knew Taran wasn't with her. Whether the Court Artesan featured in the wastrel's plans, Seth didn't know, and he wasn't going to ask any more questions. He would concentrate on what he was told and leave it at that. He led the way into the storage barn and deposited the cold, limp body onto a pile of clean straw.

✣ ✣ ✣ ✣ ✣

Sir Regus and Lady Corina were on their last legs, too weak even to shiver by the time they saw Loxton's Forest Gate looming out of the darkness. Corina, who had been sobbing with cold and exhaustion for the past half-hour, gave a faint cry of relief and swooned in her husband's arms. Sir Regus grunted under her weight and staggered onward. He cried out, "Ho there, the gate!" but couldn't make his voice carry. The gate was thick oak timbers; the guards in the gatehouse couldn't hear his cry.

Fury and frustration fueled Sir Regus's last steps as he staggered up to the gate. He propped his lady against the wood and searched until he found a stout, frozen branch, then pounded with all his might against the frost-slick oak.

"Guards, guards!" he yelled as loudly as he could. When he heard the welcome sound of the postern being opened, he followed his lady's example and slid bonelessly to the ground.

"It was brigands, I tell you, and they robbed us of everything we had! It's disgraceful! You're supposed the keep the forest safe for innocent travelers. Call yourself a soldier? Well, man, what are you going to do about it? My coach and team are gone, as are my rings, my lady's diamonds, and my gold. I demand recompense! I demand retaliation! I demand you give me their heads on a plate! I demand—"

Two of Denny's men called for a coach and escorted Sir Regus and his lady up to the castle from the Forest Gate. The exhausted pair found themselves fussed over and tended most gratifyingly on the ride up to the castle. Denny received them in the courtyard and called instantly for Elias's physician to see to Lady Corina, who was taken to a warm bed in the section of the infirmary reserved for the King's household. Her husband demanded the right to present his complaints to Vassa and Levant before he would even consider being checked over, so Denny brought him to Levant's apartment, where Vassa and Taran joined them.

Colonel Vassa held up a hand to forestall the noble's rant.

"Sir Regus, calm yourself, I beg you. You will cause yourself harm if you don't desist. Sit here by the fire and drink your brandy; it will do you good. You've had a bad experience, there's no doubt, and you've been valiant and strong in the defense of your lady. But you're safe now and there's nothing we can do before first light. So please, calm yourself and let us help you. Taran, hand him that brandy, will you?"

Taran extended the crystal glass tumbler toward the shivering man. He exchanged a glance with Vassa over Sir Regus's head as the furious but exhausted man collapsed into the offered chair and took the spirit. He cast a look at the Adept and muttered ungracious thanks. Sir Regus was one of those nobles who were highly suspicious of Artesans and he didn't much like being beholden to one.

The door opened and Major Denny stood there. He caught Vassa's eye.

"How is he, sir?"

Vassa left the shivering noble to Levant's sympathetic ministrations and moved toward Denny, Taran following. The Adept watched the indignant Regus, who was reiterating his demands, somewhat revived by the effects of Elias's best brandy.

The Colonel glanced at Sir Regus over his shoulder. "He's all right. He's more concerned about the loss of his gold and jewels than the danger to his person. But I have to admit, it's a serious assault. They're lucky to have escaped with their lives. We don't stand a chance of recovering any of what they've lost, so Elias will have to recompense them from the Treasury. Denny, we must be seen to be doing something positive to stop these recent attacks. The King instructed me to send out patrols after Neremiah's murder; he thinks the villain might be hiding in Loxton Forest. I want you to take two full details out first thing in the morning, no matter how foul the weather. Yes, I do know any tracks will have disappeared by then, but you might find traces of the carriage, or the clothes. Just do your best. And shut the city down, will you? I want double the security on the gates and no one to enter or leave without a search. Do you understand? No one."

Denny whistled softly. "There're a few nobles who'll kick against that, Colonel."

Vassa's look was grim. "They can kick all they like. Just remind them of Sir Regus's assault and His Immanence's murder. Elias will deal with any serious complaints when he returns, if anyone's foolish enough to challenge us. Go on, you'd best organize your men for the morning. I want those patrols out at first light. Taran's going to pass this on to the General when we've finished here, and if he has any other instructions I'll send a messenger to the garrison. I'll see you in the morning for the final details."

Denny nodded. "Tell Sir Regus the King's physician is satisfied his lady has taken no lasting harm. She should be well enough to return to her home in the morning."

Denny sketched a hasty salute and left, no doubt already picking which men would ride with him. Taran knew the Major would lead one of the patrols himself. He was affronted by the resurgence of brigands in the forest, seeing it as a personal slur on his abilities. Taran gave a small smile. Denny would see to it the ruffians were wiped out. By the time Elias returned, the forest would be as safe as the castle park.

When Vassa returned to the fireside, Sir Regus had finally run out of steam. The shock of his ordeal and the effects of the brandy combined to overcome his outrage. His speech was slurred and his eyes had glazed. Lord Levant shot a glance at Vassa as the Colonel approached.

"I think Sir Regus could do with an escort to help him to the infirmary. Let the physician check him over while he's still awake. No, Sir Regus," Levant continued as the noble tried to protest, "I've kept you from your rest long enough. We've already organized reprisals against those responsible. You can rely on Colonel Vassa to do all in his power to bring them to justice. We'll also inform his Majesty and act on any instructions he gives us. I will personally visit you and your lady in the morning, if the physician allows it, and I'll provide an escort to take you home when you're ready to leave. Come on, man, up you get. Let's get you to a warm bed."

Two servants, summoned by Vassa, appeared at the door to take Sir Regus in hand. Levant closed the door on them and leaned against it with a sigh. "Poor beggar."

Taran regarded Levant. "Shall I contact the General now, my Lord?"

Levant nodded, returned to the fireside, and picked up his own glass of spirit. "Better let Elias know as soon as possible. Not that he needs any more problems. He'll have his hands full with Lerric's usual complaints."

Taran took himself to a quiet corner and stilled his mind. He was much more proficient at this now, but the murmur of voices could still interfere with his concentration. Levant and Vassa spoke softly as Taran communed with General Blaine.

Blaine approved Vassa's arrangements with Denny, and Elias instructed Levant to make an inventory of everything Sir Regus and his lady had lost and to issue them with a promissory note from the Treasury. Taran then took the time to inform Sullyan at the Manor of the day's latest events.

I do not like these developments, my friend, she told him. *I do not like them at all. Tell Jerrim to be doubly on his guard, and tell Denny and his men to be careful. Loxton Forest is too easy a place to hide in. He will have his work cut out to find those villains.*

Taran broke the link, Sullyan's anxiety reflected in his own heart. He passed the messages on to Levant and Vassa.

"If you're done with my services, I'll go down to the garrison and see if there's anything Denny wants me to do," he said. Vassa waved him away.

He found Denny in the senior officers' hall, fellan by his elbow and the familiar pack of cards on the table. He hailed Taran as soon as he appeared. "Are you up for losing some more of your coin this evening?"

Taran was amazed to find the Major sitting calm and unruffled at the card table. "Isn't there something else you should be doing right now?"

Denny frowned before his expression cleared. "Oh, you mean shouldn't I be running about yelling orders and organizing patrols?" He grinned. "I did it earlier this evening as soon as I heard what had happened. I'm leading one patrol and Ardoch's taking the other. Valustin'll stay here in case of any disturbances in the city. Now, are you going to sit and take these cards or must I find some other fool … er, friend to fleece?"

Taran hesitated. Much as he enjoyed playing cards with Denny, he really ought to ride over to the estate and tell Jinny the latest developments. She might not even have heard of Neremiah's murder, although her servants usually picked up most of what occurred in the city. And he still hadn't taken her uncle's possessions to her. But the hour was late and he had not sent a note to tell her he was coming. After their last meeting he was unsure of his reception. Turning up unannounced late at night wouldn't endear him to her or make her receptive to his apologies.

He sighed heavily. Was he being cowardly again? Was the lateness of the hour simply a convenient excuse to put off what was bound to be a painful meeting? If he waited till the morning he would leave Vassa and Levant without the means to communicate with Elias should they need him. It would take him a couple of hours at least to ride to the estate, talk to Jinny, and then ride back. Strictly speaking, he was on duty during daylight hours and wasn't supposed to leave the castle until evening.

Denny watched him impatiently as the other card school members took their seats. He dealt the cards and pushed a hand toward Taran. "Come on, man. Let's see the color of your courage."

Taran smiled and allowed himself to be persuaded. It really was too late. By the time he had harnessed Bucyrus and ridden through the falling snow, Jinny would have gone to bed and the household would be in darkness. She would hardly thank him for rousing everyone just to give her more bad news.

He sighed and picked up his hand.

Chapter Twenty-Three

It was long past midnight and the snow was falling heavily. They had heard young Matty return to check on the horses and replenish their hay, and then they heard him go home to his bed. Then Seth watched the house from the doorway until all the servants retired for the night. All light save the faint glow of banked fires had disappeared from the mansion's windows when the wastrel glanced over at Seth. He grinned. "Time to go."

Seth's stomach churned, but he rose from his seat of straw, wrapping his cloak tight about him. "What do you want me to do?"

"First, we have to deal with the housekeeper. Have you decided whether you're up to the job?"

Seth ignored the sarcastic tone, determined not to let the vagrant rile him. The poor wretch was to be pitied; he didn't deserve Seth's anger. "I'm up to it. How do you suggest we go about it?"

The faintest ruby light could be seen deep within the vagrant's eyes. "Up to you. But if you're asking for advice, I'd say a swift knife to the throat, unless you want to keep her alive for later. No? Thought not. That kind of pleasure isn't to your taste, is it?"

Seth ignored the gibe. "Are you coming with me or shall I signal you when it's done?"

The wastrel gave a wide grin. "Oh, I'll be right behind you." The menace in his voice and the light in his eyes left Seth in no doubt as to why.

He shivered. "Let's get on with it."

The vagrant bowed mockingly and Seth led the way from the barn.

They emerged into the snow which swirled around them, settling on heads and shoulders. The whore's body was left in the barn. Seth presumed they'd deal with the mansion's two occupants before it would be required. He glanced over his shoulder as he neared the rear entrance to the mansion, the door closest to where Alice would be sleeping. The vagrant was right behind him.

Seth approached the scullery door and turned the knob. In the Baron's day this door was never locked, a convenient way back into the house for anyone staying out late. Jinella, however, was more concerned for security than her uncle had been and also had firm rules concerning her servants' private arrangements. Anyone wishing to indulge in personal relationships had to do it in their spare time and away from her house. As Seth had expected, the door was locked.

He felt around the lintel, his experienced fingers finding the loose brick. He worked it out and grasped the iron key it concealed. Replacing the brick, he opened the door. He and his companion slipped into the scullery, closing the door on the freezing snow outside.

Seth waited for his eyes to grow used to the darkness, but he knew every inch of this house and could have walked it blindfolded if necessary. He was soon moving across the room, followed by his sinister shadow.

They trod silently through the kitchens toward the stair leading to the housekeeper's chamber. There was no sound from Alice's room as they stood outside, Seth's breath coming heavy and fast. His heart beat wildly and his palms were sweating despite the chill. He took hold of the hilt of his belt knife, loosening it in the sheath.

He risked a look at his ragged companion, recoiling from the unholy light shining deep in his blank, disturbing eyes.

The vagrant raised matted brows, lips twisted sardonically. Seth felt anger rise in his breast, taking the expression as a slur on his courage and resolve. He put his hand to the latch of Alice's door and silently lifted it, pushing the door open. The door swung noiselessly and the faint glow of the banked fire revealed Alice's sleeping figure.

Seth slid his knife from its sheath and approached the housekeeper. He stood looking down at her oblivious face, allowing his feelings of resentment and indignation to flood his chest. She had no business here! She had testified against his master and betrayed him. She should have stayed in the city brothels. Seth felt his hand shake as his anger grew.

Before the vagrant could decide to take matters into his own hands, Seth dropped his weight on top of Alice, clamping his hand over her mouth. She woke at once and heaved beneath him, but he had her tightly. Her terrified eyes widened when he showed her the knife, holding it menacingly close to her throat. He felt her body's tremor and the hiss of her breath beneath his restraining hand. She whimpered deep in her throat, but could make no other sound.

The vagrant stirred. "Quickly, man. If you don't want to keep her, do it swiftly. We have no time for games."

Seth ignored the man. He needed to be fully in command of himself to do this. He had no feelings for Alice except resentment, but he wasn't a cold-blooded killer. He had never done anything remotely like this before and didn't want to botch it. Especially not before a witness.

Ignoring the girl's terrified whimpers, he set the keen steel to her throat. She read his dreadful intention and her instinctive panic lent her a surge of strength he hadn't expected. She nearly escaped his arms in her frantic struggle to get free, and the knife cut raggedly into her throat. Luckily, Seth's hand was still clamped firmly over her mouth so the agonized scream was muffled, but he had to make one more clumsy thrust before he got the job done. Revolted by the fountain of blood and his bungled efforts, Seth pushed the twitching body from him and staggered from the bed.

The vagrant stood with hands on hips. "Oh, brilliant. Very neatly done, my friend. Very tidy job."

Seth spun round to retort, sickened by his own actions, but the angry words died on his tongue. The sullen ruby light flared from the vagrant's eyes, quelling any thoughts of rebellion. Seth picked up his bloody knife and wiped it on the bedclothes, avoiding Alice's gaping throat and wide, accusing eyes.

"Let's just get on with it." he muttered.

The wastrel grinned wider and gestured for Seth to lead the way. The manservant sheathed his blade, surprised that the great gout of Alice's blood had hardly marked him. A few spots on his sleeve were all he could see. He stalked ahead of his companion toward the formal part of the house.

They climbed the carpeted stairs to the upper floor. The wastrel moved into the lead, needing no guidance from Seth. The manservant surmised that what the Baron knew, his puppet knew, which explained why Seth's advice as to where to hide the whore's body had been sought. The Baron had never taken any notice of the many barns and outhouses and would have had no idea of what they held.

They came to a halt outside Jinny's private rooms, and the wastrel turned to Seth. Silently, he indicated Seth should remain outside. Seth thought about protesting, but let the idea die. What was the point? The wastrel—or the Baron—had obviously decided he was too clumsy and inexperienced to be trusted. Resigned, he nodded.

✢ ✢ ✢ ✢ ✢

Once Seth had acknowledged him, the vagrant opened the door and slipped inside. He moved surely through Jinny's solar, glancing neither left nor right. His ruby eyes were fixed upon the bedchamber door and his heightened senses could pick out the deep, even breathing coming from the sleeping Baroness. His own heart began thumping, but it wasn't nervousness. Rather it was the increased excitement of his master, who controlled and directed all his actions.

So far, Reen was pleased with the night's events. Seth had proven useful, if a little clumsy, and the Baron knew he could rely on his former servant when he finally returned to power. Provided he ensured no one could connect Seth to this latest incident, the manservant should remain free and be able to resume his duties when the Baron returned from exile. Reen had to quell the memories of the many intimate services Seth had performed for his master in the past. There would be time enough later to revisit such pleasures. For now, he had to concentrate on this next delicate task.

Reen, seeing through his puppet's eyes, directed the man to the ornate door leading to Jinny's bedchamber. He'd been disappointed to learn Taran wouldn't be with her, but what he now had in mind would prove far more satisfying and provide yet more anguish for his archenemy. Smiling, his grin reflected on the face of his tool, he sent the vagrant into Jinny's chamber.

✣ ✣ ✣ ✣ ✣

Jinella had retired later than usual. She'd spent the entire day thinking of Taran, trying to make up her mind whether she should call a messenger and send her letter to the castle. Even had they not quarreled, she knew she wouldn't have seen Taran until evening. But their painful parting and her harsh words ensured he would be most unlikely to come to her unsummoned.

A measure of irritation entered her heart. He was *so*

predictable! Always so careful to do the right thing, so quick to be the guilty party. Why couldn't he be impetuous for once and come demanding her forgiveness?

She knew she was being unfair. He was a gentle soul who hated giving offence. He was gallant and kind, chivalrous and thoughtful. He wouldn't be the man she loved if he could come barging into her presence making demands. She knew all this and yet, sometimes, she wished he would.

She sat up late, rereading her letter, experiencing once again the emotions she had felt while writing it, and finally determined to send it in the morning. It was too late now. All the servants had retired early that night. She refolded the letter, returned it to the exquisite silver box she had brought in from her solar, and lay down to sleep, comforted by her decision.

She lay in a pleasant doze, dreaming of her coming reunion with Taran and how she would show him her love and forgiveness. She finally drifted into true sleep, the dream following her as she relaxed. She murmured half-formed words as she felt his hands upon her, smiled in pleasure at the sensations they produced. He was stroking her throat, running his fingers over the soft skin below her jaw and under her ear. He was sitting on the bed beside her—she could feel his weight pinning the bedclothes around her. She imagined him leaning over her, his handsome face poised above hers, smiling gently and passionately down at her.

She opened her eyes, searching for his face in the dim firelight. She tried to move her arms, to bring them out from under the bedclothes. As she came further out of her dream, the smell hit her. Gagging in revulsion, she struggled against the restraining weight above her, becoming frantic as her attempts failed.

She opened her mouth to scream and a hand clamped over her lips. The dreadful smell intensified and she screwed her eyes against the acrid stench. She struggled harder, but it was no use.

She was securely pinned and her assailant too strong.

He made no sound except the rasp of his breath. She blinked her watering eyes, determined to see who dared assault her in her own home. She stiffened in shock as she registered the demonic glow in the ruby orbs so close to her face, and her throat squeezed out a petrified whimper.

A voice crawled out of the darkness. "Keep still, my Lady, and you won't be hurt. There are none to hear should you scream. Your servants are too far away and the housekeeper's dead. I have orders to take you with me and I have no wish to render you unconscious, but I will if you cause me trouble. Do you understand?"

Jinny managed a nod against the pressure on her mouth. She felt his hand ease away and he raised his body upright. But he didn't release her arms.

"Who the hell are you?" she demanded, anger and fright lending her strength. "What gives you the right to come barging in here? What do you want with me?"

The man grinned nastily. Jinny shrank back with a gasp of horror as the demonic glow in his eyes intensified and the charnel reek rose again. She retched.

"Jinny, my dear niece, that's not very ladylike."

Jinny's eyes stretched wide and she stared frantically about the room. She had clearly heard her uncle's voice, yet he was nowhere to be seen.

"I'm right before you, my dear."

Now she did scream, for she'd seen the vagrant's mouth move, speaking in the tones of her uncle.

His hand clamped over her lips once again to muffle the shriek, but if what he'd said was true there was little chance of her being heard. The servants' wing was too far away for the sound to carry, especially with all the casements closed and covered with heavy drapes. The hand released her mouth then slapped her cheek as she drew breath for another scream. Shocked, she whimpered.

"How is this possible? I thought you were dead! They told me you'd taken your own life! How can you speak to me?"

Her uncle's voice came soothingly out of the dark. "Jinny, Jinny. You really shouldn't believe everything you hear. Did you think I'd let them defeat me? Did you think I'd let them take everything from me with no thought for revenge? No, my dear, I was only biding my time. And now I'm ready, and I want you to help me. You must go with my servant, Jinny dear. He'll bring you to me. Can we trust you not to make a fuss? I do hope so, for I'd hate to have him damage you."

Jinny was trembling uncontrollably. She didn't understand any of this. The man above her spoke in her uncle's voice, using words her uncle would use. Yet the Baron was dead—hadn't Taran told her so? Whatever Taran's faults, he would never lie to her about something so important. So how was this possible? It went far beyond her experience, despite the many curious things Taran had told her about his own capabilities. No, it was just too fantastical to believe. It must be a trick of some kind.

Jinny opened her mouth to protest, choking as her assailant's fingers tightened about her throat, cutting off her air. She was still smothered in the folds of her bedding, pinned helplessly by the filthy man's weight. The sudden attack, coupled with the reek of rotting flesh, overwhelmed her and flooded her with panic.

The dreadful eyes in that expressionless face hovered inches above Jinny's, a shuddering red mist seen through tears. She felt the stubble of his chin scrape across her cheek, he was so close. His breath hissed in her ear as he whispered, "My dear, did you by any chance hear about the terrible murder of the Arch Patrio in the city today?"

Jinny stiffened, struggling to breathe. The man's cruel grip bruised her delicate flesh, yet let just enough air through so she didn't suffocate.

"I feel I ought to tell you that this servant of mine was the perpetrator of that dreadful crime. He slit Neremiah's throat—slit it slowly with a ragged knife. Your whore of a housekeeper chose to be difficult, and now she's lying in a pool of her own blood. You're not so vital to my plans that I need you alive. Think on that, my Lady Baroness, and decide what you want to do. Keep quiet and come to me, or end up dead with your own throat cut. Make your choice."

Tears coursed down Jinny's face. She didn't know if she was truly speaking with her uncle, but she believed his threats. If she didn't do as she was told, she would end up dead. She was already half-suffocated and had no strength left to resist.

If only Taran were here with her! If they hadn't quarreled, if she hadn't overreacted and sent him away, he would have defended her to the end of his life. He would never have let harm come to her while there was breath in his body. But it was too late now for such realizations. He wasn't here, and it was her own fault for reacting so badly.

A great sob welled up in her breast, but she hadn't the breath for it. She gave the slightest of nods and gasped when the restricting hand was removed from her throat. Before she could catch her breath, the comforter was flung over her head and she was bundled off the bed. Something was used to tie it tightly around her body, pinning her arms, and she was slung over the filthy man's shoulder like a sack of grain.

Still struggling for air through her bruised throat, Jinny's senses reeled, casting her into a swamping well of darkness.

✤ ✤ ✤ ✤ ✤

Out in the hallway, Seth heard the single shriek and nearly left his post to see what had happened. The memory of the vagrant's ruined flesh returned to haunt him, and he thought better of his actions. Trembling, sweating, he stood and waited.

Soon he saw the vagrant moving toward him from the gloom of Jinny's solar. Seth registered the bulky burden slung over the man's shoulder, and the fact it was still alive. He opened his mouth, but the vagrant hissed sharply. "Silence, you fool!"

Seth's mouth snapped shut. The vagrant waved him back and stepped out into the hallway. "All quiet?"

Seth nodded. He knew the shriek wouldn't have carried to the servants' wing and the house had no other occupants. Not live ones, anyway.

The wastrel gave a curt nod. "Go fetch what you brought. Be quick about it."

Ignoring the imperious tone, Seth did as he was told. He used the back door rather than going through the kitchens again, and was back in minutes. The dreadful man had dumped Jinny on the floor and directed Seth into her bedchamber. As the manservant placed the dead whore on Jinella's bed, the wastrel lit one of the oil lamps and found the small pile of jewelry on the bedside table. "Does she usually wear all of this?"

Seth examined the glittering pile. He selected the items Jinella always wore and took them over to the corpse. Averting his eyes from the gray face with its grotesque, staring eyes, he fastened the necklace and pushed rings onto stiffening fingers. The whore had thicker fingers than Jinella and he had a job to force the rings onto the cold, unresponsive flesh. But he finally got the job done.

He gazed at the vagrant. "Are you leaving her on the bed?"

"Why not?"

"Well, the mistress wouldn't usually lie clothed in one of her best gowns on the bed. When she's in her bedchamber, she usually

289

wears a house robe."

The vagrant slapped his forehead. "Now he tells me."

Seth allowed what he considered righteous anger to surface. "Well, if you'd done as I asked and told me what the plan was I'd have mentioned it sooner!"

His acerbic tone failed to impress, however, and the vagrant glared at him. "I know very well the woman sometimes reads or writes in this room. I have a better authority than you to tell me what happens here, remember? It doesn't matter what she's wearing, only that it's recognizable as Jinella's. There won't be much else left to worry about. Now is the time to collect anything you might want from this house and any coin you might have. You'll be needing new lodgings after tonight's work. Take anything of value you want; the master doesn't want you to be in need because of this. But hurry, I want to be gone from here."

Seth did as he was bid. He didn't possess much he couldn't bear to lose and it didn't take him long to fetch it. He had a small room on the same floor as Jinella's, next to what had been the Baron's private suite. It had made their personal arrangements easier to manage. Once he had collected some clothes and his few belongings, he entered the Baron's old rooms and made for the large chest beneath the window. The Baron's store of ready coin was still where he had kept it, superficially hidden under the chest's contents. Grinning, Seth stuffed as much as he could carry into a pillowcase and returned to the vagrant's side.

The wasted man stood beside Jinella's wrapped body, waiting impatiently. He made no comment when he saw Seth's haul, but waved the manservant back into the room. "Dump that sack and go smash all the oil lamps. Be sure they break. And don't get any oil on your own clothes."

Seth doused the room with oil and the vagrant poured a good measure over the dead whore's body, paying special attention to the face. He made sure to leave a good portion of the gown untouched. For effect, he pulled the dead whore half off the bed, as if the woman, overcome by the fire, had fallen across it in her dying moments. He took a taper from the pot by the hearth and thrust it into the embers. It glowed a bloody red, matching the terrible flare in his eyes. He turned to stare at Seth.

"I'd get out if I were you."

The voice crawled hideously from the twisted mouth, the Baron savoring this vengeful moment. Seth didn't need telling twice. As he left the room he heard the first crackle of flames taking hold of the room's sumptuous furnishings, fueled by the volatile oil. He paused in the solar, but the vagrant didn't stay to witness his handiwork. He brushed past Seth, upsetting another lamp and tossing the taper into the leaking oil. Flames licked instantly on the pool's surface.

The two men emerged into the corridor and the vagrant closed the solar door. He indicated Jinella's trussed body and Seth resignedly picked her up, tucking his bulging pillowcase under one arm. They moved back through the mansion, the vagrant spilling oil and igniting it as he went, directing them finally into the kitchen.

"Put her down and go deal with the housekeeper's room," he hissed.

Seth did as he was told, reluctant though he was to confront the gory scene of his crime and Alice's silently accusing body. He did as the vagrant had done and watched the flames catch, their greedy crackle soon to consume the grisly evidence of his guilt.

When he returned to the kitchen the vagrant had Jinella over his shoulder. He stood by the scullery door. His disturbing eyes fastened on Seth, the sardonic smile back on the wasted lips.

"My friend, your part is done. How you play this situation is up to you. The master has no instructions for you. Just be sure to wait until the building is well alight. Then you can either play the hero and attempt to save the servants, or you can turn your back and find yourself an alibi somewhere. Go back to the brothel, if you like—the key's on the table there. Mistress Nolah won't have disturbed that room and she'll never mention one slovenly girl's disappearance—not after what she's been paid. But whatever you do, keep out of the way of those cursed witches from the Manor. It's rumored they can read your mind, tell if you're lying. You'd not want that, now, would you? I doubt we'll meet again, and the master'll reward your loyalty when he returns to claim his rightful place. Now go."

Seth, undecided as to his best course of action, grabbed his pillowcase, snatched up the brothel key, and left the kitchen, followed by the wastrel. They emerged into the kitchen yard and Seth watched the dreadful man disappear into the darkness before closing the scullery door, relocking it, and replacing the key behind its concealing brick. Casting apprehensive eyes up at the intensifying glow from the mansion's windows, he melted into the snowy shadows.

✤ ✤ ✤ ✤ ✤

The vagrant carried his burden away from the burning mansion. As he walked, he felt the Baron's controlling hand take over his soul, filling his enslaved mind with triumph and glee. Although he was way past feeling pleasure as a normal man might, the Baron's servant still experienced a wash of relief at a task well-accomplished. He knew intimately how his master punished failure or transgression, and had no wish to experience such torture again. The misery of his existence was purgatory enough. Now he lived only for the day when his usefulness was over and he would be allowed, at last, to die.

Once he was far enough away from the mansion and out into

the deserted, snow-laden fields, he halted. He felt the Baron exert his will, manipulating the substrate as his stolen skills had shown him, opening a rent within the Veils to allow his servant access.

Although furnished with the knowledge of how to use his powers, Reen had usurped them with no finesse, no thought for the training that underpinned the talents of those he'd assimilated. He had no understanding of what he did or why—only the how. The Baron's power, although strengthened by his hatred, was raw and vulgar and took no account of the effect it had upon those subjected to it.

Jinella had no innate Artesan gifts, but she had lived with a talented Adept-elite for three years. She had gradually developed an embryo sense of what occurred when those skills were used, becoming sensitive and open to power without being aware of it. Because it was involuntary, she had no defenses, no conscious shield, and so, when the vagrant entered the crude, ragged rent within the Veils, Jinella, half-smothered and swooning, was hit with the full force of the experience.

Her tortured scream shattered the night.

Chapter Twenty-Four

Taran sat bolt upright in bed, covered with sweat, trembling in every muscle. He stared wildly about in the darkness, trying to identify the source of his terror. His breath heaved painfully through constricted lungs, his throat raw and painful. He wrapped his arms about his chest, hugging himself, disoriented, sick, and dizzy.

With an effort, he mastered himself, bringing his talents to bear. His immediate senses told him nothing threatened in his room, and nothing in the castle either, so he could afford the time to calm his pounding heart. His breathing slowed, his heart rate returned to normal. But he had to use his healing abilities to reduce the burning in his throat and ease the cramped sensation in his lungs.

He leaned back against sweat-sodden pillows, wearily wondering if he had managed to contract a fever, rare though sickness was for an Artesan. But when he examined his body closely, he found no evidence. Puzzled, he shrugged into his night robe and got out of bed. The sheets and pillows were clammy with sweat, too uncomfortable to lie on. He would have to change the bedding if he was to get any more sleep this night.

As he opened the wooden blanket chest at the end of the bed, he picked over what his memory could tell him of the past few minutes. Was it a nightmare? Could a bad dream explain such depths of terror, such extreme reactions? He didn't think so and could find no traces of such a dream within his subconscious. All he could remember were sensations of restriction, of a burning throat, of suffocating breathlessness, horror, and panic.

He went suddenly cold. Dropping his armful of clean bedding, he sent his psyche arrowing out across the landscape, frantically searching for a pattern he knew well, praying he would find its imprint safe and undamaged. Thoughts of Sullyan's ordeal at the hands of Lord Rykan and her desperate attempts to reach through spellsilver to the empathic Rienne pounded in his brain. When he did finally reach her, when he touched her quiescent, glowing psyche, he breathed a huge sigh of relief. Its calm state showed she was asleep. No dreams troubled her slumber, no menace threatened.

Taran collapsed to the crumpled bed, shaking his head. He didn't disturb her, wouldn't trespass upon her rest with no better reason than the effects of a bad dream. Once again he stilled his racing heart, and stood to gather the bedding he had dropped.

He glanced to his window, trying to gauge the hour. It was dark and silent outside. Not even the sounds of the garrison preparing to ride out for their punitive sweeps reached his ears. It must still be early. So why, he thought, was there a sullen red glow in the sky?

Taran hadn't gone early to his bed. His luck at cards had changed and he had enjoyed a run of good hands. Only once had he been deceived by Denny's bluffing tactics; otherwise he'd called the Major on his bets and had reaped the benefits. He had even beaten Ardoch, which was more of a rarity than triumphing over Denny. The talk, the game, and the comradeship had kept the Adept long from his bed.

When he had finally succumbed to weariness he'd fallen instantly asleep. Yet his slumber hadn't been deepened by alcohol.

With dawn patrols to lead and the dreadful murder of the Arch Patrio uppermost in their minds, none had partaken of intoxicating liquor. General Blaine's views on strong drink were well known, and should a swordsman under the King's Oath, whatever his rank, commit transgressions of a drunken nature, he was instantly punished by dismissal with no appeal.

So Taran knew that whatever he had experienced during the night and whatever his eyes were telling him now, his senses were not dulled by drink. There was only one thing that could possibly cast such a ruddy-red glow on the underbelly of the snow-laden clouds.

Fire!

He flung off his night robe and struggled into breeches and shirt, tugging his sheepskin-lined jacket on and stamping into his boots. He ran to the window, which looked north-eastwards, trying to pinpoint the fire's location. But the glow was widespread, distributed by the cloud cover, and he couldn't tell the source of the flames.

He would have to rouse both castle and garrison. Fire was the city's most feared danger. Many of the buildings were of timber or half-timbered; if fire got hold it could decimate large areas of the city very quickly. Water they had in abundance—the port wharves gave easy access to the sea—but carrying large quantities of water to the seat of a fire would take time they might not have. The little Loxton stream ran through the castle parklands, but it was too small to be much use for quenching fires. Their main defense was speed, alerting the city and preventing the fire from getting out of control.

Taran ran from his room, pounding on doors as he went, crying "Fire!" as loudly as he could. People streamed from their rest in his wake, and Colonel Vassa heard the commotion before Taran reached his quarters.

The Colonel appeared at his door, pulling on his clothes. Taran heard a sleepy voice calling anxiously from the bedchamber. Astounded, he caught a glimpse of Madam Delinna, Elias's chatelaine, wrapping a silken robe about her statuesque figure. He raised his brows at Vassa, but there was no time for questions or amazement. Taran dismissed the incident and tersely told Vassa what he'd seen.

The Colonel wasted no time. He brushed past the Adept and headed down the hallway toward the stairs.

"Wake Levant, will you, Taran? And anyone else you can think of. I'll turn out the garrison."

Taran sped for Levant's chambers, but the First Minister had already heard the alarm. Taran gave his information and left Levant to organize the castle. The Adept hurried after Vassa, clattering down the stairway to the lower floor, shouldering through the castle's milling inhabitants, some of whom tried to waylay him with questions or pleas for information. Taran referred them all to Levant and forged his way outside.

He emerged into the castle courtyard, from where he could hear the Colonel's stentorian roar alerting the garrison and yelling orders. Running beneath the archway that led to the garrison compound, his breath streaming white in the freezing air, Taran made for the stables. Grooms and swordsmen were everywhere. Taran had to fight to reach the barn where the harness was stored. He snatched up Bucyrus's saddle and bridle and made his way to his mount's stall.

Bucyrus, like the other horses, had caught the pervading sense of urgency and snorted in alarm. Taran spared him a gentle word and a soothing hand before flinging on the saddle and slipping the bridle over the stallion's ears. He led the beast from his stall and vaulted to his back before they had even cleared the door.

Emerging into the compound, Taran was assailed by the

shouts of men, the calls of fretting horses, and the press of bodies. He touched heels to Bucyrus's sides and sent the horse out into the castle parklands, heading, like so many others, for the gates to the city. He heard Denny's yell close behind him and turned, seeing the Major leading a band of around forty mounted men, all running hard on Taran's heels. They clattered through the opened gates and into the city streets.

Taran ignored the tumult, the freezing air, the falling snow, and also the cries of the men around him. Reaching within himself for his psyche, Taran attuned himself to the element of Fire. He wrapped its signature about his consciousness, made himself part of it, sensitized his spirit to its nature. Then he cast his awareness out over the city, trying to shut out Denny's voice demanding he do what he was already doing.

The city was quiet, save for the districts nearest the castle where the inhabitants had heard the yells and were beginning to come to their doors. Puzzled, Taran pulled back his senses, turning questioning eyes to the red-hued sky. Denny sent one of his men to tell Vassa the city was safe, and turned to yell at Taran.

"Seems to be coming from the north!"

Taran looked that way. The night was still. No scent of smoke reached their nostrils; no floating soot marred the pristine white snow. What movement of air there was carried the faint tang of brine, as usual. The castle was to the north and west of the city. Beyond it were the cliffs dropping down to the sea, and the erstwhile Baron's estate.

Taran's blood froze. His whole body shuddered and a cold hand of panic gripped a heart that labored under the pang of shock. His face drained and his sight blurred. Now he knew why he had startled awake, sweat-ridden, lungs burning. He knew the name of the nightmare that had jolted him from sleep. He once again felt sick and dizzy and swayed in his saddle.

Denny noted his reaction, even in the gloom. He reached out to steady his friend. "What, Taran? What is it?"

Taran turned fearful eyes on him. "Oh, gods! It's not the city, Denny, it's the estate! It's Jinny's estate! Quickly, Denny, hurry! Oh, dear gods! *Jinny*!"

Taran dug his heels into Bucyrus's sides. The mettlesome stallion, unused to such harsh treatment, squealed as he surged forward, leaping into a flat-out gallop as Taran laid the reins across his neck, urging the great beast faster and faster through the narrow, twisting streets, Denny's men right behind him.

He dimly heard a yell from Denny—whether warning or command, he couldn't say. He didn't hear the words, had no thought for his safety. All he knew was that Jinny had called to him in her terror and, miraculously, he'd heard her. The one thing he had been hoping for during their three years together had finally happened. They'd achieved a pair-bonding, a true merging of spirit and soul—the one irrefutable indication they were meant to be together. All their passionate coupling, their enjoyment of each other's company, their ease together, had broken down the barrier of Jinella's lack of talent and allowed this incredible link to be forged. It had taken panic to release it.

And he hadn't recognized it.

✣ ✣ ✣ ✣ ✣

They labored long and hard into the dawn. Straining together, gasping for breath in the smoke-laden air, they struggled to fight the flames. Finding water wherever they could—the well, the horses' buckets, the dew-pond—their existence merged into one long chain of passing heavy buckets down the line to be thrown, hissing and steaming, into the all-consuming maw of flame.

The servants had been spared. Wakened by the roar as the fire attacked the main building, they escaped their rooms just before the inferno burst the door separating their wing from the mansion. Leaving all their possessions, fleeing in night robes and blankets, they spilled into the freezing night, screaming for help, milling frantically until someone ran to the chapel and tolled the bell. The estate's inhabitants poured from their houses to help.

Taran, Denny, and the men from the garrison arrived in the midst of this chaos. So swift had been their flight through the city that the guard at the gate hadn't been able to get the ponderous portal open fast enough. Taran, desperate to reach Jinny, had spurred his mount through an opening too small to accommodate horse and rider, resulting in his leg and the horse's flank being crushed against the stout wood. He had not stopped to assess the damage and was one of the first off his horse when at last they reached the inferno.

They soon saw it was hopeless. The mansion was completely alight. Flames roared from every window, spat from the roof beams, leaped feet into the air as internal walls collapsed. The servants' wing went the same way. There simply wasn't enough water to combat such a ferocious conflagration.

It was Matty who saved the horses. Disobeying his father's orders, he sprinted across the fields and opened the stable doors. Yelling at the frightened horses, he chased them into the yard where their own terror goaded them past the flames and out into the cold safety of the night. They would suffer in the cold, but better to shiver in the darkness than roast alive in their stalls.

Taran fought his own private battle with terror and panic as he strained his powers beyond their limits. The agony of his crushed leg was forgotten in the urgency of the moment. He wanted to run into the flames, throw himself up the charred stairs, and batter his way to Jinny's door in the desperate hope he'd find her safe and well. But the heat was too fierce and the building too damaged. The stairs were gone anyway, long since collapsed, along with most of the second floor. The flames exulted high above his head, leaping maniacally through the burned-out roof trusses, mocking him with his impotence as he strove to damp them down. As Adept-elite he could influence Fire, but he doubted even Sullyan could have banished this ravening monster.

He fought on, turning all the love in his heart, the panic in his veins, and the valor in his soul into strength of will as he pitted his inadequate skills against the unstoppable fire.

He never noticed the faint flush of dawn staining the east. He didn't realize the chain of buckets had ceased to move, didn't know the space around the mansion was now cleared of people. Denny had long since realized the task was hopeless and the best they could hope for was containment. He cleared an area around the burning buildings and removed everything that could catch alight, forming a fire-break. The mansion and the servants' wing were lost. Better to sacrifice what couldn't be saved in order to redeem the rest.

Now it was over. The fire still raged, but it was running out of fuel and could be left to consume itself. The still winter air was a blessing; no wind would blow the flames to claim further victims. Denny sent the exhausted villagers back to their homes and organized temporary care for the displaced servants. Any with wounds or burns too serious to treat in the village were transported back to the city. Denny had to return also. He was due out on patrol at dawn. Vassa wouldn't appreciate his being late, not even for this. So Denny approached Taran, who had fallen to his knees with exhaustion, but was still trying to quell the flames.

He nearly cried out when Denny touched his arm. His eyes snapped open as Denny crouched down beside him.

"It's over, Taran. You can do no more. Let it go, man, you'll kill yourself."

Taran turned brimming eyes on the Major. "It's over?" he

whispered. "It's gone? The whole house?"

"See for yourself." Denny directed Taran's gaze to the ravaged building.

The Adept stood painfully, leaning on Denny's arm. Tears streamed down his sweat-soaked face as he stared at the dreadful mess the fire had made of Jinny's home. He covered his face with his hands and stood there shaking.

Denny glanced at his men, who waited awkwardly, unsure what to do. They weren't the ones picked by him to patrol Loxton Forest today—he'd left those behind with orders to report to Colonel Vassa. He would have sent the men back to their rest until dawn. Denny was needed there to lead them. He turned once more to the distraught Adept.

"Taran, I'm so sorry, but I have to go now. I have patrols to lead. I'll leave my men here with you. They'll help you look through the house once it's cooled down a bit, see if they can find … you know … what's left. But I have to go. I have my orders. I'll make sure Vassa knows what's happened, if he doesn't already; he won't expect you at the castle this morning."

He got no response. Taran simply stared at the smoldering mess.

"Taran—oh gods, man, I'm so sorry. None of this was your fault; you could have done nothing to prevent it. It was an accident, by the looks of things—a spilt lamp, probably. You know what these old houses are like, tinder-dry, most of them. And you tried the hardest of anyone to stop the fire. Don't make yourself ill with blame. Jinny wouldn't have wanted that."

Denny's words finally seemed to register. Taran turned red-rimmed, guilt-ridden eyes on his friend, his tortured soul naked and burning. A terrible rage seemed to well inside him, and for one awful moment Denny thought Taran might strike him, might even try to kill him. The insane despair smothering his senses threatened to overwhelm all other concerns. But then he turned, faced once more the savage pyre of his love, his hopes, and his dreams, and screamed his loss to the sky. He threw back his head, fists beating at the frozen air, throat clawing harshly at the tatters of his life, and then he collapsed to his knees once again, tearing sobs muffled under futile hands—hands that had failed to save his love.

Chapter Twenty-Five

They left him to the course of his grief. It was the only thing they could think to do for him. They withdrew a polite distance and watched him, concerned lest he try to harm himself in the depths of his despair. Denny left for the garrison and made his sad report to the Colonel. Vassa had indeed learned of the night's terrible events and sent what help he could spare. Levant had been informed and the First Minister asked the Major what he thought he should do for Taran. Denny shrugged helplessly and advised Levant to send someone for Sullyan. He didn't know anyone else who might be able to help.

But sending for Sullyan would take too long without Taran's help. The King's runners took two days by fast horse to reach the Manor. With Taran out of action, they couldn't contact General Blaine or the King, either. Levant couldn't ignore this situation. Callous as it might seem, Taran was too valuable to risk losing to despair. Levant called for his horse and left at a gallop.

✢ ✢ ✢ ✢ ✢

Jinny swam in a sea of pain. Her head ached ferociously and there was a nauseating light across her closed eyes, flashing jagged barbs into her brain. She lay on her back, her limbs finally free of restraint. She could even get her breath, which was a mercy, although her throat was painfully raw. She couldn't recall ever feeling so utterly dreadful.

She was shivering. Wherever she was, it was freezing cold.

She had been wearing her night things when she was abducted, and although they were fine for her cozy bedchamber, they were no use at all against the winter cold. If she wasn't to freeze to death she would have to combat this frightening headache, rouse herself, and get warm.

Drawing in a breath, she tried to move her head. Nausea rushed over her, but she managed to contain it. Very slowly, she opened her eyes. There was a dim amber glow in the room. She could just make it out through half-opened lids. As her sight became used to the gloom, she made out a very small fire in one corner, opposite where she lay. Rustic bowls and utensils lay on the ground next to the fire, but otherwise the place was bare. Gradually, groaning at the jagged stabs shooting into her brain, Jinny sat up.

She'd been lying on a wooden shelf bed, about two feet off the ground. Beneath her was the silken comforter from her own bed that had been used to restrain her. She eased it out and wrapped it tightly about her body, but it didn't do much to warm her chilled flesh. She gazed fearfully about her, taking in the rough stone walls, the dirt-packed floor littered with old straw, the stout wooden door, and the tiny fire in the corner. She was quite alone.

There were no windows; the smoke from the fire escaped through a small, angled smoke-hole in the roof. She could hear no sound, but the smells in the room reminded her of livestock—maybe sheep. Was this some herder's cottage or hut, some shepherd's refuge from the winter winds? If so, she could be anywhere.

This thought brought tears to her eyes. She didn't understand what had happened to her. How could she have been abducted from the bedchamber of her own house? What had happened to her servants? Why hadn't Seth alerted her to intruders? Unless, she thought with a sudden shiver, he'd been killed. Hadn't that dreadful voice told her Alice had been slaughtered, her throat cut? If it had been done to poor Alice, why not Seth? Why not all her servants?

Jinella began to tremble uncontrollably, half with cold and half with terror. If her abductor could murder her household in cold blood, what lay in store for her? And when would it happen? How long would she be kept here, in fear and isolation, just waiting for her fate? Where was Taran when she needed him? Why had they fallen out so badly, why had she let things go so far?

Piteously, hopelessly, Jinella wept.

✤ ✤ ✤ ✤ ✤

Inconsolable, Taran stared at the mansion's smoking ruins in the harsh light of day. The outer stone walls still stood, soot-scarred and stained, but practically everything within them had been destroyed, eaten by the ravening fire. A few roof trusses still reared their stark, black angles to the sky, but all recognizable features of the mansion's interior were gone.

Taran limped carefully over the wet, charred mess inside the walls, his crushed leg shooting pain up his thigh, his vision blurred, his heart dead and cold. In the face of such destructive ferocity, he thought, how had these few, incongruous items survived? Here and there among the detritus were household objects, strangely untouched. A porcelain figure, intact, its delicate colors unmarred. Over there lay a book—a book!—its leather cover soaked, but its pages whole. And here, in the center of the carnage, a glint of untarnished silver.

Taran recognized that small, bright gleam and took a sobbing breath. He was looking at the finely-chased silver box he had bought as a surprise for Jinny. He remembered the look of pure joy and love on her face when he presented it to her, and how she'd thanked him for the gift.

He froze, realizing where he stood. Above his head, such a short while ago, had been Jinny's private rooms. She had kept this little box in her solar, and this is where it must have come to rest when the wooden floorboards and joists had been consumed, collapsing into this unrecognizable jumble of broken furniture and scorched, ruined fabric.

Unable to help himself, yet frightened of what he might find, Taran picked through the mess. He knew Jinny would have been in her chamber when the fire began, and the few servants he had spoken to confirmed that their mistress hadn't escaped. His desperate prayers that she'd somehow climbed or jumped from a window went unanswered. No one had seen her or heard her. And so, tears stinging the scorched skin on his face, he tried to find her.

✣ ✣ ✣ ✣ ✣

Seth watched Taran walk unsteadily through the smoldering rubble, unmoved by the Adept's grief. He might have made a pretense of helping him, curious as to what might be left for him to find, but for the arrival of Lord Levant. Taran was oblivious, lost in sorrow, and didn't see Levant as the man sat his horse, staring at the carnage.

Looking around, Levant caught sight of Seth and hailed him. With no other choice Seth approached the lord, who indicated the ruins with a wave of his hand.

"Is there any chance Lady Jinella survived?" he asked, speaking softly lest Taran hear him.

Seth glanced at the building. "I doubt it, my Lord. The servants got out, but the mistress had retired to her bed. She'd have been asleep when the fire broke out."

Levant frowned. "You were the Baron's manservant, were you not?"

"Yes, my Lord. The mistress graciously kept me on because

of my long service to her uncle."

"So where were you when the fire started?"

Seth went cold, but didn't allow himself to react. "I'd gone out earlier, my Lord. The mistress sent all of us early to our rest and I decided to visit with a … friend in the city. I heard the commotion and saw the King's Guard race by, and someone said the mansion was burning. I ran here quick as I could to help with the buckets."

This was almost true. Undecided as to his safest course of action once the wastrel disappeared with Jinny, Seth hid out of sight until the fire was well underway and too fierce to halt. He had seen Taran and Denny's men race past and stayed where he was until they began clearing the area. Smearing soot on his face for effect, he joined the final throes of the futile struggle, taking care to be noticed by his fellow servants. Then Taran began his desolate search and Seth experienced a macabre desire to witness the outcome of the Baron's plan. He thought his master might like to hear of Taran's despair when he came across what remained of "Jinella."

Levant appeared satisfied with Seth's explanation and waved him away. Seth went back to the ruins and slowly worked his way over to the distraught Adept, who was pushing at something lying beneath a blackened roof beam with the toe of his boot.

With a sharp, heartbroken cry, Taran went down on one knee, reaching into the charred, sodden mess on the ground. His hand came up holding a long scrap of green silk, once richly embroidered, and a gold ring still encircling a blackened finger bone. Seth watched as Taran clutched the forlorn scraps to his breast and once more screamed his grief at the blank, uncaring sky. He bowed his head, his body racked by sobs.

Seth approached him, pleased their deception had worked so well. He could see more tattered remnants of cloth, as well as the gleam of bone. The skull of the dead whore had been completely stripped of flesh, but pathetic wisps of blonde hair still fluttered nearby, and the expensive necklace could be seen draped around the neck bones.

Seth stopped beside the moaning Adept. "I'm a bit surprised you're so upset, sir," he said.

Taran jumped and shot the manservant a grief-filled look. "What the hell do you mean by that?"

Seth shrugged. "The mistress mentioned you and she had quarreled. She told me it was all over between you. She said you'd let her down, badly. She was quite distraught."

"Distraught?" Taran's eyes were fearful, haunted. "She was upset, of course, but it wasn't over. I loved her, Seth, she knew that."

Seth shook his head sadly, warming to his theme. He hadn't intended to do this. He'd simply wanted to remember the man's reactions so he could tell his master. But he knew how the Baron hated Taran for his support of Sullyan, and for his rescue of Prince Eadan. He knew his master would want Taran to suffer whatever torments could be devised to repay him for his actions. And now Seth was in a position to increase that suffering.

"I don't think she did, sir. I heard her last night, before she told me to send the servants away. She was almost hysterical. I could tell she'd been crying when she summoned me to give her instructions to the household. I thought then something was badly wrong and I pleaded with her to allow me to fetch one of her friends, but she wouldn't hear of it. She almost threw me out, sir. She told me she wanted everyone out of the house—she wanted to be alone."

Taran went white. "What are you saying, man? Why are you telling me this?"

"Well, sir, it's just that I overheard the Major earlier, before he left, saying he thought the fire must have been caused by a spilt lamp. But I checked all the lamps yesterday evening, as I always do, and I know they were all trimmed and safe. If it was a lamp that caused this fire, it was deliberately done."

Taran stared into Seth's face, his eyes wide with horror. "No," he cried, "she couldn't have! She wouldn't! She'd never take her own life—not like *this*!"

Seth shrugged and began moving away. "I'm only telling you what I know and what I saw, sir. I've never seen the mistress so distraught. I remember thinking she might do anything in a state like that …."

✣ ✣ ✣ ✣ ✣

Taran couldn't bear the implications. His guilt over the angry words of their last parting flared anew and his heart constricted painfully. He relived Jinny's tearful fury as she had sent him away, betrayal and anguish rolling off her in waves. It was his fault, yet he had made no attempt to see her since, to comfort her, to reassure her of his love. And now she was gone and he would never have the chance again. All his hopes for the future, for a family, for the love and companionship he'd always craved, were gone, cremated on a pyre of his own cowardice and selfishness. Jinny had paid the price of his failures.

Numb and shocked, Taran stumbled away, clutching the scrap of cloth and the ring in his hand. As he did so his foot kicked against the small silver box he had bought with such love. The sight of it lying there among the ruins of all he held dear was too much for him to take. As he bent down to pick it up, the world blurred around him and he fell on his face in the smoldering rubble.

✣ ✣ ✣ ✣ ✣

Denny and Ardoch rode at the head of their men through the Forest Gate and separated a mile into the trees. Denny took the northeastern side of the forest and Ardoch the southern. Although the snow had ceased falling, the weather was gloomy and overcast, the ever-present clouds promising more snow before the day was out. As Denny had feared, the night's heavy snowfall had obliterated all tracks save those of fox or bird. There would be no clues to help them hunt their quarry.

No clues had been forthcoming from the victims either. Lord Levant, having delivered an unconscious Taran to the physicians, made his promised visit to Sir Regus and his lady. He was gratified to find they were none the worse for their terrifying ordeal, for the only injuries they'd sustained related to their wealth. The promissory note from the Treasury went far toward healing that particular wound.

Levant had hoped they would be able to give him some idea of where their attack took place so Denny could focus his search in a general area. But apart from a vague notion of how long it took them to reach the city on foot, neither were much help. And considering neither ever walked very far, their estimations were probably way out. So Denny had no help in his task and was forced to organize his searches in wide sweeps.

Denny parted with the old Torlander and his band of twenty swordsmen at a junction marked only by a thinning of the trees in the deep snow. He watched them ride south and then led his own group northwest. They kept their eyes open for any signs of the gilded coach, traces of the horses' harness—which would likely have been stripped of its gold and silver adornments and abandoned—or scraps of cloth from the clothing taken. Denny guessed the ruffians' haul would have been reduced to small pieces, easily bartered or sold in the villages. Whole items such as gowns, the leather harness, or a complete coach, although worth more in their original state, would attract far too much attention and would be remembered. And as the coach was far too large to be taken far before being dismantled, Denny thought it might provide the first sign of the attack.

He wasn't wrong.

His riders fanned out until they were just in sight of each other, easier in the leafless forest than it would've been in summer. The barren trees and the smothering of dead bracken by the snow meant they could cover more ground in less time. On their very first sweep northward, after an hour of searching, one of his men let out a yell.

They gathered round to see what had been discovered. Denny praised the swordsman for his keen sight, for the small pieces of painted wood had been flung into a stand of evergreens and were only visible from a certain angle. If the man hadn't turned his head at just that precise instant, he might not have seen them.

Denny pulled the wood from the bushes. It was the right color, according to the description given, and Denny identified it positively. He glanced up at his men as he flung the wood back on the ground, exhorting them to be vigilant as they renewed their chase. They remounted and resumed the search.

✤ ✤ ✤ ✤ ✤

The smallest member of the ruffians' group grinned as he watched from another stand of evergreens, this one surrounded by a thick tangle of snow-laden bramble. The risk that the Major might order a search of nearby undergrowth was one he'd had to take, but the brambles would have discouraged any attempts to wade through them and, in the end, Denny hadn't even glanced that way. As the ruffians' leader had guessed, recovering bits of wood or scraps of clothing wasn't part of Denny's brief. Following a trail that might lead to the brigands themselves was.

The little ruffian shook the cold from his limbs and shinned up the stout sapling growing in the copse's center. The recent snowfall had covered his original tracks and now he crawled carefully along the overhanging branch that let him down just outside the ring of briar. He listened intently to the sounds of Denny's men before slipping after them, carefully setting his feet in the same tracks left by their horses.

✣ ✣ ✣ ✣ ✣

General Blaine, King Elias, and Robin took their leave of the innkeeper who had provided their night's lodgings, ignoring his protests at the handful of gold Robin pressed on him. Throughout Loxton Province, Elias's own demesne, the High King paid a network of tavern keepers and landlords to hold rooms available for those traveling on King's business, but these were Lerric's lands, where no such arrangement existed. And although Elias was High King and overlord of Albia, he didn't believe in taking advantage of his position when he could afford to pay his way.

The provisioning of fifty-three men and Elias's appropriation of the inn's three best rooms deserved some recompense in the King's eyes. Especially as the innkeeper went to some lengths to entertain and amuse his distinguished guests, including the offer of his young, flaxen-haired daughter to warm the King's bed. Although Elias felt real regret at turning down his host's most tempting offer, he was no barbarian. His own scruples aside, the landlord's implication that Lerric would have accepted the offer— would, in fact, have considered it his due—was more than enough to dismay Elias, who sent the disappointed girl away with more coin than she would normally see in a year. Elias retired to a cold and lonely bed, honor intact, but frustrated and angry.

Now he rode at the head of the company, wrapped tightly in his sheepskin-lined cloak, bundled beneath his warmest clothing. This far south the climate should have been more temperate, but the winter had as firm a grip here as it did in the north. Elias's hands were frozen within half an hour of riding.

Blaine could sense the King regarding him and Robin enviously. They were snug and warm in their cloaks, able to regulate their body temperature to keep feet and hands comfortably warm. Elias was aware they had to pay for their use of power, but to the King it seemed unfair they should be warm while he suffered the cold. His mood, already sour, worsened as he rode.

Blaine sighed. Elias still suffered from misplaced love and it often rendered him snappy and ill-tempered. The innkeeper's inappropriate offer last night had angered and shocked him, but Blaine could see how hard-pressed Elias was to refuse the gift once he realized he wouldn't be thought barbaric by accepting. His queen's betrayal and her removal from his life had hit Elias hard, and even after three years he still hadn't recovered from that fundamental wounding. His love for Brynne Sullyan, born of her selfless service and the wrong he did to her, only served to compound Elias's misery and sense of abandonment. If she had been free to return his love—and Blaine suspected she would have if not for Robin—Elias would have been a happy man.

As it was, he was prickly at best. This coming meeting with Lerric, never one of Elias's easier client kings, and the probable appearance of his stiff-backed, spiteful daughter, was bound to bring all Elias's baser qualities to the fore. Especially if Lerric trotted out his usual list of complaints and Sofira chose to be difficult.

All in all, thought Blaine, it was likely to be an unpleasant two days.

✠ ✠ ✠ ✠ ✠

Now that his plans were moving forward, it was necessary to increase the number of men Reen could call on to obey him without question. Of the original three sent by Lerric three months ago to pull him from the sea, one was about his master's business elsewhere and the other two were fast approaching the end of their usefulness. Although Reen had found other means of renewing his energy, there were still times when he was forced to take what they could ill-afford. Both men were little better than slack-jawed idiots, their life energies so reduced they could only be given the simplest tasks.

Reen had intended that he and Sofira would already be wed before coping with an occurrence such as this visit, but he was still learning how to use the powers that had been thrust upon him and wasn't yet ready to make his final move. Elias's God-be-damned announcement, while throwing up an interesting possibility too tempting to resist, complicated matters. And if the High King did suspect Lerric of collusion in the Baron's disappearance from the island, Reen had to be all the more careful.

He didn't believe Elias suspected Lerric. He had gone to great lengths to ensure his "suicide" was convincing, and he knew Patrio Ruvar was ignorant of the terrible but fortuitous accident that befell Reen on that hellhole of an island, as well as the true story behind Reen's "friendship" with the unfortunate Serrin.

It had been Serrin's slavish devotion to his "friend" that enabled Reen to survive the hideous flaying of his body, and the boy's unconscious use of his embryonic Artesan talents had healed the worst of the burns and kept Reen alive during those agonized days when all he wanted was to cast his ravaged body into the sea to quench the Fire that had taken root deep in his soul.

When Reen finally emerged from that hellish torment, when he learned how he'd been altered and how Serrin had kept him from death, he had laughed aloud. What irony that the Almighty should place within Reen's wracked, transmogrified body the means to wreak vengeance upon those who profaned the purity of God's given life! Serrin, that embittered and friendless boy who had given his aid so selflessly, so unknowingly, was the first sacrifice to Reen's new powers, the first to lose his life as well as his sacrilegious, Hell-given gifts.

He had realized he could use Serrin's vigorous life force to ensure he survived the perilous leap into the sea. It had been simplicity itself to drain the boy enough to keep him unconscious without killing him prematurely. The forged letter, left once the supply boat had gone, was a masterly stroke, ensuring no one looked for the boy before Reen was ready to leave. The idea of using the boy's life blood to authenticate his "suicide" was another stroke of genius, and some of the lad's stolen energy was used in disposing of his body at the site of the Baron's transformation, ensuring it could never, ever, be found.

Yet Reen, so new to his altered state, had underestimated his frailty. The boy's youthful energy was all but used up in the painful toil to the island's peak and his mighty leap to clear the lethal rocks surrounding the island's base. Despite his careful plans and the men sent by Sofira's father, Reen nearly died in the freezing sea. He had scarcely managed to hold his breath while the waiting boat strained against the waves to pull him to safety.

Since then he had refined his control over his new powers, learning each day how to hone and direct this God-given gift, this weapon of vengeance against his enemies. With this greater understanding came the realization that he would be unable to deal with Elias's visit or exploit it to his best advantage unless he had access to more men and more life force. He must increase his hold and build himself a band of loyal followers who would obey his every whim, whom he could control even at a distance should the need arise.

Once Sofira left him, taking her concerns over the King's visit to her bed, Reen summoned his first two slaves and ordered them to bring him, one by one, certain members of Lerric's forces; the swordsmen of his personal guard and those on night duty at the palace.

Each of them, knowing the men who summoned them, came trusting and unaware, succumbing to the terrible, leaching forces thrust violently into their bodies through the medium of Reen's cane. The Baron drank avidly, savoring each terrified soul, taking only enough to chain each man to his will. There were so many that his body swelled with their life force, fed on their youth and strength, exulted in the sheer physical power coursing through his veins.

He was most careful over the marks he left. Now his control was finer, the site of his violation was subtler. A small red mark was all that remained of his feeding, and he took care to vary the location of each. On the chest, over the heart, was easiest as it was the point of concentration for life force, but it wasn't his only option. He should be able to take what he wanted from almost any area of exposed flesh, and there were plenty of victims on whom to experiment.

The last thing he wanted was for Lerric to investigate the outbreak of nasty sores among his swordsmen. Not that the client king himself would be immune from Reen's control should he prove troublesome, and it was this concern that made the scarecrow so keen to bind Lerric's daughter to him legally. Once Elias's inconvenient visit was over, Reen would hold the marriage ceremony as soon as possible.

He smiled at the thought. He would have no trouble convincing Sofira. She was ready to give herself to him, although she'd get more than she anticipated on her wedding night—much, much more.

Around midmorning, Reen summoned two of his new servants. As the swordsmen stood before him, the red-haired and the black-haired, he noted the tremble of their limbs. They remembered their ordeal of the night before only as a dimly perceived sense of terror. Reen had been careful to ensure they would be incapable of giving him away, especially if any of Elias's men should question them. So although they went in terror of him and were bound irrevocably to his control and his will, they knew nothing damning about their condition, nothing that could implicate Reen. They would remember and act upon what he told them, not what they saw with their eyes.

Pleased with his night's work, Reen gave the two men their instructions. He had thought long and hard about Elias's visit and how he could turn it to his advantage, and he'd decided on a course of action that would eventually guarantee the architect of all his woes, the one true enemy of his God, would be brought before him. Scarcely able to contain his glee at the torment he intended to inflict, Reen sent his minions away, a deep ruby glint suffusing his ruined eyes.

Chapter Twenty-Six

Denny and his band continued their sweep of Loxton Forest, finding more evidence of the brigands' activities. Pieces of carriage, wrenched apart for their valuable decoration; discarded scraps of clothing, stripped of gold thread and jeweled adornment; even parts of the horses' harness scattered among brambles and snowdrifts. Some of these items were clumsily hidden, but most were just tossed aside once their valuable parts were removed. The night's snowfall had clearly been trusted to cover the wanton destruction.

The trail was leading them nearer a confluence with the southern section of the forest, the part allocated to Ardoch and his men. Denny guessed the brigands had taken the coach deeper into the forest, away from the main trail where they'd waylaid Sir Regus, and that they had probably decided to go separate ways or perhaps quarreled over sharing the spoils. He imagined each one grabbing and tearing in an effort to secure some small piece of gold or silver, tossing away the valueless remains as they went.

They would have known they wouldn't be pursued until dawn. They'd want to have gleaned all they could by the time day broke and then they could either hide their haul until the furor died down, or quit the forest for the nearest town.

In Denny's opinion, the latter was more likely. Loxton Forest was a cold and comfortless place in winter and any self-respecting brigand would rather be by a warm tavern fire supping the results of his efforts rather than camping in cold caves awaiting reprisals by the King's Guard. He wasn't hopeful of their capture.

✤ ✤ ✤ ✤ ✤

Ardoch and his twenty men were having less success than Denny. They had seen no evidence to indicate the site of Sir Regus's ordeal or the bandits' trail. They did scare up a small herd of deer, disturb a flock of ravens tearing noisily at the frozen corpse of a fox, and creep up on what a scout reported to be the ruffians' camp, but which turned out to be three peasants from the local village searching for firewood. Ardoch sent the peasants on their way, advising them of the dangers of staying in the forest with an unpredictable group of ruffians on the loose. The Torlander sent his men back to the search, muttering unflattering opinions of scouts who couldn't tell woodcutters from brigands.

✤ ✤ ✤ ✤ ✤

Around midday, Denny's scout gave a yell and the Major halted his band. He could see the scout returning, but the man didn't appear to be in distress or fear. Denny sat his horse and waited.

The swordsman drew his mount alongside. "I've found what remains of the coach, Major. The axles, wheels, and the main structure have been abandoned on the trail just ahead. It's been completely stripped out, even down to the gold tassels on the cushions. It's little better than firewood now, not worth saving. But there are fresh hoof prints around it, and horse droppings. I'd say the ruffians were here not much more than an hour ago. I reckon they dragged the coach here in the early morning, ripping it up as they went, and then abandoned it to take the horses and whatever else they'd stolen to the nearest town. We can't be far behind them."

Denny grinned. "Good man! Anyone got any idea how far the

southern edge of the forest is from here? Can't be more than a few miles, surely?"

The consensus of opinion was three miles. Denny thought it was worth picking up their pace to try to catch a glimpse of the brigands before they reached their refuge. If they were carrying gold and silver and leading four carriage horses, they wouldn't be traveling fast. He liked the idea of dragging them back to Vassa's feet for punishment. It would do his standing no harm at all.

"Come on, then," he called to his band, "let's get after them. With any luck, we can be back within the city by early evening, with hot food in our bellies and something to celebrate. This is one hand that old fox of a Torlander isn't going to win!"

He waved at the scout to lead the way to where he had found the ruffians' tracks. His men surged around him, eager for the chase, happy to warm themselves in pursuit of their quarry and cover themselves with glory. Denny barely registered the small rustle beside the track, made by some animal or other hidden predator.

✤ ✤ ✤ ✤ ✤

Wil was waiting in Lerric's courtyard when the High King's party finally came into sight. The gates were drawn back even before Robin could call out, and the honor guard in the courtyard snapped to attention. Elias and Blaine rode through the gates, followed by Robin and their escort. The gates were drawn closed behind them.

Robin grinned down at Wil as the Corporal saluted him from his position beside the captain of Lerric's forces. Captain Bassan had taken Wil's advice and arranged cleanup details to make the palace courtyard a fitting place to receive Elias. Wil had taken a liking to the man during the convivial evening he'd spent in his company. He had happily given Bassan the benefit of his knowledge of Blaine's exacting standards and even lent a hand with the courtyard's cleaning. Bassan was grateful, for some of his men, those who had been on night duty, were unaccountably slow that morning. If not for his veto against any of them drinking the evening before, he might have suspected them of being hungover. Yet he couldn't smell alcohol on their breath and none of them could give an explanation for their listless state. Bassan shrugged, telling Wil he hoped they weren't in for an epidemic of winter fever, and dismissed the worst affected to less physical tasks.

Bassan stepped forward to take the reins of the King's mount, saluting Lerric's overlord respectfully. Wil took Charger from General Blaine while Bassan send the waiting servant to fetch King Lerric. Others of Bassan's company moved forward to show the new arrivals where to stable their horses.

Robin turned to the King. "Your Majesty, I ask leave to oversee the comforts of my men. I'll join you and the General when I've inspected the barracks and stables and satisfied myself as to the accommodation allocated and the refreshments supplied to your escort."

Wil saw Bassan's eyes narrow at this implied mistrust. He caught the Captain's gaze and gave him a shake of the head to reassure him this was purely routine. In fact, it was a prearranged strategy, formulated to allow Robin to confer with Wil without being too obvious. The Corporal had been told to keep his eyes open and his wits about him and to report on anything suspicious while he was here, and Wil had a few thoughts to pass on to Robin.

Elias merely waved his hand. He stood in the newly-swept courtyard, staring disdainfully at the palace's shabby aspect and noting the neglected impression given by the walled-up windows of the ground floor.

"What has happened here, Captain?"

Bassan swallowed and glanced swiftly over his shoulder,

clearly hoping to see Lerric approaching. But the door to the tower stairs remained closed and Bassan couldn't ignore Elias's question.

"The ground floor of the palace has become rather unsafe, your Majesty," he said. "King Lerric felt it unnecessarily extravagant to spend the amount of gold specified by the stonemasons to effect repairs during the winter months. As the palace will remain largely unused until the spring, the king ordered the ground floor abandoned until then."

Elias stared at him. "You mean he's too tight-fisted to spend his gold on honest workmen who would require heating and feeding in order to do their job. Their services will no doubt be cheaper in the warmer months." He turned a disdainful eye on the General. "Lerric always was a miser."

Bassan looked uncomfortable and was relieved when a single trumpeter on the tower steps announced King Lerric's arrival.

Dressed in warm velvet finery embroidered with his hunting dog motif, Lerric descended the tower stairs and came forward to greet his overlord. Elias stood where he was and made no move toward his subject. Lerric looked older than his sixty-one years; his back stooped and his face lined and pale. Yet he smiled and bowed respectfully and his welcome seemed genuine, even if he did belabor the discourteous lack of notice.

"Your Majesty, we are most honored by this unexpected visit. I bid you welcome to my humble palace. I only hope we can cater adequately to your comforts. This weather has hit us hard and luxuries are in short supply. However, we have done our best in the very short time we were allowed. You and your escort must be frozen by your long ride. I have prepared a warming meal for you and the General. The garrison has been provisioned as best we could manage given the lack of notice, and my Captain here will see to the settling of your men. Come, your Majesty, allow me to lead the way and perhaps, over a glass or two of a very fine ruby vintage I happen to have in my cellar, you can tell me the purpose of this sudden and unexpected visit."

Lerric turned to lead the way to the tower stairs, but stopped when Elias made no reply or move to follow. He glanced back enquiringly, the brief hint of fear in his eyes quickly suppressed.

Elias spoke clearly. "Major Tamsen, I am sure King Lerric did not intentionally exclude you from his luncheon invitation. We shall expect you in his private quarters once you have satisfied yourself as to the comforts of the men. I'm sure you will find someone willing to guide you there."

Robin bowed to Elias, not allowing amusement to show on his face. Lerric apologized profusely to the King as the two monarchs and General Blaine mounted the east tower stairs and disappeared inside the palace.

"Right, Captain." Robin's decisive tone startled Bassan. "My men are tired and cold and these horses need attention. Be so good as to detail men to stable duties and have someone show us to the garrison accommodation. I hope you've laid in adequate supplies. My men are used to good food at the Manor and this foul weather has given them hearty appetites."

Wil could see Bassan was unsure how to react to Robin's curt usurpation of his authority, but as the young man was a major and Bassan only a captain, there was nothing he could do but comply. Wil rather pitied the man as he knew Robin had been instructed to find fault where he could, to goad Lerric's men into a grumbling frame of mind. Each swordsman in Elias's escort had been briefed to foster any discontent discovered among Lerric's men and to encourage its expression, thus, hopefully, learning any useful gossip there might be. Soldiers were universally similar when it came to maligning their officers or their conditions, eager to sound off to anyone who would listen. Robin's men had been told to be sympathetic in their comradeship.

Bassan obeyed Robin's orders and the horses were led away. Robin would also inspect the feed and hay offered their mounts. It was one aspect of his duties that he took very seriously. The men could complain for themselves; the horses could not. But for now he followed Bassan, questioning the man about the palace's routine, criticizing where he could and generally making himself disagreeable. Wil thought he was rather enjoying the role he'd assumed.

Once his tour of inspection was over and he declared himself satisfied as to the quartering and provisioning of his men, Robin dismissed Bassan to the stables, saying he wished to inspect the feed store next. He informed the disgruntled Captain he would join him there shortly.

When Bassan was safely out of earshot the men gathered round. Dexter chuckled softly and Wil eyed Robin, a smile on his lips. "The poor beggar. You gave him a right grilling."

Robin grinned back and dropped to one of the plain wooden beds that had been squeezed into the section of the barracks allocated to Elias's escort. He grimaced at its hardness. "What's this? Are you sticking up for him, Wil?"

Wil ducked his head. "He's all right, sir. Doesn't get enough backup from King Lerric is all. He'd be a good captain under your command."

"I thank you for the compliment, but don't think flattery will get you extra rations. Looks like you'll all have to tighten your belts over the next few days. I'll save you some scraps from Lerric's table if there are any."

There was some laughter and muttered comments as the swordsmen made themselves at home. A fire burned in the stone hearth and the tantalizing smells of food were drifting through. While Dexter went round checking the men were settled, Robin turned to his corporal.

"So, Wil, what have you to tell me? Anything interesting? Make it quick, I can't keep Lerric waiting too long."

Wil launched into the tale of his journey to Lerric's palace, the state of the courtyard as he'd first seen it, and the lax, sullen attitude of Lerric's guard. He told Robin of the reactions of both Lerric and his daughter when he delivered King Elias's message. Robin was thoughtful when he finished.

"Fear, you say? Are you sure? It wasn't just annoyance at the visit's sudden nature?"

Wil shook his head. "No, sir, I'm sure of it. Lerric didn't really react to the shortness of time, but he did seem to be afraid. And her Highness just sat there straight and rigid. She never took her eyes from her father's face. She was sort of radiating tension, if you know what I mean."

"Hmm. Well, that could just be because she doesn't want to see Elias again. They didn't enjoy the best of relationships when they were married. It must be nigh-on unbearable between them now."

"I don't think it was anger, Major. I'm pretty sure I'd be able to tell the difference. But she didn't let much of her feelings show while I was there. She didn't even acknowledge me when I greeted her." He shrugged. "I didn't pick up anything else of interest. Bassan gave me a room in the palace for the night, and although we sat talking long into the evening, I got nothing out of him except the usual grumbles about poor pay and long hours. But this morning he was very short with some of his men. He turned everyone out of their beds early to help with the cleanup, and it seems most of those who were on night duty are suffering some kind of sickness. He was really embarrassed at the state of some of them."

Robin stared at him. "Drunk?"

"That's what Bassan thought at first, but he told me he

couldn't smell liquor on any of them. He thinks it might be an outbreak of winter fever."

Robin wrinkled his nose. "Let's hope not! We don't want to take sickness back to the Manor with us. Rienne'll have my hide if an epidemic goes around the men. All right, Wil. If that's all, I'd better go and attend the King. Well done, by the way. You've been very observant."

He stood up, drawing the men's attention. "All of you, make sure you remember your orders. Do your best to mingle with Lerric's men, but don't get too close to any that seem sick. Do whatever seems right to blend in with them. Play cards, help them out, talk to them. Keep those sharp wits about you and get anything important to me as soon as you can without being obvious. Just remember—you're our main weapon here in Daret. You're much more likely to hear interesting gossip than either me or the General. I'll come and see you later before we all turn in."

✤ ✤ ✤ ✤ ✤

The trail of prints around the stripped-down carriage led southward, the direction Denny would have expected them to take if the ruffians were intent on disposing of their haul in the nearest villages and towns. They had rather stupidly used the main trail, but the Major supposed they thought themselves safe, having a long enough lead over any pursuers. He intended to show them their mistake.

"Come on, lads, they can't be too far ahead. And even if they've reached one of the villages by now we should still be able to catch them with some of their spoils. Get hold of one and he'll soon betray the others to save his miserable hide. Just watch your horses' legs in this deep snow."

The company leaped to the gallop, surging around their commander. The ruffians' tracks were plain in the fresh snow, a ridiculously easy signpost to follow. By the looks of them, there were about ten in the band, if the four carriage horses were discounted. Denny had twenty trained swordsmen—more than enough to deal with an undisciplined rabble of brigands. As he rode, he concentrated on the ground beneath his mount's hooves while still keeping his eyes open for signs they were gaining on their prey.

✣ ✣ ✣ ✣ ✣

Ardoch and his company were growing dispirited. They had found nothing at all and the incident with the woodcutters had demoralized them. The old Torlander had berated them long for that mistake. The scout in particular had a tough time. He now rode at the rear of the group.

Ardoch decided they should make a final sweep southeastward, which would bring them almost to the edge of the forest. If they had seen no signs by the time they reached the main south trail, they would abandon that section of the forest and try to join up with Denny's command. Perhaps they'd had more luck. But it was the swordmaster's private opinion that the ruffians were far too smart to stay in the area, especially in view of the current dreadful weather, and that they'd have quit the forest with what they could immediately carry and would be taking their ease in some distant tavern, replete with warm food and brown ale purchased with the spoils of the robbery.

The thought made Ardoch angry. He had always reacted adversely to oppression, believing it the duty of the strong to protect the weak, not prey on them. He also valued the rights of the populace to go about their business without having to look over their shoulders or pay others to guard them. He was one of the lucky ones. He had a skill with which to defend himself and never had to worry about personal safety.

He'd helped with General Blaine's scourge of Loxton Forest after the Baron's trial and enjoyed it. This recent resurgence of trouble was a personal affront and he knew Denny felt the same. If the Major had come across evidence of the ruffians who had waylaid Sir Regus's coach, well and good. But Denny had made a bet with him before they rode out that he would be the one to bring them to justice, and although Ardoch wasn't a hardened gambler like Owyn Denny, he couldn't resist such a challenge. Hence his bad temper when they had failed to turn up any signs.

He did his best to rally his group, realizing he'd probably been too hard on them. The mistake with the woodcutters was a bad one, but he had to shoulder some of the blame. He should have checked the scout's findings before ordering a charge. He was in command, after all. He promised them some of his winnings if they managed to beat Denny to the prize, and urged them to a faster pace as they continued their southeastern sweep.

Denny and his men entered the final mile before the track emerged from the snow-shrouded trees. The brigands' prints were still clear before them, and occasional horse droppings told the tale of their recent passage. Denny was feeling confident. Ahead of them was a sharp bend in the track and he fully expected to see their quarry in the distance as they rounded this final obstacle. Calling to his men, he urged them on.

Denny approached the bend, in the lead as usual. The trees were densely packed, as they had been for the last half-mile, surrounded by thick stands of shrubbery. The underlying land here was marshy. If not for the night's freezing temperatures, the going would have been treacherous. This was the one spot on the forest trail where heavily-laden coaches or merchants' carts often got bogged and stuck in spring and autumn, but with the marshy ground frozen, Denny didn't have to slacken his pace.

He led his men around the bend at a gallop.

Crossbows thumped and men screamed. Horses crashed and floundered, kicking up great gouts of snow. Bodies were flung to the ground, landing with sickening thuds as they pitched up against trees in a tangle of lifeless limbs. The bows thumped again and the swordsmen who had escaped the first barrage wrenched desperately at their horses' mouths, wheeling the panicked beasts, trying to see and avoid the deadly bolts. Yells, screams, and curses filled the air along with the frantic cries of the injured and dying, man and beast alike.

The crossbows having done their work and the terms of their agreement fulfilled, the band of ruffians surged from hiding, ignoring the carnage behind them and the piteous cries of their victims.

Chapter Twenty-Seven

Ardoch reined in his weary horse beside the scout to see what he'd found on the trail. The Torlander regarded the stripped wreckage of the coach, half-buried in snow, and also the profusion of tracks surrounding it. He grinned.

"Progress at last! Can you make out any of these prints, laddie?"

The scout shook his head. The snow was too badly trampled. But they could all see there had been many horses here—too many, surely, to belong to one band of brigands.

Ardoch called to the band. "Come on, lads, they may not be that far ahead!"

The whole patrol urged their tired mounts to the canter, following the old swordmaster's lead as he headed down the main trail in the tracks of those who had gone before.

They hadn't traveled more than a couple of miles when Ardoch raised his head. "What was that?"

He held up a hand as a faint sound pricked his ears. His company slowed around him, listening intently. "Did anyone hear a cry?"

They shook their heads. The horses were blowing, the thick snow made the going heavy, and they were weary after their long hours of searching. The noise of their breath made listening difficult.

"There it is again." Ardoch definitely heard it this time, and whatever had caused it was not so far away. They were only about a mile from the forest edge. "Sounds like Denny has found our prey. Come on, lads, it may not be too late to grab ourselves some glory!"

The company set heels to flanks and urged their tired mounts once more to the canter. Swords were drawn in readiness and eyes were kept keenly peeled for fleeing ruffians. With Ardoch in the lead they surged down the southern track, still following the prints of both quarry and pursuers.

Ardoch eased up on his reins, slowing his mount. He could see the sharp bend in the track up ahead and his heightened senses had already alerted him to the cessation of sound. "Careful, now. Let's not go plowing into the back of them."

Glancing over at his comrades, he pulled up even more. Obediently, they slowed with him, proceeding at the trot. A movement off to their right caught their attention. They turned as one to face their adversary, but what emerged from the blanketing shrubs was not an armed and dangerous ruffian.

"Ye gods, laddie! What happened to you?"

Ardoch's eyes went wide at the lone swordsman slumped over the neck of his lame and bleeding horse. He hissed as he registered the evil-looking crossbow bolt protruding from the man's back. The wounded horse staggered up to its brethren before sinking to its knees, completely spent. Its rider pitched over its neck and collapsed into the snow, bright red blood staining the churned ground.

Ardoch leaped from his horse to kneel beside the man. He cradled the limp body in his arms. There was nothing else he could do. The man's lung had gone; he was drowning in his own blood.

"What happened, laddie? Where are the others? Where's Denny?"

The glazing eyes stared upward, the final spark of life fading.

A weak hand made a feeble movement toward the bend in the track before falling back to the snow.

Spitting a curse, Ardoch laid the man down. There was no sound from farther up the track—no sound at all save their own breath and the horses' stamping. The beasts were nervous and Ardoch knew why. Trained warhorses always reacted to the smell of blood, recognizing the scents of battle. He stood, brushing the stained snow from his combat leathers, and remounted his horse. Glaring at his men, he motioned them warily forward.

Their caution was wasted. Rounding the bend in the track, the gory, red-stained snow and the tangle of broken bodies told its own grisly tale. Ardoch's eyes prickled as he beheld the confusion of dead men and dying horses. Walking his mount slowly forward, the Torlander surveyed the carnage, his face set and expressionless. "Two of you get on up the track, see if there's any sign. It's my guess they've made off, but make sure. Then get back here."

He dismounted, walking among the dead, his eyes hot. His men did the same, some of them granting a final mercy to those few brave beasts that had survived the attack but were too badly wounded to save. There were few; the ruffians had laid their trap well and sprung it with brutal efficiency. How that lone swordsman had managed to scramble away from the scene was a mystery. None of the others had escaped.

Ardoch stood for some time looking down on the crumpled body of Owyn Denny. The young Major had died in a volley of bolts. No fewer than four pierced his body and any of them would have been fatal. But the one through his heart ensured he hadn't suffered by seeing his company massacred. He had died before he'd hit the ground.

Ardoch couldn't get his breath. All of these men were comrades, but Denny was a special friend. Likeable, reliable, quick-witted, and amusing, he'd been a widely respected officer even before his well-deserved elevation to major. Since his promotion, he had grown into the role, impressing his subordinates and seniors alike with his sense of loyalty, fairness, and duty. And, Ardoch reflected sadly, there would be more than a few noble ladies who would mourn his passing. Not least, he thought with a sudden pang, a certain colonel in Elias's forces. He didn't envy Taran the task of telling Sullyan of her friend's demise.

The scouts returned with no sightings of the ruffians. Ardoch was aware his men were watching him, having checked all the bodies and dealt with the wounded horses. Their demeanor showed their deep unhappiness at the fate of so many comrades, and Ardoch knew there would be a few sore heads in the morning after they tried to drown the knowledge of their own mortality in spirits. It was up to him to give them back some purpose, for if he allowed them to dwell on what had happened he may well lose some to despair.

He drew a deep breath, steadying his own surge of anger at the wanton slaughter, and faced his men. "Now then, lads, we must hold up and do honor to these brave men. They died in the service of their King and in the pursuit of their duty. They didn't fail and there's no shame to their deaths. We must bear them back to the city with the respect they deserve, and then we'll give them the best gift we can—we'll go after those murdering bastards and run every one of them through!"

A muted mutter of agreement spread through the dispirited swordsmen. Ardoch gazed around them, seeing sorrow and misery in many an eye. He knew how they felt and he sympathized, but he still had to get them, plus twenty slain men, safely back to the city before nightfall. And then he had the unpleasant task of reporting to Colonel Vassa and explaining why only half the detail that had left at first light had returned. With the current feeling of suspicion pervading the castle and the jumpy mood of the people following Neremiah's murder, this news was going to please no one.

Sighing deeply, Ardoch stooped to the gory snow and pulled the crossbow bolts from Denny's lifeless corpse. He flung them away in disgust, his vision blurring. He was damned if he'd return the Major to the city with the instruments of his death still embedded in his flesh. Then he wrapped Denny's bloodstained cloak around his body, hiding his face, and lifted him to his horse's neck. Ardoch himself would bear his friend. The other members of his command dealt with the rest of the dead.

It was a sad and vengeful band that made its way slowly through the forest back toward the city.

Robin was shown into Lerric's warm, luxurious dining hall by a servant. He had led Robin through the same shabby hallways Wil had trod, and the Major's opinions on the condition of Lerric's palace were much the same as his corporal's. The sumptuous surroundings of Lerric's dining hall only served to cement Robin's conclusions, and the blatant difference between the king's part of the palace and that frequented by his servants lowered Robin's estimation of the man even further.

Despite Lerric's little speech to Elias bewailing the harshness of the season and the lack of fine things, the banquet laid out upon gold and silver platters wouldn't have disgraced the finest state occasion. Robin's eyes widened as he took in the variety of foods on offer.

There was a whole roast sucking pig, goose, and jugged game. There were fresh winter vegetables, herbs, and steaming sauces. Fresh-baked bread dripping with warm butter sent its comforting smells into the air. There was even fruit, dried but still wholesome and unwrinkled. The flagon of good red wine had already done the rounds judging by the full goblets, and the delicious smells spoke of well-planned festive celebrations rather than a hastily-arranged and scraped together meal.

Lerric himself, far from appearing put-upon by this insulting, unheralded visit by his powerful overlord who had cast off his client king's daughter for base treason, was acting the genial host and appeared relaxed and at ease. He even stood to welcome Robin as the young Major entered the room.

Lerric approached him, smiling easily, holding out a finely-chased goblet containing the same ruby vintage he had offered both General Blaine and Elias.

"Major Tamsen," he said in greeting, "I've heard tales of your reputation among the High King's forces. My men follow your exploits with great interest. I don't suppose you'd consider transferring to the southern climes of our fair realm? Bordenn is a pleasant province with much to recommend it, despite this damned spell of heavy snow. Come, man, what do you say?"

Lerric threw his arm across Robin's shoulders and the Major wasn't too sure how to take such familiarity. He was also reluctant to take the wine. He wasn't here to enjoy himself and he wanted to keep his wits about him.

"I'm flattered by your interest, your Majesty, but I'm afraid I'll have to decline your gracious offer. I'm content where I am, and I already have everything I could wish for."

Lerric chuckled and removed his arm. "Well said, well said! A pity, though. I could do with a few of your caliber here in Daret."

Robin thought he detected a genuine note of regret underlying Lerric's jocular tone. The client-king turned to his other guests. "Elias, your General here seems to turn out courteous as well as talented swordsmen. That man you sent as your messenger was most polite as well. Are all your men at the Manor so polished?"

Elias held his eye. "My Lord Blaine and I both believe that men trained to use sword or bow don't necessarily have to be peasants, Lerric. All are treated as equals in my forces. Their skill in battle determines their rank, not birth or class. We find that good pay, comfortable conditions, and firm discipline result in men proud of their achievements. Self-respect is an important aspect of life in the King's Guard. All my men are trusted and encouraged to speak their minds. And Lord Blaine has his own views on how they should conduct themselves, views I fully endorse."

Lerric narrowed his eyes at the General. "Ah yes, I had forgotten you were a Lord in your own right, General."

Mathias Blaine inclined his head just enough to be polite. Robin knew he had no love for Lerric, having faced the man during the civil war when he was spineless enough to support his more powerful neighbors against King Kandaran. The General's opinion of Lerric was only one grade higher than his opinion of the traitor Reen. He made no attempt to disguise his prejudice when he replied.

"As is my second-in-command, Lord Vassa, although he lost his lands, his home, and his family to the senseless ravages of the civil war. And my other colonel is of royal blood, of the House of Pharikian, the ruling House of Andaryon. So you see, your Majesty, the men of the King's Guard have no lack of fine examples to follow."

Lerric's sour look told of his displeasure at being reminded of the high status of Elias's senior officers. He decided against pursuing the matter and turned back to Robin, who hadn't been invited to sit, nor had he taken the proffered goblet.

"Major, won't you join us at table? And please, don't refuse this wine. It really is an excellent vintage. I'm sure neither your general nor your sovereign would deny you the chance to sample it."

Lerric didn't miss the glance Robin cast the General before receiving his nod of permission. The aging king narrowed his eyes once more as Robin accepted the goblet with gracious thanks and seated himself at the long table, farther down than General Blaine. It seemed to bother Lerric for some reason, but he cast the moment aside and turned to his overlord.

"So, Elias, to what do I owe this unexpected visit? There's nothing amiss that I'm aware of. Bordenn is in reasonable shape apart from this damnably vicious winter, and we sent our levy to the capital in good time this year. Although whether we we'll be able to afford so much next year is a worry. We're likely to lose livestock if this freeze goes on much longer, and if the fields are too frozen to plant the early spring crops we'll go sadly short—"

"You know full well the levy I set upon Bordenn is nothing if not reasonable, considering your support for the rebels who killed my father!"

Lerric went pale at Elias's sharp tone.

"And in the light of your daughter's betrayal of her husband and rightful lord, I think both you and your people were let off leniently. I'd be well within my rights to raze your entire province for what your family did to me."

"But you won't, will you, Elias?"

The new voice came from behind the High King. None of them had heard her enter and Elias froze, his face set, his eyes suddenly haunted.

"You won't because you know the people are innocent, yet they'd be the ones to suffer the most. And if you truly wanted to avenge yourself upon my father, you would have carried out the punishment already. As you have punished me, and do so still, by depriving me of my children."

The temperature in the dining hall plummeted, despite the huge log fire. The room was silent save for the crackle of flames, and all eyes save the King's were fixed upon the stern Princess as she made her way around the table to face her erstwhile husband. She stood before him, refusing any homage, challenging him to refute her statements.

Elias had gone white and Lerric was clearly terrified his embittered daughter had gone too far. Elias's tolerance was legendary, but so was his anger when roused. Every man had his breaking point and Sofira had already wounded him deeply. Wounds from which he still hadn't recovered, wounds which would probably never heal.

He made no reply, but stood, bowing his head to her in a show of respect such as she hadn't afforded him. Robin wanted to applaud the High King's restraint. His Artesan senses showed him a clear picture of the struggle for composure raging beneath Elias's outward calm. Yet he could also see an undercurrent of tension in Sofira, and remembered Wil's earlier words. He resolved to concentrate on Sofira tonight. Elias knew his business and could be relied upon to conduct himself. He wouldn't risk a demeaning quarrel in front of Lerric. But Sofira was obviously set on goading the King and Robin wondered why. Was she simply vindictive, or was there a more sinister agenda behind her deliberately cruel words? It was his task to find out.

"My Lady," said Elias, his voice admirably controlled, "I greet you. I wasn't sure whether we'd have the pleasure of your company tonight. Your father seemed confused as to your whereabouts. But I'm glad you've come, for my visit concerns our children."

The King's soft words and reference to Seline and Eadan sidetracked Sofira's venom. Sofira, galvanized by his mention of her children, dropped her arrogant pose and, just for an instant, gave Robin a glimpse of the raw wounds she bore in her heart.

"Are they well, Elias? Has anything befallen them?"

Her hands were clasped at her breast and her face was ashen. She appeared vulnerable and Robin knew this was no ploy. This was the genuine fear of a woman separated from the children she loved.

Elias saw it too and he didn't torment her.

"They are both well, Madam. It isn't their health I've come to discuss."

Lerric gave a small start, hastily covered. Robin saw it, Sofira did not. "What then?" she demanded, the shield slipping back into place. Now she knew they were well, she could afford to shut away her softer emotions.

Elias held himself in check at her continued lack of respect. She had always been able to hurt him and her refusal to even pay lip service to politeness angered him. Not surprising, thought Robin, for he was the aggrieved party here, not her. He was the one betrayed—cuckolded in his power if not in his bed. It was her own actions that had separated her from her children.

Elias could say none of this. He was the villain in her eyes for sending her away. She would never feel any different and he mustn't let himself be stung by her venom. With a visible effort, he ignored her challenging tone.

"Madam, we've been long hours on the frozen road this morning and we're tired. We shouldn't dishonor your father by ignoring this sumptuous meal. I suggest we leave our discussions until we've done justice to his kitchens and can relax in less formal surroundings. Allow me to pour you some of this excellent wine."

Sofira's eyes hardened, but she could hardly refuse in front of the General and Robin. She could see Elias was determined not to be goaded and Robin also sensed her intrigue at his motives. If he truly had proposals concerning their children, she wouldn't prejudice her position by antagonizing him. He had come a long way in foul weather to speak with her and that indicated an important decision. She needed to hear what it was. She smiled at Elias.

Robin was astounded at how a simple smile, not even a particularly warm one, could transform so stern a face. Sofira's bleached skin and hard gray eyes weren't given to softness, and the scraped-back style in which she wore her blonde hair did nothing to smooth the angles of her face. But her smile brought animation to her features and he caught a brief glimpse of the woman Elias had married: stern, quick-witted, and stiff-backed, yes, but still an attractive woman.

As if she'd sensed his surprise, Sofira turned the smile first on Robin and then on the General. She allowed Elias to pull out her chair and sank gracefully into it, arranging the folds of her expensive court gown. She accepted the goblet he poured for her and raised it to them.

"Very well, gentlemen, we will put aside our differences and our business and concentrate upon enjoying a rare occasion to indulge ourselves. This winter has been a difficult time for our province and luxuries are hard to come by. My father and I have done our best and we hope you approve of our humble attempts. Let us drink to tolerance and reason, if not to friendship."

Elias clearly didn't like her reference to hardship, echoing as it did her father's. He was also unsure as to her toast, but could think of no way to counter it. He took his place at the head of the table and raised his glass. They all drank, and Lerric signaled to the servants. As the food was served and the conversation turned to more mundane matters, Robin determined to enjoy the meal if nothing else.

✠ ✠ ✠ ✠ ✠

Ardoch and his somber band arrived at the Forest Gate just before dusk. The laden clouds fulfilled their earlier promise and flakes of white swirled around the burdened riders. The rising wind had teeth of ice. The old Torlander, huddled deep inside his fur-lined cloak, was heartily glad to see the welcoming glow of lamps as he approached the gates to the city.

"Nearly home, Denny lad," he murmured, but of course there was no response from the deadweight on his saddlebow.

The gate guards, expecting their return, had already observed their approach and registered their sorry state. The gates were hauled open before the company reached them and the four guards stood to attention, eyes hard and vengeful, saluting in silence as their fallen comrades were borne past them into the city. Ardoch took his band through the darkening streets, making no attempt to hide from the populace, most of whom were on their way home after the day's business. His dour mien and the obvious burdens he and his men carried soon attracted the attention of Loxton's inhabitants. They swarmed around the horses, exclaiming in dismay, pointing at the bodies and gasping in shock.

The news flashed ahead of them, faster than their sober pace, and crowds flocked every street they rode through. Neremiah's murder the day before was now common knowledge, as were the terrible fire at Jinny's estate and the purpose of the dawn patrols. In a bustling, cosmopolitan city like Loxton rumor worked its spell swiftly. Ardoch heard all sorts of theories bandied about.

The churchman had offended the King and the murder had been carried out by King's Guard attempting to recover gold from the Arch Patrio. Neremiah's murderer was someone with a grudge against the Matria Church, against Elias, against the city, and Loxton Forest was thronging with brigands and cutthroats. Trade was to be cut, the port blockaded, and the city's inhabitants were to be penned inside the walls until the murderer should be found. Elias had lost his reason, fleeing the city in fear of his life, taking his senior ministers with him. The King had gone to kill Lerric, suspecting him of being behind both murder and fire. Ardoch heard the rumors and saw the beginnings of panic in people's faces.

But he said nothing and his men said nothing. They rode with heads bowed in silence, honoring their dead, looking neither left nor right. They moved through the swelling, murmuring crowd, untouched by the accusations and speculations, and the crowd—like the rumors—grew and moved with them. People were drawn irresistibly in the wake of the sad procession, right up to the castle gates.

The castle guards heard them coming. The crowd's anxious muttering rolled before the procession like the outriding wind of a storm. One guard sprinted for the castle, calling Captain Valustin, and the Captain alerted Colonel Vassa. Together they raced for the gates, unable to believe the spectacle before them.

Ardoch and his men, dour and snow-covered, sat their mounts outside the gates. The guards hadn't opened the gates in case the crowd surged through. For the moment, the mob only wanted answers and reassurance. If they didn't get it soon, the mood would turn ugly and Vassa would have a situation on his hands.

Through the gates, the Colonel looked into Ardoch's haunted eyes. He took a breath, casting his gaze over the riders, taking account of each horse with its sorry burden. He focused once more on the Torlander. "All of them?"

Ardoch nodded, not trusting himself to speak. Valustin took a shuddering breath and Vassa cursed.

"We need to get you inside. Captain, get these people back."

Valustin slipped out of the postern gate, drawing the guards with him. Together they encouraged the swarming people to move back, just far enough to open the gates. The crowd fell silent, save for a few rowdier ones to the rear who couldn't see what was happening. Taciturn and somber, Ardoch led his band into the relative calm of the castle park.

Once the gates clanged shut and the cavalcade moved off, the clamor rose once more. Angry shouts and demands for explanations filled the air and the gates themselves were rattled. Ardoch roused from his lethargy long enough to glance at them.

"They followed us from the outskirts," he told Vassa. "They're frightened and they feel insecure. Someone will have to speak to them or there'll be a riot."

Vassa pursed his lips. "They'll have to wait. I have more important things on my mind."

But Ardoch was right. As they neared the castle and saw the courtyard filled with servants, ministers, and courtiers, all avid for the truth of the massacre, Vassa realized this event could be the spark to ignite the tinder of rumor. A city like Loxton was always one step from unrest, and the atmosphere of apprehension created by Neremiah's murder, the King's absence, and now the fire, was ripe for the flame of panic. He would fail in his duty to his King if he did nothing to calm the overanxious inhabitants.

He roared for assistance and swordsmen came forward to relieve their living comrades of the burden of the dead. The fallen would be laid respectfully in the castle mortuary until their pyres could be built. The men of Ardoch's command were led away to be fed, warmed, and comforted. Vassa himself led the old Torlander into the castle and up to Levant's chambers, where he was required to give the details of the day's terrible events.

✤ ✤ ✤ ✤ ✤

The wastrel, unnoticed by most, lingered among the crowd by the gates. He had received fresh instructions. Satisfied so far as to how his plans had progressed, Reen had decided to push his luck. He intended to make use of the link forged with Princess Seline, but left it up to his minion as to how this could be achieved.

The vagabond had heard the clamoring crowds accompanying Ardoch's band and joined the throng. At least the brigands had upheld their part of the bargain. Perhaps they had even gleaned sufficient spoils from their staged robbery to make up for what he had promised them in final payment. They would get no more gold from the Baron.

He scrutinized the despondent cavalcade as it bore its sorry burdens to the castle, mildly surprised at the thoroughness of the brigands' ambush. He hadn't expected them to succeed in killing the entire patrol. Their specific instructions had concerned Denny only. They were almost worth the extra gold they wouldn't receive. But enough of that. He must turn his thoughts away and concentrate on his next task. Somehow he had to contact the young Princess again, and the mob clamoring at the gates gave him an idea.

The crowd's mood was turning ugly. They had obeyed the Guards' commands to let the dead through out of respect, but once the gates clanged shut they realized answers wouldn't be forthcoming. Urged on by a few who were bolder than the rest, the mob bayed for attention. The vagrant quietly encouraged the troublemakers. A few choice remarks about the disinterest of their leaders and the contempt of the nobility for the common populace soon found fertile ground. An undercurrent of viciousness, present in any large gathering of people, crept to the fore. Within a very short time, the initially curious and nervous crowd had become a slavering beast threatening to tear down the gates.

The wastrel smiled. Elias's ministers couldn't afford to ignore such unrest. This volatile mood would only encourage the criminal element to commit atrocities, and the last thing the city needed was more trouble. Very soon now someone would come and speak to the mob, maybe invite the ringleaders into the castle. Therein lay his opportunity.

Chapter Twenty-Eight

The fine meal went a long way toward mellowing the mood between Elias and his subordinate. Even Sofira seemed willing to abandon her hostility and proved a pleasant, if quiet, hostess. She made conversation with both General Blaine and Robin, although she studiously avoided Elias's attempts to engage her attention. He was relieved the meal went as smoothly as it had. He'd anticipated long, frosty silences and awkward moments. Yet they had all managed to put aside their differences while doing justice to the truly delicious meal.

Elias complimented Lerric on his kitchen and allowed himself to be led into the comfortable, smaller room that served Lerric as both audience chamber and private living space. He was drawn over to the fire, where he and Blaine accepted their host's offer of fellan laced with brandy.

Robin accepted the fellan but refused the liquor. He also politely refused Lerric's invitation to join their discussions, saying he needed to check on his men. Blaine gave him permission to withdraw, and Elias inclined his head in approval. His stated reasons for visiting Lerric were spurious, as Robin knew, but even had they been real they wouldn't have concerned a major in Elias's forces. Lerric's obvious desire to keep both the King's Artesans where he could see them was good enough reason for Elias to deny him that comfort. Besides, Robin was technically still on duty.

Elias's security was his responsibility and it was perfectly natural for the commander of the King's escort to oversee the deployment of his men.

Accepting the Major's refusal, Lerric summoned a servant to convey him back to the barracks. He addressed the young man before he left.

"Major, I allow those of my men who are off duty to walk into town of an evening and relax in the tavern. It might foster good relations among our forces if some of your men accompanied them. What do you say?"

Robin bowed, his swift glance at the General going unnoticed by Lerric. "I will speak to the men, your Majesty, and suggest the idea. I thank you for your interest in their comfort. I'm sure they'll have made friends by now among your guard. You know what soldiers are like."

Lerric grinned as Robin withdrew, commenting to Blaine, "Are you sure you can't spare that young man? I could use a few like him, even for a season. He could teach manners to some of my ministers. Mind you, my ministers would be locking away their wives, too fearful of their virtue should they set eyes on that handsome face."

The General didn't smile. "Your ministers would have no reason to fear Major Tamsen, your Majesty. He is happily married and far too honorable to behave improperly. But I fear his wife and young son might complain if I lent him to you. And I'd be hard-pressed to replace him, even for a season. He's one of my finest officers."

Elias hid a smile. He knew the tale behind Robin's arrival and early years at the Manor and how close he'd come—on more than one occasion—to summary dismissal by the very man now singing his praises. The hotheaded, impetuous youth, a talented swordsman and the best shot with a bow the Manor had ever seen, hadn't endeared himself to the General with his undisciplined ways and reluctance to accept authority. Elias firmly believed that if not for Hal Bullen, Robin would either have found himself before a military court for insubordination or killed in some rash and ill-considered action. Either one would have been a criminal waste.

Elias regarded Lerric, the turn of conversation leading him nicely toward his goal—the duplicitous discussion with Sofira about their children. He wanted to keep both her and her father talking, prick them into indiscretion if he could. They might just let something slip if their tongues were unguarded, and mention of either Seline or Eadan was guaranteed to provoke a reaction from the Princess.

"Where are all your ministers, Lerric? I'm surprised to find your palace quite so deserted."

Lerric poured more brandy into Elias's cup, avoiding contact with his sharp blue eyes. "This dreadful winter has affected my poor province badly. Most of my ministers run estates of their own, as I can't afford to pay them enough to retain a permanent court. They always prefer to spend the middle winter months in their own homes. It's quite usual for Sofira and me to find ourselves alone at this time, so we adjust the business of the province accordingly. This year, what with the weather and the roads still being so bad, not even my closest nobles have wanted to return, so we remain as you find us. But as the inclement weather has also prevented the recommencement of trade, it hardly matters. Bordenn is a small and insignificant region, as you know, so I'm not as incommoded by a lack of advisors as you'd be in my position."

The King ignored Lerric's reference to Bordenn's poverty. "It's also fortunate, is it not, that your lack of a court means you don't have to attend to the repairs your palace needs?"

Elias's casual question seemed to catch Lerric unawares.

"Repairs?" he echoed, staring blankly at his guest. But he didn't have to struggle long before he was coolly rescued by his daughter.

"I believe my Lord refers to the damaged lower floor, Father."

Lerric flushed, but Sofira gave him no opportunity to compound his lapse. She addressed Elias. "My father isn't troubled by such minor matters, my Lord. He has more pressing business on which to dwell, especially now he's bereft of advisors. I try to carry the burden of such trivial concerns, and discuss them with the servants and the chatelaine. As the stonemasons who advised us on what was needed were reluctant to carry out repairs during this dreadful weather, I decided it would be best to abandon the lower floor entirely, make it secure, and leave it till the spring. It's not as if we need the space. We don't have the size of court you support even in summer when trade and the affairs of the province are at their height."

Elias inclined his head. "You are prudent, Madam. You always did know how to manage your affairs to your best advantage."

Silence fell and Elias wondered if Sofira would take offence at his double-edged statement. However, he'd put no inflection on his words and for Sofira to take exception would make her sound petty. The controlled stiffness in her tone as she replied was his answer.

"I thank you, my Lord, but you didn't come here to compliment me on my handling of the housekeeping. I believe you wanted to discuss our children?"

Elias was disappointed his first attempt to prick her temper had failed, but he would have ample opportunity as the evening drew on. He was particularly keen to observe her reaction as he gave her a report of Eadan's progress at the Manor. Her tantrum when he told her what Sullyan had said about Eadan's emerging talent was still the subject of after-dinner conversation among his courtiers. He anticipated something similar when she learned of her son's removal to Sullyan's care.

"So I did, Madam, so I did. But before I do, would you like me to tell you what they've been up to lately? You must be hungry for news."

Elias was well aware Sofira corresponded with Seline. He read all her letters to her daughter, as well as those Seline returned. So he knew his daughter hadn't told Sofira of Eadan's sojourn at the Manor, and she wouldn't have had any word of her son for some while. He had much to tell her, for although Eadan was learning his letters as well as his more unusual lessons, he wasn't yet able to construct a legible message.

Elias's offer to share his children's progress with her must have felt like crumbs from a beggar's table to the Princess. She couldn't refuse, however, despite her obvious outrage. He was right, she was desperate for news. Her throat tightening on the words, she managed to say, "My Lord is most kind."

Elias smiled, enjoying the verbal fencing. Sofira possessed a sharp mind. It was a shame her tongue and her temper shared the same characteristic. Facing her squarely, holding her gaze, he said, "I don't believe you know that your son has been taken for training at the King's College. He was accepted as an Artesan Apprentice nearly three weeks ago. You'll be pleased to hear that the reports I've received from Colonel Sullyan speak highly of his progress so far."

If Elias had hoped for an uncontrolled outburst, he was disappointed. Lerric gasped, but all the High King saw from Sofira was a further paling of her face and a tightening of her eyes. There must have been a very real struggle taking place within her heart, but all she did was clench her hands on the arm of her chair, striving for outward calm.

✠ ✠ ✠ ✠ ✠

In truth, Sofira wasn't so surprised to hear of this development. Ever since Elias told her, with pride and relish, her only son had somehow inherited the very gifts she so despised, she had expected such news. He was too absurdly pleased with his innovative College not to have his son patronize the place. But she hadn't expected Eadan to be sent there so young. He was only four years old, for goodness sake, far too young to be living among strangers.

Yet she couldn't speak her mind, not with General Blaine sitting there absorbing every word and nuance of her reactions. They already knew she would disapprove, so she might as well allow herself to show it. But she'd be damned if she'd give Elias the satisfaction of witnessing the full extent of her fury. Besides, if she gave free rein to her feelings, her father might say something stupid.

She took a steadying breath. "Was that wise, my Lord? Is he not too young to be sent so far from home?"

Elias smiled infuriatingly and launched into a full description of how Eadan had settled in, what he was learning, and his antics among his fellow Apprentices. And, presumably because he knew it would anger her, he especially mentioned the boy's fast-developing friendship with the young Andaryan seaman, Jay'el.

Despite her anger, frustration, and sense of helplessness, Sofira listened avidly, unimpressed by her son's achievements as an Artesan but soaking up every other item of news Elias let fall. The King, knowing her opinions on the subject of outlanders, was clearly surprised when she showed interest in the College's first non-human student, and answered her questions as best he could. Sofira couched her queries around her son, but still managed to elicit the information that Jay'el was courting the sister of the woman chosen by the Andaryan co-ruler Aeyron as his bride-to-be, and that Aeyron would probably bring his intended to the Citadel soon to introduce her to his people.

Remembering the Baron's careful instructions over eliciting what information she could, Sofira tried to be artful and casual in her manner. She convinced Elias she was concerned over the effect mixing with outlanders might have upon their son, and was so natural about it she was sure he didn't suspected her ulterior motives. His intentions for this visit were being turned on him without his even knowing.

✢ ✢ ✢ ✢ ✢

Robin was grateful for the opportunity to escape the verbal contest he knew would ensue once Elias and Sofira locked horns. He would have to return to their company once he'd seen to the men, but hoped by that time the worst of the bloodshed would be over. Maybe the embittered Princess would have retired, hopefully after giving away something they could use.

So far, Robin had seen little evidence of treasonous conspiracy between Lerric and his daughter, and certainly no traces of them hiding the Baron. He had watched Sofira closely during the time spent in her company and had detected no falsehood behind her words, only an understandable undercurrent of tension or dislike. Of course, this ability of Artesans to sense deviousness wasn't infallible, and some were better at it than others. But Robin was a Master and had been so for three years now. He trusted his instincts.

He followed Lerric's servant through the neglected hallways until they came to the east tower door. He nodded to the guard there and received an answering salute, smarter than those given the guests as they'd arrived. He smiled grimly. News of their party's efficiency and discipline traveled fast. He imagined after Bassan's humiliating treatment at Robin's hands, the Captain had gone swiftly through his men, kicking a few backsides and smartening them up. He certainly hoped so. Disgruntled soldiers were likelier to spill their grievances to sympathetic ears. He had already told his lads to fabricate grumbles of their own. It wouldn't do to appear too perfect.

Nodding thanks to his escort, he stepped out into the icy teeth of a strengthening wind. He clattered down the stairway, not wishing to stay exposed to this dreadful cold. Such conditions meant he'd have to convince Dexter and the men it really was in the interests of their King to accompany Lerric's guards to the tavern. At least it wasn't snowing, and the permission he was about to grant them—a moderate consumption of alcohol—should sweeten the pill.

He entered their quarters quietly, pleased to see a card school already in progress at the far end. Dexter sat with two of his men and four of Lerric's, and the mellow gleam of copper bits showed in front of most of them. Robin waved them down as his men stood, Lerric's rising more slowly.

"No need for ceremony, lads, you're all off duty. Dex, his Majesty King Lerric has informed me that on certain nights he permits his off duty men to patronize the local tavern. Have you heard of this?"

Dexter grinned, laying down his cards. "Yes, sir, Rhys here was just telling us about it."

Robin nodded at the shabby man, whose furtive gaze spoke volumes. He relaxed when he realized Robin wasn't angry.

"Well, I give you leave to go, if any of you want to." Robin's casual tone belied the meaningful stare he gave Dexter. "And as I've given you leave to go, I suppose I'll also have to give you leave to sample the local ale."

Dexter's lads gave a rousing cheer and Robin saw Lerric's four men glance at each other as if amazed permission was needed.

"But," continued Robin, and the voices fell away, "if any one reports for duty tomorrow the worse for drink, he'll suffer the consequences. Am I understood?"

Dexter came to his feet and snapped a salute. "Yes, sir."

The other men followed his example and Robin nodded.

"Very well. I'll leave you to your evening. All to be counted in by midnight, Captain, and it's your job to pick those who'll remain behind on guard while the rest enjoy themselves."

Dexter acknowledged the command and the Major turned on his heel, hiding a smirk. Dexter was doing a sterling job of playing the role he'd been assigned. Robin could already hear him whispering his discontent to Lerric's startled men. Dex would bewail the unfair position Robin had put him in and would wriggle himself out of guard detail. The men he would "select" to remain behind were already picked and had their own set of instructions. Dex would slope off to the tavern with his new friends, allowing them to draw various other instances of ill use from him. Robin knew he could rely on Dexter's sharp wits to stay out of serious trouble, and to see the other lads did too.

He made a swift pass by the stables, satisfying himself over the horses' care, and stayed to give his stallion, Tobias, the piece of dried fruit he'd saved from Lerric's table. The young mahogany warhorse took the treat with soft lips and blew down his nose as Robin stroked his satiny neck.

Pleased with the horses' conditions, Robin made his way back across the courtyard toward the tower stairs. A few of Lerric's men were already making their way out of the palace toward the town, their heavy cloaks, tattered and dingy, wrapped tightly against the biting wind. He heard Dexter's voice rise in triumph as the Captain won a hand of cards, and he also heard the disappointed murmurs of the players who'd lost. He grinned. Trust Dex to make himself at home among strangers. He continued on, his sharp eyes coming to rest on the walled-up windows and what appeared to be a recently fitted door to the supposedly unsafe lower floor.

There was no one in the courtyard, the last of Lerric's men disappearing into the darkness beyond the gate. His own men would wait for Dexter to win as much as he could before joining the others in the tavern. Robin was unobserved.

He moved closer to the fresh masonry filling what had once been a perfectly good window. He stared at it, wondering why it should bother him. He listened intently, but no sounds came to his ears. He even employed his Artesan senses, casting them through the empty spaces beyond the walls, feeling for anything that might be out of place. He stepped up to the stout wooden door and tried the latch. It was locked fast. He examined the door for possible peepholes, but whoever had done the work had done it well. There were no gaps in the woodwork or between door and jamb to see through. And anyway, it was dark.

Robin shrugged, as much to cast off the niggling feeling of unease as to indicate his lack of success. Nothing threatened and nothing lurked within the walls of the lower floor that he could sense. It was empty and deserted, as Sofira had said. He would mull over his reaction later and maybe discuss it with Sullyan when he reported to her later that evening.

The men were coming out of the barracks now. Dexter was being harangued good-naturedly by both his own lads and Lerric's for his multiple wins, and he promised them ale as compensation. Robin mounted the tower stairs to avoid being seen. Dex had created a mood and Robin's presence would spoil his hard work. He slipped through the tower door as the men spilled out into the courtyard cursing the cold.

The red-haired man fingering something deep in his pocket didn't warrant a second glance.

�֍ �֍ �֍ ✖ ✖

By the time Ardoch finished giving his account of the day's slaughter to Colonel Vassa and Lord Levant, the mob at the gates was in a frenzy. The noise rose to Levant's private suite. It seemed the longer they had to wait for information, the more convinced they were it wasn't forthcoming. And the common people knew there was only one reason for their betters to withhold information. There must be seriously bad news which would affect their lives, their businesses, or their safety. Maybe all three.

As the sound swelled again, Levant gazed between Vassa and Ardoch. He sighed. "I suppose it had better be me."

Vassa grimaced in sympathy. "I'll send a company with you."

Levant shook his head. "They'll only think I fear them."

Ardoch grunted. "Well, you'll not go alone. That's an ugly mood they're in. I'd not trust them. If you're going to let some of them in, you'll need our lads to stop the rest from barging in too."

Levant wanted to argue, but could see it would do him no good. He gave a curt nod. "The sooner we convince them there's nothing threatening the city, the sooner they'll return to their homes. The pickpockets and thieves must be having a field day with this crowd and all those homes left unattended. There'll be a barrage of complaints to the constables tomorrow, Jerrim, mark my words."

"As if we didn't have enough to worry about," Vassa said morosely.

"Come on, then, Ardoch. Assemble your men and let's get this over with. I'll see twenty of them, no more. Any that try to force their way in can spend the night in the garrison cells. See if that cools their heads."

✣ ✣ ✣ ✣ ✣

Princess Seline had managed to give Bessie the slip. It wasn't hard to do. Bessie was in the infirmary when the commotion started, caring for those who'd been burned in the fire.

When she heard about the mob at the gates, she went to look for her charge, but the Princess was nowhere to be seen. Bessie was irritated but not entirely surprised. The girl had been increasingly intractable since winning the argument with her father over going to the market without an escort. Bessie understood the King's motive for allowing his daughter her own way, but feared he had set a dangerous precedent. The Princess was growing more headstrong by the day, and without her father to reprimand her no one could gainsay her whims.

Seline, when informed of her father's trip to Bordenn, predictably demanded to go. Equally predictably, she was refused. Bessie didn't think for one minute Seline expected Elias to take her. A winter journey was rare enough—no one traveled far in such dreadful weather without a pressing reason—and to take a young child would have been folly. Yet even had it been summer, Elias would never have allowed Seline to go to her mother, and the young Princess surely knew it. It was Bessie's opinion the girl only wanted to prove a point, to argue with her father, to remind him she was growing up and would no longer be treated like a child. And she had wanted to make him feel unsettled and angered, to pay him back for his treatment of her mother.

In that, she'd succeeded.

Bessie eventually went back to the nursery, hoping Seline had returned there. But her room was still empty and Bessie swore in frustration. She was growing very tired of the girl's petulance and lack of respect for her elders. Something would have to be done once Elias returned.

Bessie knew how it would pain the King when she told him of his daughter's latest misdemeanors, but she had no choice. She was responsible for the Princess while her father was away, and if Seline wouldn't obey her something had to be said. Sighing in vexation, Bessie left the nursery to do yet another round of the castle, searching in vain for her wayward charge.

✣ ✣ ✣ ✣ ✣

Seline watched the angry crowd from the safety of a window. She'd found an unoccupied room on the lower floor that looked out on the park gates and slipped inside unnoticed. She was unlikely to be disturbed. The room she stood in was one of the unallocated offices, and most of the day's business was concluded. Elias's ministers would be changing for dinner or returning to their homes. If they could get out of the castle grounds.

Seline watched in apprehension. Even from her distant vantage she could feel their rage. She had never seen such an angry crowd. The mob looked like a single entity; she couldn't see individual faces or bodies. They were too far away and it was too dark. Many of the people carried torches and the flickering flames cast weird shadows over their forms, blending them together. She was thankful to be safely behind walls. She wouldn't care to be out there facing that baying mob. She found herself admiring the swordsmen on guard duty, putting up with thrown missiles and hurled abuse. She imagined her hero, Tad, coping with such ferocity and pictured him using his firm, gentle voice to reason with the crowd and turn aside their fury.

She was still lost in her personal fantasy when she realized the angry cacophony had stopped. Her eyes snapped back into focus as she scanned the parkland. Movement near the castle courtyard to her left caught her attention as a small party came into sight. She recognized Elias's First Minister, Lord Levant, surrounded by thirty or so of the King's Guard led by Master Ardoch. They made their unhurried way toward the gate, fixed by the crowd's collective stare. She considered going outside, the better to hear and see, but the risk of discovery was too great. Bessie was bound to be seeking her, and if any of the castle servants saw her alone they'd run and tell her irritating watchdog. The idea of being found and hauled back to the nursery before this was over was enough to hold her still.

She stood and stared, fascinated by the scene playing out before her.

Chapter Twenty-Nine

Levant walked confidently in the midst of the King's Guard, not wholly reliant on their presence for his air of calm purpose. Rendan Levant was no craven. In his capacity as First Minister, a post he had held for many years, he'd faced down countless dangerous opponents. In his younger days he'd been a creditable swordsman, serving in the King's Guard until injury forced him to leave. He wasn't intimidated by the crowd's size or anger.

Besides, he reasoned, these were ordinary townspeople. They weren't revolutionaries; they had no axe of oppression to grind. They were simply merchants, traders, and businessmen who had seen troubling things and heard more troubling rumors. They only needed reassurance. Levant had to admit that the assassination of Neremiah, the dreadful fire in the night, and the sight of a whole company of crack troops slaughtered were enough to spook anyone. It was only the catalyst of numbers that had caused this anxiety to escalate.

He walked quietly and stood openly before the mob when he reached the gates.

The crowd fell silent. The swordsmen moved away from Levant, showing trust in the crowd's restraint, and Levant stood forward to speak. The crackle of many torches was the only sound until he spoke, his eyes ranging over their faces, his clear voice ringing out over their heads.

"Good people of Loxton, you've come here in search of answers. You've seen and heard of troubling events in the city and you are understandably concerned for your welfare. Rumor has taken hold of you and you're unsure what to believe. So hear me now when I tell you there is no cause for alarm. Nothing threatens the city or your safety, and nothing threatens our King. He is away from the castle for a few days visiting with one of his subject kings, and my latest information is that he's safe and well. I ask you now to disperse and return to your homes. The recent sad events that have taken place in our city are unconnected and are being dealt with. Trust us to clear things up as you always have. Please. Go home."

Levant's speech was a good one and his unruffled demeanor encouraged quite a few to do as he suggested. It was cold, despite the press of bodies and warmth from the flames, and some of them were probably thinking of their shops and business premises, vulnerable to casual thieves. Gradually, from the back of the crowd, people began to slip away.

But at the front were those most aroused by the troublemakers' goading, who still muttered poison into gullible ears. The muttering rose in volume until someone spoke up.

"We're not going until we get some explanations. How do we know you're telling the truth? How can you say nothing threatens the city? A senior churchman ripped to pieces in his own Minster—that sounds like a threat to me! And now a whole company of King's Guard slaughtered like cattle, just after a violent attack on a noble and his wife! Not to mention that fire last night. Safe, are we? We don't believe you!"

The crowd jeered and catcalled, lending vociferous support to their unofficial spokesman. They jostled nearer the gates and some small stones were thrown from the back of the crowd. The missiles came nowhere near the party from the castle, but they enraged

Ardoch. He had just been through one of the worst afternoons of his life and thoughts of his friends laid out cold and dead on mortuary slabs pricked at his conscience. He was in no mood to pander to foolish townsfolk who didn't have the sense to know when they were well off.

Ignoring Levant's warning glance he drew his sword and raised his voice, a voice well used to reducing recalcitrant Guardsmen to gibbering wrecks. He used it to good effect.

"The next person to show his disrespect will get a taste of my steel. First Minister Levant has come here out of concern for your welfare to talk with you, and all you can do is accuse him of falsehood. I'd think twice about your response if I were you. Me and the lads are just itching for some action after finding our comrades slaughtered. A rabble such as you wouldn't even count as exercise. Do you hear me?"

There was sullen silence. Ardoch's reputation was well known among the townsfolk. He had been a popular figure in the King's Guard for more years than some could count and his devotion to duty was legendary. There wasn't a man among the rabble who wanted to cross words with him, let alone swords. The silence dragged on while the Torlander's gaze swept over the shamed faces before him.

Levant broke the hiatus with a discreet cough, trying to hide a smile. "Er, thank you, Swordmaster. Good people, I can see your concerns run too deep for me to assuage by a simple statement here at the gates. If you would care to choose twenty of your number to represent you, I will grant that group free audience at which they may air your anxieties. I will answer all questions openly and honestly and see what I can do to reassure you. Will that content you?"

There were murmurs of surprise. A free audience was rarely granted. None had heard of it being used in such circumstances before. But then the King had never been away from the castle when such troubles had come to light. The crowd muttered, Ardoch hovering close to the gates, his sword still naked in his hand.

"Well?" he roared.

"We accept," someone replied, to a ripple of nervous laughter.

Ardoch's incredulous expression at being misunderstood was almost comic. "Get on with it, then!" he bellowed, causing those nearest him to cower.

Men were hastily shoved forward and the Guardsmen cracked the gates, just enough for one man to slip through at a time. They clanged shut behind the last man, a shabbily dressed, dirty fellow. Levant turned back to the castle, leading the delegates with him. Ardoch stayed where he was with the majority of his men, staring meaningfully at the crowd.

They stared back.

"Go home," the swordmaster ordered.

Once again, people at the back began to obey, but those at the front were slower. Ardoch sighed.

"Lads."

The sound of twenty swords being drawn didn't reassure the crowd. The measured single pace each Guardsman took at the same time as his neighbor was the final straw. The crowd thought better of its reluctance and suddenly remembered pressing business elsewhere. People melted into the cold, dark streets like thawing snow.

✣ ✣ ✣ ✣ ✣

The wastrel lagged unnoticed behind the other delegates as they walked alongside Lord Levant, all strangely subdued now they were separated from their fellows. Their anxieties and grievances seemed less important, less meaningful, now they were to be given the opportunity to air them, and doubtless many of the twenty would have turned and headed for home, like the rest of the crowd.

The vagrant had no interest in his fellow delegates now that they'd fulfilled their function. He looked about keenly as they entered the castle doors, alert for any chance to hide until such a time as he would be free to search for the Princess. Finding her in the labyrinth of corridors and staircases would be no easy task, or so he thought.

So it was with startled surprise that, lingering forgotten behind the rest of the delegation, he came face to face with her as she stepped out of a room close by.

She gasped in shock, but before she could give him away he hissed, "Highness, I must speak with you."

He had only intended to let her know she must contrive another trip to the city, but before he registered her intent, she grasped hold of his sleeve and dragged on his arm. "In here," she murmured, "quickly."

Nonplussed, he allowed her to tug him into the deserted room she'd stepped from. She shut the door and leaned her weight against it, staring at him.

"You still smell bad. Don't you ever take a bath?"

He observed her keenly. Her initiative had surprised him, but her manner was so like the Baron's he had found himself obeying without question. He ignored her comment.

"Your Highness, we must be brief. I hadn't thought to speak with you today, but since you've precipitated events, I can tell you my errand now. Her Majesty, your mother, sends you greetings and asks if you can help in a simple matter."

Seline's eyes widened and she clasped her hands together. "You've seen my mother? Is she well?"

The vagrant shook his head. "I can only tell you what I was told, and we have little time—my absence might soon be marked.

What I need is a hiding place within the castle. Somewhere that will allow me to come and go in the night without being observed. Can you help me?"

"If I do, will I get to see my mother?"

He heard the desperate longing of an abandoned young girl in her voice and responded smoothly. "Of course you will. This is part of the plan to allow your mother to return to the castle. You want to help her, don't you?"

Seline glared at him. "Of course I do. And I have the perfect hiding place—somewhere no one goes, not even the servants."

The wastrel was skeptical. This sounded like a child's hideaway and he needed more than that. Once he was safely hidden within the castle he could devise his own methods for disguising his movements, but it had to be more than the wardrobe in the girl's room or the space beneath her bed.

Seeing his dubious look, Seline smiled slyly. "I gave my nursemaid the slip so I could come down here and watch what was happening. She never lets me see the important stuff, but I'm going to rule the realm someday—at the very least, a province. I don't need to be sheltered. I know bad things happen. And I have my own private place where I can go when I don't want her to find me." Seline reached into her gown, pulled out a pouch, and produced a key. She dangled it before the vagrant's eyes. "Do you know what this is?"

He inclined his head. "Pray tell me, your Highness."

Seline watched his face. "It's the key to the east wing, where my mother had her apartments. Now she's gone, it's deserted and locked up. No one goes there, ever. Except me."

The vagrant gazed respectfully, possibilities flooding his mind. Seeing his expression, Seline's lips tightened.

"You thought I was going to suggest something silly, like hiding you in my room, didn't you?"

He merely grinned.

She stamped her foot. "I'm not some little baby, you know! I do know what's going on. My mother sent me that letter, remember?"

He saw the sudden thought that struck her and she put aside her petulant air, becoming a lonely little girl again. "You're going to be here for a few days, aren't you?"

The vagrant nodded.

"If I write a letter to my mother, can you take it for me? My father reads all the letters I send through his runners and it's so unfair! I want to send her a private letter, like the one she sent me. Will you do that?"

The vagrant had no idea whether he would even survive this latest task, let alone when his usefulness to Reen would give out. Nevertheless, he nodded. He'd tell Seline whatever she wanted to hear if it gained him access to the east wing. It sounded like the perfect place to hide, if it truly was deserted.

Seline smiled in triumph and returned the key to her pouch. The wastrel regarded her narrowly. "How are we to achieve this, your Highness? I may have already been missed and we can't risk them searching the castle."

Seline shook her head. "We'd have heard by now if they'd discovered your absence. They'll hardly notice one less among that group. You can stay here till later. I'll come and get you to take you to the east wing. But I'd better go. My nurse … my maid will be looking for me and we don't want her blundering in here. Stay quiet and wait for me. It'll be a few hours until I can come back. I have to have supper and a b—that is, I have certain duties to attend before my maid will think I've retired. But I'll come as soon as I can. I'll try to bring you some food, too."

Before he could reply, Seline unlocked the door and slipped outside. Darkness returned to the room. He heard her quick steps pattering away and smiled into the gloom. This was turning out better than the Baron could have hoped for and his servant knew he'd bought himself a few more days of life. He settled into one of the comfortable armchairs to sleep away the hours until his coconspirator returned.

✢ ✢ ✢ ✢ ✢

"Oh, come on, man—what's the matter with you? One more ale's not going to hurt you. What's the worst he can do, flog you? Bet it wouldn't be the first time! Ain't it worth a little pain to enjoy a good drink with your mates?"

Dexter glanced over to where the red-haired guard was badgering two Manor swordsmen, Col and Pengar, into another drink. He saw the silent appeal Col sent him and gave the briefest of nods.

He and a good few of his men were sitting in the smoky bar of the local tavern, along with what looked like most of Lerric's guards. From what Dex had seen since their arrival, Lerric didn't have that many men, but the tavern was crowded with them tonight. Dex had split his own forces up among Lerric's to better the chances of hearing interesting gossip. Col and his close friend Pengar were sitting at the table next to Dexter's with a few of Lerric's men, all of whom seemed determined to get very drunk indeed.

Dexter frowned. They seemed to have no pride in themselves and no loyalty to their master. Though their conditions and their pay were poor, they were still the servants of a king. Dex thought that should count for something, but not, it seemed, among these rough and vulgar soldiers. As soon as they were free of the palace grounds they reverted to a rabble, making Dexter's instincts for discipline itch to smarten them up. But he was playing a role tonight and mustn't forget it.

He was surprised how hard it was to act the disgruntled, downtrodden minion. It made him realize just how privileged they were to be in the service of Elias, under Mathias Blaine. The General might be stern and unforgiving, and a hard taskmaster, but he was fair. He was a leader who believed in the integrity and trustworthiness of his men, and rewarded loyal service in kind. There wasn't a man of his who wouldn't give his life for his King, his officers, or his comrades.

But this lot! Dexter sighed. Underneath the grime, poor food, and lack of proper discipline, most of these lads were probably all right. Wil had told him about Captain Bassan, and Dex had come to the same conclusions as his corporal. Under a senior officer such as Major Tamsen—or Colonel Sullyan, he thought with a grin—most of these swordsmen would discover a sense of pride they never knew they had. It made him pity them and he threw himself wholeheartedly into gaining their trust.

The tavern was smoky and noisy; it was hard to make yourself heard. The other men were playing cards, arm-wrestling, hassling the overworked tavern girls, or passing around a strange-smelling pipe, which contained a strong narcotic. The hazy purple smoke it gave off got into everything it touched—hair, clothes, food, drink. It was impossible to avoid and Dexter very nearly ordered his lads to leave once he realized what it was. But he would be failing his major and his King if he did, so instead he glared meaningfully around at his men, making sure they all understood.

✤ ✤ ✤ ✤ ✤

Col took a healthy swig of his ale and wiped his mouth on the back of his hand. He frowned. "That's a different brew to the last one."

Pengar followed suit, gazing up at the ceiling as he ran the brown liquid around his tongue. "Not bad, though."

Their companions, two of Lerric's men, grinned. "Thought you'd like it," said the red-haired one who had bought the ale. "We make a fair brew in these parts, if the harvest don't fail, that is. One year we had so little corn we had to drink bloody cider all winter."

Col was partial to a bit of cider. "What's wrong with that?"

The second man, the black-haired one, stared at him in disgust. "Woman's drink, bloody cider is. Weak as rat's piss, like women are. A man needs good ale to strengthen his sword, if you know what I mean."

An obscene gesture accompanied this remark, along with general laughter. Someone slapped a passing tavern wench soundly on the rump. She squealed and let loose a slap of her own, which connected with the offending man's face. He roared with indignation and stood up, catching the girl about the waist and sending her two empty tankards flying. He carried her off to a darkened corner, to the cheers of his comrades, where he ignored her struggles, forced her to the floor and proceeded to teach her the price of her insolence.

Col and Pengar traded glances, not liking this turn of events. They had never been in a tavern where such things were permitted in full view of the other patrons, but the swarthy landlord took no notice, not even when the girl cried out at her ravisher's harsh treatment. Pengar shook his head at Col—they couldn't do anything that might turn the delicate friendships they'd forged into hostility.

Their red-haired companion saw them eyeing the grunting swordsman in the corner. "Want some of that, do you? I can arrange it if you'd like."

Col managed a smile. "Maybe later. This ale's too good to waste on tavern girls."

Lerric's man roared with laughter and clapped Col on the

back, nearly making him choke. Col rolled his eyes at Pengar, wishing they'd drawn guard duty instead.

He and Pen had been singled out by the two palace men as they walked to the tavern. Most of Lerric's men had gone on beforehand. Only the handful who had unwisely accepted Dexter's suggestion of a few hands of cards were left. Col and Pen had been lucky enough to double their original stake and the two palace men must have thought them worth the price of a drink or two. Pen generously bought the first round and Col the second, although he and Pen had made their tankards last and only bought ale for the other two. Now, as the palace men were halfway down their third tankard each, Col decided the time was ripe to probe for information.

"Drink here often, do you?"

The red-haired one stared across at Col with bleary eyes. He'd been on night duty not twenty-four hours ago and had enjoyed precious little sleep what with Bassan's damned cleanup detail.

"Are you joking, mate? Don't have the pay to do this very often. We don't get regular pay like you lot, y'know."

Pen's eyes were struggling to focus through the smoky haze. The face of the black-haired man seemed to flicker for a moment, as if a cloud had passed over his vision. "So why do you stay?"

Red-hair grunted. "Bad pay's better'n no pay! At least we don't have to ask permission to drink of an evening if we wants to. Seems to me you boys can't take a piss without asking first."

"There's nothing wrong with a bit of discipline." Col shook his head. The purple smoke was giving him a monstrous headache and his stomach was beginning to rebel.

Black-hair snorted. "Oh, don't give me that. Don't pretend you like it. That pretty young officer of yours is a right bastard by the looks of things. He's only got to sneeze and you lot jump. Poor bloody Bassan was in a right old state by the time he'd finished with him. Never seen the old bugger so worked up. Gave us a proper kicking, he did, dragged us out of bed—and us been on night duty—and told us to sweep the bloody yard. *Sweep the yard*! I'm a swordsman, not a bloody skivvy!"

Col was feeling distinctly green. He couldn't work out what was wrong with him. He'd never had trouble holding his ale before. "It's just the way we do things. Major Tamsen's all right. He's strong but fair. Like the Colonel. Now she—"

"*What* did you say? Did you say *she*? Don't tell me you lot take orders from a woman! Did you hear that, Othal? Their colonel's a bloody *woman*!"

✣ ✣ ✣ ✣ ✣

Red-haired Othal grinned at his comrade, but there was no retort from either of the Manor men. Both simply sat there, eyes open, hands on the table, completely unaware of what was going on around them. Othal's companion, Varth, returned the grin and glanced around the chaotic tavern. The room was so smoky he could barely see the men at the next table, and the noise had swelled so much that normal conversation was impossible.

"Time to go."

Othal nodded and put his hand under Pengar's arm. "Up ye get, me laddo."

Pen stood with no protest and Col rose likewise in Varth's iron grip. The four left the tavern, unobserved by anyone from the Manor.

Once outside, Varth and Othal picked up their pace, tugging at their unresisting companions. Col and Pen, eyes wide but unseeing, were led away from the tavern and into the town's back streets.

It was late and the freezing weather meant all the townspeople were indoors. Hardly any windows showed a light. Daret was a poor town and bed was often the warmest place in most people's homes. Col and Pen were guided through the cobbled streets until they reached the outskirts, where large storage barns flanked the road and hay and animal smells filled the cold, still air.

Varth dragged Pen toward the nearest barn, pulling the door open. Othal followed, pushing Col toward a wooden bench. The Manor swordsman sat heavily when released from Othal's grip, but didn't react at all to his surroundings. Othal took flint, steel, and bowl from the pocket of his cloak then knelt and struck at the tinder. When he had a glow, he lit a taper and touched it to the lamp they'd left there earlier. Varth closed the door, the feeble lamp lighting only the tiny circle where the four men sat.

Othal glanced at Varth, but his companion's eyes had gone strangely blank. Ignoring him, Othal turned his attention to Col and Pen, a nasty smile quirking the corners of his mouth.

"Now then, my friends," he said, his voice low, quite different to the rough tones he had used before. "Who'll begin? Who wants to tell me all about Major Tamsen? Let's start with something about his family and where he comes from, shall we?"

As Col began to speak, his droning voice devoid of inflection, a sullen ruby glow swelled in Othal's eyes.

Chapter Thirty

L evant returned to his private rooms after bidding farewell to the people's delegation. As a whole, the meeting went well. The hotheads were less inclined to accuse him without the mob behind them. He had answered all their questions and assuaged their fears. He sent them away to report to the city before the hour grew too late.

Vassa awaited him in his living room, sitting by the fire and sipping brandy, deep in thought. When Levant came in, Vassa rose and handed him a crystal tumbler of amber liquor. Levant took a healthy swallow before collapsing into the chair opposite Vassa.

"I could have done without that."

"Did you satisfy them?"

Levant shrugged. "It wasn't hard. They'd whipped themselves up over nothing. You know what crowds are like. Once they calmed down they were ready to see reason. I just hope nothing else happens to set them alight. We're woefully shorthanded after losing Denny and his company."

Levant eyed Vassa, seeing the other man's mouth tighten at the mention of the tragedy. "What are you going to do about that?"

Vassa sighed. "Valustin will command as acting Lieutenant Major until the King returns and promotes him, but what I really need to do is contact the Manor to request more men. I tell you, Rendan, I'm not looking forward to reporting all this to Elias. If he's having his usual trouble with Lerric—not to mention having to deal with Sofira—he's not going to be in any sort of mood to receive this news. That is, if I can report to him at all. Have you heard any more about Taran's condition?"

Levant shook his head. "I left strict instructions for both you and me to be told immediately if he wakes. The last bulletin I received said he was still deeply unconscious. That fire and the tragedy of Lady Jinella's death affected him badly. You know something of what these Artesan types are like, Jerrim, and you've known Taran longer than me. What are the chances of him snapping out of it?"

Vassa shrugged sadly. "I really couldn't say. I'm no expert on what they're capable of, despite living among them all these years. I have absolutely no talent, according to Colonel Sullyan, and I can't begin to imagine what they experience. But I've frequently heard her say they're highly-emotional people, ruled by their feelings until they learn to use and control them. It may be that without help of some kind Taran will take days to recover."

Levant grimaced. "And we can't contact Colonel Sullyan to ask for that help. It'll take two days to get a runner to the Manor. The King's due back before then. What shall we do?"

"We'll just have to wait until Major Tamsen or General Blaine tries to bespeak Taran tonight. When he doesn't report as usual, they'll know something's wrong. Maybe one of them can rouse him from where they are, but even if they can't, Sullyan will soon know of it. I wouldn't be surprised to see her arrive here in the next few hours."

"We'd better wait up, then, in case she does." Levant leaned forward to refresh Vassa's glass.

✢ ✢ ✢ ✢ ✢

Dexter counted heads as his men left the tavern, emerging reluctantly into the freezing night, tugging cloaks reeking of smoke tighter about their bodies. Dexter frowned and counted again. "We're two short. Who's missing?"

The men glanced around, checking their friends. "Col and Pen, Captain," someone called.

"Did anyone see where they went? Did they leave the tavern?"

Dexter's snappy tone indicated his annoyance. They'd all had strict instructions as to what they could do and where they could go. Slinking off on their own hadn't been part of the plan. He was surprised Col and Pengar had disobeyed his order; it wasn't like them.

He recalled Col's questioning look when offered more ale. This didn't add up. He called out names and sent some of the men back into the tavern to check the upper rooms and the storeroom. When that yielded no results, he began to get really worried.

"Come on, lads, split into teams of four and begin a search. Don't go knocking on any doors just yet. Let's check the streets, barns, and outhouses first. Work outward from the tavern. Hopefully they just felt the effects of that damned smoke and staggered outside to get it out of their lungs. Look anywhere they might have gone to get out of the cold. Maybe they were overcome and they've fallen asleep somewhere."

They fanned out and began searching, Dexter cursing under his breath. He had been certain he could rely on all his lads. Col had been with him many years and was a trusted comrade. Pengar was a more recent addition, having transferred from another garrison a year ago, but Dex would have sworn he was as reliable as the rest of them. He'd never had any trouble from the man. Swearing expressively, but careful to keep his foul language to himself, Dex urged his men to the search.

It was over an hour before word reached him the absentees

had been found. He had grown increasingly irritated and anxious. It was coming on for midnight and they would all be on a charge if they were late getting back. He shuddered to think how badly this would reflect on the King. He raced after the man who'd brought him the news and soon arrived at the barn where Pen and Col had been found.

He swore aloud when he saw the state of them. Collapsed on the floor, they both reeked of strong alcohol. Four empty bottles of grain spirit lay in the straw beside them and they had both fouled themselves in their drunken state. Dex thumped his fist into the door, furious at this flagrant breach of orders. The two men would be put on a charge and would eventually be discharged with dishonor. Such behavior was simply not tolerated. But Dex had been in command this night and his was the ultimate responsibility.

"Get them out of here!" he barked. "They'll have to be carried. Gods, just look at them! What did they have to do this for? The General will have their hides. I might even flog them myself. Come on, get on with it! We've fifteen minutes to get back to the palace before we all get some of what's coming to them. *Move!*"

It was a dispirited band that jogged up the final yards to the palace gates. Wil was on duty, along with two of Lerric's men, and he was watching anxiously. He had the gates open before they arrived, and frowned in consternation as they straggled through. "What happened, Captain? Why are you so late? I expected you an hour—gods, what happened to those two?"

Dexter stared sourly at the goggle-eyed corporal as he waved the men through the gates. "Bloody disaster!" he spat. "Went and got drunk, didn't they, and against my express orders! Where's the Major, Wil? I'd better report this to him before he finds out from someone else. Lerric's lot seem to think it's funny and I wouldn't put it past one of them to make sure he hears before I get to him. That's all I need!"

Wil sent a runner to fetch Robin, and Dexter saw the two men back to their bunks. The Major strode into the crowded barracks, his feet thudding furiously on the floorboards. His face was thunderous and Dex cringed. This was likely to be all over the palace by morning, causing embarrassment to the General and the High King. He squared his shoulders and prepared to face the storm.

Robin marched over to the two comatose swordsmen and stared down at their sprawled bodies. He wrinkled his nose in disgust at the smell of alcohol and human waste combined. He transferred his fury to his captain, and Dexter tried not to look away from the disappointment he read in Robin's eyes.

"What the hell happened, Captain? Weren't my instructions clear enough?"

Dexter took a deep breath. "They were perfectly clear, sir, and all the men were fully aware of them."

"So what's your explanation for this fiasco?" Robin flung out an arm toward the unconscious men.

Dex bowed his head. "I don't have one, sir. All I can tell you is that the last I saw, Col and Pen were obeying your orders. They were sitting with two of Lerric's men, and Col asked permission to accept one more drink. I gave him that permission, as they'd only had one."

"Then they took your permission too literally, Captain. Didn't I tell you to only take men you were sure of? If these two couldn't be trusted, they should have been left behind!"

"But that's just it, sir!" Dexter held Robin's furious gaze. "I'd have trusted these two with my life. They've never given a moment's trouble, you know that. They're usually the last ones to bother with drink. That's why I deliberately included them. That's why I took my eye off them. I'd swear on my life and my sword that they wouldn't have done this on purpose. They would never knowingly let you down, let alone the King."

Robin stood in silence. He trusted Dex and trusted his judgment of the men. If Dex said they weren't inclined to heavy drinking, he had to believe him. And it was true that he'd never had to discipline either man. He gazed at the two oblivious men before turning back to his captain.

Dex held his gaze openly, willing him to believe what he'd said. It didn't alter the circumstances and wouldn't cut any ice with Lerric's men, but Dex wanted his superior officer to know he was convinced some chicanery had occurred this night—some malicious prank to discredit Elias by revealing his crack troops to be just as debauched and disobedient as Lerric's rabble. He knew they would suffer the consequences, but it was important that Robin understood none of them had deliberately let their King or comrades down.

Robin let out his breath with a sigh. He shook his head in exasperation. "Very well, Dex, I believe you. We'll wait until morning and see what these two have to say for themselves. Get them cleaned up and make sure all our lads keep their mouths shut. There's no chance Lerric's men will, but we can't do anything about that. Keep these two out of sight until I've had a chance to talk with them. I'd better go and report to the General and the King. Elias is going to be furious over this. He's trusting us to show Lerric how it's done, and he's not having an easy ride up there. I wouldn't care to speculate how he'll react.

"Carry on with your orders, and try not to let this … incident upset the lads. I still trust you all and I'll reserve judgment on these two until later. I'll see you in the morning."

Dexter saluted smartly, as did every other man standing, feeling wretched. He feared how far the repercussions of this fiasco might travel.

✢ ✢ ✢ ✢ ✢

Robin shook his head as he left the barracks, feeling exactly the same as Dexter. He could hardly conceive of a worse occurrence, except perhaps a drunken brawl that ended in a murder. He could only imagine what the General would say, and Elias's temper was vicious when crossed. And he was being crossed at every turn up in the luxurious surroundings of Lerric's private chambers.

Robin mounted the tower steps two at a time and brushed past the sentry without a word. His angry footfalls sounded loudly in the empty hallways, unmuffled by rug or tapestry. He passed into the better-lit halls and found, with a heart sinking further by the minute, that he could hear angry voices even from here. He had hoped Sofira and Elias might have calmed down before he returned. He cursed under his breath, using one of Sullyan's choicer oaths. The next few minutes wouldn't be pleasant.

He approached the door to Lerric's private rooms and reached for the latch. Before he could touch it, the door was wrenched open from inside, and the furious, white-faced specter of Sofira appeared before him. Her eyes snapped fire and two spots of color flamed high on her cheekbones. She breathed heavily and her eyes were red-rimmed, although there was no hint of tears. She froze when she saw Robin, and then turned slowly, deliberately, back to face the room.

"You are cruel, Elias," she said loudly, her voice quivering with rage or pain. "You must never have loved me if you can come here offering false hope. You can't deceive me with your soft words and empty promises. You hold out your hand then snatch it back just when I begin to believe you! It's a dishonorable trick, and unworthy of you, to use my children against me."

She turned to Lerric. "Father, if you love me at all you'll withdraw your hospitality from this man. He has degraded me, both as a Queen and a mother. It shames me that you sit there with him, sharing your fireside and the comforts of your house. Well, you may do as you like, but I won't suffer his torments any longer. I've taken as much abuse as I can stomach and I'll speak with him no more."

Sofira trembled as she delivered this speech. She half-turned as if to leave, then stopped and raised her head. She glared at Elias, her voice low and full of menace as she said, "You do wrong to dismiss me so lightly, my Lord, and you have shamed me for the last time. I say to you now, for I hope we never meet again: Look to your safety, Elias of Albia, and look to your throne."

The Princess turned on her heel and strode past Robin, her shoulder striking his as she went. She didn't acknowledge the contact and Robin chose not to react. He looked in dismay at the King's rage-reddened face, wondering how on earth he could deliver his report now.

He could see Elias controlling himself with difficulty. The meeting had degenerated as soon as the subject of their children was broached, and far from causing Sofira to lose her temper and let slip information, she had turned on him immediately, accusing him of ill-treating their children, of withholding letters, of poisoning their minds against her. It was all patently untrue, but it had put Elias on the defensive and he'd ignored General Blaine's attempts to bring him back to the visit's purpose. As Blaine had feared, Sofira had turned the tables on them, playing on Elias's wounded emotions as easily as Sullyan played her harp. Robin was forced to watch in discomfort as Blaine eventually despaired of Elias and retired into resignation, nursing his drink and trying to block out Sofira's harsh, grating voice.

An awkward silence descended. Elias sat unmoving, his breast heaving with the effort of controlling his towering anger, his hands gripping the arms of the chair so hard the knuckles were white. Lerric sat to his left, his eyes on his drink, his face inscrutable. General Blaine was waiting for Lerric to speak, but when it was obvious he wouldn't, not even to apologize for his daughter's behavior, Blaine turned to Robin.

"What was it, Major? No trouble, I trust?"

Robin swallowed. He wasn't going to blurt out what had happened in front of Lerric, although the king would hear of it soon enough. And with Elias in his current state of mind, he didn't think it politic to add to the High King's distress. Yet his news couldn't wait. He took a breath.

"May I speak with you, sir? In private?"

Blaine raised his brows and very nearly broke his own rule by initiating contact with Robin. They had agreed before their arrival that contact through the substrate was to be avoided unless vital. The policy was a hang-over from years before when Sullyan thought the Baron had discovered the means to monitor substrate communication. The thought there might be others who could eavesdrop on supposedly secure conversations was hard to shake off. Blaine controlled himself before he went too far.

He was saved from replying by Lerric, who rose to his feet. "Gentlemen," he said with false cheer, "it's been a long evening and you must all be tired. I have had comfortable rooms prepared for you. I suggest we allow our overheated emotions to calm down before we enter into any further discussions."

He bowed to Elias. "With your leave, my Lord, I'll bid you goodnight. There is a servant outside who'll convey you to your rooms when you're ready. I will see you again at breakfast."

Elias didn't react to Lerric's words or otherwise acknowledge him. It was left to the General and Robin to accept Lerric's homage and return their own as the subject king left, closing the door behind him.

Robin eyed the King warily as he moved farther into the room. General Blaine gestured for Robin to sit. "Well, Major? What's wrong?"

Robin took a seat opposite the General and related what had happened in the tavern, keeping his account factual and free of emotion. From the corner of his eye he saw Elias come out of his funk and pay attention. Robin would almost rather he stayed oblivious until the sorry tale was done, but a narrowing of the eyes was the King's only reaction—that and the paling of his reddened face.

Blaine, however, was another matter. "Idiots!" he burst out, thoroughly disgusted. "How could they do this to us? Especially now, when we need their utter obedience! I thought you'd brought men you could trust, Major? Or is it your judgment that's failed here?"

Robin tried to ignore the General's comment. A couple of years ago he would have reacted hotly. Now he knew better. He knew the General was only letting off steam. He told Blaine what Dexter had said about the two miscreants, and of the Captain's suspicion there had been foul play.

The General narrowed his eyes. "How likely do you think that is?"

Robin shrugged. "From what I've seen of Lerric's men, I wouldn't discount it. I've told Captain Dexter I'll withhold judgment on the two men until they're capable of being questioned. I'll soon be able to spot whether they're covering up a lapse of conduct. If they are, they deserve to be punished and dismissed. But, sir, isn't this exactly the sort of thing we thought might happen? Didn't we discuss the possibility of someone pulling such a stunt to put us off the scent? What better way to prevent us from snooping than by causing trouble among our own troops? And we have made it rather easy for them. It was putting a lot of responsibility on the men, allowing them to go off with Lerric's lot. I'd say they held up remarkably well under the circumstances. From what Dex has told me, Lerric's men tried every trick in the book to distract our lads and lead them astray. They even trotted out a particularly nasty brand of inhaled narcotic and flooded the tavern with it."

"And what effect did it have?" The General's manner had calmed in the light of Robin's words.

"None of our lads succumbed, sir, unless that was what finally got to Col and Pengar. We'll know more after I speak with them."

"How are the rest of the men, Major?"

Robin started at Elias's voice and turned to the King, noting the febrile glitter in the man's eyes. His temper might be under control, but its effects were still apparent.

"They're subdued but fit to serve, your Majesty. They were all distressed by what's happened. They fear they've let you down. They fear your anger."

Elias shook his head. "If this was some kind of attack I'd say they handled it well if only two of them were affected. I agree with you, Major. We'll save our censure until we know the facts. Mathias?"

General Blaine nodded and Robin sighed in relief. Elias was prepared to be reasonable and, disaster though this was, it might actually have helped restore the King's common sense, which had deserted him during Sofira's spiteful tirade. If this incident had been calculated to embarrass and discommode their party, it had failed—at least in part.

"Major," said Blaine, "will you contact Taran for his report from the city? We might was well do this now, before we retire."

Robin cleared his mind and drew deeply on the power of his psyche, allowing his metaforce to flood along the lines and spirals, helixes and twists, reaching for the familiar pattern of Taran's personal imprint. He tried twice before casting anxious eyes at the waiting General.

"Sir, I can't get a response from him. Something's happened

to him. He's either unconscious or drugged, I can't be sure which. But whatever is causing his insensibility isn't good news."

✤ ✤ ✤ ✤ ✤

King Lerric staggered into his daughter's bedchamber, looking haggard and worn. She turned from her mirror to regard him, laying down the gold-backed hairbrush. She watched him in silence as he sagged to the great bed and sat there, breathing heavily and staring at the floor.

Lerric raised his head to look at his daughter, her figure softened by a wine-red satin night robe and the unbound cloud of her long hair. He wished she would leave it loose more often. It suited her face.

Sofira's mouth thinned. She turned her back and continued brushing, watching him in her silver mirror. He gradually recovered his composure and straightened his posture.

"Gods, I'm glad that's over. How did I do, Sofira? Do you think he's satisfied with our performance?"

Sofira's spine stiffened, a sure sign she was angry. "And why wouldn't he be? You were your usual whining self. Why should he have any suspicions you harbor his greatest enemy beneath your roof?"

Lerric's blood froze in panic. "Sofira! Keep your voice down. Any of his escort could be sneaking around the place, listening at doors. What if they heard you? What if they search the lower floor and find the stairs to his cell? We'd be carted off for summary execution. We might even suffer the fate decreed for Reen!"

She tossed him a withering look. "Oh, *please*! Stop thinking just of yourself. Didn't I tell you Elias had come to see *me*? Didn't I tell you he has no reason to suspect you? No reason at all, unless your spineless gibbering gives him one. You did well enough tonight. Stick to your usual complaining ways and Elias will dismiss you from his mind, as he always does. Go to bed, Father, and leave me to mine. I must write a message to Hezra and inform him of what passed between us. He has forbidden me to see him tonight, so I am denied comfort until this charade is over. If we are fortunate, I've managed to so enrage our noble High King he'll be unable to stomach any more and will leave early. I certainly hope so—I have a wedding to arrange. Now go. Leave me alone."

Stung by her tone, Lerric stood. She was growing ever more waspish, more independent of him, more caught up in that dreadful scarecrow lurking like the specter of a tortured death beneath the palace. The thought of those two finally being wed, joined by hand and by body, almost made Lerric physically sick. For one pivotal moment, he considered fleeing back to the High King and confessing all—throwing himself on Elias's mercy and begging him to rid them of that sinister parasite.

Later, he would wish that he had, with all the strength of his soul.

Chapter Thirty-One

Mathias Blaine and Robin meshed psyches, flinging out their combined strength and taking hold of Taran's unresponsive pattern. No matter how hard they tried, how strongly they called, they couldn't make Taran hear them. They returned to themselves, the General cursing freely.

"What the hell's the matter with him? Why can't anything go right for once? We're only away two days. You'd think things could remain in working order for two days."

"What do you think has happened, Mathias?" the King demanded. "Is there anything wrong in the city?"

The General heard the worry in Elias's tone, but couldn't completely bite back his irritation. That was the problem with relying on a specialty, he thought. Sooner or later it would let you down. Although he had surrounded himself with others of his kind for as long as he could remember—first Hal Bullen and then the deceased Major Anton before Sullyan and Robin joined the Manor—their scarcity of numbers always persuaded him it was safer to use conventional means of communication. He was well aware how fragile Artesan-led logistics could be. The advent of the College and Taran's acceptance of the posting to Port Loxton had accustomed him to instant communication. This occurrence, long feared by the General, only served to show how wrong he'd been.

"I don't know, Elias. We can't raise Taran so we have no way of knowing. Major, bespeak Sullyan, will you? Although I doubt she knows anything either. She'd have told us by now if she did."

✣ ✣ ✣ ✣ ✣

Sullyan was relaxing with Bull in the suite she and Robin shared on the Manor's top floor. It was adjacent to General Blaine's rooms and was much larger than her previous chambers. Although they'd occupied it for three years now, she was only just becoming used to it. It was more suitable for their needs, as it had an extra room for Morgan, but she still didn't feel as comfortable here as in her old rooms. Too much had happened there for her to easily forget.

She was thinking over those old times, a mug of Bull's strong fellan by her elbow and her old friend by her side. She gazed at him as he sprawled in her comfortable chair, legs stretched out, eyes closed. She frowned. He wearied easily these days, and his hair was more gray than brown. When had that happened? She couldn't recall. He was, of course, nearly sixty years old, and teaching Apprentices in the study of Earth while trying to control Prince Eadan's talent for pranks must take its toll, but she thought it was more than that. She really ought to speak to him about slowing down. He still trained with her every morning and his physique was as impressive as ever. But within that barrel chest beat a weakened heart that no amount of healing could repair. He'd already had one near-fatal heart seizure. She couldn't bear to think he might have another.

She was about to broach the subject when Robin's psyche impinged on her mind. She caught his tone of anxiety and became instantly alert. Prodding Bull, she included him in her mind as she acknowledged Robin.

What is it, my love? Is something wrong?

Her eyes widened as she heard Robin's news. He ran through all that had happened at the palace, and she didn't need his telling to feel the impatience and concern that flooded her psyche, emanations coming from the General and Elias. But it was her life mate's news about Taran that worried her most of all.

I last heard from him yesterday, she said, *when he reported the attack on one of the King's junior ministers. I have heard nothing since. Does Elias wish me to go to the city?*

She sensed Robin's mental shrug. *He hasn't asked, but if something's happened to Taran, our lines of communication are down. After Neremiah's murder and our suspicions as to the possible culprit, the King's feeling more than a little jumpy. The last thing he needs is to be out of touch with Levant and Vassa. And we're getting nowhere here, apart from leaving ourselves open to snide attacks from Lerric's troops. I don't know how much longer we're going to stay.*

This wasn't what she wanted to hear. *Robin, if Lerric has given his men instructions to undermine the King's escort, he has good reason for it. Tell Elias I recommend he stay for the agreed period, no matter how uncomfortable he might feel. It may be that Lerric is more rattled than he seems and is using these attacks to force you all to leave. A protracted stay might just flush out some rats.*

Sullyan sensed Robin's dubiety through their link. *I'll tell him, but Sofira was pretty vicious to him this evening and he still hasn't recovered from what she did to him. I don't know how much more he can take.*

She could appreciate Elias's discomfort. *Sofira never does anything without good cause. If she is being vicious, she is doing it to hurt Elias. Maybe she also hopes to force him to leave. You must try to convince him that by staying and taking her venom, he is refusing to play her game. She will soon lose her nerve. Sofira is not strong without someone behind her, and it cannot be Lerric. He is too weak.*

Robin's doubt didn't fade, but he promised to pass on her

advice. They broke their link, Sullyan agreeing to contact Robin as soon as she arrived in the city and learned why Taran wasn't responding. Neither the General nor the King would go to their rest until they knew the city was safe, and she understood why. A small worm of anxiety twisted her own heart on hearing Robin's news.

"Bulldog ..."

"Don't worry, dear heart, I'll stay and look after the boys. You go. It's past midnight already. You'll probably have to wake old Anjer up to tell him what you're doing."

"I have no intention of disturbing the Lord General. I have no time to waste observing the niceties, so I will not trespass on Andaryan soil."

Sullyan smiled at the huge man, grateful, as on so many occasions in the past, that his ready acceptance of her decisions and his comforting presence enabled her to act without wasting precious time. She knew her son and Elias's heir were safe in Bull's capable hands. She didn't even need to say the words.

She shrugged into her jacket and took her sword from its peg on the wall, slipping the weapons belt over her shoulder. Swinging her heavy cloak across her back, she strode from the room, leaving Bull to clear away the fellan cups and check on the two boys, sleeping like curled puppies in the next room.

Sullyan made her way through the silent Manor, descending the two marble staircases to the ground floor. She emerged into the kitchen courtyard where lamps hung to light the way for those on night duty. No one was about right now and she made it to the horse lines before she encountered anyone else.

The night duty stable hands saw her coming and had Drum bridled before she entered his stall. The enormous black warhorse whickered a soft greeting and she fondled his ears as the lads completed the harnessing. She led the stud from his stall and out into the freezing night, blessing his even temperament. He didn't even snort as he was made to leave his warm stall and journey into the cold. Vaulting to his broad back, her sword rearing over her shoulder, she trotted him out of the horse lines and into the lane beyond.

Reaching for her psyche, she manipulated the substrate as Drum bore her away from the Manor. Without forming a way through, she sent her awareness out toward the distant city, probing the castle parklands for the imprints of people. Finding none, she constructed an Earth-based aperture in the substrate and rode through it into the realm of Endormir.

Endormir was the first of the four realms, a grassy panorama of open space, a vast country of rolling steppes bordered by sheer mountains. Its indigenous people lived a nomadic life of tents and herds and hunting, and they frequented neighboring Albia in the winter months whenever possible. Endormir suffered ferocious winters with saw-edged winds scything down from the mountains, and those with the talent to escape took their families to warmer climes.

The night-bound snowscape that appeared as she and Drum emerged from the substrate was at least twenty degrees colder than the one she'd just left. Breath froze instantly and her eyes stung from the extreme cold. Swiftly, she constructed another tunnel, guiding Drum into it before the blood could congeal in their veins. It was a relief to feel the harsh winter air of Port Loxton when they emerged onto the snow-covered grass of the castle parklands.

The gate guards didn't see her or the brief shimmer of the trans-Veil construct. Neither did the men patrolling the wall. The first anyone at the castle knew of her arrival was when she cantered Drum into the garrison stable yard and slithered down his ebony shoulder. The man who had been crossing the yard startled when he saw her.

"Colonel! No one told me to expect you."

Captain Valustin was doing late rounds of the garrison. Sullyan took one look at his red-rimmed eyes and haggard face and laid a hand on his shoulder.

"What has happened, Captain?"

"You haven't heard, then? No, of course you wouldn't have. I think you'd better go see Lord Levant right away. Colonel Vassa's with him. I imagine they'll be very relieved you're here."

Sullyan's eyes narrowed. Nothing seemed amiss at the castle. There was no sign of strife and no untoward military activity. The city was quiet beyond the castle walls. But Valustin's demeanor was strange and she sensed his extreme distress.

"Tell me quickly, Val. Why are you out here tonight? It is not your usual duty. Where is Major Denny?"

Valustin closed his eyes and swallowed. Sullyan was dismayed to see tears glittering when he opened them again. "The Major's dead, Colonel."

She reeled. "Denny, dead? How?" She froze, suddenly fearful, and gripped Valustin's arm. "What of Taran?"

The Captain shook his head. "I don't know how he is."

Sullyan could see his grief. He had been a good friend of Denny's, his second-in-command, for a long time. His heart would be sore over the man's death, as was hers. Yet she needed details and he was in no condition to give them. She clasped his shoulder gently.

"Forgive me, Val. Distressing events have clearly occurred. I will attend Lord Levant and come and speak with you later."

To give him something to do, she cast him Drum's reins. Caring for the stud would calm his aching heart and allow him to regain his composure. For herself, her heart was hammering in her breast, as much for the unknown as for the tragedy that had befallen one of her oldest friends.

She raced for the castle doors, brushing past the astonished guards huddled over their brazier. As she made for the stairway she nearly collided with Princess Seline, who was coming down. The young Princess pulled up sharply, her face turning white. She carried a covered basket and stared at Sullyan with fear and dislike.

Sullyan was astonished to see the young girl up so late. "Princess. What on earth are you doing down here? Should you not be in your bed?"

Seline cast her gaze about, as if looking for something, then drew herself up, a hard look in her eye. "I am about my own business, Colonel Sullyan. I am not required to answer to you."

Sullyan regarded the young Princess. She could hear her underlying tension and surmised she was about some mischief or other. Yet she could hardly come to harm within the castle walls, and not even Seline could bully the guards into letting her outside on her own at this hour. This issue would keep. Sullyan had more pressing business.

"Then do not let me detain you, your Highness." The chill in Sullyan's tone matched Seline's. She carried on up the stairs, ignoring the Princess, and after a moment heard Seline continue down.

Sullyan made for Levant's rooms and entered after the briefest of knocks. Levant and Vassa started up at her entry, relief showing plain on their faces. She wasted no time on greetings.

"Gentlemen, tell me everything."

✤ ✤ ✤ ✤ ✤

Seline tried to calm her thudding heart after her narrow escape. Another few minutes and she would have been caught going in the side room, for which she had no reasonable explanation. Not that she'd given one for being on the stairs, either, though she knew she had the urgency of Sullyan's mission to thank for the Artesan's lack of curiosity. Yet the meeting gave Seline pause and caused her to change her plan. She couldn't take the risk Sullyan might find time to check on her, or—and this was more likely—that she'd alert Bessie to her whereabouts. Seline must be back in her room and innocently in her bed before anyone could check.

At the foot of the stairs, she glanced about. No one was in sight. She ducked into the room where she'd left the vagabond, shutting the door behind her. It was pitch dark and she waited for her eyes to adjust. A faint glow from the door guards' brazier gradually illuminated the square of window and she stood with her back to the door, listening intently.

She heard nothing. No rustle of clothing, no breathing. Was he still here? Had he left? Had he been discovered? No, the latter wasn't possible. If he'd been discovered the whole castle would be roused. She drew a little breath. "Well? Are you still here?"

She jumped as his voice crawled out of the shadows right beside her. "I'm here, your Highness."

She was amazed and rather irritated. How could someone so foul-smelling have crept so close without her knowing? She put aside her vexation in favor of haste. Delving into her pocket, she brought out a key and gave it to him.

"Here's the key to the east wing. I can't take you there now. Something's happened and I might be missed. I have to get back to my room. If I tell you the way, can you get there by yourself?"

The vagrant grinned, dimly seen in the darkness. "I'll do my best, your Highness."

She glared at him, fearing he was mocking her. "If you're discovered, I'll say I've never even seen you!"

"And how will you explain this?" He held up the key, swinging it before her eyes.

She nearly stamped her foot. "No one knows I have that. Now do you want to know the way, or shall I just leave you here?"

He bowed to her, and she told him.

393

"Thank you, your Highness. Now I think you'd better go."

She placed the small basket she'd brought on the table. "Here's some food. It's not much, but it was all I could get without arousing suspicion. I can bring you more tomorrow if you like."

His eyes flashed in alarm. "No, your Highness, that wouldn't be a good idea. What if you're seen? I think it best if you forget all about me. Don't attempt to enter the east wing; don't even think about it. I can't risk you getting into trouble. Your mother the Queen would be furious if anything should happen to you. Just leave it to me. If I need your help again, I know how to contact you."

Seline pouted. This wasn't what she wanted. Now that her mother had sent someone to aid her in her return, Seline wanted to do more, wanted to be involved. Yet the look on the vagrant's face discouraged her from voicing the protest that rose to her lips. She relented petulantly.

"Oh, very well. Just don't forget your promise. My letter to my mother is in that basket. Make sure she receives it."

He bowed again as she flounced to the door, moving away from the soft light that entered as she left.

✢ ✢ ✢ ✢ ✢

Sullyan sat in silence, her head in her hands. She simply couldn't believe what had happened over the past couple of days. First the brutal murder of Neremiah, then the attack in Loxton Forest on two noble citizens. Then the tragedy of the inferno and Jinella's awful death, and now the massacre of an entire company of King's Guard, including a very dear friend. Not to mention Taran's retreat into catatonia. No wonder Robin and Blaine had been unable to raise him. He had sunk so low into despair it was possible he might never recover.

Levant and Vassa watched her helplessly. She had taken the

catalog of disaster with no comment, the only indication of her emotions being the tears that filled her eyes. Finally, once they'd told her all, the tears spilled over and she put her head in her hands. She made no sound, and when she finally raised her head her eyes were bleak but dry.

"Gentlemen, you will excuse me while I bespeak General Blaine. He and the King are anxious to know what has occurred here."

The two men sat drinking their brandy while her eyes lost focus and she passed the distressing news to the General. She was drained when she returned to herself.

"They will return tomorrow evening," she said. "The meeting with Lerric is not going well and Sofira is proving difficult. There has been an incident involving two of the King's escort, not serious but enough to cause Elias some embarrassment. Major Tamsen thinks it may have been a scheme of Lerric's, intended to undermine the integrity of his men. He will investigate further in the morning.

"Jerrim, the King has ordered you to abandon the forest patrols, but he requires you to provide a full armed escort for anyone with pressing business beyond the city walls. All other unnecessary traffic is to cease forthwith. I will order a replacement company sent to you when I contact Bull in the morning. Elias intends to promote Captain Valustin to Lieutenant Major when he returns."

Vassa nodded and she turned to Levant.

"My Lord, will the city be content with your reassurance of their safety, or do we need to provide a greater show of force?"

Levant considered. "The representatives were happy enough when they left earlier. The mob was dispersed by Ardoch and we've heard no more from them. It'll be quiet enough as long as nothing else happens. But it would only take one more incident, one more attack or murder, and the whole place could erupt. You know what the common people are like when they feel under threat. And the King's absence doesn't help. Ardoch heard some of them muttering a ridiculous rumor that he'd fled the city in fear of his life."

Sullyan pursed her lips. "Perhaps I had better send you two companies from the Manor. I will speak to the General about it. Meanwhile, I will go to the infirmary and see what I can do to help Taran. I will stay here until the King returns, and I will be here to honor Denny and his men."

Her voice broke and she turned away, too saddened to say more. The funeral pyre for a company of twenty men would stain the air black and do nothing to reassure Loxton's people. Yet it couldn't be helped. The mortuary couldn't keep the bodies long enough for the city to forget the tragedy, and those brave, loyal swordsmen deserved their due. She left Levant's rooms with a tired, heavy heart.

The day's events ran through her mind as she made her way to the mortuary. She was beginning to suspect she might have made a mistake thinking Bordenn was the place to look for clues as to whether their old adversary had resumed his vindictive activities. The city now seemed to be the focus of attention, and although she was pleased Elias was out of the way, she knew she would never convince him to stay away, to stay safe. Not until she could prove beyond reasonable doubt Reen was behind these harrowing incidents.

The King's safety was paramount and she would do everything in her power to ensure that either General Blaine remained by his side, or that she was appointed to the duty herself. Unconnected though these events seemed to be, still they pricked her mind with insistent fingers, telling her there was a pattern, something to be read from the tragedies, even though she might not yet see it.

She woke one of the mortuary attendants, demanding to see where the bodies of the slain were laid. The sleepy attendant showed her to one of the lower rooms, kept constantly cold by its depth below ground and aided by the snow and ice brought down by the mortuary boys.

She stood in silence beside the row of lifeless corpses—all laid out the same, all cleaned and ready to be dressed in formal uniform for their final journey, all draped in shrouds bearing Elias Rovannon's sun-circled crown. The gold and red of his colors contrasted starkly with the gray of their unresponsive features, and the flicker of lamps in the windowless crypt lent a cruel semblance of life to their dull, staring eyes.

She moved along the line of men, standing at the foot of each, remembering the deeds and character of every individual, saying farewell to those she'd known as friends. Finally, she came to the end. There, slightly apart from the others, his sword laid carefully on his breast, was the corpse of Owyn Denny.

Sullyan's sight blurred as she gazed on his familiar features, recalling his quick and easy humor, his light laughter, his zest for life and gambling, and his warm but fickle heart. His good-natured face and his slim but muscular body had won him many admirers among the nobler ladies of Loxton, and not a few would bewail his demise with genuine sadness. He had broken a few hearts in his time by refusing to commit himself, but she knew his easy manner and free ways had ensured none of them harbored any bitterness.

Her own heart jolted with sorrow as she stroked one finger gently along his cold cheek. She remembered the cocky young cadet who befriended her, who never quite got to grips with the discipline demanded by his superiors. Nothing seemed to touch Denny, although Glinn Parren tried his vicious best, often causing Denny to be given punishment details he didn't deserve. Parren even tried to sabotage Denny's final tests, the failure of which would have seen him dismissed from the Manor. But Sullyan had succeeded in foiling Parren's plans, and she and Denny became firm friends, despite her constant rejections of his hopeful advances. Finally, he got the message and they found a level of friendship that survived.

Tears rolled down her face as these memories replayed. Absently, she drew the sumptuous shroud from his naked chest, wanting, for reasons she couldn't name, to see the wound that had stilled the beating of his youthful heart. She hissed in shock and anger when she saw the ragged wounds in his breast—four of them, all caused by crossbow bolts.

She was stunned. She hadn't yet heard the details of the attack and she'd assumed his company had run into a large band of brigands and fought a losing battle. But crossbows meant ambush and organization. Fleeing brigands, whether on foot or horseback, had no time to wind and load crossbows. Indeed, it was rare for casual ruffians even to carry crossbows, as the powerful weapons were cumbersome.

Swiftly, her mind reeling from the ugly implications of what she'd just seen, she examined the other men. Her face was drained and bleak when she was done. Turning from the silent corpses, she almost ran from the room.

Chapter Thirty-Two

The vagrant waited another hour before judging it safe to move. He had heard nothing since Seline's departure but the faint sound of his own jaws as he ate the food in the basket. Although the sustenance was welcome, he almost wished she hadn't brought it. If he left the basket there it would be discovered, and she would be required to account for it. If he took it with him, it might hamper his movements. In the end he had no choice. Sighing, he picked it up as he moved to the door.

He hadn't needed Seline's instructions on how to find the east wing. As the Baron's tool, he knew what Reen knew, and Reen was intimately familiar with Loxton Castle. Opening the door a crack, he peered out. No one in sight. The castle doors were closed against the cold, the guards no doubt huddled around their brazier. He wouldn't get a better opportunity.

He slipped from the room, closing the door behind him. Keeping to the shadows, he ghosted up the stairway, his ears straining for the slightest sound.

The second floor was also deserted and silent. His feet made no sound as he drifted toward his goal—the locked door leading to the disused east wing. It was fortunate the King wasn't in residence, for there was always a guard on his suite at the far end of the hall. It was a long way down, but the wastrel doubted even he could have reached this door without the guard seeing him. As it was, no one was about.

He stopped outside the door and listened intently. The apartments of Lord Levant and Colonel Vassa were on this floor, as was the nursery. But they were all farther down the long hallway and he heard nothing from any of them. He slid the key from his pocket and inserted it into the lock. It turned easily. Seline must have been using the east wing often enough for the lock to work smoothly. The vagrant slipped through the door and closed it behind him, relocking it silently.

He stood in the total darkness, allowing his eyes to adjust. But he had no need of light; the Baron knew this place well, and his servant moved confidently into the dark to wait for the right time to complete his master's instructions.

✣ ✣ ✣ ✣ ✣

Sullyan headed for the garrison. She had intended to see Taran after paying her respects to the dead, but he would keep. He wasn't going anywhere. This was more important. Her instincts, both military and Artesan, were thoroughly aroused by what she had seen on the bodies of the slain and she needed firsthand accounts of what had happened. She intended to get one from Ardoch.

She used a side entrance leading directly into the garrison courtyard. One of the King's swordsmen on his rounds saw her as she emerged into the freezing night. Valustin must have alerted the garrison to her arrival because the man merely saluted her and continued on his way. She returned the homage before she entered the barracks.

Ardoch had a private town house but also kept permanent rooms above the barracks, where he could most often be found. She knew he wouldn't be away from the castle on such a day. She mounted the wooden stairs to the officers' quarters and approached his door.

The door was open. As she came abreast of it, she could see

the old swordmaster sitting before his fire, nursing a glass of his favored tarn liquor, staring blankly into the flames. She entered quietly, so as not to startle him, and drew the door closed behind her. He glanced up, unsurprised to see her, but didn't speak.

She crossed to his table and poured herself a small measure of the peat-colored grain spirit. Sullyan rarely drank alcohol, but the sight of those proud, brave men laid out in the mortuary left her feeling wounded and weakened. A shot of Ardoch's liquid fire would warm her burdened heart. She took it to the opposite side of the hearth and seated herself.

She sipped at the burning liquor, trying not to cough. It wrought a trail of stinging heat down her throat and into her belly, and she savored its raw taste. They sat in silence, neither disturbing the memories of the other. Eventually, Sullyan stirred.

"Ghyllan, will you tell me how it happened?"

The old Torlander raised his grizzled head, staring at her from sore eyes. She had to lower her gaze from the explicit sorrow mirrored there. He clasped his hands about his glass, as if for comfort, and spoke in his gentle Torland burr, recounting the whole tale of the ill-fated patrol with military precision and attention to detail. She listened in silence until he was quite done.

"You were close enough to hear the start of it?" she asked. He nodded. "Yet by the time you arrived it was all over and the brigands were gone. So it was no chance occurrence. They were killed immediately, with no quarter or mercy. It was a carefully planned and efficiently executed ambush."

Ardoch ducked his head. "Looks that way. Only one poor sod out of twenty managed to get away before collapsing from loss of blood. Bastards must have seen or heard Denny's company and realized they were being hunted. Must have lured them toward the road and cut them down to prevent themselves being taken."

"You think it was arranged that quickly?"

Ardoch's head snapped up, eyes blazing. "What're you suggesting?"

She held his gaze. "It was a convenient coincidence, was it not? Patrols were sent out to scour Loxton Forest for Neremiah's murderer and Sir Regus's attackers. They thought to look for remnants of the haul and behold, remnants were found. Obvious tracks led down the south road. And at a sharp bend in that road, where visibility is at its lowest, an ambush was sprung. Twenty trained and experienced members of the King's Guard cut down in the first volley—horses too—*by crossbows*. No chance of survival. And no sign of the culprits when you arrive on the scene not more than a few minutes after the bloodbath. Come on, Ghyllan! Does that ring true? Where is your nose for intrigue? I cannot believe this was a random attack. No, my old friend. This was a planned maneuver, formulated by a tactical mind. This was a deliberate act."

Ardoch stared in horror. "Are you saying the two incidents are linked? That Neremiah's murderer was involved in the massacre of Denny's men? Why would he want to do that? Why wait around to kill one company of Kingsmen? Wouldn't he simply flee the area, get as far away as possible?"

She didn't relinquish his gaze. "It needs further thought, Ghyl, but that is exactly what I am saying. And if I am right, what of this terrible fire? What of the death of Lady Jinella?"

Ardoch's face turned pale and his eyes widened, but he remained silent. She sensed his confusion and how weariness and grief had taken their toll on his usually sharp mind. He needed rest. She stood, placing her glass on the table.

"Try to sleep, Ghyl." She laid a gentle hand on his shoulder. "Your experience and fortitude will be needed tomorrow when we say farewell to those who died. The men will take heart from our stoic acceptance of what we all know is a daily possibility when we take the King's Oath. We must not show weakness. We will send Owyn and the others off with respect and honor."

She left him, seeing the glitter of tears in his eyes and knowing the outward expression of deep grief was the beginning of healing, painful though it was. She closed the door behind her and made her way back into the castle.

It was too late to see Taran now. She was weary and heart sore and that was no condition in which to approach his wounded psyche, especially if what she suspected should prove true. She needed a clear head and strength of spirit if she was to help him deal with the pain of his loss. She made for the apartment kept ready for her, next to the one allocated to Taran.

Walking the length of the upper hallway, she passed the iron-bound door to the disused east wing. She was deep in thought, trying to sort through her suspicions and pin down the many niggling inconsistencies her tactical brain refused to let go of. She stopped moving and put her hand on the latch before she was aware of her actions.

The door didn't give and it brought her fully alert. She stared at the stout oak planks in surprise. Why had she stopped here? Why had her feet turned toward this door when the one to her own rooms was not only twenty feet away, but also on the other side of the hall? She stood and listened, calming the beat of her heart, silencing the whisper of her breath.

Nothing moved, nothing sounded. All was peaceful. She cocked her head, remembering another time, nearly three weeks ago, when she had felt drawn to what lay behind this door. Perhaps she ought to take note of her instincts and investigate further. There must be a reason why she was suddenly affected by this section of the castle.

She shook her head and took her hand from the latch. She was tired and needed to rest. She would wait until she had leisure to deal with this, and that was likely to be after the King returned. Tomorrow would be a busy day. Let it wait till then.

* * * * *

In the silence of deep night, once the stir created by the King's escort died down, the scarecrow's newest servant was summoned. The man called Othal made his glassy-eyed way to the Baron's retreat, unremarked by any of his fellows. The man himself, red hair slick with grease and sweat, heart hammering painfully, was scarcely aware why he felt such terror.

The palace's ground floor was in total darkness, the empty rooms deathly cold and silent. Only one room contained life of sorts, deep below this floor and protected from an Artesan's senses by the solid rock from which it was hewn. And it was there that Othal was bound. He descended the stairs and approached the closed door with trepidation, his hand shaking as he reached for the latch.

The lamp's dim glow barely reached his eyes as he pushed the door open. Nothing stirred, no sound could be heard. Yet Othal knew where his master was, and he walked forward until he stood facing the specter that had summoned him. He held out the parchment the Queen's maid had given him.

The grim figure raised its head, the dreadfully slumped and ruined features accentuating the dread menace of its eyes. Othal shuddered. This show of fear and revulsion elicited an evil smile, and the scarecrow rose to his feet, leaning heavily on his gnarled cane.

"So, my friend," he drawled as he took the proffered parchment, his voice echoing unpleasantly off the stone walls, "you've performed your first task well. I have another for you now, one of vital importance, and if you do this well, you will please me. I might even reward you. But first, I need your strength.

I have deeds to perform that require more energy than I possess. You are young and strong. You have the vitality I lack and you will lend it to me. Come here."

Othal tried to resist. The tendons and cords in his neck stood out as he strained to make his body obey him. The tremor of his muscles grew more pronounced as he struggled and sweat sprang out all over his face. His fists clenched repeatedly, drawing the amused gaze of the scarecrow, who eyed his minion meaningfully.

Finally, Othal succeeded in moving one foot an inch away from the figure before him. Reen raised his brows in astonishment, passing breath in a shocked gasp. "Ah, such strength! Would that I'd known your qualities earlier, my brawny friend. I could have used you well. But no matter. You are already mine and I will have what I require."

The scarecrow's consciousness entered Othal's mind, penetrating easily, subsuming the man's will. Briefly, feeling the stirrings of lust swell in him at the man's terror, Reen considered taking his pleasure as well as the vibrant life force. But he needed to concentrate on the business at hand and leave the slaking of such desires until he had leisure to savor them. He was nearing the culmination of his preliminary plans and speed was of the essence. One slip would see it all go to waste. If it did, at best he'd have to try again, contending with heightened caution. At worst, he'd be discovered too soon. And that would never do.

The act he intended to perform tonight was one he hadn't attempted before, although his stolen knowledge told him it was possible. All he required was the strength to reach so far, and he didn't intend to fail for lack of it. He forced the intense physical desire away and fixed his ruby eyes on the horrified features before him. Holding the man immobile with his gaze, the Baron raised the dreadful cane, the desiccated flesh of his claw-like hand merging horribly with the slimy gray wood. Its tip pulsated menacingly in the gloom. The swordsman gibbered in fear, but Reen's iron will grasped the cords of his throat, and the best he could do was whimper pathetically.

Reen grinned. Gone were the days when he needed to gag his victims. Now he held their souls with the power of his eyes and drank avidly of the terror that flowed like a river of life toward him. The silent, tearing scream as the cane came to rest over the swordsman's heart sounded only in the abyssal depths of the scarecrow's mutilated mind.

✻ ✻ ✻ ✻ ✻

The castle in Loxton was still shrouded in darkness when the kitchens began preparing the morning meals. Bread was baked and trays made up for those who chose to break their fast in their rooms. The lesser nobles who had apartments at the castle usually ate together in the dining hall, where a selection of meats, bread, and fruits was laid out fresh each morning, and a large copper kept boiling over the breakfast hearth for tea and fellan. But the senior ministers, lords, and the King's household all had their meals taken to them at the same hour each day, unless there were orders to the contrary.

This made it easier for the vagrant to carry out the next part of his master's plan.

He waited just behind the door to the east wing, which he had already unlocked. The torches burned low in their sconces and the lamps were dim. They would not be tended until the breakfasts were delivered.

First to receive his food was always the King himself, but as he was absent the nursery was the destination of the soft-footed servant who passed the vagrant's hiding place. He carried a laden tray on which balanced two meals: one for the Princess and one for Bessie, her nursemaid. The Princess ate lightly at breakfast, preferring fruit, a little bread spread with honey, and milk. Bessie, on the other hand, liked to build up her strength for the day ahead and preferred cooked meats, eggs, freshly-toasted bread dripping with honey, pastries, and a huge pot of tea. The serving man who carried the nursery tray was one of the strongest in the kitchens.

He had already passed the east wing door and didn't see the ragged figure slip into the dimly-lit hallway. The first he knew was the soft touch on his arm and the quiet whisper in his ear. It was so gently done the man looked into those ruby-tinted eyes and was mesmerized before he knew it. The touch on his arm burned, but he didn't feel it. He didn't see the dirty, nimble fingers crumble brown powder onto one of the platters he bore, and he was held enthralled until the figure disappeared and those terrible eyes ceased to grip his soul.

The servant stopped in his tracks. He shook his head, trying to clear his mind. Had someone spoken to him? Hadn't he felt a touch on his arm? But that couldn't be. He was alone in the hallway and there was no sound. He wrinkled his nose, wanting to sneeze. But it wasn't done to sneeze when carrying food. Palace servants risked dismissal from indoor service should it happen. So he controlled the urge and moved on. If he delivered a cold tray he would be ordered to return for a fresh one. And he still had Lord Levant and Colonel Vassa to serve.

He reached the nursery and tapped on the door. Hearing Bessie's usual sleepy call, he entered and deposited his tray on the table in the center of the main nursery room. Then he walked back to the kitchens, still puzzling over the strange feeling in the hallway, rubbing absently at an irritated spot on his right arm. He hoped he hadn't picked up lice from someone at the market. He had no time to worry about it now; the cook had Lord Levant's meal ready and he took it up, making the same journey as he had countless times during the course of his service.

This time, he didn't even register the lapse. The soft voice and light touch didn't impinge upon his mind, so subtly was he attuned. The vagrant could hardly feel his master working through him, and the servant had no suspicions and no defenses against the violation. The Baron was growing in confidence and strength, the wastrel thought as he crumbled yet more powder onto the hot food. He smiled as he released the servant and watched him continue on his way, completely oblivious.

A faint sound alerted the vagrant and he sprinted for the door to his refuge as someone emerged into the hallway from farther down. His heart racing in terror, he pushed the door shut as soundlessly as he could and rested his back against it, panting.

✢ ✢ ✢ ✢ ✢

Robin was also up early that morning and left his chamber before the servants arrived with the summons for breakfast. He had slept well enough, reasoning Lerric wouldn't dare allow anything to happen to them under his roof. Nevertheless, Robin and the General had shared watches during the night while Elias slept, and there were two of their own guards outside the door to their rooms. Robin nodded at them as he passed, descended the staircase, and strode on toward the east tower door.

He passed the dining hall and heard the murmur of voices. It seemed Lerric and his daughter were both early risers, and they were talking together over their meal. Robin didn't stop to eavesdrop. He had more important things on his mind, and besides, one of Lerric's serving men stood near the door and had seen him. He nodded to the man and continued on.

The barracks was noisy, and the smell of warm food greeted his nostrils. There seemed to be some sort of argument going on, but all sound ceased as he entered through the door. The swordsmen stood to attention, saluting smartly, all except two sorry figures lying slumped and green-faced in their beds. Robin stared around the men, noting their grim expressions and stiff backs.

"Stand easy, men. I haven't come to reprimand you."

There was an almost audible sigh of relief, although no one actually made a sound. They relaxed their rigid stance and Dexter came forward as Robin moved toward the sick men.

"How is the King, Major?"

Robin heard the unspoken query behind the innocent question. "He's willing to reserve judgment, Dex, as is the General. How are Col and Pen?"

"Not good, sir." The Captain looked worried as he accompanied Robin. "They've been throwing up all night and they're very weak. They can't seem to keep any liquid in their bodies, not even their own water, and they're becoming very dehydrated."

"Are they lucid? Can they remember what happened?"

"We haven't been able to get any sense out of either of them, but they've both had terrible nightmares judging by the noises they were making."

"Nightmares? What kind of alcohol sickness brings nightmares?"

"None that I know of, sir." Dexter's expression was grim. "No one's ever seen anything quite like this before."

Robin looked down at the two stricken men. Both were green and pallid, both sweating unpleasantly, both had buckets by their beds to cope with the vomiting. The smell around them was none too savory and Robin could see the damp cloths that had been used to cool their skin during the night. He looked up at his captain as he sat on Col's bed.

"None of you've had a restful night, have you?"

Dexter shrugged. "We took it in turns to watch over them. But they weren't peaceful, it's true."

Robin looked down at Col's fever-damp face and took up the man's clammy hand. Col moaned and opened his eyes. Robin frowned at the filmy appearance of his pupils. They had developed a milky sheen the likes of which he'd never seen. He murmured the man's name and Col frowned, as if trying to place his voice. "Major?"

The swordsman's voice was faint and raw, and Robin glanced up at Dexter, who shrugged again. "Col," Robin repeated, "do you know where you are? Do you remember what happened? Can you tell us?"

The young swordsman's eyes darted to and fro as if he couldn't see. But then the mist cleared as if a veil had been drawn aside, and he took a shuddering breath.

"Look out, sir!" called Dexter. Robin only just moved aside as Col heaved forward and vomited violently into his bucket. "They've been doing that all night," said Dex, his nose wrinkling at the smell. He took one of the dampened cloths and held it to Col's lips, wiping away the foul-smelling bile which was all the man could bring up.

Once the groaning swordsman was back on his pillows, he seemed more in control of his faculties. He stared at Robin in embarrassment and shame.

"Major, I'm sorry I've let you down."

Robin shook his head, still unwilling to judge. "Can you remember what happened?"

Col glanced at the unresponsive man lying next to him, then back at Robin. "I can't tell you very much, sir. All I remember is talking to two of Lerric's men and sharing a tankard of ale. I remember thinking it tasted different, but the room was full of that weird smoke and it got everywhere. Pen didn't seem to think his ale was strange. I remember feeling a bit lightheaded, and I was going to suggest to Pen we go outside to clear our heads. And that's all I remember until I woke up in the middle of the night, not knowing where I was."

Robin heard the note of fear in the man's voice. He was about to reassure him when Pengar, lying on Col's right, groaned, heaved himself noisily over the side of the bed, and unfortunately missed the bucket.

There was frantic activity whilst the floor was cleaned and the buckets emptied. The stench was raw and vile, and Robin wondered why. This was something more than alcohol poisoning, that much he knew. He had dealt with drunken men before and never come across such extreme reactions. Especially as, by all accounts, the two men had drunk no more than two tankards of ale apiece. Although there were those empty spirit bottles in the barn.

Once Pen was comfortable, Robin sat again on Col's bed. The two sick men eyed each other, clearly fearing the direst of consequences from their actions. Robin spent a few moments questioning Pengar, whose memories were similar to Col's. He recalled nothing of the ale tasting strange, but he'd been troubled by the narcotic smoke that had permeated the tavern's atmosphere. When Robin asked how it had affected him, he turned white.

"Nightmares," he whispered, as if he was afraid to remember. Col glanced at him as he said the word.

"Can you remember what they were about?" pressed Robin.

Pengar couldn't meet Robin's gaze, his expression guilty and shamed. "Eyes," was all he said, and his voice was barely audible.

Col gave a great gasp, drawing Robin's attention. "Yes!" he breathed, his own eyes troubled and fearful. "Eyes, red eyes, staring at us—compelling us. Gods, they were dreadful." He shuddered again.

Robin glanced at Dexter, who could throw no light on the revelation. Reluctantly, Robin stood, moving away with Dexter, leaving the other men to gather round their sick comrades.

Robin kept his voice low. "I don't think there's any doubt these two have been the butt of some malicious prank. They've been slipped something to make them appear drunk, probably in the hope Elias would be forced to discipline them in front of Lerric's men. We're fortunate more weren't affected. I'll be reporting my conclusions to the General and the King, and I doubt any further action will be taken. That'll be my recommendation, and you may tell Col and Pen. They're excused from further duties until they're fit. And remember we're due to leave this evening. See if you can have them on their feet by then. I would rather they rode out, even sitting double, than carried in litters. We'll put it about they've got the flux. It's partially true, in any case."

Dexter nodded, his expression indicating he appreciated the weak joke. Robin smiled. "Don't look so glum, Dex, you did well yesterday. You noticed they were missing and you found them in good time. You didn't let me down. I never expected you to watch all of them all the time. They were all given the same instructions and were trusted to carry them out. By your own words, Col and Pengar were doing just that. I can hardly fault them for being slipped a forbidden substance. There's no shame, Captain, and there'll be no reprisals. Let's not give whoever thought this up the satisfaction of seeing us rattled."

Dexter smiled tentatively, still troubled by the whole event and not wholly reassured by Robin's lack of censure. Robin clapped him on the back before leaving him to organize the morning duties.

Chapter Thirty-Three

Jinella awoke afraid, shivering with cold, and tearful. She'd seen and heard no one all through the interminable hours of the day before, and her screaming and beating upon the door of her prison had done her no good. All she had accomplished was to further inflame her already painfully sore throat. As darkness came again, she wrapped herself as closely as she could in the comforter and cried herself to sleep.

Now, as she woke scratchy-eyed and aching after an uncomfortable night of frightening dreams and tearful prayers to be rescued, she realized it was daylight again. Her insistent bladder wouldn't allow her to return to sleep, although she badly needed rest, and she straightened painfully from her cramped position on the hard, narrow shelf.

She used the bucket she'd found beneath the shelf, wrinkling her nose at its contents. Fortunately, it had a lid, though ill-fitting, and the worst of the smell was contained. She moved over to the tiny fire, which she had just managed to keep going during the night by waking frequently to tend it, and poured a small amount of her remaining water into one of the bowls she'd found. She used it to splash her face and rinse her fingers. Then she drank some, to clear the dust and the ache of crying from her throat.

She eyed the remaining water, wondering if it was a clue to when she might be released. About half the original amount was left; she'd had the wit to ration herself and not gulp it all down.

She also still had a small amount of dried fruit and bread, now slightly stale, although it had been fresh the day before. Some cheese, too, nibbled during the night by mice she hadn't seen or heard. Well, that was one mercy. Solitude she could bear; sharing her prison with brazen vermin was something else.

Tears pricked at her eyes. What on earth was she doing, worrying about mice? They were the least of her problems. She had a tiny amount of food and water, and not much wood left for the fire. If she was reduced to burning the dirty straw on the floor, or the wood of the shelf-bed, she would be in dire straits. She didn't know whether to hope for her captors to return before that, or to hope they never came.

As she had the day before, she huddled miserably on the cold floor beside the fire, wrapped in the grubby silken comforter. Tears running down her face, she strove with all the strength of her heart and mind to reach out to Taran. She'd convinced herself she could make him hear her if she only had the strength. He must be looking for her. Surely he had heard of her disappearance by now? And surely someone had found poor, dead Alice? One of the servants must have tried to rouse her the day before to see why the kitchen was cold. And Seth would have noticed something wrong when he returned to the house. Or had the tale of Alice's murder been a lie, told to cow her into submission?

She had no answers to her questions, only more uncertainty. The eerie phenomenon of hearing her dead uncle's voice from another's mouth now seemed like a distant nightmare. She had convinced herself it was a figment of her frightened imagination. She must have been kidnapped for ransom. Someone with a grudge against her had sent that filthy vagrant to spirit her away and lock her in this cold, lonely hut while they demanded money for her return. She could only hope the King or Taran would pay the ransom swiftly. She simply couldn't bear another night in this place.

Cold, alone, and frightened, Jinella gulped back tears as she lay down and tried to will herself to sleep.

✛ ✛ ✛ ✛ ✛

Despair pressed down on Taran, shutting his mind inside a prison of recrimination. Images swarmed around him like flies on a corpse. Jinny's angry tears when he had told her why she hadn't conceived. Ravening flames dancing around him, refusing his attempts to dampen them. The bleak, burned ruins of Jinny's house and her wretched skeletal remains. A flash of silver as he found the box he had bought for her, back when she believed he loved her. Through these images her figure flitted; loving, gentle, smiling, passionate, proud. All the things he loved about her came to taunt him, showing him how his actions had thrown her love back in her face.

The heat of shame swelled in him, echoed by the nightmare flames surrounding him. He heard Jinny calling, crying out for him, begging him to save her. Her voice sounded so real, her terror visceral. In his torment he strove to reach her, stretching arms impossibly heavy, urging leaden legs to run. Her piteous image wavered as he struggled to move, heart floundering, blood pounding. A shattering cry ripped through his throat as she faded from sight and he lost her all over again.

Blackness and depression ate at his soul. He ached with loss and self-blame. What use was he when he couldn't make her happy, couldn't keep her safe, couldn't even reach her to let her know he hadn't abandoned her? She was better off without him … yet his love for her remained.

He grasped at the emotion, desperate to stave off the specter of despair. She would have told him he was better than this, this wallowing in failure and self-recrimination. His powers had grown, and his confidence too. What use was that if he couldn't rule his own emotions? Why should he let the darkness take him, and thereby validate his father's low opinion of him? Hadn't he already shown he was worth more than that?

As these thoughts nudged their way through alternating veils of flame and darkness, Jinny's face appeared once more, smiling as if to encourage him. His heart surged at the sight, tenderness flooding his soul. He might have made mistakes, might not have been completely honest with her, but that didn't mean he loved her any less. It didn't mean he had to give up. If he did, he would be letting Jinny down all over again.

He thought he heard her voice once more, calling for him, crying his name. It tore at his heart, but instead of beating him down with his failures, the sound brought a measure of calm to his soul. He was an Adept-elite, not some weak and feeble fool. He had resources and he could fight this, be the man she had once loved. He owed her that, at least.

Resolve flooded his spirit and his heart gave a lurch. The image of her face gazed at him, as if through the veil of death. A solid sense of purpose tugged at him and he beat at the flames of his nightmares, quelling them as he had been unable to do at the mansion. He reached out toward her image, stretching, pleading, and felt her take his hand in hers. It was warm, vibrant, and firm. It anchored him, showing him a way back from despair.

I love you, he told her, his voice echoing in the void of his mind. He heard her sob and felt her arms come around him. Their warmth bolstered him, comforted him, giving him strength. This is how it would feel if she had forgiven him. Might she have forgiven him? Would she, even though she was gone? Had her spirit heard him, as he thought he had heard hers?

A sob caught in his throat and he gasped, choking. He snatched a breath and opened his eyes, seeing a familiar face inches from his, feeling comforting arms around his shoulders.

✤ ✤ ✤ ✤ ✤

As Taran finally stirred and woke, Sullyan released him and sat up, blinking back tears for his pain and the loss of Jinella. His cries had cut to her heart. She watched as he came fully back to himself, realizing who she was. He pushed himself upright, wincing at the pain of his crushed leg.

"Brynne. Oh, I'm sorry ... I've been ... I shouldn't have let myself go like that. Have you been here long?"

She smiled. "Only a few minutes. I thought I might have to help rouse you, but you did it all on your own."

He gathered himself with an effort, breathing hard. She sensed his awful memories of that terrible night as they surged to the fore.

"Jinny ... I thought I heard ...."

He wasn't fully over his trauma, she could see that. To help ground him in the present, she asked, "Do you know how the fire started?"

He looked up sharply. "Denny thought it must have been an accident, an overturned lamp. But Seth said ... he said ... he said she'd been desperately unhappy since our row, that she'd sent the servants off early and that she'd been crying. He offered to get one of her friends, but she refused and sent him away. He said he checked all the lamps that night and they were all safely trimmed. He said"—Taran's increasingly agitated voice fell to an anguished moan—"she must have done it deliberately."

Sullyan frowned. "What, he thinks she burned the house down to take her own life?"

Taran nodded miserably, and Sullyan shook her head. "That does not sound like Jinella to me. And you believe him?"

Taran shrugged, hugging his chest. "Why would he say it if he didn't think it was true? She must have hated me for what I did to her, and now I can never put it right. I'd just found that silver box, and then … and then, her body ….."

He couldn't go on. She regarded him while she thought over what she'd heard. The silver box he'd mentioned was on the bed between them and she idly picked it up, running her fingers over its delicate tracery.

She knew how upset Jinny had been by her belief she was barren, and could understand the girl's anger when Taran told her the truth. Betrayal hurt, especially so when the perpetrator was a loved and trusted partner. But suicide? Sullyan was damned if she would believe their row caused Jinny to contemplate taking her own life. The Baroness would have spoken with Taran once her temper cooled. She wouldn't have thrown away everything they had together because of one mistake. Jinny was too openhearted for that.

But if the fire wasn't a suicide attempt, why should the manservant say it was? Even if it was, it was a cruel thing to taunt Taran with. The Adept had obviously been in great distress, and finding Jinella's charred remains would have been traumatic enough. Why lead him to believe the fire was a result of his actions? Why drive him further into despair? Unless …

She stilled, recalling her suspicions concerning the brigand ambush and Neremiah's death. Turning eyes now clear of introspection upon the grieving Adept, she asked, "Did you and Seth ever disagree? Can you think of any reason why he would wish you harm?"

Taran raised a pale face, eyes dark with pain. His brow furrowed, his glance falling to the gleaming box she turned in her hands. "No, not really. I never had much to do with him. I got the impression he didn't like me much, but we never spoke more than a few words to each other."

Sullyan eyed the box, her thoughts speculative. She casually raised the lid, looking at the skillfully-worked design along the rim, admiring the silversmith's art. "And Jinny never expressed any dissatisfaction with—oh, what is this?"

A thick, folded parchment pressed up against the loosened lid. Sullyan glanced across at Taran, who shrugged listlessly when she offered him the box.

"I don't know. Probably a letter from her mother. She was always asking Jinny for more gold."

Sullyan took out the parchment and scanned it as Taran continued. "I was going to see her, you know. The evening before the ... fire ... I was going to see her. I wanted to make sure she'd heard about the death of His Immanence, and I hadn't yet taken her uncle's possessions to her. But instead I let Denny persuade me to play cards. It was too late, really, to go calling on her unannounced. It was an excuse, I suppose. I really should have gone. And then, in the early hours, I heard her call to me."

"What?"

Sullyan's head snapped up. She had been reading the parchment, eyes growing wider by the minute, and hadn't been paying attention to Taran. But on the heels of her realization of what the parchment revealed, Taran's last statement suddenly registered. She stared at him, the parchment temporarily forgotten. "What did you say?"

Taran stared back, frowning. "I heard her call me."

"You mean through the substrate."

He nodded. "I was asleep, dreaming. At first I thought it was part of my dream, a nightmare. It certainly felt like one. When I realized it wasn't, I thought ... I thought it was you. But when I checked, you were sleeping peacefully. It wasn't until later, when I realized the seat of the fire was at the estate, that it hit me."

Taran paused, his face draining at his failure to recognize Jinny's call. He hugged his chest tighter, breath rasping though his teeth. "I didn't expect it. She had no talent, we all knew that. I'd hoped ... you do sometimes hear of a bond being forged between close partners, and she'd always been so eager to hear about how we work and communicate. I'd always hoped one day ... one day we might break through her mind's barriers and the impossible would happen. But when it did, when the anguish in her soul grew so great she could finally overcome those barriers, when she needed me so badly she found the means to reach me ... I failed her."

Tears prickled Sullyan's eyes and she leaned forward, placing a hand on Taran's forearm. She spoke earnestly, driving her words at him to make him hear.

"Taran, I cannot deny you failed to recognize Jinny's call, although I will refute your right to claim you failed her. You can hardly be blamed for not realizing the call originated with her. You may believe me or not, as you wish. But this you will believe, my friend. Jinella did *not* take her own life. She did not succumb to dark despair over your argument, and she did *not* die hating you."

Taran stared at her out of deep wells of pain. "How can you say that?"

Sullyan extended the parchment with trembling fingers. Taran stared blankly before he took it. Sullyan rose from the bed and moved to the window, her back to the stricken Adept as he read the words his beloved lady had written. She heard nothing but the quickening of his breath. He made no outcry, gave no gasp. When she finally turned around, he had laid the parchment on the bed and was sitting with his head in his hands, just as she had done on hearing the dreadful news the previous evening.

She crossed to him and sat beside him, her arm across his trembling shoulders. But he wasn't weeping, as she'd thought. He was past weeping, now.

"She had forgiven you, my friend."

Taran dropped his hands and nodded slightly, his face even

paler than before. "So it would seem. And that's what I felt just now, as I was waking. I thought I was just trying to comfort myself. But if it's true, she didn't start the fire, did she?"

Sullyan shook her head. She was proud of his control and inner strength, and he was beginning to think again.

The Adept just stared at her. Sullyan reached out to him, to lend him a measure of strength, but he pushed her metaforce away. "I'm all right, Brynne. I just need to understand ...."

She stood, her decision made. "Taran, could you bear to accompany me to the mansion? I need to see the place for myself."

He gave a pale smile. "I could bear it, but I don't think I'm up to riding just now. I did a very stupid thing last night, tried to force my horse through a gap too small for him. I scraped my leg and it's still very painful and ... oh, dear gods, I never checked on Bucyrus! He was injured too, and I never checked he was all right—"

"Easy, Taran. Rendan brought both you and Bucyrus back from the mansion. He will have been cared for in the stables. I will check on him myself, if it will ease you. But I have to tell you, it was not last night that you fought the fire. I am afraid you have been asleep for twenty-four hours."

This news seemed to shock the Adept profoundly. "Twenty-four hours? But ... oh, gods, Brynne, the King, the General! I should have reported yesterday evening—!"

She shook her head. "Calm yourself. They contacted me when they could not raise you, which is why I am here. I will tell you all the news once we have finished our business at the site of the fire. I have other duties to attend this morning. And you need not concern yourself with riding. Drum shall carry us both. I will leave you to get dressed and meet you in the courtyard. Can you manage to walk that far?"

Taran nodded, and she smiled as she left the room.

Chapter Thirty-Four

Sullyan had Drum waiting by the castle doors when Taran limped down the outer steps. He was stiff and sore, and not just from the lacerations to his leg. His exertions on the night of the fire hadn't been helped by a day spent languishing in bed. He wrapped his fleece-lined jacket about his body against the icy morning chill and accepted Sullyan's assistance to boost him onto Drum's broad back. She vaulted up in front of him.

"You need not worry for your mount," she told him over her shoulder as she nudged the huge stud out of the courtyard. "He has been well tended. He has a few nasty scrapes, but they will heal with time. I have given him a little help and ensured he will not scar. The hair will grow back as it should and he will be well. You both had a lucky escape, by all accounts."

She'd had the details from one of the men who had ridden behind Taran that night. She heard him give a sigh of relief that his reckless behavior hadn't resulted in more serious consequences.

He managed a humorless chuckle. "So Denny told me. He gave me a thorough dressing down all the way from the gate to the estate. I can't begin to imagine what he'll say about it the next time I see him. He wasn't impressed, to say the least."

Sullyan swallowed the lump in her throat. She had forgotten he didn't know about Denny's death, and the last thing she wanted was to give him more pain. Yet she hadn't been swift enough to suppress the grief that suffused her spirit, and she could tell Taran sensed it.

Damn him! Why couldn't he have missed her lapse, as he missed so many nuances? But she was being unfair. He was growing in control and strength, and she shouldn't condemn him just because she flinched from a painful subject.

"What is it?" he demanded, clutching her shoulder. "What's happened?"

She had to tell him, no matter how much he would be hurt. He was Denny's friend too; he had a right to know.

"Taran, Owyn Denny is dead. He was killed in Loxton Forest yesterday, along with all of his company, as he rode in pursuit of the brigands who attacked Sir Regus."

There was a brief silence. "Dead?" he whispered, unable to believe it. "Denny—all of them—dead?"

She felt his distress through the grip of his fingers. "I am afraid so."

"Even Ardoch?"

She sucked in a breath. "No, no, not Ardoch. His band took a different route to Owyn's. They were close enough to hear the ambush, but not near enough to help them. By the time they reached the site, all the brigands were gone. Ardoch brought the dead back into the city."

Taran remained silent as they rode, only the tremble of his body telling of his distress. Denny had once been the Baron's unwitting tool, used to great effect in Reen's efforts to destroy Sullyan's life, and he had caused great pain to Taran as well. But he'd also been one of Taran's staunchest friends since the Adept accepted the position of Court Artesan, and Taran would sorely miss his cheerful manner, irreverent humor, and openhearted ways. As would Sullyan.

Drum's hooves crunched through the ice-crusted snow as Sullyan told Taran what she had heard from Robin the evening before. The telling soothed her and, even if he wasn't fully concentrating on her words, the gentle lilt of her voice helped keep Taran anchored in reality, preventing him from sinking once again into debilitating grief. They watched the townspeople as they rode, going about what business they could on such a bitter day, and they wondered how life could go on so blithely, so callously, in the face of such tragedy and loss. Eventually, the somber faces and muted chatter of the townsfolk registered with the Adept and he commented on it to Sullyan.

"Yes," she said, "they are still uneasy. Who can blame them after all that has happened? The funeral pyre we must attend later today will do nothing to lighten their mood."

Her reminder of what they had lost weighed heavily on Taran and he fell silent once more as they continued to the estate.

Rendan Levant, once he had seen the unconscious Taran to the infirmary, had sent men back to the estate with orders to cordon off the mansion until it had cooled enough to be dealt with and the bodies removed. So when Taran and Sullyan finally rode up to the stark remains of the once-handsome building, they found it bleak and desolate, devoid of life.

Taran stayed atop Drum while Sullyan dismounted, eyes misting with pity for the devastation. She glanced briefly up at him and he pointed mutely to where he'd found the remains of his love. Giving him a smile intended to warm his aching heart, Sullyan moved toward the blackened ruin.

The area had been securely roped off, the servants gone to find what comfort they could with friends or family. The horses had been rounded up by Matty, and now had temporary stabling in the village. The site was silent and deserted, except for the remains of the dead.

The ground around the mansion was frozen once more, but Sullyan could see where many feet had trampled the snow and where the water, so valiantly but so futilely thrown into the blaze, had puddled and frozen in the ruts. Charred timbers and blackened stone still steamed faintly in the gray morning, idle wisps of smoke telling where some ember still clung to feeble life. The scene made Sullyan shiver.

She eyed what was left of the walls as she began her search. Her nose wrinkled in distaste, as if at some noisome smell, and she halted briefly amid the fallen floorboards and burnt furnishings.

"This whole place reeks of evil."

Taran, still on Drum, was too far to hear her clearly. "What did you say?" But she ignored him and moved forward again.

She started close to the kitchens, the likeliest place for a fire to start. The whole area had been completely devastated and both floors had burned out, the upper collapsing onto the lower. It was there she found the housekeeper. The bones were still visible among the charred metal and wood, although no scraps of clothing adhered to them. Sullyan stood in silent homage over the remains of Alice, mourning the life of the young woman who had been so badly treated by the Baron and then rescued by the compassion of the King, only to end up perishing in the Baron's former home. She resolved to give Alice the same honor due Jinella once the bodies were finally recovered.

Still feeling unease, Sullyan picked her careful way toward the point Taran had indicated. Footing was perilous; the burned and blackened rubble was unstable and often turned underfoot. Ice had formed in the cooler parts of the building, slicking over puddles that hadn't evaporated in the inferno. She had to catch her balance once or twice, to cautionary calls from Taran. Finally, she saw what she'd been searching for—a gleam of bone within the black.

Tears came to her eyes at the memory of the Baroness and she stood in silence, staring down at the pathetic remains. Wisps of blonde hair still clung to the skull, scraps of green silk lay bordered by char, and the glint of gold shone from the bones of the neck.

Something was not right.

"Taran," she called over her shoulder, "what time would you say the fire started?"

The Adept considered this. "It was in the early hours before dawn when I awoke, and it must have taken us over an hour to reach the estate. The house was well alight by then and must have been for some time. But the servants could tell you better. They only just escaped the blaze in their part of the house."

"So it would have been well into the night, then. At what hour did Jinella usually retire?"

"An hour before midnight. Why?"

Sullyan crouched down beside the remains, stretching out one hand. "And was she in the habit of wearing her jewelry to bed?"

"No, of course not. What are you saying?"

Taran slid awkwardly down Drum's shoulder, using the stud's solid body to steady him. He limped through the wreckage toward Sullyan. She watched him, a strange expression on her face.

"Or one of her best court gowns?"

Taran came to her side, his eyes fixed on the huddle of bones beneath Sullyan's hand. "What?" he whispered.

She took her eyes from Taran's face and contemplated the disjointed human remains on the ground. Her eyes were hard and her own face was pale as she laid one hand gently on the curve of bone beneath the few wispy hairs. She'd barely touched the poor thing before she gave a great gasp and snatched back her hand, rubbing her wrist.

Her reaction and revulsion alarmed Taran. "Brynne, what is it? Tell me!"

Sullyan stood, her face a mask of anger. Her mind was a jumble of confusing images, none of which made any sense. The overriding impression was of evil—putrid, rotting evil. She was trembling and she put out her hand to Taran, resting it on his forearm. He stared helplessly into her gaze, fearing what she might say. He was totally unprepared for her revelation.

"This is not the body of Jinella. I do not know who it is, but I can tell you this in all certainty. Whoever was burned to death within this house, it was not the Lady Jinella."

The End

Glossary

Albian Characters

Alice, former nursemaid at Port Loxton, now Jinny's housekeeper.

Anton, Major. Deceased Artesan at the Manor, Sullyan's early mentor.

Ardoch, Ghyllan, Master. Elias's legendary swordmaster.

Bassan, Captain. King Lerric's guard captain at Daret, Bordenn.

Bessie. One of Prince Eaden's nurses.

Brynne Sullyan. A Colonel at the Manor under General Blaine.

Bull, aka Bulldog, aka Hal Bullen. Colonel Sullyan's friend and aide.

Cal Tyler. Taran's friend, and life mate of Rienne Arlen.

Chaz. A Kingsman at Port Loxton.

Col. A Manor swordsman in Robin's company.

Corina, Lady. Wife of Sir Regus, on of Elias's nobles.

Damas, Cleric Patrio. Ruvar's predecessor on Selna Island.

Delinna, Madam. Chatelaine at Port Loxton.

Denny, Owyn. A Major at Port Loxton.

Dexter. A Captain at the Manor under Captain Tamsen.

Drum. Sullyan's black warhorse.

Durren, Frar. A member of the Order of the Wheel on Serna Island.

Eaden, Prince. Son of King Elias and Queen Sofira.

Elias Rovannon. Albia's High King.

Elisse Arlen, daughter of Rienne and Cal.

Endor. Master healer at Loxton Castle.

Fergus. A Kingsman at Port Loxton

Galt. Innkeeper at Foxdune, Serna Province.

Giel, Captain. Duty captain at small garrison in Serna Province.

Goran. Chief cook at the Manor.

Greda, Lady. A noblewoman living in Tolk.

Hal Bullen. See 'Bull.'

Hezra Reen. Exiled Albian Baron.

Jeriko. Old fisherman in Serna Province.

Jerrim Vassa. A Colonel at the Manor.

Jinella, Lady. The niece of Baron Reen.

Kandaran, King. High King Elias's father, deceased.

Kerris. Apprentice to Port Loxton's master stonemason.

Kinsey, Lord. Chamberlain to High King Elias.

Lahan. A cleric at Port Loxton's Minster.

Lerric. Client-king of Bordenn, father of Queen Sofira.

Levant, Rendan, Lord. First Minister to High King Elias.

Mathias Blaine. The Manor's senior officer and General-in-Command to High King Elias.

Matty. Stableboy at Jinny's mansion.

Morgan Sullyan. Son of Brynne Sullyan and Robin Tamsen. Also the name of Brynne's deceased father.

Neremiah, Arch Patrio. Senior churchman at Loxton's Minster.

Nolah. Brothel keeper in Port Loxton.

Odren, Cleric. One of Neremiah's junior clerics who accompanied Reen to his island prison.

Othal. Red-haired swordsman in Lerric's forces.

Parren, Glinn. A Captain at the Manor under Colonel Vassa. Killed by Robin for treachery.

Pengar. A Manor swordsman in Robin's company.

Pylock, Lord. A noble at Port Loxton.

Rafe. Bouncer at Port Loxton brothel.

Regus, Sir. One of Elias's nobles.

Rhys. One of King Lerric's men.

Rienne Arlen. A healer and Cal Tyler's life mate.

Robin Tamsen. A Major at the Manor under Colonel Sullyan.

Roshan, Senior Patrio at Loxton's Minster.

Ruvar, Cleric Patrio. leader of the Order of the Wheel on Serna Island, Reen's former prison.

Seline, Princess. Daughter of King Elias and Queen Sofira.

Serrin, Frar. Young cleric befriended by Reen on Serna Island.

Seth. Baron Reen's manservant.

Sharmel, Lady. A noblewoman at Port Loxton.

Sofira. Queen to High King Elias Rovannon.

Solet. The Manor's stablemaster.

Tad Greylin. Former kitchen boy at the Manor, now a cadet.

Tambor. Tad's horse.

Taran Elijah. Court Artesan to Elias Rovannon.

Taric, Cal and Rienne's youngest child.

Tobias. Robin's warhorse.

Valustin. A captain of King's Guard at Port Loxton.

Varian, Frar. A member of the Order of the Wheel on Serna Island.

Varth. Black-haired swordsman in Lerric's forces.

Wil Gerion. A corporal at the Manor.

Withen, Master. Port Loxton's master stonemason.

Wrekin. Coachman to Sir Regus.

Yve, a junior cleric at Port Loxton's Minster.

Andaryan Characters

Aeyron Pharikian. The Hierarch of Andaryon's son and Heir.

Anjer, Lord General. Officer in overall command of the Hierarch's forces.

Idrimar Pharikian. The Hierarch's daughter.

Jay'el. Son of former pirate Ky-shan.

Kyrie. Younger of Lord Sekayin's two daughters.

Ky-shan. Former pirate, now runs the Hierarch's shipping business.

Lirina. Daughter of Lord Seyakin and Prince Aeyron's intended bride.

Rykan. Deceased Lord of Kymer province, one time aspirant to the Andaryan throne.

Seyakin, Lord. Lord of Dalkia, father to Princess Lirine.

Timar Pharikian. The Hierarch, Supreme Ruler of Andaryon.

Ty Marik. Once Count of Cardon province, now Duke of Cardon and Kymer.

Realms of the World

First Realm—Endormir

Endormirians are sometimes known as 'Roamerlings' because of their itinerant habits. They are small and slim, dark skinned, with brown or black eyes showing hardly any whites. The Artesan gift runs only through the males, and gifted males always become clan-leaders. As Endomir suffers from severe winter conditions, its people cross the Veils into the other realms for the winter months, where they are well known as traders.

Second Realm—Sinnia

Sinnians are tall and milk-haired, with pale skin. They live in clans and were once nomadic but now live in settlements. All are born able to control their metaforce up to the rank of Adept and are thus considered 'sports'. Their race often produces highly gifted musicians and storytellers.

Third Realm—Relkor

Relkorians are small, fierce and stocky, notorious for raiding the other realms for slaves to work their mines and quarries. Their Artesans, both male and female, invariably become slave-lords.

Fourth Realm—Albia

Albia is the human realm. The Artesan gift runs through both male and female lines, each gender being equal in potential. The craft is currently out of favour due to raiding by both Relkorian and Andaryan Artesans. Albians widely believe that all Artesans use their powers only for gain and control.

Fifth Realm—Andaryon

A warlike race characterised by eyes with slit pupils. They fight constantly amongst themselves, vying for position within the Hierocracy. The Artesan gift passes only through the male line and females play a minor and downtrodden role. Only the most powerful Artesan can become and hold the rank of Hierarch. Their battles for supremacy are governed by strict, ritualistic laws.

Terms

Arch Patrio. The leader of Albia's Matria Church.

Artesan.
A person born with the ability to control metaforce and Master the four primal elements.

Brine rum.
Strong liquor, drunk by pirates on Andaryon's eastern seaboard.

Cardinal stone.
The stones in a stone circle that sit at each of the four compass points.

Cheosian Red. A fine Andaryan red wine from Cheos province.

Codes of Combat.
Strict laws governing any conflict between Andaryan nobles.

Demons.
Derogatory term used in Albia to describe those of the Andaryan race.

Earth ball.
An explosive sphere of Earth element formed by an Artesan for use as a weapon.

Fellan.
A dark, aromatic and bitter beverage brewed from the seeds of the fellan-plant.

Firefield.
A barrier formed from the primal element of Fire, through which only Artesans can pass. Firefields formed by those of inferior Artesan rank can easily be destroyed by those of a higher rank.

Firewater.
Incredibly strong liquor.

Free traders.
Another term for pirate.

Immanence, your. Form of address used when referring to Albia's Arch Patrio.

Kingsman.
Term used to describe members of the High King's fighting forces.

Matria Church.
The Minster in Port Loxton, seat of Albia's primary faith, the Faith of the Wheel.

Metaforce (sometimes also called life force).
The force of existence pertaining to all things, both animate and inanimate.

Perdition.
A state of non-being for the soul—a place where souls with no ultimate destination reside.

Primal elements.
Earth, Water, Fire and Air.

Primal Sacrament.
Andaryan name for the Pact, an agreement brokered between Andaryan nobles. Used to settle wars ending in stalemate, it involves the willing suicide of a powerful Artesan.

Primary Magister.
Chief Justice Minister of Andaryon.

Portway.
Structure formed by an Artesan from a primal element—usually Earth or Water—which gives its creator access through the Veils.

Psyche.
An Artesan's unique and personal pattern through which they can manipulate metaforce and channel the primal elements.

Roamerling.
Slightly derogatory term for the nomads of Endormir.

Sally port.
A small door within a larger fortified barrier, allowing only one person to pass through at a time.

Substrate.
The medium in which the primal elements reside, and in which the world and all things have their being.

Tangwyr.
Monstrous Andaryan raptor trained to hunt men.

The Pact. (See Primal Sacrament).

The Staff.
Mysterious and terrible weapon capable of stealing and storing

metaforce. Can only be used by Artesans.

The Veils.
Misty barriers separating the five Realms of the World. Only Artesans have the power to move through the Veils.

The Void.
Dark abyss at the end of life into which all souls pass before reaching their final destination.

The Wheel.
Central principle of Albian faith.

Velletian Guard.
Personal guard of the Hierarch of Andaryon.

Witch.
Derogatory term for an Artesan.

Artesan ranks and their attributes

Level one: Apprentice. Person born with the Artesan gift and the ability to influence the first primal element of Earth. Able to hear other Artesans speaking telepathically but unable to initiate such speech.

Level two: Apprentice-elite. Has some skill in influencing their own metaforce. Has attained mastery over the element of Earth. Able to initiate telepathic speech but only with Artesans already known to them. Able to build substrate structures, identify a person by the pattern of their psyche, and counter metaphysical attack to some degree.

Level three: Journeyman. Has mastery over Earth and is able to influence Water. Able to build portways and travel through the Veils. Has some skill in using metaforce for offense. Also able to initiate psyche-overlay and converse telepathically with any other Artesan. Possesses some self-healing potential.

Level four: Adept. Has mastery over both Earth and Water. Able to build more complex substrate structures such as corridors. Able to influence where such structures emerge. Possesses stronger offensive and defensive capabilities. Able to merge psyche fully with other Artesans. Increased healing abilities.

Level five: Adept-elite. Has mastery over Earth and Water and is able to influence Fire. Possesses great healing powers which can even aid the ungifted (with their permission). Able to initiate powersinks and merges of psyche. Able to construct such structures as Firefields.

Level six: Master. Has mastery over Earth, Water and Fire. Able to control the power of an inferior Artesan against their will. Control over personal metaforce now almost total. Possesses incredible healing powers.

Level seven: Master-elite. Has mastery over Earth, Water and Fire and is able to influence Air, the most capricious primal element. Able to absorb a lesser or even equal-ranked Artesan's power and metaforce provided some link or permission (however tenuous) can be found.

Level eight: Senior Master. Has complete mastery over all four primal elements. Is able to absorb another Artesan's power by force, even sometimes without a link. Possesses a high degree of metaphysical (and usually spiritual) strength.

Level nine: Supreme Master. It has never been fully established whether this rank actually exists. Supreme Masters are supposedly able to influence Spirit - largely regarded as the mythical 'fifth element.' Ancient texts refer only to the possibility; no mention has ever been found of a being attaining Supreme Masterhood.

Sport or lay-Artesan. Freaks of nature, sports are thought to be able to control their own metaforce from birth, to whatever level of strength they inherently possess. As they receive no training their working is often undetectable. They are also believed to be able to 'hear' the thoughts of those around them; gifted or ungifted, and directly, not through the substrate.

Cas Peace was born and brought up in the lovely county of Hampshire, in the UK, where she still lives. On leaving school, she trained for two years before qualifying as a teacher of equitation. During this time she also learned to carriage-drive. She spent thirteen years in the British Civil Service before moving to Rome, where she and her husband, Dave, lived for three years. They return whenever thay can.

As well as her love of horses, Cas is mad about dogs; especially Lurchers. She currently owns two rescue Lurchers, Milly and Milo. Cas loves country walks, working in stained glass, growing cacti, and folk singing. She is currently working on writing and recording songs or music for each of her fantasy books. The song associated with *King's Envoy* is "The Wheel Will Turn"; for *King's Champion* it is "The Ballad of Tallimore"; and for *King's Artesan* it is "Morgan's Song (All That We Are)." For *The Challenge* it is "Meadowsweet", for *The Circle* it is "Larksong," and for *Full Circle* it is "Beyond the Veils."

All Cas's book songs can be found at and downloaded (free!) from her website, see below. Also find Cas on www.reverbnation.

Cas's first novel, *King's Envoy*, was awarded a HarperCollins Authonomy Gold Medal in 2008. Her *Artesans of Albia* fantasy series has won the critical acclaim of US fantasy, sci-fi, and non-fiction author Janet Morris. Cas is a member of the British Fantasy Society and had a short story included in their 40th Anniversary commemorative anthology Full Fathom Forty. She's also a contributor to the Janet Morris-edited anthology *HEROIKA 1: Dragon Eaters.*

Cas has written a nonfiction book, *For the Love of Daisy*, which tells the lifestory of her mischievous and beautiful Dalmatian. She is also a freelance editor and proofreader. Details and other information can be found on her website: www.caspeace.com.

Other Books by Cas Peace:
Artesans of Albia Fantasy Series:

Trilogy One: *Artesans of Albia*
Book One: *King's Envoy*
Book Two: *King's Champion*
Book Three: *King's Artesan*

Trilogy Two: *Circle of Conspiracy*
Book One: *The Challenge*
Book Two: *The Circle*
Book Three: *Full Cirlce*

Trilogy Three: *Master of Malice*
Book One: *The Scarecrow*
Book Two: *The Captives* (Spring 2016)
Book Three: *The Gateway* (Winter 2016)

Anthologies:

Full Fathom Forty:
British Fantasy Society 40th Anniversary Volume.

HEROIKA 1: Dragon Eaters:
edited by Janet E Morris.

Non-Fiction:
For the Love of Daisy

www.ingramcontent.com/pod-product-compliance
Lightning Source LLC
Chambersburg PA
CBHW051509250626
47156CB00001B/25